She touched the hair curling at the nape of his neck, wanting the kiss to never stop.

At the sound of Max ringing the chow bell, he let her go. She drew back, shaken by the kiss. "We shouldn't have done that."

"I'm not going to apologize for kissing you. I've wanted to since the first time I laid eyes on you. Only back then, I was just a boy who thought the way to get a girl's attention was to give her a hard time."

"I'm still a married woman," she said, hating that she sounded breathless. Had she ever been kissed like that? "And I'm your boss."

He nodded. "If you're saying that I have bad timing, I couldn't agree more." He grinned. "But I'm still not sorry." With that, he touched her cheek, a light caress before he rose, retrieved his shirt from the tree, pulled on his boots and left, saying, "I'll see you back in camp, boss."

B.J. Daniels is a *New York Times* and *USA TODAY* bestselling author. She wrote her first book after a career as an award-winning newspaper journalist and author of thirty-seven published short stories. She lives in Montana with her husband, Parker, and three springer spaniels. When not writing, she quilts, boats and plays tennis. Contact her at bjdaniels.com, on Facebook or on Twitter, @bjdanielsauthor.

Books by B.J. Daniels

Harlequin Intrigue

Cardwell Ranch: Montana Legacy

Steel Resolve
Iron Will
Ambush Before Sunrise

Whitehorse, Montana: The Clementine Sisters

Hard Rustler
Rogue Gunslinger
Rugged Defender

HQN

Montana Justice

Restless Hearts
Heartbreaker

Sterling's Montana

Stroke of Luck
Luck of the Draw
Just His Luck

Visit the Author Profile page
at Harlequin.com for more titles.

NEW YORK TIMES AND USA TODAY BESTSELLING AUTHOR

B.J. DANIELS

AMBUSH BEFORE SUNRISE
&
GUN-SHY BRIDE

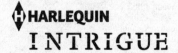

HARLEQUIN
INTRIGUE

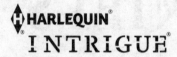

INTRIGUE

Recycling programs for this product may not exist in your area.

ISBN-13: 978-1-335-21398-3

Ambush Before Sunrise & Gun-Shy Bride

Copyright © 2020 by Harlequin Books S.A.

Ambush Before Sunrise
Copyright © 2020 by Barbara Heinlein

Gun-Shy Bride
Copyright © 2010 by Barbara Heinlein

This edition published by arrangement with Harlequin Books S.A.

For questions and comments about the quality of this book, please contact us at CustomerService@Harlequin.com.

Harlequin Enterprises ULC
22 Adelaide St. West, 40th Floor
Toronto, Ontario M5H 4E3, Canada
www.Harlequin.com

Printed in U.S.A.

CONTENTS

AMBUSH BEFORE SUNRISE

This book is for anyone who's fallen for
the wrong person—and gotten lucky
and found the right one. It's never too late for love.

Chapter One

JoRay "Jinx" McCallahan stormed into the sheriff's office, mad, frustrated and just plain beside herself.

Sheriff Harvey Bessler looked up from his desk in surprise, saw her and groaned good-naturedly. "Let me guess. T.D.?"

"What am I supposed to do about him? I'm already divorcing him. I've got a restraining order against him—like that does a lick of good. I've run him off with a shotgun. But short of shooting him, he just keeps coming back."

"All you have to do is call when he breaks the restraining order on him and we'll pick him up."

"And he'll be back on the street within hours even madder and more determined to drive me crazy."

Harvey nodded sympathetically. "Unfortunately, we don't have anything else we can hold him on. Unless he is caught in the act doing something illegal…" The sheriff motioned her into a chair before he leaned back in his own to eye her over the top of his cheater glasses. "How are you doing other than that?"

She scoffed as she took a seat. She'd been coming to this office since she was a child. Her father and Harvey had been best friends up until Ray McCallahan's recent death. Because of that, Harvey was like a second father to her. She'd been fortunate to have such good men in her life.

Until T. D. Sharp.

The sheriff got to his feet and came around his desk to call out to the receptionist. "Mabel, get this girl a cola from the machine. Get me one, too." He turned back to Jinx. "Remember when you were little and you'd come in here with your papa to visit? I'd always get you a cola. It always made you feel better."

Just the mention of her father made her eyes burn with tears. She missed him so much and she knew Harvey did, as well. "That was back when the worst thing that happened to me was falling off my bike and skinning my knees."

He laughed. "True enough. Not that you let a little thing like a skinned knee stop you. You've always been strong, Jinx."

She didn't feel strong as she heard Mabel come to the door with two bottles from the old-timey machine in the break room. Harvey took them and gently closed the door.

"I'm afraid this is the best I can do right now," he said as he handed over her cola. "What's T.D. done now?"

She took the drink, feeling embarrassed for the way she'd barged in here. T.D. wasn't Harvey's problem; he was hers. She took a sip from the bottle Mabel had opened for her. It was ice-cold. For a moment she felt like a kid again as the sheriff went around behind his desk and lowered his weight into his chair with a creak and groan.

"Other than bad-mouthing me all over town? He's got it where I can't find anyone to work out at the ranch and I've got cattle that if I don't get them to summer pasture…" Her voice broke. She took another sip.

"I don't doubt T.D. did everything you're saying," Harvey said quietly. "He been out to your place again?"

She waved that off, knowing if Harvey picked him up it would only make T.D. worse, if that were possible. She hadn't come here for that. She knew she had just needed to see him because she needed to vent and she knew that he'd listen. "I keep getting offers on the ranch even though it isn't for sale. T.D. is determined to take half of whatever I could get for the place, even though we were married such a short time. He actually thinks he deserves half the ranch."

Harvey shook his large gray head. "I'm sure you had your reasons for marrying him."

Jinx laughed. "You know that you and Dad tried to warn me but I was in...*love*." She practically spat the word out. "How could I have been so blind?"

"It happens, especially when it comes to love. T.D. can be quite charming, I've heard."

"Not for long." She took another long drink of her cola. "What does that leave me?" she asked, her voice sounding small and scared even to her. "I'm going to have to sell the ranch to get rid of him. My only other option is to—"

"You're not going to shoot him."

She smiled. "You sure about that?"

Harvey sighed. "I know things have been rough since Ray died. Maybe you should think about getting away for a while. Maybe take a trip somewhere. Give T.D. time to cool down."

She narrowed her eyes at him. "Or maybe I should sell the cattle and take a loss and forget about driving them up into the mountains to summer range." But that would be admitting defeat and she wasn't good at that.

When backed against a wall, her tendency was to come out fighting, not give up.

He said nothing for a moment. "What did your father want you to do?" he asked quietly.

Jinx felt the shock move through her and realized of course her father had told his best friend what he wanted her to do once he was gone. "I'm going to have to sell the ranch, aren't I?"

"Sweetie, I know it's not what you want. Are you that determined to keep ranching?"

"It's all I know, but it's more than that. That place has been my home since I was born. I don't want to give it up just because of T.D."

"That's the real thorn in your side, isn't it? T.D. has you against the ropes. But I can't believe you're not that set on ranching it alone. Then again, you're so much like your father," Harvey said, smiling across the desk at her. "Stubborn as the day is long and just as proud. But if you're keeping the ranch to show T.D. or people in this town…"

"It isn't right that T.D. should force me into this or worse, take half."

"I agree. You hired yourself a good lawyer, right?"

She nodded. "He says T.D. can ask for half of what the ranch is worth on paper. No way can I come up with that kind of money. I don't have a choice. In the meantime, T.D. has it where I can't even find any wranglers to work for me."

His expression softened. "I'm worried about you. If T.D. breaks the restraining order again, you call me. I can pick him up, maybe even keep him overnight."

She shook her head, finished her cola and stood. "Thanks."

"I didn't do anything."

Jinx smiled at the older man. "You listened and the cola tasted just like it did when I was a kid. I do feel better. Thanks."

The sheriff rose, as well. As she started to take the empty bottle back to the break room, he said, "I'll take that." She handed it to him, their gazes meeting.

"I'm going to go have a talk with T.D.," he said and rushed on before she could say it would be a waste of time. "He's a cocky son of a bitch and I would love nothing better than to throw him behind bars—that's just between you and me. Maybe we'll get lucky and he'll take a swing at me."

She laughed. "Good luck with that. In the meantime, somehow I'm going to get my cattle to summer range. I'm not going to let T.D. stop me even if it means taking the cattle up there by myself. Don't worry, I've advertised out of state. Maybe I'll get lucky. After that…" She shook her head. She had no idea.

Her hope was that T.D. would give up. Or his girlfriend would keep him busy and away from her. Her father used to believe time healed most things. But with a man like T. D. Sharp? She had her doubts.

"Jinx?" She turned at the door to look back at the sheriff. "Just be careful, okay?"

T. D. Sharp threw his legs over the side of the bed and hung his head. A cool breeze dried the sweat on his naked body as he sat for a moment fighting his mounting regrets and frustration. At the feel of a warm hand on his bare back, he fought the urge to shake it off.

"Come on, baby," Patty Conroe purred. "You don't have to leave. You just got here."

He reached for his underwear and jeans, anxious to escape. Coming here tonight had been a mistake. After his run-in with the sheriff earlier, he'd thought what he needed was a kind word and a soft, willing body. But it hadn't worked tonight. His body had performed but his mind had been miles away—out on the Flying J Bar MC Ranch.

"I need to go out to the ranch and talk to my wife," he said as he stood to pull on his jeans, foolishly voicing the thought that had been rattling around in his head. The sheriff thought he could threaten him? That old fool didn't know who he was dealing with. If T.D. needed to go talk to Jinx, he damned sure would. She could take her restraining order and stuff it up her—

"She isn't your *wife*," Patty snapped. "She's your *ex*."

"Not yet." He heard her sit up behind him. "We don't sign the papers until the property settlement is finished and it sure ain't finished. Which means she's still my wife. And I can damn well go see her if I want to."

"What about the restraining order? You go near her and she's going to call the sheriff."

"Let her. She already went whining to him, but there isn't a thing he can do to me. Anyway, I'm not afraid of Harvey Bessler."

"He's the law, T.D. You better watch yourself or he'll trump something up and lock you behind bars. Have you forgotten that he was her father's best friend? He would love nothing better than to put you in one of his cells."

He scoffed, more than aware how tight Ray McCallahan had been with the sheriff. But Ray was dead and gone and if Harvey kept harassing him, he'd get the old fart fired. "Let him try."

"You think he won't arrest you? Well, I'm not getting

you out of jail this time. You hear me? *Let Jinx go.* She sure didn't have any trouble letting *you* go."

Her words were like a gut punch. He wanted to slap her mouth. "Watch it," he warned. He wouldn't put up with her saying anything bad about Jinx, whether the woman was his almost-ex-wife or not.

He looked around for his boots, knowing that if he didn't get out of this apartment and soon, they were going to fight. He was already fighting with Jinx. He didn't need another woman on his case.

"Why do you need to talk to her *tonight*? Anyway, shouldn't your lawyer be handling this?"

He didn't answer, knowing better. He wished he hadn't brought the subject up about his soon-to-be ex to start with. But she'd been on his mind. Nothing new there. Jinx had caught his eye and he'd fallen for the woman. Fallen hard. When she'd told him it was over and sent him packing, he'd been in shock. The woman needed him. How was she going to run that ranch without him?

But somehow she'd managed in the months since he'd been booted out. He'd put the word out that no one he knew had better go to work for her if they knew what was good for them. He chuckled to himself since he'd heard she was having trouble hiring wranglers to take her cattle up to summer range.

That would teach her to kick him to the curb. He'd thought for sure that after a week or two she'd realize the mistake she'd made and beg him to come back. So he'd made a few mistakes. Like hooking up with Patty.

But Patty wasn't even the reason that Jinx had thrown him out. She'd said she didn't care about his girlfriend, his drinking, his not working the ranch like he should have. She said she was just over him and wanted him gone.

Maybe as his friends said, the only reason he wanted her back was because of his bruised and battered ego. But he knew in his heart that wasn't all of it. He still wanted Jinx. She was the sexiest woman he knew. He was crazy about her.

If she hadn't made him feel like he was a hired hand, he wouldn't have needed Patty. But from the day they married, he'd been too aware that it was her ranch. Not that she didn't always tell him that it was their ranch and that was why she wanted him more involved. But he knew better.

Once she threw him out, though, he threw her words back at her. *Our ranch, huh? Well, then I want half of it.* Not that it was even about the ranch and the property settlement anymore. He couldn't stand that he'd let a woman like her get away. Just the thought of another man touching her drove him insane.

He told himself he could change. He could be the man she needed. She had to give him another chance. He figured if the two of them could just talk—or even better, hit the sack together—they could work this out. Once he got her in bed, she'd listen to reason.

"You're bound and determined to go out there, aren't you?" Patty said behind him, sounding close to tears. She was wasting her time. Her tears no longer moved him. For months she'd been trying to get him to divorce Jinx and marry her. The woman was delusional.

"Maybe I should drive out to that ranch myself," she said, sniffing dramatically. He heard the threat, the anger, the spite, dripping with jealousy. "I'd like to tell her what I think of her."

T.D. refused to take the bait as he found his boots

and began to tug them on. Now, if he could just find his shirt…

"I think it would do her good to know that you've been sneaking over to my place the whole time you've been married to her. Her lawyer might want to hear about it, too."

The words swung at him like a baseball bat to the back of his head. He spun around, going for her throat before he could call back his fury. The woman was threatening to ruin *everything.* Before she could move he was on her. He saw the shock and fear in her eyes as his large hands clamped around her scrawny neck. She opened her mouth, gasping like a fish tossed up on the bank, but no sound came out.

He'd known about the bad blood between Jinx and Patty. Apparently, they'd gone to school together. Jinx had dated Patty's brother in high school. When the fool had gotten drunk and driven off the switchbacks on the highway west of Jackson Hole, Patty was convinced that he'd done it on purpose because of his breakup with Jinx.

T.D. had known how jealous Patty was of Jinx. He'd always suspected that was the reason she'd come after him, determined to get him into her bed not long after his marriage to Jinx. As if it took a lot of effort on her part. Patty was a nice-enough-looking woman with willing ways.

But tonight she seemed to have forgotten her place in the scheme of things. Leaning closer, he tightened his hold on her throat and, pressing his lips to her ear, whispered, "You listen to me. You won't go near that ranch. You won't go near Jinx. You ever say a word to her and I'll…" He felt her go limp and let go of her, dropping her back on the pillows.

For a moment he thought he'd killed her, but then she came to, gasping, eyes wild, hands going to her red and bruising throat. He watched her wheeze for breath as she scooted across the bed out of his reach.

Good, he thought. She needed to know exactly what she was dealing with if she ever betrayed him. She'd been getting a little too cocky for her own good lately. All that talk about the two of them getting married as soon as his divorce went through. Like he would tie a noose around his neck again, especially with a woman like her.

He found his shirt and pulled it on. As he walked out, he didn't look back. Let her wonder if he would ever return. Women like Patty Conroe were a dime a dozen. Women like JoRay "Jinx" McCallahan were another story.

Regret flooded him as he climbed behind the wheel of his pickup. He'd blown it with Jinx. Talk about cocky. Once he had that ring on her finger, he thought he could just coast with her. He'd been dead wrong.

Letting out a snort, he still couldn't believe that she was going to divorce him, though. But then again when Jinx threatened to do something, look out, because the woman was going to do it, come hell or high water.

As he started the engine, he reached over and pulled a can of beer from the near-empty six-pack he'd left on the seat. He told himself that he'd get Jinx back because he couldn't live without her. He knew that now, he thought as he opened the beer and took a long pull on it.

Admittedly, he shouldn't have cheated on her. He should have helped out around the ranch more. He should have done a lot of things differently. With a second chance, he would.

Not that it was all his fault. Jinx wasn't an easy

woman. She was too damned independent. Truth was, she didn't need him and that stuck in his craw.

But now with her daddy in his grave, Jinx was all alone except for Max, that old cook of hers—and all those cattle that needed to be taken up to summer range in the high country.

Maybe she would realize that she couldn't live without him, either. He'd heard that she was so desperate she had even advertised for wranglers out of state.

T.D. smiled to himself. Thanks to him, she was high and dry right now. No one around here was going to work for her. He knew most of the wranglers for hire because of all the years he'd gone from ranch to ranch as one. Unless they wanted to get on his wrong side—a bad place to be—they'd stay clear of Jinx and her ranch. And they had.

What better time to have a talk with her, he thought feeling good. He'd make sure it was just the two of them, restraining order or not. He'd charmed her into marrying him. Surely, he could charm his way back into her life—and her bed.

JINX MCCALLAHAN SLOWED her pickup as she spotted two trucks and horse trailers sitting in her ranch yard. She didn't recognize either of them. After parking, she climbed out and took in the group waiting for her.

She shoved back her Western hat as she considered what looked like a straggly bunch of wranglers standing in the glow of her yard light. She told herself that beggars couldn't be choosers since she had several hundred head of Herefords to get into the high country and time was running out.

Normally, she had no trouble hiring on help this time

of year. She was no fool. Her inability to find local help was T.D.'s doing. He'd put the word out, forcing her to look for help much farther from home, but hadn't heard anything. Unfortunately, word traveled fast among ranching communities about her "problems" with her soon-to-be ex-husband. She couldn't blame anyone for not wanting to get into the middle of it, especially if they knew anything about T. D. Sharp.

But after stopping at the sheriff's office, she'd run some errands, bought herself some dinner and made up her mind. She wasn't going to let T.D. put her out of business even if she had to take the herd to summer range all by herself—just as she'd told the sheriff. Maybe she wouldn't have to if any of these wranglers were decent hands, she thought now.

She stepped to the first cowboy who'd climbed out of the trucks and stood waiting for her. As he removed his hat, she looked into the bluest eyes she'd ever seen and felt a start. Was it the scar on his chin or something about his eyes? What was it about him that made her think she knew this man? Or had at least run across him sometime before? Surely, she would have remembered if she had stumbled across such a handsome cowboy.

Stress and lack of sleep, she told herself. Her mind was playing tricks on her. Or her body was. Because she felt strangely close to him as if they'd once shared something almost…intimate? She knew that was crazy. There'd never been that many men in her life.

Jinx shook her head. Her father's illness, his death, T.D.… All of it had taken a toll on her, she knew. She couldn't trust her mind or her body or her instincts. And if she and this man had met, wouldn't he have said something?

"What's your name?" she asked him.

"Angus Cardwell Savage, ma'am."

"Cardwell?" Her eyes narrowed. "Any relation to the Cardwell Ranch in Montana?"

"Dana Cardwell Savage is my mother."

She considered the tall, lanky, good-looking cowboy for a moment, telling herself that she had to be wrong about having met him before and stepped to the next one. "And you're…"

He quickly removed his hat. "Brick Cardwell Savage, ma'am."

She felt a start as she did a double take, looking from Angus to Brick and back. "You're twins?"

"Identical," Brick said with a chuckle. "Except I'm more charming."

Jinx ignored that. A charming cowboy was the last thing she needed. She'd married one and look how that had turned out.

She considered the two for a moment. Angus had a small scar on his chin in the shape of a crescent moon. Other than that, she couldn't tell the brothers apart. She moved on to the next wrangler.

As the cowhand removed the weathered straw hat, a long blond braid tumbled out. "Ella Cardwell," the wrangler said, lifting her chin in obvious defiance.

Jinx shook her head. "I said I needed men. Not—"

"I can do anything these two can do," Ella said, aiming her elbow at the two cowboys next to her who were also from Cardwell Ranch. "Usually better," the cowgirl added, lifting her gaze until Jinx was staring into emerald green eyes that flashed with fire.

She shot a glance at the two Cardwell men, expecting

them to object. Neither did. Turning back to the young woman, she said, "Ella Cardwell, huh?"

"My mother's Stacy Cardwell. Dana's my aunt."

"What are you doing riding with these two?" Jinx asked, indicating Ella's cousins.

"I like wrangling. I'm more at home on the back of a horse than anywhere on this earth." She shrugged. "My cousins watch out for me and I watch out for them."

Jinx studied the young woman whom she estimated to be in her late twenties, early thirties—about her own age and that of her cousins. They were all young when what she needed was seasoned help. Unfortunately, there was none to be had right now because of her almost-ex-husband. It was why she couldn't afford to be picky and yet...

"Why aren't you all working on your family ranch?" she asked, concerned about their ages and lack of experience. Also their possible safety, given what was going on.

"I will someday, but in the meantime, we wanted to see more of the country and experience life before we settled down," Angus said.

Brick chuckled. "Just sowing some wild oats, ma'am."

That was what she was afraid of. "There won't be any of that on this cattle drive. We have to get my herd up into the mountains for the summer and I'm already running late. If you're looking for fun, you've come to the wrong place."

"We're good hands and we aren't afraid of hard work, ma'am," Angus said, giving his brother's boot next to him a kick. "Don't mind my brother. He likes to joke, ma'am."

She'd had more than enough of this ma'am stuff. "Call me Jinx," she said as she moved to the next two wranglers who'd answered her help-wanted ad.

"Royce Richards," said the fourth cowboy. At least he was older. "Cash and me here used to wrangle for—"

"Huck Chambers," Jinx said, nodding as she eyed the men more closely. She'd seen them around Jackson Hole. Cash looked to be in his early forties, much like Royce. He removed his hat and said, "Cash Andrews." While Royce was tall and wiry-thin with a narrow, pinched face and deep-set dark eyes, Cash was larger with a broad face as plain as a prairie. But when her eyes met his pale brown ones she felt something unsettling behind them.

She tried to remember what she'd heard about the men and why they were no longer with Huck. She thought about calling Huck, but told herself if they didn't work out, she'd pay them off and send them packing. She only needed them for a few days, a week at most, depending on the weather and how long it would take them to move the cattle.

Looking the lot of them over, she reminded herself that she was desperate, but was she *this* desperate? She hesitated. She could use all of them, but hiring a young woman wrangler? That seemed like a recipe for disaster on a cattle drive. She thought of the spirit she'd seen in the young woman's eyes, a spirit that reminded her of herself.

"All right," she said with a sigh, hoping she wasn't making a mistake—not just with the Cardwell bunch but with Royce and maybe especially Cash. What was that she'd seen in his gaze? Just a flicker of something she couldn't put her finger on. A lot of cowboys didn't like taking orders from a woman. She hoped that was all she'd seen.

"See your way to the bunkhouse. We ride out at first light in the morning. I notice that you brought your own stock," she said, glancing at the two pickups parked in her yard and the horse trailers behind them. "You can bed them down for the night in the barn or that corral. Cook will rustle up something for you to eat. I wouldn't suggest going into Jackson Hole tonight." *Or any other night*, she thought. But since they would ride into the mountains early tomorrow, they'd have little chance to get into trouble.

At least that was what she told herself as she headed inside the ranch house to talk to Max about feeding them. She found him in the kitchen finishing up washing some pots and pans, his back to her. The cook was short and stocky as a fat thumb with a personality as surprising as what he often cooked. He'd been with Jinx's family for years. She didn't know what she would do without him. Or vice versa if she sold the ranch.

But as she studied the man from behind, she realized Max was getting old. He wouldn't be able to handle a cattle drive much longer. For him, her selling the ranch might be a relief. He could retire since she knew her father had left him well-off.

The moment he turned around and she saw Max's face, she knew he'd seen her wranglers. "They might not be as bad as they look," she said defensively.

"Didn't say a word."

"You didn't have to." She leaned on the counter. "Can you rustle up something for them to eat?"

He nodded and began digging in the refrigerator. He came out with a chunk of roast beef. She watched him slice it and said, "They're young, I'll admit."

"Unless my eyes are going, that one looked distinctly female."

She sighed. "I like her."

Max laughed, shaking his head. "Bet she reminds you of yourself."

"Is that so bad?" He said nothing, letting that be his answer. "You hear anything about Royce Richards and Cash Andrews?" she asked, changing the subject. "They used to work for Huck Chambers."

He looked up from the beef he was slicing. "If you have any misgivings, send them on down the road."

"I can't. I have to take a chance with them. I need the help and at least they're older and probably more experienced." She looked toward the window and wondered what her father would have done. In the twilight, the pine trees were etched black against the graying sky. Beyond that, the dark outline of the mountains beckoned.

She told herself that she had to follow her instincts. First, she would get the herd up to the high country to graze for the summer. It would buy her time. Then she would decide what to do. She couldn't think about the future right now.

But of course that was all that was on her mind. "Once this cattle drive is over..." She didn't finish because she didn't know what she would do. Just the thought of ever leaving this ranch brought her to tears.

"I'll run sandwiches over to the bunkhouse," Max said. "You should get some sleep. You worry too much. You have five wranglers. With a little luck—"

"My luck's been running pretty thin lately." If the wranglers had heard what was going on at her ranch, they wouldn't have wanted anything to do with the Flying J Bar MC and she'd really be out of luck.

"I have a feeling your luck is about to change for the better," Max said as he picked up the plate of sandwiches and started for the door. "You're due. You want one of these sandwiches? I don't remember you eating much for dinner earlier."

She shook her head. "I'm not hungry, but thanks. Max," she called, stopping him at the door. "You didn't have anything to do with those three showing up from Cardwell Ranch, right? You didn't call Dana Savage, did you?"

He didn't turn as he said, "Go behind your back? I know better than to do something like that. I'm no fool." With that he left.

Jinx sighed, still suspicious. Her mother had been friends with Dana and it would be just like Max to try to help any way he could. She let it go, telling herself not to look a gift horse in the mouth. She had five wranglers, and tomorrow they would head up into the high country. Maybe Max was right and her luck was changing.

Still, she stood for a long time in the kitchen, remembering how things had been when both of her parents were alive. This house had been filled with laughter. But it had been a long time ago, she thought as she heard Max leave the bunkhouse and head out to his cabin. Her father's recent illness and death had left a pall over the ranch even before she'd finally had it with T.D.

You need a change. Don't stay here and try to run this ranch by yourself. I don't want that for you. Her father's words still haunted her. Did he really think it would be that easy just to sell this place, something he and his father had built with their blood, sweat and tears?

She shook her head and was about to head up to bed when she heard the roar of a vehicle engine. Through the kitchen window, she spotted headlights headed her way—and coming fast. "T.D." She said his name like a curse.

Chapter Two

After they took care of their horses, Angus could tell that something was bothering his cousin and wasn't surprised when Ella pulled the two of them aside.

"Maybe we should have told her the truth about why we're here," she said, keeping her voice down. The other two wranglers were still inside the bunkhouse.

"I thought the plan wasn't to say anything unless she didn't hire us," Brick reminded her. "She hired us, so what's the problem?"

"It doesn't feel right keeping the truth from her," Ella said more to Angus than Brick. She knew how Brick felt. He'd found them a job up by the Canadian border where one of his old girlfriends lived on the ranch. The last thing he'd wanted to do was come to Wyoming instead. Especially knowing the circumstances.

"We don't want to stomp on the woman's pride," Angus said. He knew firsthand where that could get a person. "Jinx needs three good wranglers and that's what we're doing here. Once it's done you can go anywhere you want to go."

Brick sighed as they reached their pickup and unloaded their gear before continuing on to the bunkhouse. Angus found himself looking out into the growing darkness. He'd felt it the moment they'd driven into the ranch yard. He wondered if the others had, as well, but wasn't about to ask. Trouble had a feel to it that hung in the air. An anticipation. A dread. A sense of growing danger. It was thick as the scent of pines on this ranch.

He understood why his brother hadn't wanted to come—and not just because of that cowgirl up by the Canadian border. "Don't see any reason to buy trouble," Brick had argued. "I know this woman's mother was a good friend of our mother's, but *Wyoming*?" Brick had never seen any reason to leave Montana. Angus felt much the same way.

But Jinx McCallahan was in trouble and their mother had asked them to help her—but to keep in mind that she was a strong, independent woman who wouldn't take well to charity. She just needed some wranglers to get her cattle up to summer range, Dana had said.

While Brick had been dragging his feet, none of them was apt to turn down Dana Cardwell Savage. But what his brother and cousin didn't know was that he would have come even if their mother hadn't asked them. The moment he heard that JoRay "Jinx" McCallahan needed wranglers, he'd been on board.

"Once she can get her cattle up to summer range, things should get better for her," their mother had said. News among ranch families traveled like wildfire, but Angus had the feeling Dana had heard from someone close to Jinx. "The trouble is her ex-husband. He's got all the local ranchers riled up. She can't get anyone to work for her other than Max, the ranch cook, and while he's like family, he's getting up in age."

Angus had talked Brick into it. All it had taken was

the promise that when the cattle were in their summer grazing area, they'd hightail it back to Montana.

Ella hadn't needed any talking into it. "The woman just buried her father? She's running the family ranch single-handedly and now the ex-husband is keeping her from getting her cattle to summer pasture? Of course we'll go help."

Dana hadn't been so sure that her niece should go, but Ella wasn't having any of that. She'd been riding with her cousins since college. She wasn't sitting this one out. So the three of them had packed up and headed for a small community south of Jackson Hole, Wyoming.

Angus had been looking forward to seeing Jinx again. He remembered her red hair and her temper and was intrigued to find out what had happened to that girl. *That girl*, he'd seen tonight, had grown into a beautiful woman. Her hair wasn't quite as red, but her brown eyes still reminded him of warm honey. And those freckles... He smiled to himself. She didn't try to hide them, any more than she tried to hide the fact that she was a woman you didn't want to mess with.

For a moment earlier he'd thought that she had remembered him. But why would she? They'd just been kids, thrown together for a few hours because of their mothers.

He'd seen her looking at the scar on his chin. If anything could have jogged her memory, the scar should have, he thought as they entered the bunkhouse.

"It's more than Jinx needing wranglers to get her cattle up to summer range," Ella said quietly beside him.

He nodded, having felt it since they'd reached the ranch. Jinx had more trouble than a lack of hired help.

Back in the bunkhouse, he'd just tossed his bedroll

onto the top bunk when he heard a revved engine growing louder as a vehicle approached the ranch.

"Stay here," he said to Ella, signaling to his brother to stay with her.

He picked up his weapon from the bed, strapped it on and stepped out of the bunkhouse into the darkness to see the glow of headlights headed straight for them.

JINX PICKED UP the shotgun by the front door on her way out to the porch. The moment she'd heard the engine, she'd known it was T.D. and that he was going to be a problem. By now he would have had a snoot full of beer and have worked himself up. She didn't need to see her ex-husband's pickup come to a dust-boiling stop just short of the house to know that he was in one of his moods.

The driver's-side door was flung open almost before he'd killed the engine. *Drunk again*, she thought with a silent curse. Tucker David "T.D." Sharp stumbled out of the pickup, looking nothing like the handsome, charming cowboy who'd lassoed her heart and sweet-talked her all the way to the altar.

"You get out here, JoRay!" he yelled as he stumbled toward the house. "We need to talk."

"I'm right here," she said as she stepped from the dark shadows of the porch. She saw his eyes widen in surprise—first seeing her waiting for him and then when he spotted the shotgun in her hands. "You need to leave, T.D. I've already called the sheriff."

He smirked at that. "Even if you did call him, it will take Harvey at least twenty minutes to get out here."

"That's what the loaded shotgun is for," she said calmly, even though her heart was racing. Just seeing him in this state set her on alert. She knew firsthand what he was capable of when he got like this. He'd torn up the kitchen, breaking dishes and some of her mother's collectibles during one of his tantrums.

"Come on, JoRay. I just want to talk to you," he whined as he took another step closer. "Remember what it was like? You and me? You *loved* me. I *still* love you." He took another step. "I deserve another chance. I swear I can change."

"That's close enough." She raised the shotgun, pointing the business end of the barrel at the center of his chest.

He stopped, clearly not sure she wouldn't use it on him. She saw his expression change. "You had no business kicking me off this ranch," he said, his tone going from wheedling to angry in a heartbeat. He spat on the ground. "I got me a lawyer. Half this ranch is mine and I intend to take what's mine. This ranch and you, if I want it. You're still my wife. I can take it all." He started toward her when a voice out of the darkness stopped him.

"Not tonight you aren't."

A wrangler stepped from the shadows into the ranch-yard light by the bunkhouse. She saw the faint gleam of the scar on his chin. She also saw that Angus was armed. He hadn't pulled his gun, but it was in sight and T.D. saw it, too.

"Who the hell are you?" her almost-ex-husband demanded.

"The lady asked you to leave," Angus said, his voice low, but forceful.

T.D. scoffed. "You going to make me?"

"If it comes to that, yes." The cowhand still hadn't moved, hadn't touched the gun at his hip, but there was something like steel in his tone.

She could see T.D. making up his mind. He'd come out here looking for a fight even if he hadn't realized it. But with T.D., like most bullies, he preferred better odds.

He swore and shot Jinx a lethal look. "This isn't over. You might have hired yourself some…cowboys," he said as some of the other wranglers came out of the bunkhouse and watched from a distance, "but when they're gone…" She heard the promised threat, saw it in his gaze. He'd be back for more than the ranch.

Jinx felt a shudder. How could she have not seen the mean side of this man before she stupidly married him? Because he'd kept it well hidden. Drunk, he was even worse, filled with an unexplained rage. She'd felt the brunt of that anger. He'd never hit her. He wasn't that stupid. But he'd beat her down with his angry words every time he drank until she'd had enough and sent him packing at gunpoint.

Her father, Ray, had been in the hospital then. Once he died, T.D. got it into his head that he deserved a second chance. When that didn't work, he'd decided the ranch should be his. And so should Jinx. He'd refused to sign the divorce papers until she settled up with him.

The problem with the man was that he never took no for an answer. Egged on by his friends he drank with and some of the other ranchers he'd grown up with who'd tried to buy her out the moment her father had died, T.D. felt both the ranch and she were his legal right.

Legally, he might have some right to the ranch, unfortunately, because they were still husband and wife technically. She hadn't had the sense to get a prenuptial agreement signed before they'd married. She'd been in love and stupid. But no matter how much of a fight T.D. put up, she was divorcing him. And while he might get his hands on half the proceeds from the ranch, he would never get his hands on her again if she could help it.

T.D. started toward his truck, stopped and tilted his head as if listening. With a smirk, he turned back to say, "If you called the sheriff, he's sure taking his time getting here." His gaze locked with hers for a moment. "Liar, liar, pants on fire, all Miss High-and-Mighty. You didn't even call the sheriff."

"If I'd called the sheriff," she said quietly, "he would have stopped me from shooting you, if you'd taken another step in my direction."

The words seemed to hit T.D. like a strong wind. He wavered, his gaze locking with hers. "So why'd you bother with a restraining order, then?" he snapped, thinking he was smarter than she was.

"Because it will look better in court after I kill you. 'I tried to keep him away, but he just wouldn't listen.'"

"Best keep it loaded and beside your bed, then," he said, smirking at her. "Because I'll be back."

She didn't doubt that. He would come back when it was just her and Max alone on the ranch. "And I'll kill you before I let you touch me again."

Her words inflamed him—just as she knew they would. But he wasn't the only one with a temper. She'd put up with all she was going to from this man. She didn't want him to doubt that she would pull the trigger on both barrels when he came back.

T.D. slammed his fist down on the hood of his pickup as he stumbled to the driver's-side door and jerked it open. He shot her a hateful look before climbing behind the wheel. The engine revved. He threw the truck in Reverse and tore off down the road, throwing dirt and gravel.

Jinx let out the breath she'd been holding. Moments before, she'd half expected T.D. to turn and charge her like a raging bull, forcing her to shoot him or pay the price for even a moment's hesitation. She figured the only reason he hadn't was because of Angus.

As she turned to thank him, she saw that the spot where he'd been standing was empty. Like the others, he must have gone back inside the bunkhouse. Apparently, he hadn't wanted or needed thanks. But now he'd put himself in the line of fire. T.D. wouldn't forget.

ANGUS STEPPED AROUND the side of the bunkhouse, listening to the sound of T.D.'s pickup engine fading in the distance. He hoped the man had enough sense not to come back, but he wouldn't bet on that.

He thought of the way that Jinx had handled the situation and he smiled. Angus had come down here believing that it was to save not just Jinx's cattle—but the woman herself.

After seeing her with that shotgun tonight, staring down her husband, Angus realized Jinx McCallahan could take care of herself. It didn't surprise him. He thought of the girl he'd met just that once. She'd made an impression on him all those years ago. She'd done it again tonight.

Her almost-ex-husband thought he could bully her. Well, T. D. Sharp had picked the wrong woman to try to intimidate. Angus could have told him that just based on knowing her a few hours years before. You didn't want to mess with that redhead, he thought, smiling to himself.

So as he stood in the dark, pretty sure T.D. wasn't headed back this way—at least not yet, he reevaluated what he was doing here. Helping Jinx get her cattle to summer range, but after that…he wasn't so sure.

Angus thought of the woman standing on the porch with the loaded double-barrel shotgun trained on her not-soon-enough-ex-husband. He realized he wasn't here to rescue her. She could rescue herself. But maybe, with some luck, he could keep her from killing T.D. and going to jail.

PATTY STOOD IN front of the bathroom mirror inspecting her throat. It was still red in spots and bruised in others. She could make out T.D.'s fingerprints where he'd choked her. She touched the spot tenderly and cursed Jinx. Just the mention of her name sent T.D. in a tailspin. Until he was done with that woman, he wasn't himself. She had to remember that.

Stepping out of the bathroom, she thought she heard a vehicle. T.D. would come back. He'd be all apologetic and loving. He'd done it before another time when he'd gotten rough with her. And like tonight, it had been over Jinx McCallahan.

Oh, how she hated that woman, she thought, fisting her hands, fingernails biting into her palms. She'd give anything to get that woman out of their lives.

And now T.D. had gone out to her ranch to see her as if he could talk her into giving him another chance. The damned fool. It would serve him right if he got himself arrested—or shot. She wouldn't put it past Jinx to shoot him. Maybe then he'd realize that she didn't give two hoots about him.

Tears burned her eyes. What was wrong with the man? He had a woman who loved him unconditionally and still he couldn't stay away from that…ranch woman. He'd left her to go to Jinx. It burned at her insides. What if he didn't come back tonight? What if Jinx gave him a second chance? The thought made her sick to her stomach. Why couldn't she just let T.D. go?

She felt bitterness roiling in her stomach. If only Jinx would sell her ranch and leave town like most people thought she would after her father died. Let her move far away. Then T.D. would come to his senses. As long as Jinx was around, she'd keep him stirred up.

Her phone rang. For a moment she thought it would be T.D. Maybe he'd gone down to the bar and had started feeling guilty about their fight and was now calling to apologize. Or maybe invite her down to the bar to have a drink with him. Wouldn't it be something to be able to go out in public together? That would show Jinx.

She checked her cell phone, instantly disappointed. It was only Wyatt, T.D.'s friend, probably calling to ask if she knew where the man was. "Hey," she said, picking up. Maybe T.D. had asked him to call her.

"Are you all right? I saw T.D.'s truck down at the bar. Figured you'd be alone. You two have a fight?"

Patty's heart dropped. If T.D. was at the bar, then maybe he *wasn't* planning to come back tonight.

"You okay?" Wyatt asked.

She felt touched by his concern. The shy cowboy was so sweet. Too bad she couldn't fall for him instead of T.D. "Wyatt, you have to stop worrying about me." He'd found her sobbing her eyes out the last time she and T.D. had had a bad fight. He'd run a clean washcloth under the cold-water faucet in the bathroom, wrung it out and handed it to her. He'd asked if he could get her anything to eat, something to drink.

He was so thoughtful. She wished T.D. was more like

him. And while she appreciated the fact that Wyatt cared, at the same time, it felt a little creepy. Sometimes she wondered if he watched her apartment just waiting for T.D. to leave in one of his moods.

"I could come over," Wyatt said now.

She touched her throat. It still hurt. Wyatt would notice the bruises and the dark spots that looked like fingertips. "I don't think that's a good idea. You know how T.D. is. He wouldn't like it." Who was she kidding? T.D. wouldn't care.

"Was he alone at the bar?" she asked.

"I don't know. I didn't go inside. Patty, what do you see in him?"

It was a question she'd asked herself many times over the year she'd been seeing T.D. He'd never made it a secret that he loved his wife and yet, she'd been convinced that one day he would leave Jinx and marry her. Instead, Jinx had thrown him out and now T.D. was determined to get the woman back.

"I'm in love with him," she said simply. "You know that."

"I know. It's just that…he doesn't treat you right, Patty. You need a man who values you for who you are. You have so much to offer a man. A man who deserves it."

She couldn't argue that. Like tonight, she didn't need Wyatt to tell her that it was mean of T.D. to come by only to leave right after they'd had sex. She knew he was using her and it broke her heart, but what could she do? The alternative was to not see him at all.

"You have to know how I feel about you. What can I do to show you? Just name it, Patty," Wyatt pleaded. "I would do anything for you."

She walked back into the bathroom and stared at her

reflection in the mirror for a moment. Wyatt was right. She deserved better. "There *is* something you could do. Where are you now?"

"Just down the street." His voice sounded hopeful and she knew he'd meant it about doing anything for her. With a little persuasion, she thought she could get Wyatt to do the one thing she might ask.

"Come on up. But make it quick. T.D. will be coming back soon."

AFTER LEAVING THE RANCH, T.D. had considered going back to Patty's. But he wasn't up for another fight. Nor was he up for apologizing. Patty just didn't get it. He wanted Jinx, as much as he hated her right now. His wife thought she had the upper hand at the moment. Maybe she did. Maybe that was why he was so angry.

He'd driven straight to the bar, telling himself that maybe he would sneak back out to the ranch later tonight and surprise Jinx. A need stirred in him like none he'd ever felt, and he kept reminding himself that she was still his wife. She'd better not be seeing anyone else. Just the thought of that cowboy who'd come out with his six-shooter strapped on his hip...

He ordered a beer even though he could tell Marty hadn't wanted to serve him at all. But Marty also didn't want any trouble, as if he could sense that T.D. was just spoiling for a fight. It had been a long time since he'd broken up a bar.

"One beer, T.D., and then you head on home," the bartender told him.

"Home? And where exactly would that be, Marty?" he asked angrily as he picked up the cold beer the man had set in front of him. He took a long drink. It did little to cool down his fury. Jinx had no right to treat him this way. She'd made him the laughingstock of town. He couldn't let her get away with it. Half that ranch was his and damned if she wasn't going to give it to him. If she thought they were finished, then she didn't know him very well.

He smiled to himself and took another gulp of beer. From what he'd seen out at her place, she was planning to take that herd of hers into the mountains tomorrow. It would take her a few days of good weather and good luck to get them up to the high country.

T.D. had made that trip with her last year. He knew the route she took and where she camped each night. As he finished his beer, he realized that he hadn't believed she would get anyone to help her take her cattle up to summer range. Now that she had, she'd forced his hand. He could no longer just threaten to follow her up into the mountains. He had to do it. He had to show her. And he knew just how to do it.

WYATT FELT SHAKEN to his core as he left Patty's apartment. His hands actually shook as he started his truck. On one hand, he couldn't believe his good luck. On the other… He left, driving aimlessly through town, his mind whirling.

He'd had a crush on Patty since grade school. Not that she'd ever noticed him except on those few occasions when he'd stopped into the café where she waitressed. She was nice enough then, smiling and chatting him up. He wasn't stupid. He knew she was like that with everyone because she hoped for a good tip.

Over the years, he'd watched her go through a couple of bad marriages and twice as many equally bad relationships. But nothing had cooled his ardor for her. He'd always known he was what she needed. He'd only hoped that one day she would realize it.

Now he had finally told her how he felt and to his surprise, she'd made him an offer. The offer was less than what he'd hoped for and yet more than he'd expected. He felt as if full of helium. This must be what people meant when they said they were floating on cloud nine.

Of course, there was a catch, he thought, feeling himself come back to earth with a thud.

"Word is that Jinx is driving her cattle up to summer range tomorrow," she'd said once they were seated on the couch in her living room. She'd sat so close to him that her perfume had filled his nostrils making him feel weak. He couldn't help but notice that she'd forgotten to button the two top buttons on her blouse, making it gap open. Sitting this close he could see the swell of her full breasts above her lacy black bra.

He'd also seen the red marks on her neck, a couple of them deep bruises, but he'd known better than to say anything. He'd figured it was why she'd invited him up so he waited for her to bring up the subject.

"Wyatt, you're his best friend," she'd said, leaning toward him. "You know T.D. is planning something. Once Jinx gets those cattle to the high country, T.D. will lose his leverage—or at least what he sees as leverage."

He'd nodded, surprised that Patty knew this about T.D. and yet still wanted the man. "He's threatened to follow her up into the mountains," he'd admitted. "But I think it's just talk."

She'd scoffed at that. "He'll get himself all worked up tonight after a few beers and then he'll want you and Travis to go with him since he doesn't have the guts to do it alone, and the two of you don't have the guts to turn him down."

He'd winced, knowing it was true and that she was right. He'd agree to go once T.D. started pressuring him. You just didn't say no to him, and Wyatt hadn't since they were kids growing up. T.D. had gotten him into so much trouble over the years. But like she said, the man was his best friend.

What she'd said next had floored him. "I want you to make sure that Jinx McCallahan never comes out of those mountains."

At first he'd thought he'd misunderstood her. "I don't know what you mean."

And then Patty had leaned toward him, her full breasts brushing his arm as she kissed him. "Do this for me and I promise you won't regret it." She kissed him harder, giving him a little of her tongue. He'd about lost it right there.

But when he'd reached for her, she'd pushed him away. "Not until you do me this favor." Then she'd taken his hand and put it on her warm breast. He'd felt her nipple harden under his palm. And just as quickly, she'd pulled it away. "Now you should go. You wouldn't want T.D. to catch you here."

He'd stumbled out of her apartment to his rig and started driving aimlessly. She wasn't serious about any of it, he told himself. Not the offer. Not the favor she'd made him promise to think about as he was leaving. The woman didn't realize what she was asking. Or what she was offering.

"If you and T.D. get up in those mountains trying to sabotage Jinx and her cattle drive, anything could happen," Patty had insisted as she'd walked him to the door. "Accidents happen. No one even knows who did what."

There was no mistaking what she'd asked him to do for her. Kill Jinx. As if the woman was Patty's only problem. It astounded him that she didn't know T.D. at all. Even if Jinx wasn't in the picture, T.D. wasn't going to marry her. He'd string her along until he found someone else he thought he deserved more. Then he would break her heart all over again. But this time Wyatt would be there to pick up the pieces. Unless he let Patty down now.

He saw T.D.'s pickup parked in front of the bar and their friend Travis getting out of his rig to go inside. He pulled in, honked his horn and Travis stopped to wait for him.

That he'd even given a second thought to Patty's favor was insane. He couldn't kill anyone, especially his best friend's wife, he told himself as he climbed out of his truck in the glow of the neon bar sign. Why would Patty think he was capable of such a thing?

Because she knew how much he wanted her.

Patty was the only woman in town who saw him as anything but a shy, awkward cowboy who lived with his mother when he wasn't working on some ranch or another. She was offering him something he'd only dreamed of for years. He could still taste her on his lips as he and Travis pushed into the bar.

Chapter Three

As T.D. finished his beer, he tried to understand where he'd gone wrong. Too bad his father wasn't still around. His old man would have told him how worthless he was, happily listing every mistake he'd ever made, and the list was long.

He'd thought marrying Jinx would change him. Even his father would have been surprised that a woman like Jinx would have given two cents about him, let alone married him. But now she was divorcing him, proving that his father was right. He didn't deserve Jinx. He really was worthless.

But Patty aside, he wanted to argue that he'd been a pretty good husband. Just not the one Jinx wanted. He ground his teeth at the thought. What the devil had she wanted anyway? A man she could boss around? Or one who would take over the ranch and run it the way he saw fit? He could run that ranch with one hand tied behind him—if she'd give him another chance. So he'd made a few mistakes when she'd let him run it. He wouldn't make those mistakes again.

He fumed at the thought of the way Jinx had treated him at the end. He'd looked into her beautiful face and he'd seen the disgust he'd grown up with. He wasn't good enough for her, never had been, her look said. He saw that look every night when he closed his eyes to try to sleep.

The only thing that kept him sane was drinking. If he drank enough, sometimes he'd pass out and didn't have to see that look.

"Another beer," he said, banging his empty bottle hard on the bar and getting a side-eye from the bartender.

"You've had enough," Marty said as he came down, a bar rag in his hand. He picked up the empty bottle. "I told you I was only serving you one. Why don't you call it a night, T.D.?"

"What don't you—" The rest was cut off as his two friends came in on a rush of spring air. He could see how this was going to go if he stayed. He was in one of his tear-this-place-apart moods.

"Let's get out of here," he said to his friends, sliding off his stool before they could join him. "If they don't want our business here, we'll take it somewhere else. Anyway, there's free beer at Patty's. She's a little mad at me, but I still have my key." He picked up his change, leaving no tip for Marty as he pocketed the few coins. Marty acted as if he didn't care. He seemed glad to see him go.

"Why don't we go to my place?" Travis suggested. "I've got beer and there's no one there to give us any trouble."

T.D. laughed. "Good idea. I need to let Patty wonder where I am for a few days anyway."

Outside, the cold spring night air took his breath away for a moment. Warm, summerlike weather was a good two months away in this part of Wyoming. He started toward his pickup when he spotted the sheriff standing across the street leaning on his cruiser. He swore under his breath. The SOB was just waiting for him to get behind the wheel. Harvey had been laying for him, hoping to catch him at something so he could throw his butt behind bars.

T.D. laughed. "Let's walk. It's a nice night," he said to his friends.

"Are you kidding?" Travis squawked. "It's freezing out."

"Man up," T.D. said as he gave Travis a playful shove and then the three of them were making their way down the street, leaving their vehicles parked in front of the bar. It wasn't as if they hadn't done that before on those nights when they were too drunk to drive home.

"You're awfully quiet," T.D. said, throwing his arm around Wyatt's shoulder. "I'd suspect you had woman trouble if I didn't know you better." He laughed at his own joke as Wyatt shrugged off his arm.

"I might surprise you someday," Wyatt said.

"Right," T.D. said with a chuckle. "But in all seriousness we need to talk about tomorrow. I hope you're both ready to ride up in the mountains. We've got to catch up with Jinx and do a little damage."

"What kind of damage?" Travis asked, sounding worried.

"You know," T.D. said, feeling the alcohol he'd consumed. Sometimes it made him feel invincible. He was going to show everyone, especially Jinx. "Get ready for some…high jinks."

WYATT HAD BEEN hopeful that Patty was wrong and T.D. would give up on trying to stop Jinx's cattle drive. He should have known better. T.D. was at loose ends after the breakup. One day he was determined to get her back;

the next he just wanted half the ranch so he could get on with his life.

Going up into the mountains after Jinx and her herd, though, was just plain crazy. Nothing good could come of that. Someone could get killed. Wasn't that what Patty was hoping? The reminder sent a chill through him. That he would even consider her request... Was he so desperate for anything that Patty offered that he'd even consider it?

Once they reached Travis's trailer, they consumed more beer and listened to T.D.'s account of what had happened earlier tonight, first at Patty's, then out at the ranch with Jinx. Wyatt watched as T.D. worked himself up for tomorrow. Just as Patty had said, the cowboy was talking about chasing after the herd and Jinx as they headed for the high country and doing anything he could to ruin her life.

"It's time I showed Jinx what was what," T.D. blustered, fueled by the booze and the anger he had going.

"Come on, T.D., what's the point in going all the way up there after her?" Travis argued. "Sounds like it could get us all killed or thrown into jail and for what? Just to mess with your ex-wife?"

T.D. swore. "She's not my ex yet. I need to show her that I mean business. And up in the mountains, the sheriff won't be watching me like a hawk. That old fart is out to get me because of her."

Wyatt had to ask, "You got a plan?" He still held out hope that all this was just the booze talking. Maybe by morning, T.D. would be so hungover he'd have changed his mind. The thought both relieved him and upset him. He hated to think how it would disappoint Patty. Wyatt couldn't stand the thought of her thinking less of him.

T.D. grinned. "You know how dangerous a cattle drive can be. Accidents happen. And let's face it. Jinx is due for some bad luck the way I see it. She can't just toss me out without a dime. Before I'm through with her, she'll be begging me to take half the ranch. Maybe more. If something were to happen to her… Well, we're still legally married. That entire ranch could be mine…if my wife should meet with one of those accidents."

"I don't like the sound of this."

"Damn it, Travis," T.D. snapped. "Stop your whining. You don't want to come with us? Fine. Stay here and work at your old man's hardware store. Or you could tell him that you have a cattle drive to go to and won't be back for a few days."

"You're going to get me fired, T.D."

"Quit. Once I get the ranch, I can offer you a good-paying job and you won't have to put up with your old man ever again. How does that sound? You, too, Wyatt."

Wyatt couldn't imagine anything worse than working for T.D. "Sounds great," he said, which seemed to be what the cowboy needed to hear right now.

"Sure," Travis said, sounding about as enthused by the idea as he was.

He had to hand it to Travis for trying to talk sense into T.D. But ultimately, Wyatt knew that Travis would come along with them. T.D. would beat him down. Just as he would Wyatt if he'd raised objections. So he hadn't bothered, because as T.D.'s best friend, it was a foregone conclusion that he was going along.

"Then we should get some sleep," Travis said, climbing to his feet.

"Mind if I stay here, Trav?" T.D. asked as he finished his beer and stood.

"Take the guest room down the hall."

T.D. laughed. "Guest room. That broom closet of a room? You're really living large, Trav."

"I'm going home," Wyatt told the two as he got to his feet.

"I'll pick you up first thing in the morning," T.D. said. "Be ready." It wouldn't be the first time T.D. had sat outside Wyatt's mother's house, honking his horn and yelling for him to get moving.

And just as quickly, T.D. changed his mind. "Wait, first we should have one more beer to celebrate," he said, pulling Wyatt to him as Travis went to the refrigerator for the beers. "A toast to us!" he said, putting his arm around each of their shoulders. They clinked beer cans together, T.D. sloshing his own beer on the floor.

"We're going to need to pick up a few things in the morning before we head out. I promise you, this is going to be fun," T.D. said. "Something all three of us will remember when we're old men. Isn't that right, Wyatt?" He pulled him closer.

Wyatt hoped the cowboy didn't smell Patty's perfume on him. He could still smell it on his shirt, still remember the feel of her lips and the sweet touch of her tongue in his mouth. He swallowed, afraid he couldn't do what she asked. More afraid he could.

ANGUS HADN'T SLEPT WELL. Seeing Jinx now grown-up and so beautiful and self-assured, he'd felt a sense of pride. *I knew her when*, he'd thought. But that wasn't all that stole his sleep.

Last night he'd seen how strong and capable Jinx was when facing down her soon-to-be ex-husband. He worried that if he hadn't been here, T. D. Sharp would have called her bluff and gotten killed. Unfortunately, that would have been something Jinx would have had to live with the rest of her life.

Now Angus had found himself lying awake, listening for the sound of a pickup on the road into the ranch. The one thing he'd learned about T.D. last night was that he wasn't through with Jinx and that made him dangerous—just as dangerous as the situation he, Brick and Ella had ridden into.

He must have drifted off, though, because the clang of the breakfast bell brought him up with a start. By then, Ella and Brick had been already dressed and headed for the chow hall. Angus had quickly followed. The other two wranglers had straggled into the ranch kitchen a little later.

"I'd like you to ride point with me," Jinx told him at breakfast.

"Happy to," Angus said. He and the ranch woman would be riding at the head of the line of cattle. He'd felt her studying him as if trying to understand why he seemed familiar, he figured. Maybe he'd tell her once they were alone on the cattle drive. Not that she would probably be happy to hear their first meeting story, he thought, touching his scar.

Jinx turned to Ella and Brick. "I thought the two of you could work the flank and swing positions farther back." She considered Royce and Cash. "You'll be the drag men bringing up the rear, picking up stragglers and keeping the line moving."

"Whatever you say, trail boss," Cash had said with a smirk.

Jinx seemed to ignore him. "We'll see how that works out. Max will be bringing up the rear in the chuckwagon."

At daybreak Angus and the rest of the wranglers saddled up and began to move the large herd of cattle toward the mountains. They left the valley floor for the foothills dotted with tall pines. Angus felt a sense of relief to be riding away from the ranch.

The days ahead would be filled with long hours on horseback, herding cattle up into the towering mountains of western Wyoming. He loved cattle drives and always had. It was a peaceful existence. *At least for the moment*, he thought as he looked back down the road. Soon they would start the climb up into the mountains.

He found himself looking over his shoulder, wondering how long it would be before he spotted riders coming after them. How long it would be before he saw T. D. Sharp again. By then, they would be far from civilization. They would be on their own since Jinx had said their cell phones wouldn't work until they reached the top of the mountain—and even that was sketchy.

They moved cattle all morning and now trailed them along a creek through the pines. Cattle tended not to trail in a group, but string out in a long line. There were natural leaders who would take their places in front, while all the rest trailed behind. A head of a thousand could stretch out a mile or two so the wranglers worked in pairs on each side of the line.

The day had broken clear and sunny, reminding Angus how much he loved this work. He breathed in the spring air, rich with sweet pine, the scent of bright green spring grasses. It mixed with the scent of dust and cattle on the warm breeze. He lived for this and couldn't imagine any other life, he thought as he turned his face up to the sun. He knew his mother hoped that one day he would return and help run Cardwell Ranch in the Gallatin Canyon near Big Sky, Montana.

Lately, the ranch had been calling him. He could feel his time of being a saddle tramp was almost over. He just wasn't sure his brother Brick realized it. Or how his cousin Ella would take the news. Knowing her, she had already sensed his growing need to return home.

He'd grown up on Cardwell Ranch, fished the blue ribbon trout stream of the Gallatin, skied Lone Peak and ridden through the mountains on horseback from the time he could sit a saddle. But as he took in this part of Wyoming, he thought nothing could be more beautiful than its towering snowcapped peaks.

His gaze shifted to the woman who rode opposite him. He could see her through the tall pines. Like him, she, too, was smiling. "Beautiful, isn't it?" she called to him as if sensing him watching her.

"Sure is." Jinx in her element was more beautiful than the country around her. Her long, copper-colored hair was tied off low on the back of her neck. Her straw cowboy hat was pushed back and her freckled face turned up to the morning sun making her brown eyes sparkle. He couldn't help staring.

At a sound behind him, he turned as his brother rode up, all smiles. "You have a nice herd here," Brick called to Jinx. "Excuse me for saying it, but you look real pretty this morning." With that he spurred his horse before he turned back to his flank position.

Angus rolled his eyes at him and rode off to pick up one of the cows that had wandered off, before falling back into line. He saw that Jinx had dropped back to say something to Brick and shook his head. His brother.

If there was a pretty woman around, Brick was going to try to charm her.

But Angus suspected his brother was wasting his time. Jinx had already fallen for one cowboy whom she was now trying to get rid of. He didn't think she was in the market for another.

ELLA SAW THE exchange and chuckled to herself. Her cousins were so competitive that her aunt Dana said they had probably arm wrestled in the womb. Ella wouldn't have been surprised. She'd grown up with the two of them always trying to outdo each other as boys and now as men—especially for the attention of women.

She wasn't worried this time, though. Jinx, she suspected, could see through anything the two did to impress her. She just hoped they all knew it was only for fun. Maybe she needed to remind Angus of that, though. She'd seen the way he had looked at Jinx earlier this morning. It surprised her and worried her a little.

Right now both Jinx and Angus were vulnerable. Jinx, because of her father's death and her upcoming divorce. Angus, because he'd finally gotten over his heartbreak from the last woman he'd fallen for and he now exhibited signs of a growing restlessness. She suspected he would be returning to Cardwell Ranch soon to stay.

Ella turned in her saddle to look back, making sure they hadn't lost any cattle. In the distance she could see the chuckwagon bouncing up the trail behind a team of two horses with Max at the reins. Closer, Royce and Cash were riding next to each other, appearing deep in conversation. As if sensing her watching them, they separated to move some of the slower cattle up into the line.

She didn't like the vibes she picked up from the two

men and planned to sleep with her sidearm handy. She'd been a little surprised that Jinx had taken them on. But the ranch woman was desperate or Ella and her cousins wouldn't be here.

"First cattle drive with a woman wrangler," Royce said as he rode up next to her. But when he saw Jinx riding in their direction, he pretended to turn back to look for cattle.

"Doing all right?" Jinx asked her as she brought her horse alongside Ella's.

"Just fine."

Jinx rode astride her for a few minutes. "You let me know if anyone bothers you."

Ella laughed. "I can handle myself."

"I don't doubt that. But there's two of them and I don't trust either of them, do you?"

"No. Don't worry. I've been keeping an eye on them. I'm not sure why, but I don't expect them to stay with us long."

"Funny you should say that. They both hit me up for an advance on their wages before we left this morning," Jinx said. "I turned them down, but I suspect I'll be paying them off before we ever reach summer range."

If that was the worst they could expect, Ella thought. They rode along for a few minutes, the herd of cattle a rust-colored mass of slow movement. "I heard about your father," Ella said without looking at the woman. "I'm sorry."

She felt Jinx's surprised gaze on her for a long moment before the woman said, "I wondered how much you all knew about my...situation." Ella said nothing. "I suppose it's no secret that my mother and Dana Cardwell Savage were friends." Ella knew that the two women had met at cattlewomen conferences and stayed in touch until Jinx's mother's death. "I suspect that's why the three of you showed up on my ranch."

Ella kept silent, riding along through the spring morning, glad, though, that Jinx knew. She didn't like keeping anything from the woman. She liked Jinx.

"I guess what I'm saying is that I appreciate you being here, but it could get...dangerous."

Ella looked over at her and smiled. "Then I'm glad we're here to help."

The ranch woman chuckled at that. "We'll see how you feel when the shooting starts—so to speak."

She met the woman's gaze. "We know what we're up against. We didn't come into this blind."

"I just hope you don't regret it." With that, Jinx rode off.

STILL HALF-DRUNK and sound asleep in Travis's spare bedroom, T.D. came awake with a start at the sound of someone banging hard on the door.

"Tucker David Sharp, we know you're in there," a deep male voice called from outside.

He froze, wondering how they'd found him. He considered going out the only window large enough that he could fit through. Then he swore under his breath, realizing that going out the window wasn't going to help. He needed to try to settle this and hope for the best.

"Give me a minute," he called as he rolled over to look at his cell phone. He couldn't believe he'd slept so late. He swung his legs over the side of the bed and put his throbbing head in his hands. The cattle drive. Jinx would have been up before first light. Who knew how far she'd managed to get by now. Cussing his hangover along with his bad luck, he wondered when his fortune would change. Trouble just seemed to dog him.

"Goin' to bust down the door if you don't open it," said the voice on the other side.

"What's going on?" Travis asked from the spare room doorway. "You know this guy?"

Pushing past Travis, he said over his shoulder, "Don't worry. I'll take care of it." In the living room, T.D. took a deep breath, let it out and stumbled to the door.

The man standing outside was big and beefy with a bulldog face and dark eyes as hard and cold as a gravestone.

"Shawn, come in," T.D. said as the man pushed his way in sans an invitation. He closed the door and turned to face him, a little surprised that Shawn had come alone. Little did he doubt that there were more men, probably waiting in the car in case T.D. caused any trouble. "Look, I know I owe you money."

The man laughed, setting his jowls in motion. He stopped abruptly to narrow those death-like eyes on him. "You *owed* money. Now it is past due. Perhaps you didn't read the fine print when you took out the loan."

"This is a small town so I assume you know what's happened to me." He waited for Shawn to say something. When he didn't, T.D. continued even though he knew his words were falling on deaf ears. "My wife is divorcing me. I have a lawyer who says I can get half of her ranch. You know the spread, so you know how much money we're talking about here. So it shouldn't be that long before I'll have what I owe."

Shawn smiled at that. "Don't forget interest and the late fee that is added every day you don't pay. But here's the problem. My boss doesn't want to wait."

T.D. remembered his father's expressions when bill collectors came around. *They can't eat you.* But they darned sure could mess you up. *Can't get blood out of a turnip.* Another of his father's expressions. But Shawn wasn't your normal bill collector. It was T.D.'s blood that was going to run free if he didn't come up with a plan and quickly.

And it wasn't as if he'd taken out a loan at the bank. He'd gambled on being able to pay what he owed, just as he'd gambled away any money he could get his hands on. "Five thousand. I can get you that by the end of the week."

Shawn raised a brow. "You don't have two nickels to rub together. Where will you get five grand?"

"Leave that to me. One week. Five thousand to hold your boss until I can pay him everything I owe him."

"With interest and late fees."

"Right," T.D. said, thinking how large a chunk that was going to take out of his half of the ranch. But when he considered the alternative, what choice did he have? Jinx had no idea just how deep his gambling debts had gotten. Not that she was going to bail him out again. She'd made that clear before she'd thrown him out.

His future looked bleak. Unless he got the entire ranch. Like he'd told his friends, anything could happen on a cattle drive.

Chapter Four

The day passed in a blur for Angus as they worked the cattle up through the pines and began the long climb to the high mountain range. Saddle sore after eating the dust the cattle kicked up, they had stopped midday for a quick lunch and to let the cattle drink from the stream. Then it was back in the saddle. Jinx had said she wanted to make it up to the old corrals the first day so they pushed ahead and reached the spot by the time the light began to fade.

Angus climbed off his horse now to close the gate to the corral that held the horses. The herd lowed from a large vibrant green meadow, the cattle glowing in the last of the day's light.

He felt the hours in a saddle. But it was a nice tired feeling of accomplishment. Also, he was thankful that they'd gotten the herd this far without any trouble. He'd actually been a little surprised. But then again, T. D. Sharp might be the kind of man who made threats when he was drinking, then didn't follow through on them.

At least he hoped that was the case. He'd seen Jinx watching the trail behind them. She expected her ex to make trouble. But they'd been moving at a pretty good pace all day. He figured T.D. would wake up with a hangover this morning and not be anxious to jump on a horse and head for the hills.

But Angus didn't doubt that the man wasn't through making trouble for her. He just didn't know how or when the cowboy would strike, only that he would if he could get some friends together to buoy his confidence. Angus had met men like him before.

All day he'd kept an eye on Jinx—as well as Royce and Cash. He'd seen Jinx's expression when she'd hired the two. She'd hesitated more with Royce and Cash than she had with Ella. That told him a lot. She didn't trust them and neither did he.

After unsaddling his horse, he left it in the fenced enclosure and headed for the chuckwagon, following the smell of something good cooking. He could see flames rising from a large campfire not far from the wagon where Max was dishing up dinner. There was steak, potatoes and beans with fresh homemade sourdough bread to soak up every bite.

Angus took his plate over to the fire, pulled up a log and sat down next to Ella and Brick.

"Good grub," Brick said as he cleaned his plate and went back for more.

Royce and Cash were still taking care of their horses. Angus didn't see Jinx. Max was busy in his wagon kitchen slopping more beans and potatoes on Brick's plate along with another steak.

"How are you doing?" Angus asked Ella quietly. He knew she never complained and that she could hold her own. He also trusted her instincts. She had a sixth sense about some things, especially people. But sometimes he worried about her. She would get quiet and he'd know that something was bothering her. Like now.

"I'm doing better than your brother," she joked. "He is getting nowhere with Jinx."

He smiled and shook his head, letting her deflect his question for the moment. "You know Brick. He'll keep trying."

"She likes you, though," Ella said, glancing over at him. "She isn't sure she can trust you, though. I've seen her watching you and frowning."

Angus chuckled, knowing trust wasn't the problem. But he said, "I would imagine she won't be trusting any man for some time to come. However, I asked how you were doing."

Ella smiled, but it didn't quite reach her eyes. "I'm fine."

"Well, if you want to talk about it…" He let that hang, seeing that whatever seemed to be bothering her, she wasn't ready to share it.

Over by the chuckwagon, Brick had struck up a conversation with Jinx as she came to get her plate. Ella shook her head as she and Angus watched him. "She sees right through him and yet he still thinks he can charm his way into her good graces. You, however, haven't tried to charm her."

"Nor am I going to try." Jinx wasn't like the other women he and Brick met. He wasn't interested in making it a competition. The other women had recognized it as a game and had enjoyed the attention. But none of the other women were Jinx.

He ate and watched the flames rising into the wide-open sky overhead. It wouldn't be full dark for another hour or so, but by then, he figured most everyone would be out for the night except for those assigned to stand watch over the herd.

"I'm worried about Royce and Cash," he said. "You let me know if they give you any trouble."

Ella chuckled. "You sound like Jinx. But like I told her, I can take care of myself."

"I'll still be watching them both," he said and followed her gaze to where the two men had finally finished putting their horses and tack away by the old corral. Rising, he took his cousin's empty plate and his own and started toward the chuckwagon.

Brick was headed back to the campfire and stopped him. "We made good time today, don't you think?" his brother said. "Another couple of days and we'll be in the high country." Brick looked toward the towering peaks, dark against the fading light. "This job isn't going to last that long. I was thinking we could still go north for the summer and work that ranch up by the border."

Angus laughed and shook his head. "You know you aren't serious about that woman up there."

Brick cut his eyes to him. "Who says I have to be serious?" Jinx had been talking to Max at the chuckwagon, but now made her way toward them and the campfire. Brick had seen her, too.

Angus grabbed his arm to detain him for a moment. "I'd tell you that you're wasting your time but that would only make you more determined," he said with a sigh. "Emotionally, Jinx is no place good right now. The last thing she needs is a wolf like you tracking her. In case you care, I'm not interested in her so let's not make this a contest."

Brick grinned at him. "Nice speech, my brother. But I've seen the way you look at her."

"I'm worried about her and what T. D. Sharp is going to do next. You should be, too, since the man is dangerous."

"You're just *worried* about her." His brother laughed. "I turn on the charm and get nowhere while you just quietly worry. I've also seen the way she watches you. Come on, we've been doing this since grade school." He glanced toward Jinx, who'd stopped to turn back to say something to Max. "But you should know. I could be serious about a woman like Jinx."

Angus shook his head and muttered, "I knew I was wasting my breath. You aren't serious about this woman or even the one up on the Canadian border and we both know it. Leave Jinx alone." With that he turned and walked over to the wagon where Max was watching Brick get a log for Jinx by the fire. What made him angry wasn't even his brother, but the surge of jealousy he'd felt.

"She forgot her bread," Max said, more to himself than Angus.

"I can take it to her."

Max studied him for a moment before handing him the plate with the bread on it. As he handed over his dishes and walked back to the campfire, he thought about how protective Max was of Jinx. The woman seemed to bring that out in all of them. He reminded himself that this was just a job, even though he knew it wasn't. They were here because Jinx needed their help and not just with her cattle, he feared. But his cousin and brother were right about one thing. He was determined to protect Jinx, for old times' sake, he told himself. It was more than a job for him.

"Happy with the progress we made today?" he asked Jinx as he handed her the plate of bread Max had sent for her.

Jinx took a piece and he set the plate down on a spare

log and sat across the fire from her. Brick had taken a log between the women.

"We're on schedule but last I heard there's supposed to be thunderstorms tomorrow," she said. "We won't be able to get any cell phone service until we get to the top of the mountain, so there is no checking to see if the storm has been upgraded or not." She sighed. "Spring in the mountains. I'm hoping we can beat the bad weather to the next large meadow where we have another corral at least for the horses."

She took a bite of her meal. Angus suspected she didn't even taste it. A lot was riding on getting the cattle to summer range. But he knew it was also a distraction from what had been happening down in the valley with her ex.

"That's why I want to leave at daybreak. To get as far as we can before the bad weather hits us," Jinx was saying. "If you could let the others know?"

"I'd be happy to," Angus said. He could tell that she was exhausted from more than the cattle drive. He wished there was something he could say to make things better for her, but unlike his brother, he thought Jinx probably needed silence over sweet words.

"I'll go tell Cash and Royce," he said and rose.

"Tell them chow's on, too," Max called as Angus headed over to where the men were standing and talking next to the corral holding the horses. He felt every mile in the saddle as he stretched his long legs. Walking through the tall green grass, he found himself looking forward to turning in early. They'd gotten through the first day without any trouble. No disgruntled almost-ex-husband. But a thunderstorm could change all that. Lightning was the major cause of stampedes on cattle drives.

Even if T. D. Sharp didn't show his face, they were in for a rough day tomorrow.

JINX WATCHED ANGUS GO. She still hadn't figured out why he seemed so familiar. Nor had he said anything. She sighed and rose to take her dishes back to Max.

"I can take those for you," Brick said, shooting to his feet.

She smiled but shook her head. "Stay here by the fire with Ella." She was glad when he sat back down. She needed to be alone. Brick was sweet and a good wrangler. He amused her with his blatant attempts to charm her, but he was wasting his time. While he resembled his brother, they didn't seem to be anything alike. Angus was a mystery to her.

The more she was around him, the more she felt a strange sense that they'd been here before. She couldn't shake the feeling that she knew this man, as in another life. It was crazy. Sometimes she'd find herself studying his face as if a memory was so close she could almost touch it.

"He's handsome, isn't he?" Max asked, startling her. She hadn't realized that she'd reached the chuckwagon. Her mind had been miles away.

"Pardon?" she asked, turning to face him as she conjured up her most innocent face.

Max laughed. "You were staring at Angus Savage—and not for the first time, I might add."

"I don't know what you're talking about. I was...thinking."

"*Thinking*? I can just imagine." He turned back to his cooking.

She didn't want to know what he'd imagined. Nor did

she want to continue this conversation. Still, she asked, "Have you ever run across someone you felt as if you knew in another life?"

He chuckled. "That your story?"

"I'm serious."

Max turned to look at her. "I can see that. I suppose it's possible the two of you met before. Your mother and his were good friends." The cook frowned. "I think she took you with her up to Cardwell Ranch once years ago." So that could have been it, she thought. "You don't remember?"

She shook her head and yet as he said it, she had an image come to mind of mountains shooting up from a green river bottom and a large red barn set against a wall of rock and pine trees. A memory teased at her. "How old would I have been?"

"Eight or nine," he said as he turned back to his cleaning up. "You didn't stay long, just overnight, I think. That's probably why you don't remember."

But she did remember a little. Now it really nagged at her. It wasn't just that she'd seen him before. She couldn't shake the feeling that something had happened during that visit; she was sure of it.

She turned to look at Angus again. He'd rejoined his brother and cousin on a log by the fire. His face shone in the campfire light. Max was right about one thing; the cowboy was handsome as sin. Had he remembered her? He would have been a little older than she was by a couple of years at least.

"Why don't you just ask him?" Max said with a laugh. "Otherwise, it's going to drive you crazy."

He was right about that, as well, but what if Angus didn't remember her? She'd feel foolish. Then again, what if he did? What if he was just waiting for her to say something?

"While you're making up your mind, why don't you hand me your dishes?" Max said with a shake of his head as he took them from her.

Leaving camp, she checked the cattle, glad that Brick and Royce had volunteered to take the first shift. She didn't expect trouble. Not tonight. T.D. was angry and vengeful, but he never planned ahead. He knew she was taking the herd up into the high country for summer grazing today. Maybe he would even wait until she returned to continue threatening her, rather than try to catch them. His laziness might pay off for her.

But unfortunately, she also knew that her being up here in the mountains put her at a disadvantage. T.D. wasn't stupid. He would realize how vulnerable she was up here. Anything could happen in the mountains on a cattle drive. People got injured. Others died. And T.D. was desperate to get his hands on her ranch. He would come after her.

In the distance she heard a coyote howl. Another answered, then another. She was more worried about wolves and bears, than coyotes. But she could only protect her herd so much. It was the nature of the business.

The camp was quiet as she walked back toward the fire. From out of the dark shadows, she spotted a lone figure still illuminated in the flames. Ella gave her a nod as she pulled up the log next to her again. The heat of the blaze felt good this high in the mountains since it was only early June.

Jinx could feel the long day in the saddle in her muscles. She yearned for sleep, but it had been hard to come by for some time now. It wasn't just T.D. who haunted her dreams. She didn't want to think about any of that. Instead, she was curious about this young woman and her lifestyle.

"If you don't mind me asking, why this life?" she asked after a few moments.

Ella smiled. "Probably same as you. I was born into it. When you're raised on a ranch, you do what you know." She shrugged. "I like what I do."

"But you aren't working your home ranch."

She shook her head almost wistfully. "It would have been too easy just to stay there. But I wasn't ready to settle down. I wanted to experience other places, other people. It's tougher as a woman to find that kind of freedom. That's why traveling with my cousins works. They give me space. I give them space."

Jinx looked toward where Angus had spread out his bedroll in the fallen dried pine needles beneath a stand of pines some distance away. "They seem nice enough," she joked.

Ella chuckled. "They'll grow on you."

"That's what I'm afraid of," Jinx said.

"Brick can be a little much."

The ranch woman shook her head. "He doesn't bother me. Has he ever been serious about a woman?"

"Not to my knowledge," Ella said. "A sure sign of fear of intimacy, huh?"

She waited a beat before she asked, "And Angus?"

"Oh, he's been in love. Got kicked in the teeth not all that long ago, so he's gun-shy."

"Aren't we all?" Jinx considered the young woman. "What about you?"

"If you're asking if I've ever met someone who made me want to settle down…" Ella shook her head. "By my age my mother had been married a few times. I'm hoping I'm a whole lot pickier than she was."

"Sorry. I didn't mean to pry. I thought everyone met someone, got married, lived happily-ever-after. That's what my parents did. They were high school sweethearts. That was the kind of marriage I'd wanted. The kind I'd just assumed I would have."

"Everyone makes mistakes when it comes to love. I'm sure I will, too."

Jinx eyed the woman, thinking how much she liked her. If they didn't live in different states, miles from each other, they could be good friends. She was going to be sorry to see Ella go when the job was over. "You seem like a woman with her head squarely set on her shoulders."

Ella laughed. "Maybe. At least when it comes to some things. I've seen my cousins make fools out of themselves over love. I swear I'm not going to do it, but then again no man has ever swept me off my feet. I've seen what love has done to some of my seemingly normal friends, as well."

Jinx knew the woman was trying to make her feel better. Just talking to her did. She stared into the flames, letting them lull her for a while before she pushed to her feet. She had no idea what tomorrow would bring other than thunderstorms, but she needed to at least try to sleep.

"You'll put the fire out?" Ella nodded. "Sleep well. We leave again at daybreak." With that, she turned and left.

The weight of the job ahead and the day in the saddle pressed on her. Taking her bedroll Jinx found herself a spot some distance from the others. Spreading it out, she lay down and stared up at the night sky through the pine boughs. She'd never seen so many stars—even back at the ranch—as she did up here. Breathing in the last scent of the campfire and the pines, she closed her eyes. She found herself smiling, glad she'd hired on the Savage brothers and their cousin Ella.

Exhausted, she fell asleep, only to be awakened to what sounded like gunfire and yelling.

Chapter Five

Angus woke to what he soon recognized as the banging of pots and pans, followed by cussing. He sat up abruptly, afraid T.D. had found their camp already. He turned in the direction of the racket. Through dawn's thin haze he saw Max standing next to the chuckwagon, his shoulders hunched in anger, a large dented pan in one hand and a huge spoon in the other. He was beating the bottom of the pot and staring off into the trees. What the—

Rolling out of his sleeping bag, Angus pulled on his boots and strapped on his gun, then headed for Max. "What happened?"

"The son of a bee broke into the wagon, made a mess and took most of our food," Max said, toning down his cussing as Jinx quickly joined them.

"Who broke into the chuckwagon?" she asked, sounding as confused by what she'd awakened to as he'd been.

Max huffed. "Dang black bear. Made a hell of a mess. I heard someone moving around in the wagon." Max slept under the wagon, but was clearly a heavy sleeper. "I looked in half-asleep and there are these red eyes staring out at me. 'Bout scared me out of my wits."

Angus chuckled and relaxed. He'd been afraid it was T.D. or someone in camp who'd gotten into their food.

"I thought you kept the food up so the bears couldn't get into it?"

"Had it locked up, but these bears… Smart as whips. Figured out how to get into the container, I guess. I should have hoisted it up in a tree, but I thought for sure it was safe in the metal box."

"How bad is it?" Jinx asked.

"You mean other than the mess?" Max rubbed his grizzled jaw for a moment. "Bear got all the meat. I'd say that was enough, wouldn't you? We have at least two more days up here before we head back. It can't be done on empty stomachs."

"Can we make do with what the bear didn't get?" she asked quietly as if not wanting the whole camp to know about this.

Angus figured it was too late for that given the racket Max had made. He could tell that the older man was still shaken by coming face-to-face with the bear. As he looked over his shoulder, he saw Brick and Ella were headed this way.

Max stared at the ground for a moment. Angus could tell that the bear had startled the cook. Max had scared it away by banging the spoon on the bottom of the pan— which now looked like the surface of the moon.

"We still have flour and sugar, salt and lard." Max raised his head. "I hope you like biscuits."

"I *love* biscuits," Angus said. "Also, I can get a couple of blue grouse and my cousin Ella is one hell of a fisherwoman." He turned and caught Ella's eye. She nodded and turned back to her gear. If he knew her, she'd have some fish from the creek for Max to fry in minutes. "We'll be fine," he said, turning back to Jinx and Max. "It's only a few days."

"Three to get back out of the mountains." Jinx smiled at him and mouthed "Thank you," before turning her attention to Max again. "We'll make do."

Max nodded sullenly. Clearly, he hated being outwitted by a bear. Not to mention the rude awakening he'd had. Jinx was also visibly upset about the loss of the food, but she appeared to be holding it in as if afraid that letting it out would only make things worse.

"Get some breakfast going," Jinx said. "I'll get the others up. If they aren't already." As she started to walk away, she touched Angus's arm. "Can I speak to you for a moment?"

He followed her away from the chuckwagon and Max for a short distance before she stopped and turned to him. "A *bear*." She shook her head as if relieved it hadn't been T.D. "Sure gave Max a scare." She let out a huff of a laugh. "I had expected trouble but I figured it would come from T.D. and his buddies." She sobered. "I know him. He won't be far behind, though. Still, my first thought was that maybe Cash or Royce was behind it. Maybe T.D. didn't put them up to hiring on with me. Maybe I'm just overly suspicious now."

Angus nodded. "You're not."

"I should send them packing right now." She met his gaze. "Problem is, we could use them. Especially with thunderstorms coming today. We only have two more days before we reach the high country if nothing slows us down."

"If you're asking my advice, I'd keep them where we can see them until then."

Jinx sighed and smiled. "I was and you're right. Fine, but I'll be watching them."

"You won't be alone," he said and walked back to

where Max was still swearing as he stood looking at the mess in the wagon. "Let me help with breakfast."

The older man turned to stare pointedly at him. "You ever cooked on the trail?"

"I have," Angus said. "You want me to make the biscuits or the fire?"

Max's face broke into a grin. "We got trouble enough without you making the biscuits, son. See to the fire." He climbed back into the wagon, mumbling to himself.

"I make some damned fine biscuits, I'll have you know," Angus called after the cook. Inside the wagon, Max huffed, but he was no longer cussing.

Angus smiled as he set about making the fire. Brick joined him. Ella had gone down to the stream. She always carried fishing line and had a knack for catching things. Angus figured it was her infinite patience. Brick went to help Max clean up the mess the bear had made.

When he had the fire going, he looked up and caught Jinx watching him.

AFTER A BREAKFAST of fried trout and biscuits, they rounded up the cattle and traveled higher into the mountains. Ella had proven her skill at catching pan-size trout. This morning he and Brick cleaned them before turning them over to Max, who dusted them with flour and dropped them in sizzling lard.

"Good breakfast," Jinx had said as she finished hers and thanked Ella for the fish before her gaze shifted to Royce and Cash. "I'd like the two of you to ride pickup again today. Keep an eye out for stragglers. If the thunderstorm is bad, I'll need you to help keep the herd from spooking."

Both men nodded. Angus had noticed that Royce and

Cash had eaten plenty of fish and biscuits. There was nothing wrong with their appetites. What did surprise him was that they hadn't asked about the ruckus this morning, keeping to themselves as usual. He found that strange. Also suspicious. He wondered if there was a reason the bear had been able to get into their supplies so easily. The men made him nervous, just like they did Jinx and Ella.

But after breakfast and the excitement of having a bear in camp, they'd gotten a fairly early start, riding out as they had the day before. The sun rose and moved lazily across the canopy of sky above the treetops.

As the morning and early afternoon slipped away, the sun began its descent into a horizon filled with gunmetal-gray storm clouds.

Just as Jinx had predicted, a thunderstorm was headed their way. Angus could hear the low rumble in the distance. He rode over to join her. "How far to the next corrals?"

She shook her head as she glanced at the storm moving toward them. "We can't make it in time. There's a large meadow a half mile from here. I don't think we have a choice but to try to hold them there."

As Angus rode point again on his side of the herd, he saw Jinx riding back to give the others the news. He could feel the electricity in the air. It made the hair quill on the back of his neck. He could smell the scent of rain.

Behind him, he felt the lightning strikes growing closer along with the thunder and rain as he found the meadow and circled back to help with the herd. He knew what could happen if even a few of the cattle spooked and took off. He'd seen a herd stampede in a thunderstorm and knew that was Jinx's greatest fear.

Or maybe her greatest fear was what T.D. might do if he'd decided to follow them into the mountains. If T.D. took advantage of the thunderstorm to hit just then, Angus doubted they could keep the herd from stampeding.

PATTY HAD BEEN so sure that T.D. would have come by her apartment last night—if he wasn't in jail. She needed to know what had happened so she dressed in her uniform for work, but left early so she could stop by T.D.'s favorite bar.

Sliding onto a stool down the bar from several regulars having their morning coffee, she asked Marty if he'd seen T.D. last night. She and Marty had gone to school together. He was older and had married young. He had three kids and another on the way with his wife of many years.

She'd always liked him. Always thought how different her life would have been if she'd married someone like him and now had a home and kids.

Marty poured her a fountain cola and set it down on a napkin in front of her before he answered. "He was here. I let him have one beer and then asked him to leave. From the marks on your neck, I probably don't have to tell you that he was in one of his moods."

Self-consciously, she touched her neck. She'd thought she'd covered the worst of it with makeup. "Did he say where he was going when he left?"

"Yeah, he wrote down his entire itinerary for me." He shook his head. "He left with his minions, Wyatt and Travis."

Well, at least he hadn't been thrown in jail after going out to Jinx's ranch. Maybe she hadn't called the law on him. Or maybe he'd changed his mind and hadn't gone. Maybe he'd just come here to the bar.

She took a sip of her cola. "So you don't know where they went after they left? T.D. didn't say what his plans were?" She had to get to work soon, but first she had to know if T.D. had mentioned going after Jinx.

Marty seemed to study her for a moment. "They stopped in this morning for…supplies for a trip. They were all in T.D.'s truck with a horse trailer and three horses in the back. I would imagine you know as well as I do where they're headed." Marty leaned toward her on the bar, his gaze locking with hers. "Why do you waste your time on him?"

She chuckled and looked away, embarrassed. "I need something to do while I'm waiting for you to ask me out."

"I'm married, but I know that's like bear bait for you." Marty shook his head. "Patty, I'm serious. You're better than T.D., better than any of the men I've seen you… date. Come on, Patty, wise up. There are some good men out there. Try one of them for a change."

She put down her glass of cola a little too hard, splashing some out onto the bar. "We all can't be like you, Marty," she snapped. "In a dead-end job, with a mortgage on your double-wide and a bunch of kids."

He sighed. "Sorry, you're right. It's none of my business and what do I know anyway, right? But I'm happy, Patty. Are you?" He turned to go down the bar.

"I'm sorry. Marty? *Marty!*" But he kept walking. What made it worse was that she knew he was right. She thought her problem was Jinx. Or that her problem was T.D. She knew it was her and always had been. She was like her mother. She always went for the lowest denomination when it came to men. But that didn't mean she loved T.D. any less.

As she finished her cola and left Marty a tip, she felt her chest tighten as she thought about what she'd asked Wyatt to do. Too late to change anything, she told herself. Wyatt probably couldn't do it anyway.

For a moment, though, she felt the enormity of what she might have put into motion. She'd known Wyatt'd had a crush on her for years. She'd seen it in those puppy dog eyes of his and the way he shuffled his boots, dropping his gaze to them when he was around her, as if half-afraid to meet her eyes.

Until last night. It did amaze her how easy it had been to seduce him. All it had taken was one kiss and he'd been ready to do anything for her. He hadn't said he'd do it, though. He might chicken out. But at least she'd put the notion into his head and had given him a taste—so to speak—of the payoff if he did it.

Now, though, she felt nervous and worried. She told herself that what was done was done. Too late for second thoughts since there was nothing she could do about it. And if something did happen up there in the mountains and Jinx didn't return… Well, T.D. would be free of Jinx—and he'd have the ranch. And he'd have Patty to thank for it.

Sheriff Harvey Bessler pushed through the door as she was leaving. "Patty," he said. "I'm hoping I heard wrong." She had no desire to talk to him. Also, she was running late for work. But he was blocking the door.

"Sorry?" She made a point of looking at her phone to show him that she was on her way to work—that was if he didn't notice the waitress uniform she was wearing.

"I heard T.D. and his buddies have gone up into the

mountains. But you wouldn't know anything about that, right?"

She shook her head. "Did you ask his wife?"

Harvey gave her a sad smile. "I hope he's smart enough not to go after Jinx and make trouble."

Patty glanced again at her phone. "I wouldn't know, Sheriff, but if you don't move I'll be late for work. I'd hate to tell Cora that I was late because of you. Who knows what she'd put in your food the next time you come into the café."

He sighed and stepped aside. "You have a good day, Patty."

"I'm going to try, Sheriff." As she stepped out of the bar, she saw the dark clouds moving swiftly across the valley. She glanced toward the mountains where by now T.D. would be. The air smelled of rain and the wind had picked up, swirling dust up from the gutter to whirl around her. She shielded her eyes, Marty's words still stinging her.

As the first drops began to splash down, she made a run for the café wondering where T.D., Wyatt and Travis were right now. She knew it was too early, but she couldn't help wondering if maybe Wyatt might already have Jinx in his sights.

Chapter Six

Lightning splintered the sky in a blinding flash. Thunder followed on its heels, a boom that seemed to shake the earth under their feet.

Angus pulled on his slicker to ride the perimeter of the herd. He could feel the wind at the front of the storm kicking up. The pine trees swayed, creaking and moaning as dust devils whirled around him.

Clouds moved in, taking the light with them as the sky blackened. It was like someone had thrown a cloak over them, snuffing out the light, going from day to night. In a lightning strike, he saw the woods illuminated for a moment in sharp relief before going dark again.

When the rain came, it slashed down horizontally in hard, huge drops that pelted him and cascaded off the brim of his Stetson. Through the downpour, he could barely see Jinx on the other side of the herd, running point. He watched as the cattle began to shift restlessly. It wouldn't take much for them to panic. All it would take was for a few of them to take off at a run and spook the others and soon they would all be stampeding.

The wind tore at the trees, ripping off pieces of the boughs and sending them airborne. The rain fell in sheets, obliterating everything. A bolt of lightning zigzagged down in a blinding path in front of him. His horse reared and he had to fight to stay in the saddle as thunder exploded directly overhead in a boom that set some of the cattle at the edge of the storm running.

The herd was already jumpy. It wouldn't take much to set off more of the cattle. Too many of them running would be impossible for the two of them to turn by themselves. They would be caught in the stampede.

Angus spurred his horse as he went after them, hoping to cut them off and turn them back before the others began to move. He rode blind, the rain painful as it pelted him. The wind lay over the grass in front of him, moving like ocean waves in an angry sea.

He turned the handful of spooked cattle, steering them back toward the herd. As he did, he spotted Jinx through the rain. She and her horse appeared almost ghostlike in a lightning flash. She'd ridden out and had turned the others. The rain was so loud that when it suddenly stopped, he felt as if he'd gone deaf.

He looked over at Jinx. She sat on her horse, glancing around as surprised as he was. Just as quickly, it began to hail. Ice pellets the size of quarters fell in a wall of white that blotted out everything. He ducked his head to it, the noise as deafening as the thunder and rain had been. The hail pummeled him and the side of the mountain, quickly covering the ground and the backs of the cattle.

He rode his horse under a high, large pine tree to wait out the hailstorm. As he did, he could hear the lightning and thunder moving off over the mountains. It wasn't until the hail began to let up, that he saw Jinx again. She sat astride her horse under a pine tree only yards away. He saw the relief on her face.

More than relief. She smiled with the kind of joy that

comes with knowing you made it through something challenging. He returned her smile as he took off his hat and shook off the melting hailstones. The herd stood, backs coated white, the storm over. Angus settled his Stetson back on his head and felt himself relax a little as droplets of moisture fell from the sodden pines as the storm moved on as quickly as it had appeared.

WYATT WATCHED THE storm pass from under a large pine tree low on the mountain. Next to him, Travis Frank wrung out his hat. "This has to be one of your worst ideas ever, T.D."

"Quit complaining," Wyatt said as he looked around the sodden camp. "It isn't like that was your first thunderstorm—or your last if you're lucky." Travis grumbled under his breath as T.D. emerged from the tree he'd been under, stretched and walked over to them.

"One hell of a storm," the cowboy said, laughing. He'd clearly used the time trapped under the tree while waiting for the hail to stop to take a nip or two from one of the bottles of whiskey he'd brought along.

"You realize that he's going to get us killed or thrown in jail," Travis said under his breath to Wyatt.

"Ready to ride?" T.D. asked jovially. The man had never made it a secret that he loved storms. T.D. loved loud and boisterous, disorder and confusion. He loved chaotic frenzy—and often caused it. It was no wonder the cowboy would enjoy a storm like the one that had just moved through, Wyatt thought as he and Travis left the shelter of the tree.

"What now?" Wyatt asked, clearly not enjoying this. Like him, Travis had noticed that T.D. had been hitting the bottle. His face was flushed, his eyes bright. Sober, T.D. was trying. Drunk, he was hell on wheels.

"Now we catch up to the herd and let the fun begin," T.D. said, grinning. He looked excited, anxious to do whatever he could to cause trouble. Wyatt knew that Jinx would be expecting nothing less. He wondered if T.D. realized that or if he thought he was really going to surprise her when he showed up.

Wyatt hated to think what mayhem T.D. was planning. More than likely the man was playing it by ear, which was even more frightening. He hated to think how drunk T.D. might be by the time they reached Jinx and the herd.

He went to the large pine where he'd tied his horse, swung up into the damp saddle and looked to the towering pine-covered mountain ahead of them. How long before they caught up to the herd? Like T.D., he was anxious. He'd brought his hunting rifle with the scope. Patty's favor rode with him, like a secret tucked in his jacket pocket. A secret that warmed him all through the storm and chilled him the closer they got to catching up to Jinx.

AFTER THE STORM PASSED, the sun had shone bright. They moved the cattle farther up the trail, making better time than Angus had expected. With the storm over, there was a more relaxed feeling in camp that evening when they finally stopped. They'd reached some more of the old corrals along the trail to summer range.

He'd gone out and killed two blue grouse. Though out of season, he didn't think anyone was going to turn him in after Max fried up the birds until they were crisp on the outside and juicy in the middle. Max had made gravy out of what was left of the cracklings in the huge cast-iron skillet and served it with a large batch of homemade biscuits. Nothing went to waste.

"We're sure as the devil eating better than I expected," Cash said and stuffed half a biscuit into his mouth. "You know what I mean," he said as he swallowed the mouthful. "After the bear got into our grub."

Angus saw Jinx and Max share a look. He had a pretty good idea what it was about. Max had been so sure that he secured the box with the metal meat cooler in it. When Angus had a chance, he'd gotten a good look at the box. He knew that bears were much smarter than most people thought.

He'd once had a cooler stolen off his cabin porch at the ranch by a grizzly bear. That bear did everything possible to get into that old rounded-edge metal cooler, much like the one in the chuckwagon. When Angus had found it, the grizzly had scratched and clawed and even rolled the cooler down a hillside, but still hadn't been able to get inside it.

There was only one way the black bear had gotten into the one in the chuckwagon. Someone had propped it open like a calling card for any bear in the area. Max was lucky he hadn't awakened to the noise to find a grizzly staring out of the wagon at him.

"Excellent meal," Brick said and everyone around the campfire agreed. This high in the mountains, the temperature began to drop even though it was early June.

After everyone had finished, Royce pulled out a well-used pack of cards and challenged anyone who wanted to play with a poker game. Angus passed, but Brick and Cash said they were in. Ella announced that she would watch and make sure no one cheated.

Jinx got up and walked with Angus to the chuckwagon

where Max was seated, watching all of them after cleaning up the dishes. As they approached, the older man rose from where he'd been lounging and announced he was calling it a night.

"I'm sleeping in the woods tonight," Max said. "No more sleeping under the chuckwagon." With that he took his sleeping bag and disappeared into the darkness beyond the campfire.

"Max isn't wild about bears," Jinx whispered with a laugh.

"Hope he doesn't run across one then out in the woods." They both chuckled as she and Angus sat on a log with their backs to the chuckwagon.

"With his luck, Max will run across one on its way to the chuckwagon," she said.

They grew quiet as the campfire popped and the card game grew louder. "I think that's the second time I've heard Royce speak," Jinx said. "You think he deals off the bottom of the deck?"

"I think you can count on it," Angus said with a laugh.

"Your brother—"

"Can take care of himself. Anyway, Ella is looking after him." He smiled to himself, thinking about the three of them working their way across the west from ranch to ranch, camp to camp. It wasn't Brick's first card game. Nor the first one that Ella had watched to make sure he wasn't cheated.

"I'm going to miss this," he said, surprising Jinx—and himself—that he'd spoken his thoughts out loud.

"Are you quitting wrangling?" she asked, turning to him. Her brown eyes had darkened with concern.

"I'll never quit ranching. My parents are counting on me coming back and pretty much taking over running

Cardwell Ranch. It's what I was born to do." He smiled and shook his head. "I'm looking forward to it. But I will miss this. Who knows what Brick is going to do. He wants nothing to do with running the ranch."

"You two look so much alike and yet you're so different." He could feel her gaze on him. "What about Ella? What are her plans?"

Angus glanced toward the campfire. Ella's pretty face was lit by the golden firelight. "I don't know. She's welcome to help with the ranch. She's family. But you know how that goes. She could meet some man in a three-piece suit and follow him to the big city."

Jinx laughed. "Can't see that happening, but like you said, you never know. The big city definitely isn't for me. Then again, I have no idea what my future holds."

At the poker game, sparks rose up from the campfire to burn out in the velvet starlit sky overhead. Angus stretched out his long legs, content after a good day in the saddle and a good meal. It didn't hurt that he was sitting here with a beautiful woman, one who intrigued him and always had.

Jinx seemed as relaxed as he felt. He told himself not to get any ideas. The woman needed him. He was a hired man. Once the cattle were at summer pasture, his job would be over.

Still, as he breathed in the night scents that floated around him, he was aware of Jinx next to him in a way he hadn't been aware of a woman in a very long time. The night air felt heavy and seemed too busy with that feeling that anything could happen. He wondered if Jinx felt it or if it was all his imagination.

The thought made him smile. Whatever it was he felt right now, he knew that this was where he belonged at this moment in time. Fate had brought him here. Brought him to this woman whom he'd never forgotten.

"You almost look as if you're enjoying this," Jinx said as she also stretched out her legs to get more comfortable.

He chuckled. He loved nothing better than being in the mountains, listening to the lowing of the cattle and feeling tired after a day in the saddle. But there was also something about Jinx that drew him to her and it was more than a chance meeting all those years ago. It was also more than his being protective.

"I guess it shows, how much I enjoy this," he said, looking over at her. Her brown eyes shone in the ambient firelight; her hair seemed to catch fire, reminding him of how red it was when she was but a girl.

"It does show," she said. "This life gets into your blood. It would be hard to give up."

"I don't plan to. What about you?"

She seemed to be watching the flames of the nearby campfire, the light playing on her face. "After my mother died, my father lost interest in the ranch," Jinx said. "He lost interest in life and went downhill fast. I buried him earlier this spring. I've been running the ranch alone since then. T.D. was supposed to help take up the slack." She looked away. "But I realized right away that all he wanted to do was sell the ranch and live off the profits."

"I'm sorry," Angus said as he focused his gaze on where Brick tossed another log on the fire. A shower of sparks rose up in a flurry of bright red to disappear into the sky overhead.

"This ranch has been in my family for only two generations," she said. "Around here that doesn't mean anything. Most of these people are at least fifth generation ranchers."

"That doesn't mean you aren't wedded to the life and the land. It's hard to let go of something you love. Or someone," he added, remembering what his brother had said.

She smiled over at him. "I let go of T.D. months ago. Unfortunately, getting rid of him isn't as easy as I'd hoped. I filed for divorce but he's contested it, determined to force me to sell and settle with him." Jinx shook her head. "We've only been together less than two years and yet that's enough, according to my lawyer, that T.D. can force me into a settlement. I can't believe what a fool I was."

Angus chuckled. "We've all been there, trust me." Only the crackle of the fire and the occasional burst of laughter or curse broke the stillness around them. He wasn't surprised that in a few minutes, Jinx changed the subject.

"I can't believe my good luck, getting three good hands from Cardwell Ranch," she said, lightening the mood. "Your cousin Ella is just as good as she says she is."

He smiled. "Yep, she can ride circles around me and Brick."

Jinx glanced over at him, the firelight dancing in her eyes. "The two of you let her."

Angus grinned. "Maybe a little, but don't underestimate my cousin. She's special, that one."

"I love how close you three are. Do you have other siblings?"

"An older sister, Mary, and older brother, Hank. And lots more cousins."

"I always wanted a large family."

He studied her in the firelight. "Maybe you'll have one of your own someday." She looked skeptical. "Just because you climbed onto a rank horse once, doesn't mean you quit riding."

She laughed at his analogy. "Rank horse covers T.D. well. I know there are good horses out there as well as men. I'll be much more discerning next time. If there is a next time."

"There will be," he said and met her gaze. He held it, wishing he could take away the hurt he saw in those eyes.

"Your father is a marshal, right?" He nodded. "Your family must miss you."

He smiled, thinking of his mother. "If my mother had her way, we'd all live in the main house and would park our boots under her dining room table every night for dinner."

Jinx nodded. "I've heard about Dana Cardwell Savage. Our mothers were friends, both involved in the cattle-women's organizations, but I'm sure you already know that. What about Ella's parents?"

"Just her mom, Stacy. She's always taken care of all of us and helped Mom running the house rather than the ranch. She lives on the ranch in one of the cabins up on the side of the mountain." He could feel Jinx's curious gaze on him.

"I'm sure your mother can't wait to have your boots back under her table."

"There's no hurry," he said, chuckling at the truth in her words. "My family, especially my mother and uncle Jordan, have everything under control. My sister takes care of the books for the ranch. They don't need me yet."

"But when they do?"

"I reckon I'll head on home."

Jinx stared up at the swaying pines overhead for a moment. "When my father got sick, I promised myself that I would keep the ranch or die trying."

"Is that what he wanted you to do?"

She seemed surprised by the question. "No, actually, on his deathbed, he made me promise two things. Get rid of T.D. and then the ranch. He thought it would be too much for me and that I would kill myself trying to hang on to it. I guess it's no wonder so many ranchers are selling out to those large companies that move cattle with helicopters and are owned by even larger corporations."

"Ranching isn't an easy way to make a living, that's for sure," Angus agreed. "So your father gave you good advice."

She chuckled. "You mean by kicking T.D. out?" She shook her head, looking rueful. "I'd kicked him out of my bed a long time before that. I should have kicked him off the ranch sooner. But I think I just hated to admit what a mistake I'd made."

"What about selling the ranch?"

Jinx stared again at the campfire for so long, he didn't think she was going to reply. "That's the hard part. I'm not sure I can do it." She let out a bitter bark of a laugh. "But I'm not sure I can keep it, either. T.D. is forcing my hand. I think I'm going to have to sell it just to settle up with him."

"I'm sorry it's come to that."

"My own fault. And maybe my father was right and it's for the best. Just doesn't feel that way right now. Admittedly, T.D.'s got me digging in my heels just out of orneriness." She sighed and seemed glad to see the poker game break up. Angus noted that neither Cash nor Royce looked happy as they headed off to bed. Brick, however, was grinning and joking with Ella, which told him that she'd kept the game honest. That was his cousin. Now his brother had the two men's money in his pocket and had probably made enemies in the process.

"It's going to be another early morning tomorrow," Jinx said but didn't move. "I heard that a male grizzly was seen in this area recently. I thought I'd put Royce and Brick on first watch. Brick's already volunteered."

Angus just bet he had. "I can relieve Brick."

She nodded. "I'll let them know." Like him, she must have hated to leave this quiet spot. There was an intimacy to it. When she looked over at him, their gazes locked for a few long moments.

Jinx pulled her gaze away first and rose to her feet. "I best get some shut-eye," she said. "It was nice visiting with you."

"You, too. Sleep well," he said as he watched her stop by the campfire to speak with Brick and Ella. Jinx was chuckling to herself as she went to find Royce and Cash before heading to her sleeping bag spread out in the dried pine needles some distance from the fire.

Angus watched her go, telling himself that there was nothing he could do to help Jinx other than to get her cattle to the high country. But even as he thought it, he knew that wouldn't be the end of her problems. And they hadn't gotten the cattle to the high country yet, he reminded himself as he made his way to his own sleeping bag.

All they needed was another long day of moving the herd and then a short one without any more trouble than they'd had and the cattle would be on summer range. Then it would be just a matter of returning to the valley. The job would be over.

As he walked through the darkness of the pines toward where he'd dropped his sleeping bag earlier, he saw Royce ride off with Brick and then part company as they split up to take the first night shift.

He looked around but didn't see Cash. The two worried him, especially after the incident with the bear in the chuckwagon. Since then, though, nothing had happened. So maybe Max had gotten forgetful and left the box holding the meat locker unlocked and cracked open just enough that a bear caught wind of it.

He told himself that in another day and a half they would have completed the job they were hired on to do. He and Ella and Brick could head back to Montana. They would have accomplished what they'd come here for.

Unless Jinx's almost-ex had other plans for them before then.

ELLA COULDN'T SLEEP. She felt restless, even as tired as she was. For a while, she lay staring up into the darkness. Clouds from the aftermath of the storm hung low over the mountainside, blocking out the stars like a thick, dark cloak.

Finally, she rose and walked away from the camp, feeling as if she couldn't breathe. She wasn't sure what was causing it. Earlier she'd tried to reach her mother. But she couldn't get cell phone coverage.

From as far back as she could remember, she'd "sensed" things. She'd been uneasy when they'd stopped by Cardwell Ranch before heading down here to Wyoming. Her mother had been acting strangely. It wasn't anything she could put her finger on. Just a sense that something was wrong.

That feeling had only gotten stronger. Her instincts told her she should saddle up and go home. But she'd signed on to this job and she would stick it out. Especially after meeting Jinx. She wasn't about to leave the woman shorthanded. In a few days they would be headed home. She just hoped that would be soon enough, as she reached the horse corral.

With the clouds hanging so low over the mountainside, she could only make out dark shapes behind the corral fence. She leaned against the railing, breathing in the cold night air, and tried to still her growing unease. She and her mother had always been close since from the beginning it was just the two of them—and of course the rest of the Cardwell/Savage family. As to her father, she knew little about him, only that he'd never been in the picture.

Not that she hadn't had an amazing childhood growing up on Cardwell Ranch. Her mother had seemed happy there after having split with her family years before over what would be done with the ranch following Mary Cardwell's death. Ella knew only a little about the argument that had caused the siblings to fight over the ranch. Apparently, Dana had refused to sell it, while Ella's mother, Stacy, and her uncle Jordan wanted the cash from the sale.

When their mother's will was finally found, it settled the squabble, but by then the damage had been done. It had taken time for Stacy and Jordan to come back to the ranch. Stacy had come back after she had Ella.

She felt fatigue pull at her and started to push off the corral fence when she heard a sound that made her freeze. Someone was moving through the darkness in her direction. Instantly, she was on alert, aware that whoever was moving toward her was moving cautiously, as if not wanting to be heard.

Whoever it was hadn't seen her. She stayed still as the figure grew larger and larger. She knew it wasn't an animal because an animal would have picked up her scent by now.

The shape grew larger and larger until the man was

almost on top of her. She watched him look around in the darkness as if to make sure that no one had seen him. She could tell he was listening because the night was dark; he couldn't see any farther than she could.

Then, as if believing he was alone, he reached for the latch on the corral holding the horses.

"Cash?"

He jumped and then froze for a moment before he slowly let go of the latch. Turning just as slowly, he squinted into the darkness. He took a few steps in her direction. "Oh, it's you. I didn't see you standing there." He sounded winded as if she'd scared him. Or worse, she'd caught him.

"What's going on?" she asked, even though she had a pretty good idea.

"Nothing," he said as he moved closer. "Just checking on the horses."

"Looked like you were going to open the gate and let all the horses out."

He let out a nervous laugh as he closed the distance between them. "Why would I do that?"

"I was wondering the same thing." He was close now, so close she could see the dark holes of his eyes.

He glanced around and then said quietly, "I thought everyone was asleep."

"I figured you did."

His gaze settled on her. His lips curled into a smirk. "What's a woman like you doing up here on this mountain with a bunch of men anyway?"

"You have a problem with it?"

"Me?" He leaned toward her. "Naw, but some men would think a young, good-looking woman riding with a group of males was just asking for it."

His words sent a chill through her, but she didn't let it show. Except for the fact that she'd eased her hand down to the holstered gun at her hip. "Men like that end up dead. Good thing you're not one of them. Otherwise, I'd advise you to sleep with one eye open."

He cleared his throat as his gaze dropped to her hand resting on the butt of her pistol. "That sounds like a threat."

"Only to men who don't respect women."

Ella heard a soft chuckle from the darkness before Jinx materialized out from behind Cash.

"There a problem here?" the trail boss asked, startling the already nervous Cash.

He spun around. "Not from me," Cash said quickly and took a few steps away from Ella.

When Jinx shifted her gaze to her in question, Ella simply shook her head and said, "I believe Cash was just on his way to bed. He's thinking about sleeping with one eye open."

He shot her a mean look before checking his expression and turning to Jinx. "In case either of you care, I'm a light sleeper." He touched the gun at his hip.

"Sleep well," Jinx said.

As Cash headed toward camp, Ella heard him mumble something about women not knowing their place.

Jinx sighed as she watched him disappear into the darkness before she turned back to Ella. "Now, what was really going on out here?"

"I couldn't sleep. Cash didn't see me out here in the dark. I think he was planning to release the horses. He was starting to open the gate when I spoke up. He said he was just checking his horse."

"But you don't believe him." Jinx nodded. "Best get some sleep."

Chapter Seven

Wide awake now, Jinx saddled up her horse. Royce had offered to take the first watch, along with Brick. So far it had been quiet. Other than the black bear that had gotten into their larder, they hadn't seen any more bears.

But with the grizzlies out of hibernation and hungry, they were a threat to the herd. She'd seen how easily one could take down beef on the hoof. She and the others had to be cautious, especially of the ones with cubs, she thought as she rode out toward the south end of the herd.

But the wild animals weren't the only threat. She thought about what Ella had told her, trusting the woman's instincts along with her own. Cash needed to go. But maybe after being caught, he wouldn't be a problem. Jinx sighed. She needed him just a little longer. If he'd hired on to cause her trouble, then maybe he was already working with T.D. Otherwise, there was a good chance he would turn on her once her almost-ex did show up. It was only a matter of time before that happened. T.D. was too predictable not to follow her up here.

Pushing thoughts of him away, she considered what to do about Cash. As the last of the clouds passed, the night sky was suddenly ablaze with stars and a sliver of moon. Nothing seemed to move in the dark stillness as she rode south along the edge of the herd.

On nights like this, she couldn't help but think of her father. She missed him so much it took her breath away. He'd been everything to her since she was a girl. He'd always been there when she needed him. When her mother had died, he'd comforted her more than she could him. He would have known what to do about Royce and Cash.

Just as he'd known that T.D. was all wrong for her. He'd tried to talk her out of marrying the cowboy, but she'd been in love.

Love. She could laugh now at how starry-eyed she'd been. T.D. had definitely charmed her. He'd made her feel beautiful. Her feelings for the few boyfriends she'd had seemed silly in comparison. T.D. had been her first honest-to-goodness love affair. He took her to fancy restaurants in Jackson Hole, getting her out of her jeans and boots, making her feel like a desirable woman.

That thought made her heart ache. She'd felt like a princess with T.D. Why wouldn't she marry him? He'd said and done all the right things.

"I know you want your father to walk you down the aisle," T.D. had said one night. "I want that for you. That's why I don't think we should put off getting married."

She'd been dragging her feet. There'd been little red flags. T.D.'s credit card not working. Times when he'd forgotten his wallet. She'd been happy to pay. Another time there'd been the man whom T.D. had purposely avoided at the rodeo, saying the man was a poor sport at cards. Later, she would learn about his gambling habits. But back then, there'd been enough that she'd been wary of when it came to marrying T.D. He had talked a good line, but she questioned how much help he would be on the ranch.

But then her father had gotten sick. T.D. had been right. She'd dreamed of her father walking her down the aisle. They'd decided to get married, rushing into it even as her father was telling her to wait and be sure this was the man for her.

An owl hooted down at her from a tree limb, startling her out of her thoughts. She reined in her horse, realizing that she still hadn't seen Royce. He was supposed to be riding herd tonight along with Brick. She could hear Brick to the north playing his harmonica, but there was no sign of Royce.

A horse whinnied from the darkness. She spurred hers forward, following the sound to find Royce's horse tied to a tree. Quietly, she slid off her mount and approached the man on the ground, gun drawn, only to find him sound asleep under the large pine.

Walking up to him, she kicked the worn sole of his boot. He shot up, fumbling for his gun as he blinked wildly and tried to wake up.

"Sorry," he said, scrambling to his feet. "Mother Nature called. I got off my horse and sat down for a minute. Guess I fell asleep."

"Guess so," she said. "Go on back to camp. I'll take it from here."

Royce picked up his Stetson from the dried pine needles and, head down, untied his horse. He hesitated for a moment as if he wanted to say something more in his defense. But apparently, he changed his mind, swung up on his horse and left.

Jinx watched him go, figuring she knew why Huck Chambers had let the two go. If just being lazy was all she had to worry about, she could live with that a few more days. But she feared there was more when it came to those two, especially after Ella's earlier suspicions about Cash.

ANGUS WOKE SHORTLY before he saw Jinx ride out. He rolled out and headed for his horse, figuring he'd relieve his brother so Brick could get some sleep. It didn't take much to find him at the front of the herd. Angus simply followed the sound of Brick's harmonica. His brother always carried the musical instrument in his hip pocket, seemingly lost without it.

As he approached, his brother kept playing an old Western song that their grandfather Angus had taught him. He and Brick had been named after their grandfathers. Angus Cardwell played in a band with his brother Harlan, while Brick Savage had been a marshal, like their father.

Brick finished the tune, holding the last note until Angus rode up alongside him. "We've got company," his brother said quietly. His first thought was a grizzly. "Three of them. I spotted their fire. It's almost as if they want us to know they're down there."

"T.D.," Angus said. He'd been expecting him before this. Three riders on horses could easily catch a slow-moving herd. The question now was what happened next.

"What do you think his plan is?" Brick asked.

T.D. didn't seem like a man who would have a plan. Instead, he bet the cowboy made decisions on the spur of the moment. It was another reason, Angus knew, that the man was dangerous. He'd learned from his marshal father that one of the most volatile situations involved a domestic dispute. And now he and his brother and cousin were right in the middle of Jinx and T.D.'s.

"I would imagine he plans to surprise us," Angus said.

"You sure we shouldn't go down there and surprise them?"

He shook his head. "Short of shooting them, all we would do is play into T.D.'s hands. He wants to torment Jinx. Better to ignore them as long as we can. Otherwise, I'm afraid there might be bloodshed."

His brother nodded, but looked disappointed. Brick wasn't one to back down from a fight. He'd gotten his namesake's temper and his other grandfather's musical talent, while Angus had taken more after their father. Hudson Savage was easygoing, solid as granite and just as dependable. He thought before he spoke and it took a lot to rile him.

"Get some sleep," Angus told his twin. "Jinx said we're moving out early again."

He saw his brother glance down the mountain to where the men were camped.

"Let's not say anything to Jinx," Angus said. "Not yet. No reason to worry her when so far, T.D. and his friends haven't done anything."

"Not yet," Brick said as he pocketed his harmonica and rode back toward camp.

T.D. TOOK A DRINK from the pint of whiskey he'd brought and stared into the flames of the campfire. He felt antsy but he knew that Wyatt was right. They'd had a long day on the trail, pushing hard once they finally hit their saddles at almost midday. They'd caught up to Jinx and the herd before sundown.

Wyatt had insisted that it wouldn't be smart to do anything until they'd rested their horses and come up with a plan. *Wyatt and his plans*, he thought with a silent curse as he raised his gaze from the fire to consider his friends.

"You really hit the bottom of the barrel with these two, didn't you, Junior?" his father had said when he'd begun running with Wyatt and Travis at a young age. "But then I guess it isn't easy to find two dumb enough to tag along with you given where you're headed."

He thought of his father's smirk, his words harder than a backhand and more hurtful. Tucker David Sharp Senior had never given him any credit. The man had been convinced early on that his namesake wasn't going to amount to anything and neither were his friends.

Well, all that was about to change. At least for him. Once he got the ranch…

The more he'd thought about it, the more he wanted the whole thing. Half would force Jinx to sell her precious ranch, which should have been satisfaction enough, he supposed. And it would put a good chunk of change into his pocket—temporarily. Once he paid off his gambling debts, he wouldn't have all that much left. Also, he knew himself well enough to know that money burned a hole in his pocket. He'd gamble, trying to use the money to make more money and probably lose it all.

But if he had the whole ranch, then he could show his father that he'd been wrong about him. Too bad the senior Sharp was in his grave, but he could watch from his special place in hell. *Look at me now, Dad. See how wrong you were?*

He would rename the ranch after himself and make it the best damned ranch in the valley. He took another sip of the whiskey. Or maybe he'd just sell it and live off the money. Maybe he'd have to sell it to pay his gambling debts. If he couldn't borrow against it. He imagined walking into the bank and asking for a loan against his ranch. *His* ranch. He liked the sound of that.

"You might want to go easy on that stuff," Travis said from across the fire as he watched him take another slug from the whiskey bottle. T.D. shot him a dark look. "Just sayin' I agree with Wyatt. We should have a plan so we don't get our fool selves shot. Jinx ain't alone up there."

"Don't you think I know that?" T.D. snapped. He thought of the cowhand who'd come to his wife's rescue the other night at the ranch. He'd seen the others, as well. A motley bunch if there ever was one. He'd recognized two of them, Royce Richards and Cash Andrews, both worthless as the day was long. Working for Jinx was probably the only job they could get after Huck had booted them off his place.

But dumb and worthless aside, they'd all be armed. And Jinx was no fool. She'd know he'd be coming after her—if she didn't already. He got up to throw another tree limb onto the fire. He couldn't wait until tomorrow. When he got the ranch he was going to buy himself a brand-new pickup, the best money could buy. He'd show them. He'd show them all. T. D. Sharp was somebody.

Chapter Eight

The next morning Jinx pulled Royce aside. "Here's your pay," she said, handing him the money she'd brought along, already anticipating that Royce and Cash wouldn't last more than a day or so. "I think it's best if we part company now rather than later."

"You have to be kidding me. Just because I fell asleep?" Royce said incredulously. "I suppose you've never done that while on watch?"

"No, I haven't, and I've been doing this since I was six."

He shook his head. "I guess we all can't be as perfect as you, Ms. Trail Boss. By the way, how'd you get the nickname Jinx anyway?"

"It was just something my father called me, if you must know."

"Oh, I thought it was because you brought bad luck to everyone around you," Royce said, his eyes narrowing angrily. "Seems all those things T.D.'s been saying about you are true."

She didn't bother to comment as she turned. Over her shoulder, she said, "You're welcome to have breakfast before you pack up and leave."

"No, thanks," he said to her back. "I've had enough.

At least now I understand what your husband had to put up with."

Jinx kept walking. It was hard not to take the bait. Royce had a lot in common with T.D. Both blamed other people for how their lives had turned out. They really seemed to think that if their luck changed, everything would come up roses. They preferred to blame luck rather than their lack of hard work.

As she was headed down the side of the mountain to where the chuckwagon sat, she saw Max and knew, even before she heard him carrying on, that something else had happened.

By the time she reached him, Angus and Brick had joined him. Angus was squatting on the ground in front of one of the wagon's wheels.

"What's wrong?" she asked as she moved closer.

"Someone sabotaged the wagon," Brick told her.

"Don't worry. Angus thinks he can fix it," Max said, disbelief in his tone. "Then again, he thinks he can make eatable biscuits."

She caught Angus's amused grin. "I'm going to have to make my biscuits before this cattle drive is over just to show Max," he said to Jinx.

"If you must," she said, unable not to smile.

"My honor is at stake," he said as they all stood around the wagon wheel in question.

"So you think you can fix the wheel?" she asked.

"A couple of spokes were pried loose," Angus said. "Brick and I can knock them back into place. They should hold enough that we can get the wagon off the mountain. You can get it fixed once we get back to civilization, though."

"Civilization? You do know this is Wyoming, right?" she joked, then sobered. "So this was done purposely?"

Angus nodded. "There's something else you should know." He hesitated as he saw Cash headed their way. "T.D. and his friends have caught up to us."

"You think they did this?" she asked.

He shook his head. "It was someone in camp."

She let out an angry breath. Turning, she saw Royce riding off. Did he do this?

Cash joined them. "What's going on?"

JINX CONSIDERED CASH, wondering if she shouldn't send him down the mountain with his pay, as well. But she figured Royce had done this after her encounter with him last night. "My ex-husband and a couple of his friends have followed us. It could be a problem."

"Looks like it already is a problem," Cash said, eyeing the wheel on the wagon.

"We aren't sure who did that," Angus said as Royce disappeared over a rise.

Cash followed his gaze. "So you paid off Royce?"

"I did," Jinx said, half expecting Cash to quit and go with his buddy. "I'm saying it could get dangerous. I know you didn't sign on for that."

He nodded his head in agreement before shrugging. "I hate to ask what's for breakfast," he said, as if losing interest in the conversation.

"Ella caught more fish and I know there are biscuits," Brick told him.

"That'll do," Cash said and started toward the fire Max had already laid that morning. "It's just another day and a half, right?" he asked over his shoulder.

"Right," she said to his retreating backside before

looking at Angus. He shook his head as if to say it was her decision whether or not to keep him on.

The news about T.D. hadn't come as a surprise. She'd known he couldn't leave well enough alone. It gave her whiplash the way one moment he was begging for her to take him back and the next threatening to sue for half the ranch. More and more, she just wanted it over.

"Should have killed T.D. when I had the chance," Max mumbled under his breath.

"And what would I do without you while you went to prison?" she demanded.

"Starve," he said flatly.

"Exactly." She coaxed a smile out of him as he dished up her breakfast and she went to sit near the campfire. Cash got up without a word to go stand in line for his breakfast. She told herself it was just another full day and night. They would reach summer pasture with the herd by noon tomorrow and then head off the mountain.

Not that it would be over for her, but at least she didn't have to worry about her wranglers and Max up here in the mountains with T.D. and his friends. She felt anxious, though, knowing that he was so nearby. She would double the patrol tonight. Knowing T.D., he just might decide to strike once he was drunk enough.

"YOU'RE AWFULLY QUIET," Angus said as he sat down next to his cousin after getting his breakfast plate. Everyone else had eaten while Angus and Brick had worked on the wagon wheel. They would be moving out soon.

"It hit me that this is probably the last time that we'll do this together, the three of us," Ella said.

"Why would you say that?" he asked, surprised.

She shot him a don't-con-a-conman look. "Because

it's time. I've suspected you've known it for a while." Her gaze left him to find Brick. "I'm worried how your brother is going to take it. But I'm sure he'll fall in love, get married, have a passel of kids and be just fine."

Angus shook his head. He couldn't see it. Brick loved women. Loved the chase. But once he caught one, he was already looking for his next challenge. He studied his cousin for a moment. It would take a very special woman for him to ever settle down.

"What about you?" he asked. Ella looked surprised. "There a cowboy out there for you?"

"A cowboy?" She chuckled. "I'm thinking more like a banker or a stockbroker, someone who wears a three-piece suit to work. What are you smiling about?"

"You. I know you, cuz."

"Maybe I'm tired of cowboys and want something different."

"Maybe a man who drives a car that has to be plugged in."

"Nothing wrong with saving the planet."

Angus scoffed. "Seriously, what would you do with a man who didn't know how to drive a stick shift or back up a trailer or ride a horse?"

"Anything I wanted," she said with a laugh.

He shook his head. "Well, I hope you find him, but it's not going to be on this mountain."

"I know." She met his gaze. "So you're saying it's time we grew up and settled down. I guess this is the last time for the three of us to be wrangling together."

"It makes me sad to think about it," Angus said and took a bite of his breakfast. He didn't have much of an appetite after seeing what someone had done to the chuck-wagon wheel. Talking about this wasn't helping. "We've had some good times. I wouldn't take anything for the years we've been on the road."

Ella nodded. "What will you do?"

"Go home. The ranch needs some young blood." He studied her out of the corner of his eye as he ate. "I know your mother wishes you would stay on the ranch. You know there is a place for you in the business."

"I know. I don't know what I'll do. But I'm not worried. It will come to me."

He shook his head. "You amaze me. You have so much faith in how things will work out. Don't you ever worry?"

"Of course I worry. But I do think a lot of it is out of my hands."

"Stacy will be disappointed if you don't stay on the ranch."

Ella smiled. "My mother can handle disappointment. She's had plenty of it in her life. Anyway, she's told me repeatedly that she just wants me to be happy."

He laughed. "My mother told me the same thing."

"You don't think she means it?"

"She does. And she doesn't." He shook his head. "Dana has her heart set on me coming back to the place. Fortunately, I'm a born rancher. It's what I want to do, always have."

"You're thinking of Brick."

Angus nodded. "He doesn't want to ranch. But he doesn't know what he wants."

"I predict that one day he'll meet a woman and everything will be clear to him. But that doesn't mean it will be easy."

"You see that in the campfire flames?" he joked.

"Pretty much." She met his gaze, smiling. "Same thing is going to happen to you. If it hasn't already."

Angus finished his breakfast and rose, laughing. "I trust your instincts, cuz, but a woman isn't always the answer and from what I've seen, love is never easy."

Ella merely nodded. But as he walked away, he heard her say, "We'll see."

THROUGH THE MORNING mist hanging in the pines, T.D. saw Royce coming and picked up his rifle where he'd leaned it against a tree. He ratcheted live ammo into the chamber as the man rode toward him. "That's far enough," he said, raising the weapon.

"Take it easy," Royce said and reined in to lift his hands in surrender.

"What do you want?"

"I just got fired by your wife. What do you think I want? A kind word, a soft bed, a decent meal?" he said sarcastically. "I want to get even with her. Then I want the other stuff along with a stiff drink or two. I heard you were offering a…reward of sorts for anyone who…didn't help your wife." Royce chuckled. "I've done my part."

"By hiring on to help her get her cattle to summer range?" T.D. demanded.

"Maybe I made it more difficult for her. They're probably trying to figure out how to fix one of the wagon wheels right now."

T.D. smiled. "Why don't you swing down out of that saddle and we can talk about it? I do have a little whiskey."

"I just thought you might," Royce said as he dismounted and tied his horse to the closest tree limb.

Resting his rifle against the tree again, T.D. dug in their supplies for another pint of whiskey. "Have a sip and then tell me what's going on in the other camp."

Royce took the bottle, unscrewed the lid and gulped.

T.D. snatched it from him. "I said a sip." He wiped the top off with his hand and took a drink.

"Where are the others?" Royce asked, looking around.

"Doing some surveillance work. How many men does Jinx have?"

The cowboy pulled up a log next to the fire. "Four at the moment, not counting the old cook and the woman she hired on."

"I thought I saw a cowgirl by the bunkhouse the other night." He laughed. "She's that hard up, is she, that she had to hire a woman?"

"The woman's good. Definitely wouldn't underestimate her," Royce said.

"That's it?"

"Cash Andrews is up there. At least for the moment. She's only got another day and a half and she'll have the cattle to the high country. Cash will do what he can to make it harder for her." Royce smiled. "He was going to let the horses out but that…cowgirl, as you called her, caught him."

T.D. shook his head. "Sometimes it feels as if women will take over the world unless we do something about it."

"I'd take another drink. The trail boss didn't allow liquor."

He laughed, knowing all about Jinx's rules. He'd played hell living by them. He handed the whiskey bottle to the man, ready to grab it back.

But this time Royce took a drink and passed it over to him again. "She's already been having some bad luck," he said, grinning as if he knew this was music to T.D.'s ears. "A black bear got into the food. Seems someone left the metal box with the meat and eggs in it open. This morning the chuckwagon wheel had been worked over. Thought you might like to hear that."

"Poor Jinx." He eyed the cowboy. "If you're not in a hurry to get back down to the valley, maybe you'd like to hire on with me."

"You're offering me a job?"

"I'm going to be running the Flying J Bar MC soon," T.D. boasted. "But this job is more about getting even. The wages aren't good, but the satisfaction is guaranteed."

Chapter Nine

The day passed without any trouble, surprising Angus.
When Jinx rode over to him late in the afternoon, he
mentioned his surprise to her.

"He'll wait until tonight," she said. "He'll wait until
he thinks we are all asleep. It could be a long night since
I plan to double the patrol tonight. But tomorrow will be
an easy day and then it will be over."

It just wouldn't be over for Jinx. Not that Angus
thought they would get by that easily. T.D. had ridden a
long way. He wasn't going to let them get away without
making trouble for Jinx and the herd.

It was dusk by the time they made camp and Max
cooked the grouse Angus and Brick had shot. Cash straggled in, limping.

"Stepped in a hole," he said as he plopped down on
a log by the fire. "It's killing me." He turned as Jinx
walked up and asked what was going on. "I don't think
I can ride watch tonight. I can barely walk. Hurts like
hell even in the saddle."

Jinx seemed to study him for a moment. Like him,
Angus figured she had been expecting something like
this. "You quitting, Cash?"

He shook his head without looking at her. "Just not sure I'll be much help."

She nodded. "I'll settle up with you in the morning. Unless you're thinking of taking off tonight?"

"Mornin' will do," he said, still not looking at her.

All day Angus had seen her watching for T.D. while keeping an eye on Cash. The wrangler had seemed restless. When they'd stopped for lunch, Angus had noticed that Cash barely touched his biscuit sandwich of leftover fried fish from that morning. Normally, the man ate as if he feared it would be his last meal.

"I'll be glad to have Cash gone," Jinx said later as she and Angus rode out to take first watch. "I'm kicking myself for hiring him and Royce."

"You did what you had to do," Angus told her. "Anyway, they haven't caused that much trouble."

"There is still tonight," she said as she looked down the mountainside.

He'd seen the campfire below them. He'd also seen four men standing around it. Royce had joined ranks with T.D. and his friends. *No big surprise there*, he thought. That just left the question of Cash. He made Angus nervous, like he did Jinx.

To make matters worse, the night was dark, the clouds low. A breeze in the pines made the boughs moan woefully. It was the kind of night that you wouldn't see someone sneaking up on you until it was too late. Worse, they'd had to leave Cash in camp alone except for Max. Brick and Ella were on patrol on the other side of the herd.

Angus felt anxious and he knew that was what was really bothering Jinx. Knowing T.D. was out there and not alone... "Cash'll be gone in the morning."

She nodded, but still looked worried as they rode slowly around the northern perimeter of the herd. "What if Royce hooks up with T.D.?"

He hated to tell her. "He already has, I'm pretty sure."

She let out a bark of a laugh. "Cash is bound to join them, as well. They'll outnumber us."

He couldn't argue that. "We'll do what we have to do." He'd been thinking about what they could do if T.D. attacked them. He thought the cowboy would be more sneaky than that. But neither of them knew what the man would do.

"I just don't want to have to kill anyone," she said.

He didn't, either, but what neither of them said but both knew was that they would if they had to.

JINX CONSIDERED RIDING down the mountain and confronting T.D. But they would merely have the same argument. Worse, he'd be with his friends so he'd show off. She couldn't chance making things worse by embarrassing him in front of them. At this point she had no idea how to handle T.D. He'd gone off the rails and she couldn't see this ending any way but badly.

She wondered what he had planned. As if he ever planned anything. Maybe he thought he could intimidate her by simply following her up here. If he'd hoped his presence would rattle her, well, it did. She'd been waiting for the other shoe to drop for some time now. T.D. was nothing if not determined. He wouldn't give up. Now more than ever he had to save face with his buddies and everyone else in the county. Too bad he didn't put that kind of determination into a job.

She thought of T.D.'s father and what little he'd told her about him in a weak moment. The man had sounded horrible, which she knew could explain partially at least why T.D. was the way he was. He saw himself as a victim. Right or wrong, he believed his actions, no matter what they were, were warranted.

Like now, it was clear that he felt he had to do something to make this right when this was the worst thing he could do. But there would be no reasoning with him. The only thing she could control were her own actions. Keep fighting T.D.? Or give in?

Giving in meant putting the ranch up for sale. She couldn't afford to borrow against it, not when she knew that she and Max couldn't run it by themselves.

Before her father died, he'd seen the handwriting on the wall. "I'm getting too old to do this anymore," he'd told her. "Even if T.D. was worth his salt, this place takes more hired hands than we can afford. It's why so many families are selling out. Even the ones with a half dozen sons who could run the place are being sold because younger folk want more out of life than feeding cattle when it is twenty below zero, calving in a blizzard or branding in a dust storm or pouring rain."

"We've done all of that and survived," she'd argued. "I love this life. I'm not ready to give it up."

"It's dying, Jinx. I need you to promise me that when I'm gone, you'll put the place up for sale and move on with your life."

She hadn't been able to do that. "I'll try." That was all she'd said that time and then again later when her father was on his deathbed. He'd known how hard it would be on her to let go of the ranch—especially being forced to by her soon-to-be ex-husband. The property settlement was the only thing holding up her freedom. But if it meant giving up the life she loved, what kind of freedom was that?

She'd already been offered a fair price for her herd—if she got the cattle to summer grazing land. She wouldn't even have to bring them back down in the fall. Also, there were several ranchers around, interested in her place. A local Realtor had come out not long after Jinx's father's death.

"With what you'd make off the ranch, you could do anything you've ever dreamed of," the woman had said.

"What if running this ranch is what I've dreamed of?" Jinx had asked her.

The woman had nodded and given her a pitying look. "Then I guess your dream has come true." She'd handed Jinx her card. "In case your dream changes," she'd said and left.

WYATT SMELLED DINNER cooking and felt his stomach roil.

"You goin' to have one?" Travis asked. T.D. had put him in charge of the food they would need. "Just a couple of days' worth. Keep it simple," T.D. had said foolishly.

"Hot dogs again?" Wyatt asked.

"Hey, T.D. said to keep it simple. I cut you a stick to cook yours on. What more do you want?"

Real food, he wanted to say. Like his mother cooked every night. He picked up the stick with the sharp end Travis had whittled with his pocketknife and looked around. "Where's T.D.?" Travis shrugged. Digging a hot dog out of the insulated pack, he wondered how long they could survive on hot dogs, cookies and trail mix. Not long since the supply was dwindling fast.

"Maybe he changed his mind." Travis sounded hopeful.

Like him, Wyatt figured Travis was ready to get off

this mountain. It was cold at night this time of year and hot during the day. They'd spent hours in the saddle following Jinx and her herd of cattle, only to stop when Jinx did and make camp below the mountain. T.D. had done nothing but drink and complain about his soon-to-be ex-wife. Hopefully, this foolishness would be over soon because they were running out of food and now they had Royce to feed, as well.

Speaking of the devil, the wrangler ambled out of the woods. "I'll take one of those," Royce said of the hot dogs. Travis pointed at the stick he'd made him. "Where's T.D.?"

They both shrugged. Wyatt saw that his hot dog was pretty much black and pulled it out of the fire. Travis tossed him a bun and a plastic squeeze container of mustard.

"You have any ketchup?" Royce asked.

"We're roughin' it," Travis said. "It's mustard or nothing. We didn't know we'd have…company."

Royce laughed at that. "Well, when the fireworks start, you're going to be glad you have my company."

Wyatt shared a look with Travis. What had T.D. told Royce? Fireworks? He didn't like the sound of this.

At the sound of a twig breaking off to their right, they all froze for a moment. Wyatt was going for his gun, thinking the smell of the hot dogs cooking had brought a bear into camp. It wouldn't be the first time.

Fortunately, it was just T.D. He came walking into camp, grinning.

"The fun is about to begin," he announced and looked at Travis. "That one for me?" he said of the hot dog Travis had cooked perfectly.

Travis looked from the hot dog to T.D. and back before he sighed and said, "Why not?"

"Then we'd better pull up camp," T.D. said, taking the hot dog and bun and reaching for the mustard. "We might have to move fast."

Oh, hell, Wyatt thought. What has the cowboy done now?

Chapter Ten

Angus caught a whiff of something on the breeze that froze his blood. *Smoke?* Jinx must have caught the scent, as well. She shot him a look and then the two of them were yelling for the others as they raced toward the smoke rising on the horizon.

Angus hadn't gone far when he saw the flames licking at the grass along the tree line—and in the direction of the herd. He jumped off his horse, pulled off his jacket and began beating the flames back. Next to him, Jinx was doing the same.

As Ella and Brick joined them, they formed a line, pushing the fire back. Had it been fall, they wouldn't have been able to stop the wildfire. But with the new grass mixed in with what was left of the dried fall vegetation, the fire wasn't moving fast.

The four of them worked quickly, beating back the flames. Angus had no doubt who had started the fire. He'd seen firsthand what T. D. Sharp was like that night at the ranch. He'd expected trouble, but not this. The man was a damned fool. Didn't he realize that he could start a forest fire that could spread through the mountains— killing everything, him included?

Every year forest fires burned across this part of the

west. They often grew even with the states throwing everything they could at the flames. Most weren't put out until the first snows in the fall. That was Angus's fear now. If this fire spread, it would kill more than Jinx's herd.

At first it appeared that they would never be able to hold the fire off. Then as if granted a miracle, a spring squall came through just before daylight, drenching them and the mountainside with a soaking rain shower. The rain did most of the work, but they still had to finish putting out hot spots.

By then it was midday. But they'd kept the fire away from the herd and they'd put it out. With most of the mountainside wet from the rainstorm that had come through before dawn, T.D. would play hell getting another fire started until everything dried out. By then they would have the cattle in the high country and have returned to the valley.

Angus figured T.D. would lose interest once Jinx was no longer on the mountain. There would be no reason to kill a bunch of cattle, especially when it sounded as if he would get half the ranch in the divorce. So half the cattle would also be his. That was if the man had thought that far ahead.

But first they had to get the herd rest of the way to summer range. What else did T.D. have planned for them before they all went back down into the valley?

"Here's where it started," Brick called. Jinx walked over to where his brother was pointing at the ground and Angus followed.

He knew what he was going to find even before he reached his twin. Boot tracks in the soft, wet, scorched earth and the charred remains of a bandanna soaked with fuel oil.

"Whoever started the fire had planned this," Jinx said with disgust as she took a whiff of the bandanna. The cowboys wouldn't have had fuel oil on them. They had to have brought it with them. She shook her head, planting her hands on her hips as she looked out across the pasture to where the herd moved restlessly. If Angus hadn't smelled the fire so quickly… If the flames had gotten away from them…

"What now?" She sounded close to tears but quickly cleared her throat. "What's he going to do next?" She looked at Angus, but it was Brick who spoke.

"What if it wasn't your ex?" Brick said as he looked around. "Anyone seen Cash?" Angus realized he hadn't seen Max, either.

They made their way back to camp. Angus wasn't surprised to see Cash's horse gone. Max was busy finishing making breakfast. "I thought you might all be hungry," he said as he took them in. "Figured I was better here than fighting the fire."

"When did Cash leave?" Jinx asked.

"Soon as he smelled smoke," Max said. "He high-tailed it out of here. Said he'd catch up with you at the ranch to get his pay."

Jinx mumbled something under her breath.

"I think we should end this now," Brick said and looked at him. "Let's go pay them a visit."

"No," Jinx said, her gaze on Angus. "We have cattle to move. That's why we rode up here. That's what we're going to do. We've lost some time, but we're going to get these cattle to the high country. But first I'm going to

wash some of this soot off. Thank you all for being here."
With that she turned on her boot heel and walked away.

"I think we're growing on her," Brick said with a
chuckle.

Angus smiled. "That is one determined young woman
and she's right. We take care of the herd. That's our job."
He felt his twin's gaze on him.

"She likes you," his brother said.

"I'm not trying to—"

"That's just it, Angus. You don't have to try." With
that, Brick turned and walked away.

Angus sighed, tired of his brother's need to compete. He doubted it had anything to do with Jinx. Brick
just liked to win. Angus was determined, though, that it
wasn't going to be a problem between them. After this
job was over...well, as Ella said, maybe it was time that
the three of them went their own way.

Smelling of smoke and covered with soot, Angus
headed for the creek. He needed to cool down anyway.
He and Brick weren't that much alike sometimes. He had
wanted to go after T.D., too, which told him that Jinx was
right about ordering them not to. He'd never been impulsive. Now wasn't the time to start.

And what if some of T.D.'s men hit the herd, scattering
it, while he and Brick were off looking for him?

Reaching the creek, he stopped under a large old pine
tree and pulled off his boots. Pulling his gun, he pushed
it down in one of his boots and then took off his belt and
tossed it beside the boots.

He considered stripping down, but realized his clothing could use a wash. Or at least a dip in water. He
stepped to the edge of the stream, picking a dark spot

where the water ran deep and then in a few strides dove headfirst into the shimmering pool.

He'd known it would be freezing cold. Just as he'd known it would take his breath away. But knowing was one thing; feeling it clear to his bones was another.

He shot up out of the water and let out a yell and then a laugh.

"How's the water?" asked Jinx from the shadow of the large pine.

"Warm," he lied, grinning as he watched her pull off her boots, then her holstered gun, before she did what he had done.

He moved aside to give her plenty of room. She dove in and came up fast, spitting out the icy water as she did. He couldn't help but laugh.

"Cold enough for you?" he asked, still grinning even though he realized he couldn't feel his lower extremities.

"I've felt colder," she said and then laughed as the two of them rushed to the shore, grateful to be out of the snow-fed water.

Angus pulled off his shirt and hung it over a limb to dry in the sun. A warming spring breeze rippled over his bare flesh.

Jinx had sat down on a rock, leaning back to close her eyes. "Maybe your brother is right," she said.

"Brick is seldom right," he joked. "That you even think he might be proves you've lost your mind."

She smiled and opened her eyes to look at him. "If anything happens to you and the others because of me…"

"We knew what we were getting into."

She studied him on the rock where he'd sat down beside the stream. He'd stretched out his long legs in the hopes that his jeans would dry some in the sun without him having to remove them. "Ella told me. Your mother asked you to come help me?"

"It's what neighbors do."

She laughed at that and she freed her hair from the braid she'd had it in. The wet coppery mass of curls fell around her face, dropping down past her breasts. "We're hardly neighbors."

"We're ranchers. Ranchers help other ranchers."

"Maybe where you live."

"Don't blame the other ranchers. They're in a tough spot."

She met his gaze. "Do you always give everyone the benefit of the doubt?"

"Hardly. But I try," he admitted. "Few people want to get in the middle of a family squabble."

"Is that what this is?" she asked, holding his gaze. "But the three of you did."

He chuckled. "By now you must realize that we lack good sense."

She pulled her gaze away to look toward the stream. "I hate that everyone knows my troubles."

"Don't. We all need help sometimes."

She smiled, shaking her head. "You must be wondering what I saw in T.D. What would make me marry someone like him?"

"That's your business."

"Still, you must think me a fool."

He laughed softly, turning his face up to the sun. "If you'd met my last girlfriend… We all have a mistake in our past that we'd like to forget."

"You're an awfully nice man, Angus Savage."

He could feel the sun warming his chest and hear the quiet babble of the stream. But what really warmed him were her words. Sitting here with her, he felt a contentment that he hadn't felt in a long time.

His eyes opened as he sensed her closeness. She stood over him for a moment, before she sat down next to him and turned until she was facing him only inches part. He held his breath as she reached toward him. His heart thundered in his chest as he felt her cool fingertips trace the scar on his chin.

"I'M CURIOUS," JINX SAID, her voice sounding strange even to her. "How did you get that scar?"

She watched Angus swallow, then seem to relax, his blue eyes bright with humor. "Well, it's kind of an amusing story." He smiled. "I got pushed out of a barn loft when I was eleven."

"That's awful."

He sat up straighter until they were eye to eye. "It was my fault. I asked for it."

"You asked to be pushed out of a barn loft?"

"I was teasing her. She warned me that if I didn't stop she would knock me into tomorrow."

"She?" Jinx felt goose bumps break out over her skin and for a moment she could smell the fresh hay in the barn, feel the breeze on her face, remember that cute cowboy who'd taunted her. Her heart began to pound.

His smile broadened. "She was a spitfire, as fiery as her hair back then."

Jinx felt heat rush to her cheeks. "Tell me her name wasn't JoRay McCallahan."

"Sorry, I'm afraid so," he said and laughed. "I wondered if you would remember."

"When I saw you, I thought I'd met you before, but I couldn't think of when that might have been. Then Max told me that my mother took me up to the Cardwell Ranch for a short visit when I was about nine." She groaned. "Your mother must have been horrified by what I did to you." Jinx didn't think she could be more embarrassed.

He shook his head. "My mother said, 'What did you do, Angus?' I confessed that I'd been giving you a hard time and that you'd warned me what would happen if I didn't knock it off."

"Oh, I can imagine what my mother said."

"Actually, both mothers had trouble hiding smiles, once they realized that no one was hurt badly. Your mother told you that you couldn't go around pushing boys just because of something they said or you'd spend the rest of your life fighting them."

"You'd think I'd have learned that lesson."

He grinned. "When your mother said that, you replied, 'Well, if the boys are smart, they won't give me a hard time—especially standing in front of an open window two floors up.'"

She laughed with him. "Oh, that sounds so much like me. I'm so sorry."

"Don't be," he said as he seemed to fondly touch the scar. "It was a good learning experience for me." His blue eyes hardened. "And I never forgot that girl."

"I suppose not." She shook her head in disbelief. "Still, you came down to help me get my herd up to summer range."

"Like I said, it's what neighbors do," he said and grinned again. "Also, I was curious to see the woman that girl had grown into."

She couldn't help the heat that rushed to her cheeks wanting to blame it on the sun beating down on them. "Now you know."

He smiled. "Yes. I wasn't disappointed." He leaned toward her and she knew even before his lips brushed hers, that he was going to kiss her—and she was going to let him.

The kiss started out soft, sweet, delicate, but as her lips parted for him, he looped his hand behind her neck and pulled her down for a proper kiss. She felt the warmth of his bare chest against her still-damp Western shirt. A shiver moved through her as he deepened the kiss. She touched the hair curling at the nape of his neck, wanting to bury her fingers in his dark hair, wanting the kiss to never stop.

At the sound of Max ringing the chow bell, he let her go. She drew back, shaken by the kiss. "We shouldn't have done that."

"I'm not going to apologize for kissing you. I've wanted to since the first time I laid eyes on you. Only back then, I was just a boy who thought the way to get a girl's attention was to give her a hard time."

"I'm still a married woman," she said, hating that she sounded breathless. Had she ever been kissed like that? "And I'm your boss."

He nodded. "If you're saying that I have bad timing, I couldn't agree more." He grinned. "But I'm still not sorry." With that, he touched her cheek, a light caress before he rose, retrieved his shirt from the tree, pulled on his boots and left, saying, "I'll see you back in camp, boss."

JINX WATCHED HIM GO. Her face still felt hot, her cheeks flushed, and her heart was still doing loop-de-loops in her chest. She touched her lips with her fingertips, remembering the feel of his mouth on hers, and couldn't help but smile. Of course the kiss had been wrong. But she was glad that Angus hadn't apologized for it.

As he disappeared into the pines, she couldn't remember ever feeling this good. This free. And if she was being truthful, it hadn't been the first time she'd thought about kissing Angus. He was handsome as the devil. Just the image of his broad chest as he'd come out of the stream, the water rippling over taut, tanned muscles... She shivered, realizing that she wanted more than just a kiss.

That, too, surprised her because for months she hadn't given men, let alone sex, a thought. But that Angus had released this in her, didn't surprise her. She liked him, trusted him, felt close to him. Now that she knew about their earlier connection, she thought with a laugh. But Angus was also the kind of man her father would have approved of. Too bad he hadn't come along before T.D.

Shaking her head, she reminded herself of the mess her life was in right now. She was a woman who'd foolishly married a handsome, smooth-talking man. Now she was living a bad country song, she thought as she rose and pulled on her boots.

The best thing she could do, she told herself, was to keep her distance from Angus. The cattle would be settled into summer range by tomorrow. Once they reached the ranch, he would no longer be in her employ.

But didn't that mean he would be headed home to Montana? He'd told her he was going back to help run Cardwell Ranch. It was just as well, she knew. She certainly wasn't ready for even a man like Angus.

But she felt a shiver as she thought of the way he'd cupped the back of her neck, drawing her down as he deepened the kiss. She found herself smiling again.

She pulled her long hair up into a ponytail and tried

not to think about Angus or the kiss or her uncertain future. He would return to Cardwell Ranch. She would sort out the mess she'd made of her life.

Her cheeks still felt hot, though, and she could still taste him on her lips. One look at her and would everyone know when she returned to camp? She realized that she didn't care.

T.D. had failed in his attempt to get the mountain on fire and scatter her herd. She felt ready for whatever else he had up his sleeve, determined to get through this or die trying. Soon she would be free of him. Her step felt lighter as she followed the smell of freshly baked biscuits.

ANGUS HAD WALKED away from Jinx, telling himself to be careful. He thought about the last woman he'd let get this close and how that had turned out. Jinx...well, she was a whole different rodeo in so many ways, including, he reminded himself, that she was married with a crazy not-yet-ex-husband.

He finished buttoning up his shirt. It had dried nicely. As he neared the camp, his brother stepped out of the trees.

"Have a nice swim?" Brick asked, grinning.

"I did." He saw his brother look past him toward the creek. "Don't even think about it."

Brick gave him his best innocent face. "I don't know what you're talking about."

"Jinx. She isn't some prize to be won. She's got serious problems and is in no shape to even think about getting involved with another man."

Brick cocked his head. "Is that what you keep telling yourself?"

Angus sighed. "We're almost done here. Once the cattle are in the high country, there will be nothing keeping us here."

His brother shook his head. "And you'll just be able to leave her knowing that her jackass of a husband isn't through tormenting her?" He didn't give Angus time to answer. "That's what I thought. You don't want a part of this, brother, trust me. How do you even know that she's over him?"

He thought about the kiss still tingling on his lips. Jinx was over T.D., that he was sure of. But that didn't mean that she was ready for another relationship, especially after her last one. "I'll cross that bridge when I come to it, but you definitely won't have to stay. You and Ella can go back home and—"

Brick was shaking his head. "The three of us signed on and the three of us will leave together. You stay here and you'll get yourself killed."

He wanted to argue that his twin didn't know squat, but unfortunately, Brick was right. He would only make things worse if he stayed. But how could he leave knowing the kind of trouble Jinx was in?

"I just hate to see you falling for her," Brick said. "You're dead right that she's not ready for another man. Hell, she hasn't gotten rid of the one she has."

"There's no reason to be talking about this," Angus said as he started past his brother. "Let's just get these cattle safely up to the high country. That's the job we're being paid for. That's enough to worry about since I really doubt that T.D. and his friends are through with us."

His twin caught his arm to stop him. "I'm just worried about you, Angus."

"Maybe it's time you quit worrying about me."

Brick laughed. "We're brothers. Womb mates. I'm

going to worry especially when I see you headed down a dangerous path. You just can't stand to see a woman who needs rescuing and not try to rescue her. It's in your DNA. But you almost got killed the last time you got involved in a domestic situation that wasn't any of your business."

He'd gotten between his girlfriend and her former boyfriend, a mistake in so many ways. "This is different."

"Is it? Jinx can divorce T.D., give him what he wants and be done with him. But maybe she's dragging her feet on the property settlement because she is still in love with him. Like you said, she needs time to figure it all out."

"I know that," he said as he stepped past his brother and started again toward camp. He glanced back. It had crossed his mind that Brick might go down to the creek. But to his surprise, his brother now followed him.

"He'll hit us again," Brick said, thankfully changing the subject. "Maybe we *should* try to find him no matter what Jinx says."

"We can't leave the camp unprotected. Jinx is right. With two of us gone, it would be a perfect time for T.D. to strike."

Brick said nothing, but Angus could tell his brother was chewing it over. He just hoped Brick didn't do anything impulsive.

WYATT THOUGHT ABOUT riding out of the mountains and not looking back. T.D. had sent him out to see what damage had been done to Jinx and her herd after the fire. He hated to report that Jinx and her crew had put out the fire with the rainstorm finishing the job. He knew that news was going to put T.D. into a tailspin. He'd thought he was so smart starting the fire.

"Well?" T.D. demanded as he dismounted. "Took you long enough. I thought I was going to have to come look for you."

Wyatt already anticipated the cowboy's reaction to what he had to tell him. "They fought the fire, putting it almost out. Then the rain did the rest. The fire's out."

"What about the herd?" T.D. demanded. "Surely it scattered some of them."

He shook his head. "Sorry."

T.D. swore and stomped around the wet camp. Royce was trying to get a fire going again but everything was soaking wet after the squall that had come through. He and Cash were arguing, Cash saying he was hungry and might ride down to town.

"We should all ride out of here," Travis said, watching them. He looked wet and miserable. "I don't know what we're doing up here anyway."

T.D. turned on him so quickly Travis didn't have a chance to react. The blow sent him sprawling onto the wet ground. "I'm sick of your whining. Nothing is keeping you here and while you're at it, take those two with you."

Royce looked up, seeming surprised that T.D. meant him and Cash. He'd managed to get a small blaze going. He continued building the fire. Cash, Wyatt noted, had gone silent.

"That's all you saw?" T.D. asked as Wyatt hung up his slicker on a tree limb to dry in the sun. "I thought for sure that the fire would spook the herd. Or at least scatter them."

Wyatt shook his head. All the way back, he'd debated telling T.D. what he'd seen through his binoculars near the stream. Maybe it would end this once and for all. Or maybe it would make T.D. even crazier.

He had no idea what T.D. would do if he told him that he'd seen Jinx and one of her wranglers down by the stream swimming together, then talking while sitting in the sun and then kissing.

Wyatt had watched, unable to pull his eyes away. The two had been so close, so intimate. He wouldn't have been surprised if they'd stripped down and made love right there beside the water. The scene had been so passionate, it had made him wonder if the kiss was the first between the two of them.

He saw that Travis had gotten to his feet and was now busying himself hanging his wet clothing on a tree branch, his back to the rest of them. After T.D. had punched him, why hadn't Travis left? Wyatt told himself he would have gone with him, but he knew that was a lie. T.D. would expect him to stay. Even if he wouldn't, Wyatt wasn't finished up here, was he?

After what he'd seen, he'd been telling himself that Jinx deserved what she was going to get. She was cheating on T.D. Not that it was his place to do anything about that, Wyatt told himself. But if he told T.D., he knew the cowboy would go ballistic, riding up to the camp, guns blazing.

He thought of Patty and the promise she'd made him— and the one he'd kind of made her. T.D. was pacing, worked up because his fire had fizzled out and his attempt to hurt Jinx had failed. So far, nothing that anyone had done had stopped the woman. Suddenly, T.D. stopped pacing and looked at him. "We're going to have to stampede the herd."

Travis turned to glance back at him, but then quickly turned away again. Royce threw a handful of dry dead pine needles onto the fire. "Count me in," he said. Cash just looked uncomfortable but nodded.

Wyatt realized that everyone was waiting on him, including T.D. He told himself that now was the time to put an end to this if he was going to. If he rode back to town now, he suspected the others would follow. He knew Travis was just looking for an excuse to bail but wouldn't unless someone else did first.

He could stop this before it was too late.

Before anyone got killed.

Chapter Eleven

"Hey! Watch out!"

Patty felt the plates of food she'd been carrying tilt dangerously as she collided with one of the café customers. "Sorry."

The man was busily looking at his sleeve and then his pants to make sure that none of the café's evening special had spilled on him. Patty heard his wife say from the booth, "It was your fault. You got up right in front of her."

"Are you kidding?" the man demanded. "She wasn't watching where she was going. If you'd been paying attention, you would know that she's been in a daze this whole time. She screwed up the orders at that other table."

"Seems one of us has been watching the waitress with a little too much interest," the wife snapped.

Patty felt the heat of embarrassment on the back of her neck as she delivered the orders to a far table. The man was right. Her mind hadn't been on work for some time now. She put on her plastic smile, tried to say all the right things, but she was only going through the motions and at least one person had noticed.

"Everything all right?" her boss asked when she returned to the kitchen.

She had no idea. "Fine." Her mind was in the mountains with T.D. Had he caught up to his wife? For all she knew, the two of them could have made up. She kept seeing a campfire and the two of them rolling around on a bedroll next to it. The image burned through her stomach like acid.

Not that she believed it. Jinx wouldn't take him back. There was no way the two of them were reconnecting, not with all those others up there on the mountain with them. Not only did Jinx have wranglers working for her apparently, but she also had several hundred head of cattle to tend to. She wasn't rolling around with T.D. on any bedroll.

But not knowing what was happening was driving her crazy. Wouldn't she have heard if T.D. and the others had returned to town? Of course she would have. Which meant they hadn't.

So T.D. was still up there in the mountains. Which meant Wyatt was still up there, as well. For a while, she'd forgotten about that.

She thought of the promise she'd made him—and what she'd asked him to do. She'd seen the way he reacted to her. He would do anything for her—just as he'd said. Just as she'd known he would.

A thought made her heart begin to pound.

By now Jinx could be dead.

Unless Wyatt chickened out.

She went to pick up an order for a table that had just come up and tried to still her nervous anticipation. Wyatt wouldn't let her down.

"Don't you think we should call the sheriff on T.D.?" Ella asked as she joined her cousins around the campfire later that evening. Max was busy in the chuckwagon and Jinx was seeing to her horse.

They'd spent the day moving cattle, getting as far as they could. Tomorrow was their last day. They should reach summer range before noon, Jinx had said. "And tell him what? I'm sure he knows T.D. followed us up here, but there was little he could do. It's a free country and a huge mountain range," Brick said.

"Brick's right. Nor can we prove he started the fire," Angus said. "I'm not even sure the sheriff could arrest him on the restraining order. T.D. hasn't gotten close enough to break it yet. Also, Jinx said we wouldn't be able to get cell phone service until we reached the high country above the tree line and even then, she said it would be sketchy."

She knew they were right and yet she couldn't shake the bad feeling she had. "You know he's not finished."

"He'll hit us tonight. He has to," Brick said. "This time tomorrow we'll be in Jackson Hole. I don't know about the two of you, but I plan to kick up my heels. But first I'm going to treat myself to a big fat juicy beef steak and all the fixings. Maybe find me some sweet-smelling woman who wants to dance."

Ella shook her head. "I wouldn't be counting your chickens just yet."

"She's right," Angus agreed. "I don't think the fire did the kind of damage T.D. was hoping for. Whatever he has planned it will be tonight and I suspect it will be much bigger."

Ella poked the fire with a stick, sending sparks into the air. "I don't get why he's doing this. Just to torment her?"

Angus shrugged. "I'm not sure T.D. has a point. He's

angry, probably drunk most of the time and feeling he has to do something to save face."

"It's stupid and dangerous," Brick said. "If that fire had gotten away from us or that rain squall hadn't come through when it did..." He shook his head. "The cowboy's crazy."

At the sound of someone coming out of the darkness, they all turned. "Brick's right. T.D. is crazy, stupid and dangerous," Jinx said. "That's why we aren't going to get much sleep tonight."

"I still think we should pay him a visit," Brick said.

"Don't you think they're expecting that?" Ella asked only to have her cousin shrug.

"Also, there's five of them now," Angus said, having earlier seen them trailing the herd. It didn't surprise him that Cash had joined their ranks. "Riding into their camp would be more dangerous than staying where we are and waiting for them to hit us."

"Except we have several hundred head of cattle," Ella said. "If I were him, I'd try to use them against us."

Jinx looked over at her and nodded. "My thought exactly. He'll try to stampede the herd tonight when he thinks we're all asleep. He'll drive them right at us."

"Unless we stop him," Brick said. "That's why we have to hit him first."

Ella saw that Angus was studying Jinx and smiling as if they'd just shared a secret. "You have a plan?"

"Once it's dark enough where we can't be seen, we booby-trap one side of the perimeter," Angus said and Jinx gave him a knowing smile.

Brick caught the exchange and said, "Bro, why do I get the feeling you told her about what we used to do when we were kids to catch critters?"

"Subject must have come up some time or another," Angus said.

"They have us outnumbered," Jinx said, clearly warming to the plan. "We have to better our odds. I suspect they'll come riding in fast, yelling and shooting to spook the herd. To drive the herd right at us, they'll come in from the north. We just need to be waiting for them, subdue the ones we catch and quell the attack. Any we can get on the ground, should be fairly easy to tie up and gag, right?"

Brick laughed. "I like the way you think. Less bloodshed."

"Hopefully, no blood will be shed." She looked at Angus. "It's going to be another dark night. We weren't going to get any sleep anyway. At least this way we'll be ready for them."

Unless we're wrong and T.D. came at us another way, Ella thought. She wondered how far she'd have to ride to get cell phone coverage should things go as wrong as she feared they would.

"You mind staying here with Max and making sure everything is all right?" Angus asked her as the others rose to go to work.

Ella nodded, knowing exactly what he was telling her to do.

THEY WORKED QUICKLY and quietly, setting up the traps some distance from the herd in the path T.D. would have to take to stampede the cattle into their camp.

Angus checked with Brick to make sure he was ready before he went to the spot where they'd left Jinx. He let out a soft whistle as he approached to let her know it was him coming through the trees and was careful not to trip any of the booby traps.

"You ready?" he asked when he reached her. He could tell she was nervous. They all were. "It's going to be all right."

She smiled. She really did have the most beautiful warm smile. There was a gentleness to her along with strength. He found himself drawn to her in a way he hadn't ever been with another woman. He didn't believe in love at first sight and yet he hadn't forgotten how taken he was with that redheaded girl who'd turned up at Cardwell Ranch, all those years ago.

He touched her cheek, unable to stop himself any more than he could hold back the feelings that swam to the surface when he saw her. He felt connected to her in a way he couldn't explain. He would have said fate had thrown them together not once but twice, years apart, if he believed in it.

Ella would have understood what he was feeling better than he did. She believed in a lot of things he didn't including love at first sight and destiny and true love. But this feeling was so strong that had he believed in true love, he would have been tempted to call it that.

Brick always said that falling in love was like falling off a horse. You had no choice but to get back on. Well, Angus much preferred falling off a horse. To him, falling in love was like jumping off a cliff and not knowing if you would survive. He knew one thing. The landing could be hell.

He'd survived his last breakup, but even as strongly as he felt, he knew he wasn't ready to make another leap. Especially if that leap involved Jinx McCallahan, he told himself. Even if she wasn't married and in the middle of a divorce and didn't have a crazy, dangerous ex who wouldn't let her go. Jinx was a mess. It didn't matter that she'd kicked T.D. out months ago, filed for divorce and didn't want him back under any circumstances, apparently. Her husband wasn't through with her yet. Angus feared she might lose more than her ranch because of T.D.

"Is everything all right?" Jinx asked quietly, no doubt seeing the battle going on inside him.

"Fine," he lied. "How about you?"

"Fine."

He could see that she was as confused as he was. "We're going to get through this," he said, hoping what he was saying was true.

"I hope so," she said as if she knew he didn't just mean tonight.

He was so close, he could see the pain in her face even in the darkness. He knew what it felt like to have a failed relationship. His hadn't even involved getting to the altar. His relationship hadn't lasted that long. But he recalled the pain quite easily. He knew that Jinx wasn't ready for another man any more than he was ready for another woman.

He breathed in the cold mountain air, feeling tired from a long day in the saddle and working hard to get the traps set. It wouldn't be long now. He should get back to his spot.

Yet, he didn't want to leave her. A premonition? He was worried about her and would be until she was free of T.D. In the meantime, he knew she would stay in his thoughts. What was it about her? Those few seconds when she let down her guard and let him see how vulnerable she was? At those moments it took all his strength and good sense not to step to her and take her in his arms, everyone be damned if they didn't like it.

"I should go," he said. Her ex was going to show up at any time. Crazy bitter and probably drunk, nothing good was going to come out of it when T.D. did strike again.

Every time a lock of her coppery hair came loose from her braid and fell over those big brown eyes, he wanted to push it aside. But he knew if he touched her, he'd kiss that mouth again with its bow-shaped full lips.

He realized the trail his thoughts had taken and reined them in with a groan. His brother was right. Something about this woman had him twisted into a knot. His gaze followed her whenever she was around. He couldn't quit thinking about her.

Worse, if he was being honest with himself, he'd been smitten with Jinx from the moment he'd laid eyes on her when they were nothing but kids. It had only gotten worse when he'd seen her again. He recalled the way she'd come out of her house that night at the ranch, shotgun in hand, facing down her ex with courage and determination. She'd shown a strength that had chipped away a corner of his ice-encased heart.

Since being on the cattle drive, he'd felt his heart melting at just the sight of her. She refused to show weakness even when he knew she had to be as exhausted as he was at the end of the day. More and more he felt drawn to her in a way that made him both scared and exhilarated.

He felt like one of the bears that had come out of a long hibernation. He was hungry again in a way he'd never experienced before. Bad timing be damned. He wanted this woman.

JINX SHIVERED IN the darkness. She was so close to Angus that she could look into his blue eyes. This was it, she thought. They could all die tonight. She yearned for Angus to take her in his arms.

He brushed a lock of her hair back from her face. She felt her eyes widen, but she didn't move. "Why are you looking at me like that?"

"I'm counting your freckles. I've wanted to since I first laid eyes on you," he whispered, so close now that she could hardly breathe.

She smiled to hide how nervous it made her. "I take it you have a lot of time to kill?"

He met her gaze and smiled. "Not as much as I'd like right now," he whispered. "You don't have any idea how beautiful you are."

She chuckled self-consciously and dropped her gaze. "Angus—"

With his warm fingers, he lifted her chin until their eyes locked. "You're beautiful, Jinx, and I haven't been able to take my eyes off you this whole time."

Her pulse jumped as he bent to brush his lips over hers. The heat of her desire rushed through her veins, hot as liquid lava. She'd never felt this kind of need before, knowing only one man could satisfy it.

Angus pulled back to look into her eyes for a moment before he dropped his mouth to hers again. She surrendered to his kiss as he parted her lips and delved deeper. His arms came around her, pulling her against him until she could feel the beat of his heart in sync with her own.

She opened to him, no longer fighting her feelings. Desire flared, his kisses fanning the flames. She lost herself in his kisses, in the strength of his arms drawing her to him, in the low moan she heard escape his lips as she pulled back.

"Jinx," he whispered her name on a ragged breath.

"Jinx." Angus said it low, soft, a caress that sent a pleasurable shiver across her skin. Then his fingers touched her face, drawing her closer until she was looking into his eyes, losing herself in them.

His mouth was dropping to hers again. Her lips parted, as if there had been no doubts between them. One arm looped around her waist, pulling her into his solid body. She felt his need as much as her own. Like her, she knew that he feared tonight might be their last.

She surrendered to him, needing this man's strength as well as his gentleness. What surprised her was the fire he set ablaze inside her. T.D. had never ignited such passion. He'd been rough and demanding, believing that was what every woman wanted.

Angus seemed to know what she needed, what she desperately desired, as if he knew instinctively that she hadn't been truly satisfied. Because of that, she felt vulnerable and exposed. Had it been any other man other than Angus…

His breathing was as labored as her own as his hand slipped up under her coat to her warm flesh. She arched against him, wanting and needing more, as she let out a moan of pure pleasure and whispered his name.

They both froze at a sound in the trees lower on the mountain. For a while, she'd completely forgotten T.D., forgotten everything but the feel of this cowboy's arms around her.

Angus groaned quietly and let go of her, drawing back. "When this is over," he said on a hoarse breath. "Jinx, I promise, when this is over…"

She touched her finger to his lips and shook her head. They couldn't make promises. Not tonight. Not under these circumstances.

Angus looked as if he couldn't bear to leave her. She knew the feeling. She gave him a gentle shove.

Nearby, they heard one of the traps being sprung. Then silence.

ANGUS WAS FURIOUS with himself as he rushed back to his spot on the mountain only to find that a deer had tripped one of his traps. The pretty doe bound off into the distance. But it could have just as easily been T.D. or one of his men. He shouldn't have left his traps unattended. He wouldn't again.

He'd let himself get carried away. It wasn't like him and yet when he'd looked at Jinx… He thought of what he'd seen in her eyes. A need like his own. A fear matching his own. Tonight everything could go wrong and there could be bloodshed.

Forcing that thought away, he told himself it was why they'd both been vulnerable. Just the thought of the two of them on the side of this mountain in the dark and what he'd wanted to happen… He knew it was insane, but he'd felt as if they were the last two people in the world. Neither of them had wanted to stop, but fortunately, when the deer tripped the trap, they had.

What if it had been T.D. instead of a deer? What if he'd seen the two of them? He shook his head at his own impetuousness, let alone his foolishness. He could have gotten both Jinx and himself killed.

Tomorrow they would reach her grazing land with the herd, then… But that was the problem. Then Jinx would be back at her ranch dealing with her problems and there would be no excuse for him to hang around. That was if they lived through tonight, he reminded himself.

He heard a meadowlark whistle close by. "You all

right?" Brick whispered as he came out of the darkness of the pines. "I heard one of your traps go off."

"Deer. A little doe." His voice sounded strange even to him.

"You all right?" his brother asked suspiciously.

"Just jumpy. You should get back to your traps."

He nodded but didn't move for a moment. Angus wondered if his twin could tell from his expression even in the darkness what he'd been up to.

"We'll be done tomorrow," Brick said.

"I was just thinking about that," he said, honestly.

"I bet you were."

"I'm looking forward to going home to the ranch."

"Glad to hear that." Brick slapped him on the shoulder. "Be careful."

"You, too." He watched his brother disappear back through the pines and tried to concentrate on staying alive tonight.

Chapter Twelve

As they waited for the cover of darkness, T.D. thought about sneaking into camp, finding his wife and collecting on at least some of what she owed him. She hadn't just kicked him off the ranch. She'd kicked him out of her bed months ago.

He'd been fine with it at the time. He'd had Patty, and Patty was always willing. But she wasn't Jinx. Patty couldn't fill a need in him that had little to do with sex. Jinx had filled that need. He'd been married to her and the ranch. He'd felt he finally belonged somewhere.

What bothered him was that he'd thought Jinx would come begging for him after a few weeks, let alone a few months, without him.

But she hadn't. It seemed impossible that she hadn't seemed to miss his lovemaking as if he hadn't been giving her what she needed. Was that true? If so, it shook the very foundation of what he believed about himself. All he'd ever had was his looks and his way with women. That Jinx might have found him lacking drove him insane with fury.

Patty never complained, he told himself. And yet the fact that Jinx didn't want him back ate at him. When he got the chance again, he'd remind Jinx what she'd been missing.

"Let's get ready to go," he ordered everyone gathered around the fire. He sensed they weren't as into this as he was and that annoyed him.

"Don't you think she's going to be expecting this?" Travis asked without moving.

He didn't bother to answer him. Travis was right about one thing, though. Jinx knew him too well. She'd know he'd come for her tonight, their last night on this mountain. But not even Travis knew what he had planned. In the dark there would be confusion. At least that was his hope. Jinx would anticipate what he had planned. Too bad there was nothing she could do about it, though.

Still, it made him wonder if he was too predictable. Is that why she thought she could live without him? Maybe it was time to prove to her that he could still surprise her. He smiled to himself.

"Here's what I want you all to do," he said and told them their part of the plan, keeping his own to himself. He knew he couldn't depend on Travis or Royce or Cash. But at least he had Wyatt here with him. They'd been buds since grade school. Wyatt would have his back.

Stepping away from the dying coals of the campfire, he pulled his binoculars from where he'd left his saddle-bag to look toward her camp. He couldn't see a damned thing, it was so dark tonight. He thought about last night when he'd spotted Jinx and he'd felt his pulse jump like it always did when he caught her unawares.

She'd been standing not far from the light of their campfire. He'd been studying her when he realized that she wasn't alone. His heart had begun to pound wildly. He'd felt weak with shock and fury. She'd stood talking to one of her wranglers—the same one who'd come to her rescue back down at the ranch.

He'd seen the way she was standing, the way she had her head tilted to look up at the cowboy. She liked him. Maybe more than liked him. He realized that he hadn't even considered what his wife had been doing all these months when she wasn't letting him into her bed. How many other wranglers had there been since she'd kicked him out? Did everyone in the county know what had been going on but him?

His blood had pounded so hard in his head, he'd felt dizzy.

That was when he knew that he could kill her. She'd humiliated him for the last time. When he'd seen her standing with that cowboy, he could have grabbed his rifle and taken a shot right then, but suddenly a cold calm had come over him. As his wife had stepped away from the cowboy, he'd lowered the binoculars. For possibly the first time in his life, he hadn't gone off half-cocked. He was going in prepared this time because now he knew what had to be done.

He would find her while the others kept everyone else busy. He'd find her and finish this.

ELLA PUT OUT the campfire as planned and watched the smoke rise slowly into the darkness. Quiet fell over the mountainside. The plan had been to make everything seem as it had been other nights. As predicted, clouds had rolled in, smothering any starlight tonight.

She listened, knowing it wouldn't be long before this moment of peace was interrupted. Brick, Jinx and Angus had left to be ready. Jinx was closest to camp but Ella couldn't see her. She thought about their traps. They didn't have time to dig holes or pits, but would use the pine tree boughs to make a swinging log that could be released as a rider passed. Another one would have a large rock that swung down from a tree.

"Even if some of them miss, they will be enough of a distraction that we can attack," Brick had said, clearly enjoying this.

"We need to immobilize as many of them as we can before they reach the herd," Jinx had said.

Ella had opted to stay in camp to set up some booby traps of her own just in case the others were wrong about how and where T.D. would strike.

"You're a smart woman," Max said now as he left behind his beloved chuckwagon to take refuge in an outcropping of trees next to a wall of rock some distance from the camp. She'd talked him into it, wanting him out of the line of fire no matter what happened tonight.

"You should have a good view from there," Ella had said as she'd tried to sell him on the idea. "But you'll also be armed so if any of them decide to come this way..."

The older man nodded, clearly seeing what she was up to. "I would love to get that man in my sights."

She gave him a disapproving look. "We're supposed to wound them unless we have no other options."

"I'll be sure to keep that in mind."

Leaving him, she went back to where the campfire had died to nothing but a tiny stream of smoke before climbing into the chuckwagon to get the pots and pans she needed. Her trap wasn't lethal, but it would alert them if T.D. and his men were circling around behind them. Max would be safe as long as he stayed out of sight.

ANGUS FINISHED THE last of the swinging branch booby traps and looked through the trees to where he could barely see Jinx. He knew that like him, she was waiting and listening. Jinx thought that T.D. would come roaring in, all liquored up, shooting and yelling and out of control.

They wouldn't have any trouble hearing them coming, if that was the case. Jinx didn't expect T.D. to approach this rationally. She just assumed he would be drunk, angry and acting out rather than having a plan.

But Angus thought that she might be wrong and that expecting him to act as he usually did could be a mistake. T.D. knew this was his last night to stop them from reaching summer range—or at least cost them another day or so, if he scattered the herd. So Angus stood listening, suspecting T.D. would try to sneak up on them instead.

He couldn't help but worry. Ella had stayed back at camp to take care of things there. She'd looked worried but he knew she would take care of Max and herself.

They were all worried, he thought, as on impulse, he moved quietly through the pines to where Jinx was waiting. He drew her into his arms, unable to fight the bad feeling that had overcome him. She leaned into him as if glad to let him take some of the weight off her—at least for a moment.

At the sound of something moving slowly, cautiously toward them, they separated. Brick came out of the darkness, whispering, "Is it safe?"

Angus wasn't sure if he meant from the booby traps or because he had spotted Jinx in his brother's arms. "We're as ready as we can be."

Brick nodded. "I'm going back up the mountain to my spot." He pulled some strips of leather from his jacket pocket. "If I get one down, I'll make sure he won't be any more trouble until I untie him at daylight." He pulled out the wad of torn dish towels he planned to use as gags.

His brother gave him a grin before disappearing back up the mountainside.

Angus just hoped this worked and that no one got hurt or worse, killed. But that would be up to T.D., he thought with a shudder as the darkness seemed to take on a life of its own. "They're coming," he whispered as he heard a horse whinny in the distance.

Chapter Thirteen

As Brick hurried back up the mountainside, Angus returned to his spot. Jinx could tell he hadn't wanted to leave her. The night felt colder not being in his arms. She tried to concentrate on what had to be done, rather than the wrangler.

With luck, this would work. Even if T.D. stampeded the cattle into their camp, the only thing that would be destroyed was Max's beloved chuckwagon. A chuckwagon could be replaced. Max, in the meantime, would be safe away from camp, Ella had assured her.

She knew they were as ready as possible and still she couldn't help being scared. With a man like T. D. Sharp… Had he followed her up here just to torment her? To keep her from getting her herd to summer range? Or was his motive even more treacherous? She remembered the look in his eyes the other night at the ranch and knew at that moment, he'd wished her dead.

Jinx swallowed the lump in her throat, telling herself the man didn't scare her even as she knew it wasn't true. There was something about him, a feeling that he'd stepped over some invisible barrier and now he felt he had nothing to lose. If he ever got her alone again…

She shivered and pushed the thought away. His attack on them tonight would get him sent to jail. At least temporarily. With luck, she could get a loan against the ranch until she had it sold. Dangling that kind of money in front of T.D., she thought she could get him to sign the divorce papers. She wanted this over.

Right now the thought of losing the ranch didn't seem so overpowering. Standing here in the dark, trying to gauge what T.D. would do next, she had a whole different set of priorities. She wanted to live. Angus had made her realize there were more important things than a piece of land or a herd of cattle. There could be a life after T.D., after losing her mother and father, after even losing the ranch.

Not that she was ready for that life. Not that Angus might even be in it. But he'd made her see that her mistake in marrying T.D. wasn't the end of the world. It was only the end of this life. She could put this all behind her without knowing what the future held for her—just that she had one.

If she lived past tonight.

Waiting in the dark, the night getting colder, she regretted her own stubbornness. She should have sold her cattle, taken a loss and put the ranch up for sale. She'd put not just her life in jeopardy. Now Angus, Brick and Ella along with Max were in danger because she was so damned determined to get the herd to summer range.

As much as she hated to admit it, she'd done it not just out of stubbornness. She'd wanted to show T.D. that he wasn't going to run her life, let alone ruin it. Her stubborn pride could get them all killed. She couldn't bear the thought. Angus, Brick and Ella had answered her ad because Dana and Jinx's mother had been close. They should never have had to come all this way. None of them should be on this mountainside right now knowing there was a madman out there in the pines set on vengeance.

Another horse whinnied from deep in the pines above her on the mountain. She heard a branch snap under a horse's hoof. They were moving more slowly than she'd expected. Did they expect a trap?

She pulled the weapon at her hip, hoping she wouldn't have to use it. The plan had been to cause enough confusion to drive them back—if not subdue any who fell into their traps. By cutting down their numbers, it would make T.D. think twice. At least that was the hope. She knew he was basically a coward. He needed his two close friends to bolster his courage—that and alcohol.

Unfortunately, he had them and two more men who would follow his orders if he offered them the right incentives.

The sound of the riders grew closer. She could hear the creak of saddle leather, the brush of tree boughs and whisper of high grass against the horses' legs as their riders kept coming.

Jinx found herself holding her breath. She knew how quickly everything could go south. Behind her, the cattle lowed softly. If she was right, the approaching riders would begin firing their weapons and yelling as they tried to stampede the herd back toward the camp.

And if she was wrong?

ANGUS FELT THE hair rise on the back of his neck as he realized the riders had spread out and at least one would soon be almost on top of him. Even in the pitch blackness of the spring night, he waited for the shapes to materialize out of the dark.

The trick, he knew, was to stay calm until it was time

to attack. The booby traps were spring-loaded. All a horse had to do was trip the rope hidden in the tall green grass and all hell would break loose. Jinx could handle this, he told himself. At the same time he was reminded that all of this was about her.

T.D. had ridden all the way up here with his friends to cause her trouble. He wanted to torment her. To make her pay for not taking him back. To hurt her.

And that was what scared Angus the most. If T.D. got his hands on her, how far would the man go?

He couldn't see her through the trees, but he knew she was still there. He hadn't wanted to leave her alone, still didn't.

A swishing sound off to his left on the mountain-side was followed by a cry of pain. He could hear what sounded like a struggle, then silence. He listened hard for the all-clear signal and finally heard his brother whistle a meadowlark's call.

He tried to relax. Brick had one of them down. Four to go.

The riders seemed to be quickening their pace through the pines. One of his log swings snapped in the darkness. He heard an *oouft* sound followed by a loud thump as a body hit the ground. An instant later, a horse ran past him—sans its rider.

Angus sprang into action, moving quickly toward where he'd heard the man fall. As he neared, he heard mewing sounds. Gun drawn, he pounced on the man only to have him cry out in pain.

"My arm," the man cried. "It's broken." His eyes widened as he saw the gun in Angus's hand. "Don't kill me. None of this was my idea." The man began to cry.

Angus saw that there was no way to tie the man's

hands, so he took the man's weapon and tied his ankles together along with the wrist of his good arm.

"You have to get me a doctor," the man pleaded. "I don't want to die out here."

He hurriedly put his hand over the man's mouth. "Where's T.D.?" he asked the man quietly and released his grip on the man's mouth long enough to let him answer.

"I don't know. I thought he was with us, but I haven't seen him since we left camp."

He quickly gagged the man, fearing it was too late. The others could have heard him. But none of them had come to his aid. At least not yet.

In the distance he heard another of the booby traps snap off to his left. Brick had another one down, followed by the meadowlark whistle. As another booby trap went off, he waited but heard nothing. That one must have missed. Or maybe the man had wised up and gotten off his horse.

To Angus's count, they had three down. That left two men. Did Brick have T.D.? If not, was he one of the two left? He hoped they'd heard what was going on and had headed back. He listened, hearing nothing but the pounding of his own heart.

That was until he heard an earsplitting racket coming from camp and then dead silence.

THE FIRST SIGNS of daylight cast an eerie dark gray shadow over the mountainside. From her perch in one of the large old pines, Ella saw that a riderless horse had set off her alarm in the camp. She watched the horse head for the corral where their horses whinnied and moved around restlessly.

So where was the rider? She felt anxious, worried about what was happening in the forest beyond the camp. But she wasn't about to leave Max. She'd promised Jinx she would make sure he was safe.

He sat with his back against the rock rim, his shotgun resting in his lap. She watched from her tree perch. The clouds had parted some. The sky to the east lightened in the area around her, and she wondered how long before dawn. Her eyes felt dry and scratchy from staring into the darkness of the pines.

She listened but heard nothing but the cattle lowing in the meadow higher up the mountain. Closer, she heard the steady beat of her heart as she waited and prayed that the others were all right. And yet as she waited, she feared something had gone wrong. She kept thinking about the horse that had set off her alarm—and its empty saddle. Where was the man who'd been riding it?

JINX TENSED AS she heard the noise coming from camp, but before she could react, she heard a rider bearing down on her. She had her gun ready, hoping she didn't have to use it. A riderless horse burst out of the darkness and ran past her.

She let out the breath she'd been holding and tried to relax. The horse had come from the direction of the camp. She told herself that Ella would take care of whoever had set off the alarm back there—just as she would make sure Max was safe. If she was able.

Listening, Jinx heard nothing. The quiet was more unnerving than the racket had been. She had no idea how many of the men were down. Or if any of them had turned back. All she knew was that unless they had T.D., he was still on this mountain somewhere. Maybe even closer by than she knew. That thought sent a shudder through her. She feared how badly things could go on this mountainside.

The sound of the gunshot made her jump. It had come from higher up on the mountain. *Brick*. Her heart dropped. She knew Angus would go to him. She could hear movement through the pines off to her right. It was still pitch black in the pines, but the sky was lightening in the distance. Soon the sun would rise. Soon she would be able to see who was coming at her.

A closer sound made her freeze. She sensed T.D. even before she heard the swish of his boots through the tall grass behind her, followed by the smell of the alcohol on his breath as she swung around, leading with the pistol in her hand.

T.D. was on her so quickly she didn't have time to even pull the trigger. He covered her mouth with his gloved hand before she could scream as he ripped the pistol from her grip. Tossing the weapon away into the darkness, he put his face against the side of hers and whispered, "Hello, wife. Don't you wish you'd just paid me off when I asked nicely?"

Chapter Fourteen

Angus ran through the pines toward the sound of the gunshot, knowing where it had come from. His brother was in trouble. There hadn't been the meadowlark whistle as hard as he had listened for it. The clouds had moved off, leaving a lighter ceiling overhead as daylight peeked through the pines.

He could make out shapes through the trees. He saw two horses, both tied to a limb. That meant three men down, just as he'd thought. He hadn't heard another trap being sprung. What had happened that there'd been a gunshot?

Because there were still two men out there, he reminded himself as he ran through the pines. He'd known at once that the gun report had come from the spot where Brick had set up his booby traps. As he ran, he prayed for the sound of his brother's meadowlark whistle. But it didn't come to let him know that Brick was all right. Because in his heart, he knew he wasn't.

He didn't even consider that he might be running into a trap. All he could think about was getting to his twin. He'd felt that shot as if the bullet had entered his own body. Because they were identical twins, they'd always shared a special bond. Not that they'd dressed alike or were alike in so many ways. They'd never had a special language that was all theirs. Nor had they ever sensed when the other was in trouble. Until now.

Angus was almost to Brick when he heard the second gunshot. He burst through the pines, shoving aside boughs to find his brother lying on the ground next to two bodies. In that instant, he saw that Cash had been gagged and tied up but had managed to free himself.

At the sight of Angus, the man jumped up, ran to his horse and pulling the reins free, took off down the mountain as if the devil himself was after him. On the ground next to Brick, Royce lay dead from a gunshot wound to the chest. There was a gun dangling from the man's fingertips even though his wrists were bound.

He saw what had happened as clearly as if he'd witnessed the whole thing. Royce had pulled a second gun that Brick hadn't found on him before his brother had tied the cowboy up.

Angus dropped down beside his brother. Brick was trying to say something. There was a dark blood spot on his upper chest that was getting larger and darker. Angus quickly pulled off his coat and pressed it to the wound.

As he did, he heard someone coming through the trees. He didn't go for his gun, knowing he wouldn't have time to pull it. He picked up Brick's gun and turned it as the figure burst through the pines.

Ella. He eased his finger off the trigger as she dropped to the ground beside Brick. "Help is on the way," she said as she took over holding the coat to her cousin's wound. "I was able to get cell service from the top of a pine tree."

Angus felt a surge of relief. Help was on the way. But her next words turned his blood to ice.

"I think T.D. has Jinx," she said. "She's not where she's

supposed to be and there are drag marks going down the mountain. His horse set off my alarm. I had a bad feeling so I called for help, then climbed down the tree. I was on my way to check when I heard the second shot."

His heart had dropped to his boots. Brick was shot and T.D. had Jinx?

"I'll take care of Brick," his cousin said. "Go find her. Before it's too late."

As T.D. DRAGGED her through the woods, Jinx tried to fight him. He held her by the throat, his boozy breath next to her ear as he told her what he was going to do to her. When he'd first jumped her, he'd thrown her down, knocking the air out of her.

She fought him, scratching and kicking and biting, only to have him slap her so hard she saw stars. He'd sat on her and quickly bound her wrists and gagged her with her bandanna. He'd thought she would scream for help. She could see that T.D. was just hoping someone would come to her rescue so he could kill them.

With his arm locked around her neck, he dragged her. When she tried to fight him, he cut off her airway until she quit struggling. At first she'd been terrified, knowing at least in part, what he planned to do to her. But the more she fought him, the more furious she got. How dare he think he could treat her this way?

She knew she needed to save her strength for when she had a chance of actually getting away from him, but the mad she had going felt good. And it was so much better than terror right now.

He stopped under a large old pine tree far from the camp. Throwing her down, he climbed on top of her. She glared at him, putting all her disgust into the look.

"It's not rape," he said as if reading her gaze clearly enough. "You're still my wife, which means you are still mine to do whatever I want with." His idea of marriage astounded her. She tried to tell him what she thought of him through her gag but he only laughed, not understanding a word.

"Come on, you like this," he said as if he could still charm her. "I love you. I just want to show you how much, remind you of what you've been missing. You have been missing it, haven't you?" His gaze narrowed for a moment. "Don't you remember what it was like with the two of us? You know you still love me. We can stop this right now. All you have to do is admit it was a mistake when you threw me out. It isn't too late for us."

She knew it was a lie, but she wondered if T.D. did. Maybe he believed everything he said. If she submitted to him, it wouldn't be over. Even now, she could see that he didn't trust her. Didn't trust that he could charm her anymore. She could see the fear in his eyes. Even if she were stupid enough to take him back, his anger and insecurity would make their lives a living hell. He'd always said, when he was drinking, that she thought he wasn't good enough for her. He was the one who believed that until he'd proven to her he was right.

T.D. wasn't good enough for her. He wasn't the kind of man she wanted in her life. Not now. Not ever.

He stared at her in the growing light. Was he having second thoughts about this? Was he wishing like she was that none of this had ever happened?

Slowly, he leaned down to kiss her, but she moved her head from side to side each time he tried and attempted to buck him off. But he was too strong for her. She wouldn't submit to him. She couldn't.

Swearing, he said, "Fine. We don't have much time so let's get right to it." He unzipped her coat and then grabbed her Western shirt and unsnapped it in one quick, hard jerk. "I'll just take what's mine. You want it rough? Well, too bad, because that's the way you're getting it."

She'd told herself that she would kill him if he ever touched her again. He'd bound her wrists behind her with duct tape and had her lying partially on her side. She felt a little give in the duct tape. He'd been in a hurry and he hadn't done a good job.

As he leaned over her, grabbing her chin to hold her head still while he kissed her hard, she moved her hands down her side and pulled her legs up until she could reach her boot with the knife in it.

Drawing the knife from the sheath, she clutched it tightly in her fist. She knew she could do little damage with the knife the way she was bound. But right now just getting him off her would be a start. Leaning back, she got the blade between her wrists and felt it cut through most of the tape. Just a little more.

T.D. took her movements as her getting into what was happening. He deepened the kiss as he groped her through her bra. The tape gave. Her wrists free, she swung the knife.

He must have sensed that her hands were free because he moved just enough that the blade cut into his side—rather than his back. He let out a howl of pain, grabbing her wrist with such force that she dropped the blade before she could stab him again. Still on top of her, T.D. snatched up the knife, his blood staining it.

Her breath caught in her throat as he leaned over her, flashing the blade in her face. She closed her eyes as he wiped the blood off on her cheek. "You stupid bitch," he breathed, sounding as if in pain. She knew it was only a flesh wound. She had succeeded in only making him angrier with her.

But she opened her eyes, defiantly glaring at him. If he didn't know before, he did now. She would rather die than let him do this to her.

Holding her wrists down above her head with one hand, he laid the cold knife blade against the bare skin of her chest for a moment, before he cut her bra open. She felt the cold night air on her exposed breasts and heard his chuckle when he saw her puckered nipples.

It's the cold, you idiot, she wanted to say, even more contempt in her gaze.

He recognized it because he growled, "I could cut your throat just as easily."

Please do, she thought.

"Maybe I will cut you, once I'm through with you," he said, so close that she wanted to gag on the alcohol fumes. He pocketed the knife and rolled her over, duct-taping her wrists again, this time more roughly.

Flopping her back over, he held her down with his body as he stared at her for a long moment. She felt a chill because the look was clear. This was goodbye. He would never let her leave this mountain alive.

She heard him unzip his jeans before he began fumbling to get hers undone, shifting to one side as he did. Jinx brought her knee up hard and fast and caught him in the groin. As he let out a howl and leaned to one side, she bucked him the rest of the way off and rolled to the side to scramble to her feet.

He reached for her, grabbing a handful of blue jean fabric and dragging her back. She kicked at him, but he pulled himself to his feet and slapped her so hard she tasted blood.

His voice was hoarse with fury and pain as he locked one arm around her throat again, pulled his pistol and held it to her head. "You're a dead woman."

WYATT TRIED TO hold the rifle steady. His finger brushed over the trigger. All he had to do was pull it. Pull it and Jinx would be history. Patty would be grateful.

At the thought of her, his finger hovered on the trigger. If only he could quit shaking—and get his crosshairs on Jinx. Since the moment T.D. had grabbed Jinx, he hadn't had a clear shot.

Just when he had the crosshairs on her, they both moved. He swore. He could feel himself sweating profusely under his coat even though the early morning was freezing cold. The sky around him was lightening. He had a clear view of the two and wasn't sure how much longer he would.

He hadn't heard any of the others for some time now. Not since the sound of that gunshot had broken the silence. Earlier T.D. had spelled out the plan to them. Even as he was talking, Wyatt knew he was lying. T.D. wanted them to quietly sneak up on the herd before they started shooting and hollering and scattering them.

But just before they left camp, T.D. pulled him aside to tell him that he had a different plan for him. "I'm going to sneak into the camp from the other way, find Jinx and finish this. I want you to cover my back."

Wyatt had nodded numbly, thinking that the cowboy's plan worked out perfectly for his own plan. They'd ridden for a way with the others and then cut off through the pines to ride up almost to the camp. It had been T.D.'s idea to let his horse go into camp as a decoy. The man wasn't stupid. He knew Jinx was expecting the attack.

Wyatt had hung back but kept his eye on T.D.

Now he stood some yards away. The rifle was getting heavy. He didn't know how much longer he could wait to take a shot. Worse, he thought he'd heard a helicopter in the distance.

When he'd lowered the rifle, then lifted it again, he'd been shocked to see that Jinx had almost gotten away from T.D. The rifle wavered in his hands. Surely he hadn't missed his chance at a clean shot.

He fought now to get the crosshairs on her. T.D. had his arm around her neck and a pistol to her head. What the hell? Was he only threatening her? He couldn't believe that this situation might solve itself. If T.D. killed Jinx, he wouldn't have to and yet he could take credit when he saw Patty. T.D. would be going to prison...

Wyatt felt a surge of hope that everything might work out for him. But T.D. had to pull that trigger. He watched as Jinx tried to fight him off. Any moment the wranglers working for her would be coming. What was T.D. thinking, taking this risk? *Shoot her!*

Couldn't the man feel time running out? It struck him that T.D. was crazy. He always had been, but lately he'd been getting worse. He was going to get them all thrown in jail—if not killed.

As he watched through the scope, Wyatt realized that T.D. wasn't going to shoot her. If Jinx was going to die, it would be up to Wyatt to finish this and soon. He'd missed a good shot earlier when he'd lowered the rifle for even a moment and was now mentally kicking himself. This could already be over. He could have killed Jinx.

The rifle wavered in his arms, the crosshairs going

from Jinx's face to T.D.'s as the two kept moving around. Wyatt thought of how disappointed Patty would be if he didn't do what had to be done. How disappointed he would be in himself because any hope he had of ever being with Patty would be gone.

Not that T.D. stood a chance now of ever getting Jinx back—and freeing Patty. Hadn't Wyatt been hoping that his friend would return to Jinx and break it off with Patty for good? He could have seen himself comforting the brokenhearted Patty. He'd seen it as a chance to win the woman's heart.

But now it was clear that Jinx was never going back to T.D.—not after this. T.D. had blown any chance he had by following her up here into the mountains. Not that it seemed he stood a chance anyway since now there was a wrangler in the mix. Jinx had moved on—and damned quickly, if he said so himself. Patty thought she had to get rid of Jinx to get T.D. back. Jinx was already long gone.

Through the rifle scope he tried to get a shot at Jinx. T.D. wasn't going to pull the trigger. Instead, his friend seemed to be looking back up the mountain. For a moment Wyatt feared that he'd seen him and almost lowered the rifle. No, T.D. must have heard some of the others coming. Time had run out.

He put the crosshairs on Jinx's red head and assured himself that no one would know who fired the fatal shot. T.D. would be blamed for all of it—not that he wouldn't probably get away with it, just as he had all of their lives. He'd dragged them up on this mountain, gotten him and Travis in trouble, and T.D. would somehow shift the blame.

If T.D. shot Jinx he'd go to prison and Patty would

be free. But even as he thought it, Wyatt knew the man didn't have what it took to pull the trigger.

Wyatt settled the crosshairs on Jinx as the sun caught in her red hair. "This is for you, Patty."

As DAWN BROKE over the mountains, Angus followed the drag marks down the mountain at a run, his pistol drawn, his heart racing. He had to find Jinx.

He came to a sliding stop as he saw them—and they saw him. T.D. pulled her out of the darkness of a large pine, using Jinx like a human shield. She was gagged and from what he could see, her hands seemed to be bound behind her. Her coat was open, along with her shirt, her bare breasts covered by her long hair.

T.D. had a gun to her head and was grinning as he locked his free arm around her neck, pulling her back against him. "Drop your gun or I'll kill her right now," he ordered. "I wouldn't try me on this."

Angus could see the fear in Jinx's face, but suspected that it was more for him than for herself. He felt his finger on the trigger, the barrel pointed at T.D.'s head. But it was a shot he knew he couldn't take.

He thought about what to do as he considered his options. They were limited. He could rush the two of them and hope for the best. There was a desperation in T.D.'s expression. He looked nervous, like a trapped animal, and that made him even more dangerous. The man knew that he'd never get out of this, not this time. Brick had been shot. Royce was dead. T.D. would have heard the gunfire.

What Angus feared was that the man would panic and shoot Jinx if he didn't drop his gun. He slowly lowered his pistol to the ground, knowing that there was nothing stopping T.D. from shooting him.

But Angus was ready. If T.D. even started to pull the gun away from Jinx's head, he was ready to launch himself at the man. There was a good chance he would be shot, but if he could save Jinx, it was a chance he had to take.

"I know she's been with you," T.D. said, anger marring his handsome face. "Just the thought of you and her..." Jinx let out a cry as T.D. tightened his hold on her.

Angus started to take a step forward, but T.D. quickly said, "Don't do it. I'll kill her. You know I will. If I can't have her, then no one can, especially you."

He could tell that Jinx was having trouble breathing. "You don't want to go to prison."

T.D. laughed. "I've been headed there my whole life. The only thing good I ever had was Jinx. And now that's gone." He pressed the pistol barrel harder to her temple, making her wince. "This is all your fault, Jinx. You only have yourself to blame."

The air filled with a sound of a gunshot report.

Chapter Fifteen

Angus started at the sound. He had no idea where the shot had come from—just that it had happened fast. Suddenly Jinx was on the ground and T.D. was standing over her splattered with blood. Angus was instantly moving, grabbing up his gun from the ground as he rushed toward T.D.

Another shot filled the air, biting the bark of a tree next to T.D. as the man turned and ran into the pines. Angus launched himself down the hill to cover Jinx from the gunfire. He still wasn't sure where the shots were coming from or who was firing them. He shielded Jinx, terrified that she was already badly injured by the first gunshot.

"Jinx!" he cried as he hurriedly removed the gag from her mouth. "Jinx?" As the gunfire stopped, he heard someone take off on horseback. Pulling his pocketknife, he cut her wrists free and turned her onto her back to lower her to the soft ground.

Her eyes were open. But like T.D.'s, her face was splattered with blood to the extent that he couldn't tell where she'd been hit.

"Angus," she said, her lips curving into a smile before her eyes closed.

"Jinx, don't leave me. Jinx?" He moved closer. In the

growing light of day, he could see where a bullet had grazed her temple. He checked her pulse. It was strong. She didn't seem to have any other injuries, he realized with relief. He could hear a helicopter approaching. Closer, he heard someone moving through the tall grass and trees toward him.

He spun around, pistol ready, and then relaxed. "Max, Jinx has been hit."

Max stumbled up to them and dropped to his knees next to her. Jinx opened her eyes. "Max." The older man took her hand as her gaze shifted to Angus. "T.D.?"

"He got away," he said.

"No," both Max and Jinx said almost in unison.

"A helicopter will be here in just a minute," Max said. "I'll stay with Jinx. Don't let T.D. get away."

Angus saw the worry in the older man's eyes. Unless T.D. was stopped, Jinx would never be safe. He felt torn. He didn't want to leave her, but he damned sure didn't want T.D. to get away.

"Go," Max urged him. "She'll be all right. I'll stay with her and make sure of that."

Swearing, Angus took off down the mountain, following the blood trail T.D. was leaving as the sun topped the mountain and fingered its way through the pines. T.D. hadn't come at them as they'd both anticipated. Instead, he'd sent his flunkies in while he circled around to come up the back way. He'd never planned to stampede the herd. The man had only been after Jinx, letting the others be the diversion he needed.

The bad feeling Angus had had since they'd taken this job had now settled in his bones. He had to find T.D., if it was the last thing he did. As he looked into the dark shadows of the pines, he knew it could very well be just that.

T.D. RAN, slumped over from the pain. He still couldn't believe that Jinx had stabbed him. But that was the least of his worries. He was bleeding from a gunshot wound to his upper chest and because of that, he was leaving a trail. Worse, he knew someone was behind him coming after him—just as he knew who it would be. Jinx's wrangler.

The thought turned his stomach. Earlier, he'd had a nice drunk going. He'd felt cocky and self-assured. He'd outsmarted his so-smart wife. He'd had her in his clutches.

Now he was running scared. He could just hear his father telling him how he'd really screwed up his life good this time. He was looking at jail. Maybe even prison. Why hadn't he let it go? Why hadn't he let Jinx go? But he knew the answer. She was the best thing that had ever happened to him.

But following her up on this mountain? It had been as stupid as Travis had said. He blamed his pride. Everyone in the county knew that Jinx had kicked him out. What was he supposed to do? He couldn't stand looking like a beaten dog with his tail between his legs. He couldn't just let her get away with that.

Now as he stumbled through the pines feeling sick to his stomach and scared, he didn't want to be that man anymore. He wanted desperately to be different, but he had no idea how to make that happen. He felt as if he'd been forced into his bad behavior his whole life. First, by his father's taunts. Later, by the knowledge that he wasn't any good. He wasn't good enough, especially for Jinx. It was why he drank. The more he drank, the worse things got, but he hadn't been able to stop. He'd never been able to stop himself on any of it. For the life of him, he couldn't just let things alone.

Like now. He kept running instead of doing the smart thing and surrendering. He could hear a second helicopter coming. Why not just give up? He needed medical attention. He was still bleeding. He wasn't even sure he could get away. Why not make things easier for himself?

Because there was something in his DNA that wouldn't let him. *That and arrogance*, he thought. Then again, a part of him believed he could get away. He knew this mountain. He knew how to get off it to the closest ranch. He knew how to get help from someone who wouldn't call the cops. He could get away and save himself, and knowing that was what kept him going.

What he didn't know was how badly Jinx had been hit. He'd felt her drop to the ground when he'd released her. There'd been blood everywhere. He hadn't known if it was his or hers. Now he knew that at least part of it was his. But he was sure she'd been hit. Who had fired the shot, though? Not the wrangler. Maybe one of his buddies. Or maybe even Max. Max hated him, just as Jinx's father had.

He pushed those thoughts away as he ran, one surfacing that made him stumble and almost fall. What if Jinx was dead?

The thought hit him so hard that he had trouble staying on his feet. He loved her. His heart broke at the thought that she might be gone. He knew he'd said he was going to kill her—and he might have—but it wasn't what he'd wanted. He hadn't pulled the trigger. He wasn't sure he ever would have been able to.

He'd just had to let her know he wouldn't be simply sent away like some orphan child she was tired of having around. He thought of his mother who'd deserted him when he was nine. He remembered standing at the window, snot running from his nose as he cried and pleaded for her not to leave.

His father had found him and practically tore off his arm as he'd jerked him away from the window. "I'll beat you to within an inch of your life if you don't quit crying. She's gone. Accept it. I have. I never want to hear her name spoken in this house again. Now man up. You and me? We're on our own so make the best of it."

The memory still hurt. He had to stop for moment to catch his breath. Each breath was now a labor. What if the bullet had clipped one of his lungs? What if it was filling with blood right now?

T.D. knew he had to keep moving—even if it killed him. He took off again, holding his hand wrapped in his bandanna over his wound, aware that the bandanna was soaked with his blood.

Growing more light-headed, he felt as if he'd been running his whole life. He was a runner like his mother, he thought. She had gotten away. He feared he wouldn't be so lucky.

Chapter Sixteen

Angus stopped to look ahead in the pines. Had he lost T.D.? He glanced down and saw a drop of blood on the dried pine needles. He looked for another and saw it a few yards away. The blood drops were getting farther apart and smaller, which meant the man wasn't bleeding as badly as he'd been earlier. He would soon be harder to trail. He had to find him before that. He had to find him before he got away. T.D. knew this mountain. He would know how to escape—if he was able.

Angus stared into the shadows of the dense pines, looking for movement, listening for even the sound of a twig snapping. He heard nothing, saw nothing move. He knew T.D. wasn't armed. He knew that the man had dropped the gun he'd been holding to Jinx's head. Unless he had another weapon on him, he was at a distinct disadvantage that way.

However, T.D. had one very good advantage. He was somewhere ahead, and he had enough of a head start that he could be lying in wait somewhere up there. Angus would be expecting an ambush, but would he get a chance to fire his pistol before T.D. sprung his own trap?

It was still a mystery as to who had shot T.D. and Jinx. The rifle report had echoed across the mountain. He'd thought it had come from behind him, but he couldn't be sure. The gunshot had startled them all—even T.D. Angus remembered the sound of a rider taking off not long after the second shot.

Now as he searched the ground for more blood, he worried about Jinx and his brother. He knew that Ella was with Brick, and Max with Jinx. Help had arrived and they both were getting treated for their injuries. Still, a part of him wanted to turn back even though he knew there was nothing he could do to help them.

This wasn't his job, going after T. D. Sharp. He told himself to let him go as he heard one of the helicopters lift off again. Let the sheriff handle this. Anyway, T.D. might already be bleeding to death up here on this mountain like the wild animal he was.

But Angus didn't turn back. He kept going, stubbornly, not willing to chance that the man might get away with what he'd done. Had T.D. heard the helicopters arrive and now begun to take off again? Would he head for them, choosing medical attention over freedom?

ELLA HELD BRICK'S hand in the helicopter on the way to the hospital. He was in and out of consciousness, but the EMTs had stopped the bleeding and were monitoring his vital signs. They weren't as strong as they would like, they'd said.

She kept thinking about how he hadn't wanted to come to Wyoming. How he'd wanted to go see that woman he liked up by the border. Had he sensed that coming here… She shoved the thought away, telling herself that none of them had known he would be shot. Even with all her intuitiveness, she hadn't known this was going to happen.

Brick opened his eyes. "Angus?" he whispered.

"He's fine," she said, even though she didn't know that for sure. As Jinx was being loaded into the second helicopter, Max had told Ella that Angus had gone after T.D., who'd been wounded. Max said Angus had saved Jinx's life. Then he had climbed in with her and the helicopter had taken off.

Just as Ella's chopper with Brick was about to take off, a man had come running out of the woods saying his arm was broken. The EMTs seemed to know him and called him by name—Travis. They'd let him climb in. Ella knew he was a friend of T.D.'s. He sat away from her, looking scared and avoiding eye contact as if he also knew he had more trouble than a broken arm.

Ella squeezed Brick's hand and prayed for him and Angus. It was just like him to go after T.D. Jinx had been hit but was going to make it, the EMTs had said. Angus had saved Jinx, according to Max. So why hadn't he waited and let the sheriff handle T.D.?

Because he was worried the man would get away and go after Jinx yet again, she thought. He was probably right.

JINX DIDN'T REMEMBER much of the helicopter ride to the hospital. Max had been there, telling her everything was going to be all right. She knew better than that.

Now she watched the nurse and doctor moving around the ER as she lay on a gurney in a daze. Max said Angus had saved her. She just remembered T.D., his arm around her neck, stars dancing before her eyes as he cut off her oxygen, and a gun to her temple. He'd said he was going to kill her, and she hadn't doubted that he would before Angus had appeared on the mountainside above them.

She'd thought at first that Angus had fired the shot.

But she swore it had come from another direction. She'd felt the bullet graze her temple and hit T.D. He'd shuddered behind her, loosening his hold on her throat and then letting her go.

Close to blacking out, she'd dropped to her knees, gasping for breath. As Angus had rushed to her, she'd seen Wyatt Hanson in the trees. He was holding a rifle, the barrel pointed right at them and then, as if realizing he'd been seen, he'd taken off on his horse.

The rest was a blur except for Angus's handsome face above her, his look of concern in those blue eyes and then his smile when he realized she was going to be all right.

She'd looked down to see the blood, unsure how much of it was hers and how much of it was T.D.'s. And then Max was there, telling Angus to go after T.D. She'd wanted to stop him, but everything seemed to be happening too fast.

Now her heart ached with worry for Angus. He'd gone after T.D. and as far as she knew, no one had seen him since.

When the elderly doctor she'd known her whole life came into her ER room, she asked him if anyone else had been admitted. He shook his head as he checked her pulse. "Angus Savage?"

"Brick Savage is on his way to surgery. I don't believe Angus Savage has been brought in."

"T. D. Sharp?" she asked.

The doctor shook his head. "The sheriff is here, though. Are you up to answering a few questions?"

She nodded. She kept remembering being shot up on the mountain and Max saying, "The helicopters are here. They're setting down in the meadow now. It's going to be all right."

But Jinx had known that nothing was going to be all right. Angus was still up in the mountains chasing T.D. and she was here. She mouthed a silent prayer for both Brick and Angus.

The sheriff was beside her bed, holding her hand, and she was crying hard. "It's all my fault," she kept saying in between her racking sobs. "All my fault."

Harvey tried to tell her that it wasn't, that he had to check on the others and would be back.

As he started to leave, she grabbed his hand again. "T.D. is still up there. Angus Savage went after him. You have to find them."

"We will," he promised.

"Please don't let anything happen to Angus."

The sheriff smiled and squeezed her hand. "Don't worry."

But all she could do was worry, head pounding. She thought of that young cowboy whom she'd shoved out that barn loft window. She'd almost gotten him killed that day on the Cardwell Ranch when they were little more than kids and here she was again jeopardizing his life. She thought of Angus, his handsome face glowing in the campfire light. The man was like granite, solid and strong.

She clung to that. She had to believe that no matter what happened up on the mountain, Angus would survive. He had to, she thought, her heart aching.

ANGUS MOVED CAUTIOUSLY through the pines, scanning the terrain ahead for movement. He'd seen the red marks on Jinx's throat along with the tiny specks of blood splattered there so he'd known what had happened, even if he hadn't seen T.D. holding her in a headlock, a pistol to her head.

What he didn't know is who had taken such a dangerous shot. Jinx could have been killed. As it was, the bullet had only grazed her temple. But just one wrong move by her or her shooter…

But that hadn't happened, he reminded himself, pushing away the image that lodged in his brain. Instead, Jinx had gotten lucky. She was alive. T.D. had taken the bullet and once Angus found the man, he'd put an end to this.

That was if T.D. was still alive. His hope was that he would come upon the man's body lying in the dried pine needles. He didn't want to kill him, but he would if it came to that.

Ahead, he saw movement and quickly stepped behind a tree. He could hear something busting through the underbrush on the side of the mountain.

He frowned. Too large for a man? He peered around the tree in time to see several moose that had been spooked out of their beds. He glanced in the direction they'd come from, knowing that was where he would find T.D.

Chapter Seventeen

Wyatt couldn't stop shaking. The ride down the mountain had been at breakneck speed. He'd practically killed his horse and himself. But all he'd been able to think of was getting to Patty. He didn't want anyone else telling her what had happened.

He'd heard the helicopters but had stayed in the trees hoping no one saw him. Not that it would make any difference. There was always the chance that the sheriff could tell which rifle had fired the shot. That was why the only stop he'd made was to drop his rifle into an old mill shaft at the edge of the mountain. He'd thrown in a bunch of rocks to cover it, before getting back on his horse and riding the rest of the way to the corral where he kept his horse.

Wyatt knew there was no way to cover the fact that he'd been up on that mountain. Too many people knew he'd been there. Even if he said that he'd left before they'd gone up to Jinx's camp, there was one person in particular who knew better. The person who'd seen him after he'd fired the first rifle shot. T.D. T.D. knew that he'd shot him. T.D. probably even knew that he'd fired a second shot, trying to finish him off.

That thought rattled him clear to the toes of his boots.

He told himself it had been an accident. That he'd been trying to kill Jinx. Or had he, at the last minute, lifted the rifle just a little? Had he seen T.D. in the crosshairs of his scope? Had he realized Patty would never be free as long as T. D. Sharp was alive? Is that what made him take the shot? Or had it really been an accident, his arms fatigued from holding the rifle up for so long, his finger on the trigger jittery at even the thought of what he was about to do?

It was a short walk from the corral to Patty's. He stumbled up to her door after leaving his horse at a ranch on the edge of town. As he tried to catch his breath and still the trembling inside him, he knocked, then knocked louder. He couldn't help looking around as if any minute he expected to hear sirens and turn to find a SWAT team with their weapons trained on him.

The door finally opened. "I shot them." Wyatt pushed his way into her apartment, practically falling in, his legs were so weak.

"Them?" Patty said.

He realized he hadn't meant to say that. But he had. "I shot Jinx. And T.D."

"You *what*?" Patty cried. "Is T.D….dead?"

"I don't know. I didn't mean to. It was an accident. I swear. I was doing what you asked me to. T.D. had Jinx by the throat. She was struggling…"

"Is Jinx dead?"

"I don't know. It all happened so fast." He rushed into the living room and dropped onto the couch. "She was on the ground. There was so much blood. And then I saw T.D. He was holding his chest and there was blood everywhere. That's when I hightailed it off that mountain. It was horrible."

Wyatt dropped his face into his hands and broke down in tears.

"Tell me what happened," Patty said, her voice cracking. When he didn't respond, she came over to the couch and sat down beside him to shake his shoulder. *"Tell me what happened."*

He took a gulp of air and tried to still his sobs. This was not the way he'd wanted Patty to see him. But he couldn't help himself. He was terrified of what he'd done and the price he would be forced to pay.

"Wyatt," she said as if talking to a child. "Pull yourself together and tell me what happened."

He nodded. After a moment he stopped crying, wiped his face with his sleeve and swallowed as he saw that all the color had left her face. She now stared at him as if in shock.

Wyatt cleared his voice and began. "T.D. said we were going to stampede the cattle, but they were waiting for us. They'd set up these booby traps and I heard Travis get caught in one. I think Cash and Royce did, too." His voice cracked. "I think they might be dead." He started to put his face back into his hands, but Patty grabbed one hand and, shaking her head, said, "Tell me how T.D. got shot."

"He never planned to go with the others," Wyatt said. "He sent them in the way he figured Jinx would be expecting the attack. He and I went in the back way. T.D. double-crossed the men with him. He had no intention of stampeding the cattle. He was only after Jinx. Patty, he would never have stopped going after her. *Never.*"

PATTY STARED AT the man, wanting to scream at him, but her throat had gone dust dry. She was shaking inside, afraid she knew what the fool had done. Her worst fears had been realized. What had she been thinking asking Wyatt, of all people, to take care of this for her?

"You fired the shot?" she asked, trying hard to keep her voice level.

"I told you. It was an accident. I was trying to hit Jinx."

"You did hit her, right?" He nodded, looking down as if unable to meet her gaze. "And T.D.? You wouldn't have meant to shoot him. He's your best friend."

His head came up, his eyes full of tears and he nodded quickly. "T.D. had Jinx in a headlock with his pistol to her head. They must have moved when I fired."

"But you don't know how badly either of them was hit, right?"

He shook his head. "I panicked. I just had to get out of there."

He'd killed both Jinx *and* T.D.? Her hand itched to slap him until he quit his stupid blubbering. But she knew she was partially to blame for this. She'd known the man wasn't strong.

She hadn't expected him to do something so stupid as to kill T.D. Not T.D. She fought her own tears at the thought of him being gone. For so long, she dreamed of the day that she and T.D. would be husband and wife. They'd have kids, buy a house, maybe take a trip to Disney World.

That dream burst like a soap bubble. Even if T.D. wasn't dead, he might be lost to her.

"You're a good shot, aren't you?" she asked. "I mean, you beat T.D. and Travis every time at the state fair. You always get your elk and deer every year, killing them in one shot, not spoiling any meat. Isn't that right, Wyatt?"

He nodded, but couldn't hold her gaze. She felt her heart drop. What had the man done?

Patty placed her hand on his thigh. He sniffed but was no longer crying. He wiped his face on his sleeve again and looked over at her as if the sun rose and set on her. "You say T.D. went after Jinx?"

He nodded and she listened as he told her how T.D. had been drinking and getting more angry every hour. The herd was almost to the summer grazing range. They were running out of time.

"You know how he gets when he drinks," Wyatt said, his voice hoarse. "He was crazy. There was no talking him out of it." She patted his thigh and told him to continue. "He and I went in through the camp, but then he found Jinx and started dragging her down the mountain away from the others.

"Travis got hurt first. I heard him scream. Through the trees I could see that he'd been knocked off his horse. I heard him say his arm was broken. Then I think Cash and Royce got caught. That's when I heard a gunshot, then another. I didn't know what was going on. I don't know who all were killed."

"Because you were following T.D. so you could get a good shot at Jinx," she reminded him.

He nodded and swallowed, looking guilty. "I was watching them through the scope on my rifle." He met her gaze. "I was just doing what you asked me to."

Patty removed her hand from his thigh. She could see that was exactly what he would tell the sheriff. That she'd made a deal with him to kill Jinx. She had no doubt that under pressure, he would break down. He would tell the sheriff that it had been her idea. Knowing Wyatt, the fool would probably even tell the sheriff what she'd promised him if he killed Jinx for her. She could deny it, but she feared that Wyatt would be the more believable one, especially if it went to trial.

Panic rose in her, but she tamped it back down. If T.D. was dead, what did she care if she went to prison? Her life would be over without him. But maybe he wasn't. Maybe all of this could be saved.

She tried to think. "Where is everyone now?" Wyatt was sobbing again into his hands. She shook his shoulder again. "Where is everyone now?"

He lifted his head, wiping his face with his sodden sleeve as he tried to pull himself together again. "I saw helicopters. Two of them. The medical ones. I guess the injured are at the hospital by now. I had to get out of there before they saw me."

So whoever had survived this fiasco had gone to the hospital—or was still up on the mountain. "You should stay here," she said. Wyatt brightened. "I'll go to the hospital and find out who all made it." He nodded, looking miserable again. "I'll be back. You should get some rest. Whatever you do, don't leave, okay?" He nodded. "Don't talk to anyone. I mean *anyone*. This is just between the two of us." He nodded again, looking hopeful.

She told herself that if she played this right, she might be able to save herself. If not, it would be her word against Wyatt's. She didn't even have to guess which the sheriff would believe since he'd known them both since they were kids. Which meant she was going to have to get Wyatt to lie. With a sigh, she knew what she'd have to do in that case.

Patty dressed quickly. If T.D. was alive, then he could be one of those brought out by helicopter. She imagined him in the hospital, injured, but alive. She refused to even consider that he was dead up there on the mountain along with all of her dreams.

T.D. was strong and smart and determined, she assured herself. He would survive—he had to. Once she saw him, she'd have to deal with Wyatt. That prospect had little appeal. If only he'd done what she'd asked. He'd said he'd seen Jinx on the ground. He'd said he'd seen blood. Maybe the shot he'd taken had passed through her and hit T.D., barely wounding him. That was possible.

She hung on to the hope that Jinx was dead and T.D. merely injured. Still, she wanted to throttle Wyatt. The damned fool. Why would he take a shot when T.D. was struggling with Jinx?

Because she'd asked him to kill Jinx.

Unfortunately, she feared that wasn't all that was going through Wyatt's mind during that instant when he'd pulled that trigger. The man was too good a shot to do something so stupid. So reckless. So dangerous. But if she was right, then that, too, would be her fault.

Her blood ran cold at what she might have done—signed T.D.'s death warrant. But maybe it wasn't too late. Maybe T.D. was still alive. Maybe it wasn't too late for her, either. Maybe she could cover her tracks.

Then there was Wyatt. Would the sheriff be looking for him? Not yet. She had time.

She drove to the hospital on the edge of town, trying to remain calm. But the moment she pushed in through the emergency entrance, she saw people scurrying around and felt her skin turn clammy. Spotting a young blond-haired, green-eyed woman in soiled Western attire, she stepped to her.

"Were you with the McCallahan Ranch cattle drive?" she asked.

The woman nodded.

"Can you tell me who was brought into the hospital?"

Just then the sheriff walked out of one of the ER rooms. He headed straight for her.

"Thought I might find you here, Patty." Sheriff Bessler was looking at her as if all of this was her fault.

She bristled under his gaze, but held her temper. There was only one thing she wanted to know. "Is T.D....?"

"I don't know any more than you do at this point except that your boyfriend had no business up there and now I've got two gunshot victims." He pushed past her. "Go home, Patty," he said over his shoulder. "If your boy is alive, he's going to jail."

"What about Jinx?" she asked, making the big man stop in his tracks and turn back to her.

"No thanks to T.D. she's going to be fine," the sheriff said, his face set in stone. "She was treated and released. If you see T.D., Patty, you call me or I'll slap you with assisting and abetting a wanted man. You don't think I will? Try me." With that he turned and walked away.

Patty couldn't believe the injustice. Jinx was fine. But T.D. was wounded somewhere up on that mountain? She turned around and saw the young woman wrangler. "Please, you were up there with them. Can you tell me if T.D. is okay?" she asked, hating the panic in her voice.

ELLA CONSIDERED THE woman the sheriff had called Patty. From what she'd gathered, this was T. D. Sharp's girlfriend. Right now all she could think about was Brick and Angus. Brick was up in surgery. She had no idea where Angus was or if he was still alive.

But she couldn't ignore the pain in the woman's voice. "I don't know. I heard he was wounded. That's all I can tell you." Patty started to turn away. "What I do know is that because of T.D., my cousin is fighting for his life and his brother could be, as well, up on that mountain. He'd gone after your boyfriend."

"But T.D. was alive?"

Ella heard no compassion in the woman's voice for the people T.D. had hurt and had to turn away, her sympathy for the woman waning. She walked back down the hall to wait, too worried about both of her cousins to deal with T.D.'s lover.

She told herself that both Brick and Angus were strong. They were fighters. Which meant that Angus wouldn't give up until he found T.D. and finished this. Her heart ached at the thought. T.D. could kill him up there on the mountain and they might never find him.

While she tried to concentrate on thinking positive, she was exhausted. Her senses seemed dulled down to nothing but static. Worry made her heart ache. She told herself they would both be fine, but she didn't feel it in her soul and that terrified her.

Dropping into a chair in the hallway outside the ER rooms, she closed her eyes and prayed. She thought of Brick in surgery. In the helicopter, he'd come to long enough to tell her what had happened on the mountain— how Royce had shot him after Brick had captured him and bound his wrists. Either he or Cash had had a second gun that he'd missed.

The EMTs tried to get Brick not to talk, but he seemed determined to get the words out. "I killed him. I didn't even hesitate after he shot me. I just pulled the trigger." Brick had closed his eyes. "I killed him."

"Only in self-defense," she'd assured him.

She'd heard the anguish in his words as he repeated them. *"I killed a man."*

And then the alarms had gone off and the EMTs were fighting to save Brick's life as the helicopter set down next to the hospital and he was rushed to surgery.

She said another prayer for him, terrified that she would lose both of her cousins. *Please, let them be all right.* Ella needed both men in her life. She couldn't do without either of them. And she didn't even want to imagine what Dana would do if she lost her boys.

Chapter Eighteen

Back home, Jinx felt as if she was going crazy with worry about Angus and Brick and now Max. Earlier when the doctor finally came back in her room before releasing her, she'd said, "I know you said I have a mild concussion so that could be the problem, but I swear I haven't seen Max since I was brought in."

Dr. Kirkland had nodded solemnly, making her heart drop. "I've admitted him. Now, don't get excited," he'd said quickly before she could panic. "He was having some chest pain. Nothing to worry about, but I wanted to keep him overnight for observation. I want to do the same with you."

"I want to see him," she'd said and started to get up off the gurney, but he'd laid a hand on her arm and shaken his head.

"Max is resting. Seeing your concern will only agitate him. I've assured him that you are fine. Now I've assured you that he is fine. Both of you just need rest. You've been through a lot. You can see Max tomorrow. Now please stop fighting me."

She'd lain back but was too restless to stay there. Sitting up again, she'd said, "Please let me go home. I'm going crazy here. And you know I'll sneak up and check on Max if I'm forced to stay here overnight."

Dr. Kirkland had chuckled and given her a look of disbelief. But he'd known her long enough—since the night he delivered her—that he knew her well. "I'd like you to stay, but your concussion is very mild. I see nothing in your vitals to be concerned about. The bullet wound will heal, but you'll have a scar."

She'd thought of Angus's scar—the one she'd basically given him. "I don't mind." It was the scars you couldn't see that bothered her.

The doctor had studied her. "I suspect you have a terrific headache, am I right?"

"It's not bad," she'd lied. "Please, Doc. I'd feel better at home." But she'd known she wouldn't feel better until Angus was found alive and safe and Max was back at the ranch. "Is there any word on Brick Savage yet?"

"He's still in surgery. He had a really close call. Surely there are even more things you need to worry about." He had no idea—or maybe he did.

Dr. Kirkland had finally agreed to discharge her if she promised to take it easy at home. He'd said he'd see to the paperwork.

"I'd feel better if she stayed here," the sheriff had said as he pushed aside the curtain in her ER room.

"You two work it out," Dr. Kirkland had said as he left.

"Have you heard anything?" she'd asked Harvey.

He'd shaken his head. "Since you feel good enough to go home, I'm sure you're up to some questions."

"Shouldn't you be up on the mountain looking for Angus?"

"I have deputies up there right now searching for both Angus and T.D. Anyone else I should be looking for?"

"Cash and Royce were up there. Wyatt and Travis."

The sheriff had nodded. "Travis is getting his arm

cast as we speak and from what I heard, Royce is dead. A chopper will be taking me up to the mountain soon, so why don't you tell me what happened. I've already gotten the story from others who were brought in, except for Brick. He's still in surgery."

She had given him a shortened version. When she finished, he asked, "Booby traps?" and shook his head. "You say you don't know who shot you and T.D.?"

"No, but I saw Wyatt Hanson with a rifle and he rode away right after the shooting stopped."

The sheriff had mumbled something under his breath. All she caught was "wouldn't blame one of his own for taking a potshot at him," before he said, "What the hell was T.D. thinking, going up there after you?"

"Like I know what makes him do what he does. As I told you, he started a grass fire, trying to stampede my herd, but we got that put out. We knew he'd hit again so we made some booby traps to slow them down."

His gaze had saddened. "He tried to rape you."

"But he didn't. Angus stopped him and so did whoever shot him."

Still, the sheriff had looked distraught. "I wish I could have been able to stop him from going up there. Unfortunately, there is no law against riding up into the mountains. But you could have called when you saw him. Even if I hadn't been able to arrest him…"

"What would you have done? We had no proof that T.D. had started the fire. He hadn't gotten anyone killed at that point. He hadn't even gotten close enough to me to arrest him for breaking the restraining order."

"Fortunately, Ella Cardwell climbed a tree on top of the mountain and was able to reach 911 for help. Smart woman."

Jinx had mugged a face at him. "What do you want me to say? That I should have sold my cattle at a loss and never gone up on that mountain?" She'd felt a sob climb her throat. "I wish I had."

The sheriff had laid a hand on hers. "None of this is your fault. This all falls on T.D. and those fools he got to go along with him." Harvey's radio had gone off. He'd checked it and said, "I have to go. They have a helicopter ready to take me up there. Anything else I should know?"

"Just find Angus, please."

"And T.D.," he'd added pointedly. "Until he's behind bars, you won't be safe. Which is another reason I'd like you to stay here tonight."

She'd shaken her head. "He's up on that mountain somewhere wounded. I'm not worried about him. You're going to find him anyway and lock him up." She'd smiled at the sheriff. "I'll be at the house. I have my shotgun loaded by the door."

"Great. We love it when private citizens take the law into their own hands. Nothing can go wrong with that."

"If he so much as steps on my porch, I'm going to shoot him," she'd said with a fierceness that she could see even surprised the sheriff. "He is never touching me again."

The sheriff had looked at her for a long moment before he'd drawn her to him and hugged her. "I'd send a deputy out to your house but—"

"You need them up on the mountain to find Angus and T.D. I'll be fine."

He hadn't looked convinced of that. "I'll call as soon as I know something."

"Promise?"

"Promise."

ANGUS COULD SEE a rock rim ahead. He slowed, feeling the air around him seem to still. The sun was golden against a blue sky studded with puffy white clouds. The morning was cold and crisp and completely still now that the helicopters had left.

But he knew that the sheriff could be arriving soon to search for T.D., pick up Royce's body and investigate the crime scene. The cattle had scattered with the landing of the urgent care helicopters. It was just one more thing Jinx would have to worry about. Angus was determined that T.D. wouldn't still be on that list.

The silence on the mountain took on an eerie feel that made the hair on the back of his neck prickle. He felt as if he and T.D. were the only ones left on the planet. He figured they were the only ones still alive left on this mountain.

Angus studied the terrain ahead of him. He saw no movement, heard nothing for a long moment. A squirrel began to chatter at him from a nearby tree. A jet left a contrail in the sky overhead.

He knew he should turn back and wait for the sheriff. This wasn't his job. But all his instincts told him that he was close and that if he didn't stop T.D., he would get away. Even if he didn't go after Jinx right away, he would always be a threat to her. She would have to be on constant guard, waiting for the other shoe to drop, waiting for him to suddenly appear. When he did…

Angus knew that was why he had to find T.D. and end this. His pistol ready, he moved into the pines beneath the rock rim, knowing that if T.D. was going to hide somewhere, the rocks under the rim would be the perfect place.

He'd expected an ambush. He'd expected gunfire when he got close enough. T.D. had dropped his pistol, but that didn't mean he didn't have another weapon. Angus hadn't seen any blood on the ground for a while now. T.D. wasn't mortally wounded. That meant he was even more dangerous since even if he wasn't armed, he could launch himself from a tree or a rock. T.D. would have the element of surprise.

Angus reached an open area and stopped beside a tree. A slight breeze moaned in the tops of the tall pines. He listened for a closer sound. Movement through the grass as someone approached. The snap of a twig under a boot heel. A stumble overturning a rock.

Hearing nothing, he spotted an object caught on the tall grass in the middle of the clearing. It appeared to be a blood-soaked bandanna.

Angus moved toward it, watching the tree line ahead as he did. When the warning came it was too late. He heard a rumble like thunder and looked up the mountain-side. The rocks T.D. had dislodged were bounding down the steep slope directly toward him. The man had left the bandanna on the tall grass knowing Angus would see it and believe he'd crossed the clearing. T.D. had known he was following his blood trail.

The ruse had worked. Angus had only a few seconds to decide which way to run—forward or try to double back. The rocks had dislodged other rocks and started a landslide that filled the clearing above him.

Angus realized belatedly that the clearing was an old avalanche chute. There was nothing to stop the landslide now barreling down the mountainside toward him.

In those few seconds he had, he made up his mind. He sprinted forward, hoping to get to the trees before the landslide caught him up in it.

The damp, dew-soaked new grass was slick, his cowboy boots slipping and losing purchase. Once, he almost fell when his feet threatened to slide out from under him. He ran as hard and fast as he could. His legs ached from the sudden intensity of his effort. His lungs burned. He could hear the low rumble getting louder and louder, so close he could feel the air it displaced as it roared down the mountainside.

He was almost to the trees. Just a few more yards. A large rock appeared in front of him, careening past. Then another. He tried to dodge the next one. It clipped him in the leg, knocking him to the ground.

He rolled, the shelter of the trees so close he could almost reach it. A rock hit him in the side, knocking the breath out of him as he pulled himself up on all fours and launched himself into the trees. A fist-size rock bounced just as he threw himself forward. It smacked him in the head.

The lights went out before he hit the ground.

Chapter Nineteen

T.D. stared down the mountainside. He'd seen the wrangler get hit a couple of times by the rocks tumbling down the slope. Now all he could make out was the cowboy's boots, still visible, protruding from one of the pines along the side of the clearing.

Was the man dead? Pretending to be dead? T.D. pressed his glove over his wound. He'd gotten it bleeding worse with the effort of pushing off the rocks to get the landslide started. But it had worked. The cowboy still hadn't gotten up.

He waited, unsure what to do. Go down and check to make sure the man wouldn't be after him again? Take the man's gun and finish him? Or just get the hell out of Dodge?

He felt light-headed from loss of blood. He knew he needed a doctor. Fortunately, there was someone who was fairly close to a doctor who could patch him up and would without calling the sheriff. All he had to do was get off this mountain. He was pretty sure the bullet had gone clean through his chest just below his left shoulder. With luck, he would live.

The wrangler still hadn't moved. He knew he probably couldn't trust his thinking since he suspected he might be in shock. He wouldn't have minded finishing the bastard off. The cowboy had come to Jinx's rescue not once, but again last night. He'd seen them together. He knew that look of Jinx's.

Just the thought made his blood boil. The sound of another helicopter made up his mind for him. He took one last look at the cowboy still lying at the edge of the pines unmoving and then he turned toward the game trail that he knew would lead him off this mountain to a ranch where he could get the help he needed.

He hadn't gone far when he saw a saddled horse standing in the middle of the trail. He recognized the mount as Royce's and couldn't believe his luck. The mount was dragging its reins as if it had gotten spooked and come untied. He wondered where Royce was, but the thought was a quickly passing one.

T. D. Sharp wasn't going to look a gift horse in the mouth, so to speak.

JINX WILLED HER phone to ring. The sheriff had promised he would call her the moment he knew anything about Angus Savage as well as T.D.

She knew Harvey would do as he promised. Which meant he hadn't found Angus or T.D. Just the thought of all that country up on that mountain… The men could be anywhere. T.D. was wounded, but that didn't mean that he couldn't be dangerous. Angus had come all this way to help her and now he could be dead.

She found herself pacing the floor even though the doctor had told her to take it easy. She said she would or he wouldn't have released her from the hospital. Her temple felt tender under the bandage and her head ached. She'd been going crazy at the hospital. She hated feeling like an invalid on an emergency room gurney when she hadn't been injured that badly. Worse, she hated feeling helpless.

The sheriff was right. She liked to believe she could take care of herself. She'd never liked asking for help, especially after she'd kicked T.D. out. She'd wanted to show everyone that she could handle all of this—the ranch, her father's death, T.D. and the divorce.

But as strong as she knew she was, she'd needed help. She didn't know what she would have done without Angus, Brick, Ella and Max. Her eyes filled with tears. Her stubbornness had put them all in jeopardy.

Picking up her phone, she called the hospital to check on Max and Brick.

"Both are sleeping comfortably, Jinx," the nurse she knew told her. "Ella Cardwell is on a cot in her cousin's room. Everyone is down for the night. Just like you should be."

She knew the nurse was right as she touched the bandage on her temple. Her head still ached, but it had dulled. She hung up, thinking of the scar she would have, which made her think of Angus's small one on his chin. She wished she were in his arms right now. She closed her eyes as she remembered the heat of their kisses. Stolen kisses and one of the few things she would never regret.

You're falling for him. Her eyes flew open. No. True or not, she couldn't trust her heart. Not now. Not with the divorce and knowing she was losing the ranch. Anyway, how could she possibly trust something that had happened so quickly? She couldn't. She'd leaned on Angus. He'd come to her rescue. He'd saved her life.

Of course she felt something for him. But love? She shook her head even as her heart drummed in her chest at the thought of the man, and worry nagged at her. He had to be all right. He just had to. She couldn't bear the thought that T.D. might kill him. That she might never see Angus alive again. Her heart ached with worry.

Why hadn't the sheriff called? Hours had gone by. Maybe he hadn't found either Angus or T.D. Or maybe he'd found them both. She knew Harvey. He'd never tell someone over the phone about a death of a loved one. That was something he did, hat in hand, head bowed, at the person's door.

Chapter Twenty

Angus surfaced to the sound of a helicopter. He opened his eyes. How long had he been out? Not that long, he told himself as he found the sun still glowing in Wyoming's big sky. But he had lost some time.

He tried to sit up, his head swimming. He gingerly touched the spot where the last rock had clocked him. It was painful. He looked around, blinked. T.D. Where was the man? Turning carefully, he glanced back up the mountain. Why hadn't the man taken advantage when he was out cold and finished him? Because T.D. wasn't really a killer? Or because he wanted to get off this mountain as fast as he could?

Pushing himself to his feet, he glanced down the mountain to where the helicopter was hovering before setting down. He headed in that direction although he felt dizzy, his head aching and his footsteps unsure. When he heard the rotors on the helicopter finally stop, he pulled his pistol and fired three shots into the air.

His call for help was answered by a returned three reports, one after the other. He holstered his gun and kept walking in the direction of the chopper. By now, this mountain had to be crawling with cops. Was it possible they'd caught T.D.? He couldn't bear to think the man had gotten away.

Ahead, he could make out the helicopter through the trees. It had landed in a clearing. Before he could reach it, a deputy sheriff intercepted him, demanding to know who he was.

"Angus Cardwell Savage," he said, feeling light-headed.

"Mr. Savage, are you aware that you're bleeding?"

He never got to answer because he'd seen the sheriff coming through the pines toward him and then darkness closed in again.

PATTY KNEW SHE should go home, but Wyatt was there and she wasn't ready to deal with him yet. She pushed into the bar and headed for a stool. It was early enough in the afternoon that the place was almost empty. Just the way she liked it when she was feeling the way she was.

Marty came down the bar. He looked surprised to see her. She still felt bad about what she'd said to him before. "Cola?"

She shook her head. "Whiskey. Straight up." Her voice broke and she was glad when he merely nodded and went down the bar to get her drink. She was in no mood for small talk, let alone anything deeper. She didn't need to be told again what everyone thought about her and T.D.

Just the thought of T.D. brought tears to her eyes. He couldn't be dead. Wouldn't she know it in her heart if he was? And what was she going to do about Wyatt?

Marty set a shot glass full of whiskey on a napkin in front of her and put down the bottle next to it. "Thought I'd save myself the walk back," he said.

She could tell he was waiting—just in case she wanted to talk. She picked up the shot glass and threw back the whiskey. It burned all the way down. Her eyes watered again, this time from the alcohol. "I'm sorry about—"

He waved that off. "Bartenders are just supposed to listen. No one with a lick of sense would take advice from one." He started to turn back down the bar.

"Marty," she said and reached out to touch his forearm to stop him. "I don't want to be me," she said as she removed her hand from his arm. "I hate the person I've become but I don't know how to change."

"Everyone has days like that."

"No, not like this one," she said and poured herself another shot. For a moment she merely stared at the warm golden liquid. "I'm going to have to do something I'm going to regret and yet, I don't have a choice, you know?"

Clearly, he didn't. He studied her openly. "Don't take this wrong but maybe you want to do whatever it is sober."

She laughed. "Not a chance." And threw down another shot.

JINX HAD THOUGHT she would feel better at home instead of in the hospital, but she'd been wrong. She found herself walking through the house as if lost as she kept reliving what had happened on the mountain.

She touched her throat, shuddering at the memory of T.D.'s arm locked around it. He'd cut off her air supply to the point that she'd almost blacked out. When she saw Angus appear, she'd thought she was dreaming. She'd seen the gun in his hand but thought he'd put it down. Had he fired the shot that had hit her and T.D.?

She still felt confused. Where had the shot come from? All she remembered was feeling something hit her in the head. T.D. had jerked, his arm loosening on her throat, as he stumbled back. She'd dropped to the ground, weak from lack of oxygen, blood dripping in her eyes. Hadn't there been another shot? She recalled turning to see T.D. holding a spot high on his chest.

He had looked confused as if like her, he hadn't known where the shots had come from. Then his expression had changed as if he saw something…someone in the distance. She'd followed his gaze and seen Wyatt holding a rifle and looking in their direction before jumping on his horse and taking off.

Wyatt had to have been the one who'd fired the shot— just as she'd told the sheriff. And yet, it made no sense. He was T.D.'s best friend, often his only friend. She frowned. Things had gotten so crazy up on that mountain, they might never be able to sort it out.

She just remembered that after she was shot, everything had happened so fast. It now felt like a blur. Angus she recalled had thrown his body over hers to protect her from further gunfire, flattening them both against the ground before Max had appeared and told Angus to go after T.D.

She could understand why both men wanted T.D. stopped. Hadn't she told the sheriff that she would kill him the next time he showed up here at the ranch? But all this waiting, all this worrying.

She pulled out her cell phone and called the sheriff to see if there had been any word. It went straight to voice mail. She reminded herself that Harvey had promised to call the moment he heard anything. He'd always been good to his word. He would call.

Or he'd show up at her door, she thought with a stab to her heart.

Walking to the window, she looked out. It was dark

outside. She blinked in surprise. Exhaustion pulled at her. She knew she needed sleep because she couldn't account for the missing hours. Had she been pacing the floor all this time?

As she started to turn from the window, she heard the wind howling along the eaves. One of the fir trees scraped against the outside of the house as the others bent and swayed against a darkening sky. Another thunderstorm?

Jinx hugged herself, suddenly chilled. T.D. was still out there. For all she knew he was dead. But then again, she knew the man. He could be determined to the point of obsession when it was something he wanted.

If he could, he would survive and when he did, he would come after her.

Jinx shivered, hugging herself as she looked out into the darkness. Was Angus still up on the mountain? Why hadn't she heard anything? Just the thought of him made her heart ache. He'd gone after T.D. because he'd known—just as she had—that T.D. wouldn't stop. Not until she was dead.

She assured herself that by now half the county had gone up into the mountains looking for T.D. They'd find him. They'd find Angus. Angus would be all right. They would find T.D. alive. He would be arrested. This would end and when it did…

That was the part, though, that she didn't have figured out yet. But she wasn't going to get it figured out tonight. Her head ached and she felt weak and sick with worry.

She'd never felt more alone. She kept remembering that her stubbornness had causes this mess. If she'd just sold the cattle, taking a loss, and given the money to T.D.… . She knew that wouldn't have been enough for him. He wanted more than money. He wanted vengeance.

But at least she might be divorced from him by now. No longer his wife. No longer his. As long as they were husband and wife, he thought he could do anything he wanted with her. Right now she would gladly give him the ranch just to get him out of her life.

Just to know that Angus was all right.

Had Angus found T.D.? She knew T.D. would never fight fair. What if he'd seen Angus tracking him? What if he'd waited in ambush and killed him?

She turned away from the window, telling herself she had to have faith that Angus was all right. She had to because he'd made her want to go on when she'd felt like quitting, not just ranching, but life.

Max was getting too old for this. She knew that he wouldn't quit as long as she needed him. She thought about calling the hospital again, but knew she'd get the same report. She needed rest. If she could escape for even a little while in sleep…

Her cell phone rang, making her jump. She saw it was the sheriff and quickly picked up.

"Angus was found," he said quickly. "He's going to be fine. He was admitted to the hospital and no, you can't see him tonight. He has a concussion. Was hit in the head, but as I said, Doc assured me that he will be fine."

She felt a flood of relief that brought tears to her eyes. "And T.D.?"

Harvey was silent for a moment. "He got away. That's why I'm sending a deputy out to your place as soon as the shifts change. Most everyone has been up on the mountain looking for him."

"You don't need to send a deputy out here."

"Don't tell me how to do my job, young lady. I'm

worried about you. The deputy will just sit outside your house. He won't bother you."

"You sound tired," she said, touched by Harvey's concern for her.

"I am. You sound tired yourself. I thought the doctor said you could go home but only if you rested."

She smiled to herself. "I was just heading to bed. Thank you for letting me know."

"Sleep well."

"You, too." She hung up and headed for her bedroom. Now that she knew Angus was all right, she might be able to get some sleep, she thought as she turned out the lights as she went.

She'd reached her bedroom door and fumbled in the pitch-black room to flip the light switch. Nothing happened. *The overhead lightbulb must have gone out*, she thought. She was working toward her nightstand next to the bed to turn on that lamp when she heard a sound that stopped her cold.

Someone was in the room. In the room waiting for her in the dark. Her blood turned to slush as she said, "Who's there?" fearing she already knew.

Chapter Twenty-One

Jinx let her hand drop to the nightstand drawer. "I know you're there," she said as she eased it open and felt around for the pistol.

It was gone.

The lamp on the nightstand across the bed snapped on, illuminating Patty Conroe sitting in the chair beside the bed. She was holding the pistol from Jinx's bedside table.

"Patty?" She felt confused to see the woman for a moment. She'd been expecting T.D. But as she looked at her husband's lover, she knew she should have been anticipating this visit for some time. "What do you want?"

"What you've taken from me," Patty said.

"What I've taken from *you*?"

Patty's once pretty face showed the road map her life had taken since the two of them were in high school together. "T.D. was mine first."

"You can have him." She noticed the way the woman was holding the gun. Patty knew how to use it.

"How's your head?" Patty asked offhandedly.

"Not fatal."

"That's too bad."

"Patty, where did you leave your car? I didn't see it when I came home."

"I left it behind that old barn on the way in so you wouldn't see it. I wanted to be here waiting for you the moment I heard you were being released from the hospital. The nurse was so helpful when I called."

"How did you get in here? I know the door was locked."

"I used T.D.'s key. You need to know the truth," the woman snapped. "T.D. came to me when he wasn't getting what he needed from you. I didn't lure him away from you."

"It doesn't matter," Jinx said with a sigh. "I'm divorcing him. He's going to be all yours."

"If he's not dead because of you." Patty sniffed, the pistol wavering in her hand.

Jinx smelled alcohol. She should have known that Patty wouldn't have come out here unless she had been intoxicated. In that way, she was a lot like T.D. And that made her more dangerous. "He's not dead."

"You can't know that," she cried.

She heard such heartbreak in the woman's voice. Had she ever cared that much about T.D.? Not even when she'd married him. She hadn't known then what it felt like to really be in love with anyone, she realized. Her own heart was breaking at the thought of Angus injured and at the hospital because of her.

"Patty, put the gun down and go home. Your fight isn't with me."

The woman let out a bark of a laugh. "Are you serious? T.D. wouldn't be wounded and up on that mountain, possibly dead, if it wasn't for you," she said, her voice hoarse with emotion.

Jinx thought at least that might be true. "He's the one who followed me up there. You blame me for that?"

"You made him crazy. You have his blood on your hands."

"Enough. Go home, Patty. This is getting us nowhere."

Patty pointed the pistol at her heart. "You ruined my life and T.D.'s. You have to pay for that, Jinx."

"I TOLD YOU going to Wyoming was a bad idea," Brick said weakly as he gave Ella a lopsided smile.

Ella started on her cot next to his hospital bed. Tears instantly flooded her eyes as she shot to her feet to take his hand. "You had me so scared," she said, never so happy to see that grin of his.

"Angus?" he asked, his voice hoarse with emotion and no doubt pain as he looked around the hospital room. Of course he would know that Angus would be right here beside his bed, as well—if he could. "Ella?" There was a worried edge to her cousin's voice.

"He's going to be fine. He went after T.D., got hit in the head, but the doctor said other than a concussion and a few scrapes and bruises, he'll be fine. He's here in the hospital. You'll get to see him soon."

Brick seemed to relax. "I knew something had happened. I had this dream…" He seemed to shudder. He met her gaze. "I almost didn't make it, didn't I?" She nodded and swallowed the lump in her throat. "And T.D.?"

"He was wounded but got away."

"Jinx?"

"She was given medical attention and released. You'll hear all about it, once you've had some rest."

Brick closed his eyes. "I remember you and a helicopter?" he asked, opening his eyes again.

She nodded. "I was able to get cell phone service and

called for help. You and I were flown to the hospital. Max rode with Jinx."

"Is Max okay?"

"He was admitted to the hospital for observation. The doctor doesn't think he had a heart attack but wanted to monitor him."

"T.D. got away?"

"Half the county is up on that mountain looking for him. They'll find him."

"I hope you're right." He reached for her hand and squeezed it. "When you see Angus…"

She nodded, tears burning her eyes. "I'll tell him that you miss him."

Brick smiled. "Tell him that I love him, okay? I'll deny I said it." He shrugged.

She had to smile, knowing he was telling the truth. "Your mother just went down the hall to get some coffee. Your dad flew down to Jackson Hole to see if he could help find T.D. since there was nothing he could do here but wait."

"That sounds like him. How's Mom?"

"Worried but you know Dana. She's as strong as they come. The rest of the family has been in and out. They're going to be delighted to hear that you're conscious and your old self."

Brick met her gaze. "I don't feel much like my old self right now. But it's so good to see you." He frowned. "Ella, what aren't you telling me?"

"You just worry about getting out of this bed and back on your feet."

"Ella?"

"It's my mother." She shook her head. "It's just this

feeling. I'm sure it's nothing. Dana said she's minding the ranch while everyone else is down here."

She could see that he was drowsy and struggling to keep his eyes open. "You rest. Everything is fine now." And yet she couldn't shake the feeling that her mother was in some kind of trouble.

"Tell me you found him," Angus said as the sheriff stepped into his room. He could see that the lawman looked exhausted.

"I'm afraid not," Harvey Bessler said as he removed his hat. "We'll resume the search in the morning."

Angus swore, making his already aching head hurt more. He'd been so hopeful when he'd been told how many were up on the mountain looking for T.D., his own father included. "You know Jinx won't be safe until T.D. is caught."

The sheriff nodded. "I just talked to Jinx before I came in to check on you. She's fine. I'm sending a deputy out there to keep an eye on her. Now, get some rest and quit worrying."

He watched the sheriff leave, wishing he could quit worrying. Common sense told him that T.D. was wounded and probably still up there on that mountain. Even if he'd gotten off it, he was in no shape to be going after Jinx again. The sheriff was right. He shouldn't worry.

But he did. Glancing around his hospital room, he spotted two things that helped him make up his mind about what to do about his worry. He saw his dirty clothing piled up on a chair by the bathroom door. He also saw his mother's coat and purse. Earlier, she'd been sitting next to his bed before going to check on Brick.

Angus quickly rose from the bed. He had to stop for

a moment until the light-headedness passed. Struggling into his clothing, he questioned what good he would be to Jinx if his instincts were right and T.D. had somehow gotten off the mountain and headed for her ranch.

In his mother's purse, he found the keys for the rental car she'd told him about. He felt a little stronger. At least he told himself he did as he quietly opened the door and peered out.

It was so late that the hallway was empty. He headed for the exit sign, knowing he couldn't rest until he made sure Jinx was all right.

"PATTY, WHY WOULD you kill me?" Jinx demanded, seeing the gun waver in the woman's hand.

"Because someone has to do it!" she cried. "Otherwise, T.D. will never be free of you, and you know it."

Jinx thought of Wyatt Hanson in the trees, holding his rifle before riding away. Who had he been trying to shoot? Her or T.D.? "You think shooting me is going to free him for you? You'll be in prison." So would T.D., though she didn't mention that. "What happens when he comes off that mountain and finds out that you're in jail for shooting me?"

Tears filled Patty's eyes. "You really think he's alive?"

"Knowing T.D., I would count on it," she said truthfully.

The gun seemed to grow heavy in Patty's hand. "I don't want to live without him."

"You won't have to, unless you shoot me," Jinx told her. "Don't throw away your future." She could see that this had been a flawed plan of Patty's to start with. The woman wanted Jinx out of her life badly enough that she thought she could shoot her. Jinx understood that on some level. She wanted T.D. out of hers just as badly.

"Put the gun down, Patty." The male voice at the door made them both jump. Startled, Patty pulled the trigger, the pistol bucking in her hand. For the second time that day, Jinx felt a bullet buzz past her head. This one, though, didn't break the skin.

T.D. swore, his bellow almost drowned out by the report of the gun. He moved quickly for a man who was injured, grabbing the pistol and backhanding Patty, sending her flying to the floor at the corner of the room.

"I wasn't going to kill her!" Patty cried as T.D. turned the gun on her.

Without thinking, Jinx started to rush T.D. as if she thought she could stop him from killing the woman.

He swung the barrel of the pistol in her direction as he said, "I wouldn't if I were you." She froze where she was. She could tell that T.D. was weak from his gunshot wound even though he'd apparently gotten some sort of medical help. She could see part of the bandage sticking out of the collar of his shirt. But Jinx wasn't fool enough to think that would even the odds if she rushed him.

"Okay," he said, sounding as exhausted as she felt. "Now, tell me what the hell is going on here."

Patty was crying, still on the floor. "I just wanted to free you of her. I thought if she was dead…"

T.D. nodded, not taking his eyes off Jinx. "I stopped by your apartment before I came here," he said, without looking at Patty. Jinx heard the woman let out a cry as if he'd kicked her. "Had a little talk with Wyatt." Patty began to sob, her words lost in her tears. Jinx heard enough, though, to know that the woman had put Wyatt up to killing her up on that mountain. Now T.D. knew it, too.

"Did you really think that if you got Wyatt to kill Jinx that I would want anything to do with you?"

"We could get married," Patty said between sobs. "I would make you happy. You know I could."

"No, Patty, you and I are never getting married, especially after you almost got me killed. I will never love you the way I did Jinx. Never. You need to leave now, Patty. I don't think you want to watch what happens next."

Patty quit crying and wiped her face. "What are you going to do? You're in enough trouble. You can't kill her."

"Oh, I'm not going to kill her," he said, narrowing his eyes at Jinx. "Though she might wish I was when I'm through with her. Now, get out of here."

Patty got to her feet, hesitated and then rushed out the door.

T.D. hadn't moved. He seemed to be waiting until he heard a car engine to make sure Patty was gone before he said to Jinx, "Take off your clothes."

ANGUS DROVE UP the road to the Flying J Bar MC Ranch as fast as he dared. It had only been a few days since he and his brother and cousin had driven up this road. So much had changed in that time.

He pulled in behind the sheriff's department car and got out, telling himself this was probably a fool's errand. Just as the sheriff had said, there was a deputy watching the house.

But as he came along the side of the car, his heart began to pound. The deputy would have seen him drive up. He would have gotten out of his car to see who it was. That was if he could.

As Angus reached the driver's side, he saw the deputy slumped over in the seat and swore. His first instinct was to race into the house. But he was smart enough to know that in his physical state, he might need all the help he could get. He eased open the deputy's car door, grabbed the car radio and called it in. Once the dispatcher told him that help was on the way, he headed for the house.

JINX LOOKED ACROSS the expanse of her bed at T.D. "You know I'm not taking off my clothes."

He chuckled. "It was worth a try." He put the pistol down on the nightstand. As he did, she bolted for the door. Of course he beat her to it, knowing exactly what she would do. Grabbing a handful of her hair, he dragged her back into the room and threw her on the bed.

She could tell the effort hurt him, just as she knew it wouldn't stop him. He knew this was the very last thing she wanted from him so he was more determined than ever. He climbed on top of her, and holding her down, began to rip off her clothing as he told her—as he had on the mountain—all the things he was going to do to her. Only this time, there was no one to stop him.

Even with him injured, she was no match for him. She knew she should just submit, just as she knew she wasn't about to.

The sound of the gunshot startled her. She looked up into T.D.'s sneering face as she felt his hold on her lessen. The second shot made him jerk. The third crumpled him on top of her.

Jinx felt his warm blood spreading over her chest. She pushed him off and leaped up from the bed to see the shooter standing in the shadowed doorway of her bedroom.

"Patty?" she whispered, seeing the glazed-over look in the woman's eyes and the gun still clutched in her hand, the barrel now pointed at Jinx.

"The two of you didn't even notice me come back into the room," the woman said. "The two of you were so busy that you didn't even see me pick up the gun."

"You know I wanted none of that," Jinx said, and saw something in the woman's expression that turned her blood to ice. "Don't make this worse, Patty."

"How could it be worse?" she asked on a sob. "I loved him. I would have done anything for him. Anything. But all he wanted was…you." She raised the gun to heart level and pressed the trigger.

ANGUS HAD BEEN moving stealthily down the hall toward the sound of voices when he'd heard the first gunshot. By the second gunshot, he was running. By the third, he'd reached the woman standing in the doorway of the bedroom.

Before she could pull the trigger again, he slammed into her. The report was like an explosion to his already pounding head. The woman went down. He went down with her as he fought to get the pistol out of her hand.

"Let me kill her!" the woman was screaming. "Please… You don't know what she's done. She ruined my life." She'd broken into sobs but was still fighting for the gun as they wrestled on the floor.

Normally, Angus could have easily disarmed the woman, but his head injury had left him weak and slow as if he was moving through quicksand.

Out of the corner of his eye, he saw Jinx and was instantly thankful she didn't appear to have been shot. She stepped down on the woman's hand holding the gun, grinding her boot heel in until he heard a cry and Jinx kicked the gun away.

He sat back against the wall, the gun at his side, as Jinx dropped to the floor next to him.

"What are you doing here?" she demanded. "You should be in the hospital."

Angus could only smile because he had to agree. "I was worried about you."

"Oh, Angus." She cupped his face and bent to kiss him. The sound of sirens filled the air, drowning out at least some of Patty's sobs. The woman had climbed up on the bed and now had T.D.'s head cradled in her lap. She was smoothing back his hair and telling him about a dream she had that involved Disney World.

Chapter Twenty-Two

"What's the plan now?" Marshal Hudson Savage asked from the head of the huge family table in the dining room at Cardwell Ranch.

"Don't cross examine them, sweetheart," Dana said sweetly but strongly. "They've been through enough without having to decide their futures at my dinner table right this moment. Have some more roast beef," she said to her twin sons seated across from her.

"I'm going back to Wyoming to help Jinx get everything ready for the sale of her ranch," Angus said, passing on more roast beef.

Brick took some, though, thanking their mother. "Mom, everything is delicious," he said after chewing and swallowing. His recovery was going slowly, making them all worried about him.

She smiled. "Thank you, Brick. You know you both gave us a scare. I'm just so glad that you're home."

"But for how long this time?" Hud asked, not to be deterred. Brick hadn't looked up from his meal, eating quietly as if lost in his own thoughts.

"I shouldn't be gone for more than a couple of weeks," Angus said. "Then my plan is to come back and go to work here on the ranch." He said this to his mother. "That's if you'll have me."

His mother's eyes filled with tears. "Really?"

"Finally," Hud grumbled. "You boys are going to be the death of me."

"Are you coming back...alone?" she asked, pretending interest in the small portion of mashed potatoes on her plate.

Angus laughed. "You are so subtle, Mom."

"Like a sledgehammer," his father muttered under his breath.

"Well?" she asked, clearly ignoring her husband.

"Alone, Mom. At least for now. Jinx and I both need some time."

"What about you?" Hud asked Brick.

"I've actually been thinking about what I might want to do once I'm healed," he said, motioning to the sling that had his mother cutting his meat up as if he were five. Angus could tell that his brother didn't mind. Like him, Brick seemed to be glad to be home. "I heard you might have an opening for a deputy marshal."

His father looked up from his meal in surprise. "Are you serious about this?"

Brick nodded. "I am."

"You have to go to the law academy, but if this is something you want..."

Angus could tell that their father was delighted at the prospect that at least one of their sons might be interested in law enforcement. Their older brother Hank lived on the ranch with his wife, Frankie, and Mary did the ranch's books. It had looked like they all might be involved in ranch work in this family.

He looked over at their mother. Clearly she'd prefer

Brick not become a lawman, but she only took her husband's hand and smiled at Brick. "It will be nice to have
you boys home," Hud said.

"I'll get dessert," Dana said and got up to hurry into
the kitchen. Angus could tell that she was thinking about
all the meals the family would be having at this table in
the future. Tonight she'd wanted it to be just the four of
them. But he knew they were in for a lot of big family
celebrations at this table.

When his mother returned with a three-tiered choco-
late cake, he said, "By the way, I thought Ella was going
to be here tonight."

Dana shook her head as she began to cut the cake.
Brick already had his fork ready and was saying how
much he'd missed his mother's cooking, making her
beam.

"Ella?" she said. "She wasn't around. Hank told me
that he saw her leave." She stopped cutting to look up at
him. "I think she's gone to look for her mother."

"Stacy?" Brick said as he took the slice of cake his
mother handed him. "Where's she off to?" he asked and
took a large bite of the cake and thick fudge-like frost-
ing, one of his mother's favorite recipes.

"That's just it," Dana said. "We don't know. Stacy just
left." She looked to her husband, who shook his head.
"Maybe she just needs a break from all of us."

"Maybe," Angus said, but he could tell that his mother
was worried about her sister.

"Ella will find her," Brick said. "That woman is like
a bloodhound when she gets something in her head."

"I hope you're right," their mother said as she handed
Angus his cake. "Now, tell me about Jinx. I want to know
everything."

ON A BEAUTIFUL fall day, JoRay "Jinx" McCallahan drove into Cardwell Ranch in her pickup, pulling a horse trailer with her favorite horse inside. She slowed as she crossed the bridge over the Gallatin River to look down. The water was incredibly clear, a pale green that made the granite rocks along the bottom shine as if pure gold.

She breathed in the fall air scented with the river and the pines and looked up at the towering mountain with its rock cliffs before letting herself take in the ranch. The house was two stories with a red metal roof. And there was the large old barn that she recalled as a young girl.

Jinx smiled, thinking how strange life was that she was here again. Only this time, she couldn't wait to see that cowboy she'd pushed out that barn window all those years ago. Time heals all wounds, her father used to say. To some extent that was true. She still missed her father just as she missed the Flying J Bar MC Ranch she'd grown up on.

But it was a dull ache overpowered by the excitement she felt to be on the Cardwell Ranch again. She actually had butterflies flitting around in her stomach at just the thought of seeing Angus after these months apart. They'd talked on the phone for hours every day about everything but the future. Angus had left the door open.

"I'll be here if you ever want to come north again," he'd said. "I'll be waiting."

ANGUS WAS IN the barn when he saw the truck and horse trailer coming up the road. He stepped out, pulling his Stetson down to shade his eyes. He couldn't see who was behind the wheel. His heart leaped anyway. He'd been waiting for this day for too long not to know it had finally come.

As Jinx pulled up into the yard, he strode toward her truck, trying hard not to run. She opened the door and stepped out. Her beautiful copper hair caught the autumn sun. She reached back into the pickup for her straw hat and putting it on, looked in his direction.

By then, he was closing the distance between them, running toward their future. When he reached her, he grabbed her, wrapping his arms around her and lifting her into the air. She laughed, a sound that filled his heart with joy. Slowly, he lowered her back to the ground and looked into her beautiful freckled face. Now he would have all the time in the world to count every one of them, he thought and glanced into the warm honey of her eyes.

"Jinx," he said on a breath as light as a caress.

"Angus." She smiled, those eyes glinting. "You said to just drive up when I felt like it. I felt like it."

He laughed as his heart swelled to overflowing. "I'm so glad. Wait until you taste my biscuits."

She laughed. "You still have that bet going with Max?"

He nodded. "He promised to come up to the ranch." Angus looked into her eyes and knew that if he'd had a preacher standing by, he'd have married this woman right here and now. Looping his arm around her waist he pulled her to him and kissed her as if there was no tomorrow.

At the sound of the front door of the house banging open, he let her go. "Two seconds from now we are going to be mobbed by my family. Before that happens, I need to tell you something. I love you."

She nodded. "I love you, Angus."

"That's good because I don't have to look over my shoulder to know that the woman hurrying this way is my mother. She's going to want to know when we're getting married. I don't want to rush you but…"

Jinx looked over his shoulder, then back at him, grinning. "If that's a proposal—"

He dropped to one knee, pulled out the small velvet box he'd been carrying around for months. "It certainly is. Say yes. Please. The engagement can be as long as you want, I promise."

She laughed and nodded. "Yes."

He opened the box, took out the ring and slipped it on her finger. He heard his mother's cry of glee behind him.

"It's beautiful, Angus," Jinx said and kissed him as he rose to his feet again. "I don't need a long engagement since I've known for a long time I want to spend the rest of my life with you."

"Oh," Dana cried. "That is so beautiful." Then she was hugging the two of them as more family members began to show up.

Angus introduced his large family and extended family until the yard was full of Cardwells and Savages. It was as if they'd known today was the day to be on the ranch. He wondered if his mother had anything to do with this.

"I should have warned you about my family," Angus whispered to Jinx. "You can still change your mind."

Jinx shook her head. "Not a chance, cowboy."

"I'd like to tell you that it won't always be like this," he said.

"I love it." She looked around at all of them, most talking over the others as if her arriving had turned into a party. "I remember you telling me about your mother wanting all of your boots around her big dining room table. I want my boots under that table."

"You're killing me, Jinx," he said as he pulled her

to him again for a kiss. "I can't tell you how long I've wanted this with you."

She nodded, her eyes bright with tears. "It's strange but I feel as if I've always been headed back here. I know it sounds crazy, especially knowing how hard it was for me to sell my family's ranch, but driving in just now, I had the strangest feeling that I've come home."

Angus pulled her closer. "Welcome home. Trust me, now that you're going to be a part of Cardwell Ranch, you should know it's going to be a wild ride."

* * * * *

GUN-SHY BRIDE

From the beginning my husband, Parker, has been there for me. He was the one who encouraged me to quit my paying job even though he knew how hard it would be for us financially. He's always believed in me and takes up the slack so I can just write. He's my hero. This book, which may be my all-time favorite, is for him.

Chapter One

The wind howled down the ravine as Deputy Sheriff McCall Winchester poked what appeared to be a mud clod with the toe of her cowboy boot.

The thunderstorm last night had been a gully-washer. As her boot toe dislodged some of the mud, she saw that the pile of objects in the bottom of the gully was neither mud nor rock.

"Didn't I tell you?"

McCall looked up at the man standing a few feet away. Rocky Harrison was a local who collected, what else? Rocks.

"It's always better after a rainstorm," he'd told her when he'd called the sheriff's department and caught her just about to go off duty after working the night shift.

"Washes away the dirt, leaves the larger stones on top," Rocky had said. "I've found arrowheads sitting on little columns of dirt, just as pretty as you please and agates large as your fist where they've been unearthed by a good rainstorm."

Only on this bright, clear, cold spring morning, Rocky had found more than he'd bargained for.

"Human, ain't they," Rocky said, nodding to what he'd dug out of the mud and left lying on a flat rock.

"You've got a good eye," McCall said as she pulled out her camera, took a couple of shots of the bones he'd found. They lay in the mud at the bottom of the ravine where the downpour had left them.

With her camera, McCall shot the path the mud slide had taken down from the top of the high ridge. Then she started making the steep muddy climb up the ravine.

As she topped the ridge, she stopped to catch her breath. The wind was stronger up here. She pushed her cowboy hat down hard, but the wind still whipped her long dark hair as she stared at the spot where the rain had dislodged the earth at the edge. In this shallow grave was where the bones had once been buried.

Squinting at the sun, she looked to the east. A deep, rugged ravine separated this high ridge from the next. Across that ravine, she could make out a cluster of log buildings that almost resembled an old fort. The Winchester Ranch. The sprawling place sat nestled against the foothills, flanked by tall cottonwood trees and appearing like an oasis in the middle of the desert. She'd only seen the place from a distance from the time she was a child. She'd never seen it from this angle before.

"You thinking what I am?" Rocky asked, joining her on the ridge.

She doubted that.

"Somebody was buried up here," Rocky said. "Probably a homesteader. They buried their dead in the backyard, and since there is little wood around these parts, they didn't even mark the graves with crosses, usually just a few rocks laid on top."

McCall had heard stories of grave sites being disturbed all over the county when a road was cut through or even a basement was dug. The land they now stood on was owned by the Bureau of Land Management, but it could have been private years ago.

Just like the Winchester land beyond the ravine which was heavily posted with orange paint and signs warning that trespassers would be prosecuted.

"There's a bunch of outlaws that got themselves buried in these parts. Could be one of them," Rocky said, his imagination working overtime.

This less-civilized part of Montana had been a hideout for outlaws back in the late 1890s or even early 1900s. But these remains hadn't been in the ground that long.

She took a photograph of where the body had been buried, then found herself looking again toward the Winchester Ranch. The sun caught on one of the large windows on the second floor of the massive lodge-style structure.

"The old gal?" Rocky said, following her gaze. "She's your grandmother, right?"

McCall thought about denying it. After all, Pepper Winchester denied her very existence. McCall had never even laid eyes on her grandmother. But then few people had in the past twenty-seven years.

"I reckon we're related," McCall said. "According to my mother, Trace Winchester was my father." He'd run off before McCall was born.

Rocky had the good sense to look embarrassed. "Didn't mean to bring up nothin' about your father."

Speaking of outlaws, McCall thought. She'd spent her life living down her family history. She was used to it.

"Interesting view of the ranch," Rocky said, and reached into his pack to offer a pair of small binoculars.

Reluctantly, she took them and focused on the main house. It was much larger than she'd thought, three stories with at least two wings. The logs had darkened from the years, most of the windows on at least one of the wings boarded up.

The place looked abandoned. Or worse, deteriorating from the inside out. It gave her the creeps just thinking about her grandmother shutting herself up in there.

McCall started as she saw a dark figure appear at one of the second floor windows that hadn't been boarded over. Her grandmother?

The image was gone in a blink.

McCall felt the chill of the April wind that swept across the rolling prairie as she quickly lowered the binoculars and handed them back to Rocky.

The day was clear, the sky blue and cloudless, but the air had a bite to it. April in this part of Montana was unpredictable. One day it could be in the seventies, the next in the thirties and snowing.

"I best get busy and box up these bones," she said, suddenly anxious to get moving. She'd been about to go off shift when she'd gotten Rocky's call. Unable to locate the sheriff and the deputy who worked the shift after hers, she'd had little choice but to take the call.

"If you don't need my help…" Rocky shifted his backpack, the small shovel strapped to it clinking on the canteen he carried at his hip as he headed toward his pickup.

Overhead a hawk circled on a column of air and for a moment, McCall stopped to watch it. Turning her back to the ranch in the distance, she looked south. Just the hint of spring could be seen in the open land stretching to the rugged horizon broken only by the outline of the Little Rockies.

Piles of snow still melted in the shade of the deep ravines gouged out as the land dropped to the river in what was known as the Missouri River Breaks. This part of Montana was wild, remote country that a person either loved or left.

McCall had lived her whole life here in the shadow of the Little Rockies and the darker shadow of the Winchester family.

As she started to step around the grave washed out by last night's rainstorm, the sun caught on something stuck in the mud.

She knelt down to get a better look and saw the corner of a piece of orange plastic sticking out of the earth where the bones had been buried.

McCall started to reach for it, but stopped herself long enough to swing up the camera and take two photographs, one a close-up, one of the grave with the corner of the plastic visible.

Using a small stick, she dug the plastic packet from the mud and, with a start, saw that it was a cover given out by stores to protect hunting and fishing licenses.

McCall glanced at Rocky's retreating back, then carefully worked the hunting license out enough to see a name.

Trace Winchester.

Her breath caught in her throat but still she must have made a sound.

"You say somethin'?" Rocky called back.

McCall shook her head, pocketing the license with her father's name on it. "No, just finishing up here."

Chapter Two

Inside her patrol pickup, McCall radioed the sheriff's department. "Looks like Rocky was right about the bones being human," she told the sheriff when he came on the line.

"Bring them in and we'll send them over to Missoula to the crime lab. Since you're supposed to be off shift, it can wait till tomorrow if you want. Don't worry about it."

Sheriff Grant Sheridan sounded distracted, but then he had been that way for some time now.

McCall wondered idly what was going on with him. Grant, who was a contemporary of her mother's, had taken over the job as sheriff in Whitehorse County after the former sheriff, Carter Jackson, resigned to ranch with his wife Eve Bailey Jackson.

McCall felt the muddy plastic in her jacket pocket. "Sheriff, I—" But she realized he'd already disconnected. She cursed herself for not just telling him up front about the hunting license.

What was she doing?

Withholding evidence.

She waited until Rocky left before she got the small shovel and her other supplies from behind her seat and walked back over to the grave. The wind howled around her like a live animal as she dug in the mud that had once been what she now believed was her father's grave, taking photographs of each discovery and bagging the evidence.

She found a scrap of denim fabric attached to metal buttons, a few snaps like those from a Western shirt and a piece of leather that had once been a belt.

Her heart leaped as she overturned something in the mud that caught in the sunlight. Reaching down, she picked it up and cleaned off the mud. A belt buckle.

Not just any belt buckle she saw as she rubbed her fingers over the cold surface to expose the letters, *WINCHESTER*.

The commemorative belt buckle was like a million others. It proved nothing.

Except that when McCall closed her eyes, she saw her father in the only photograph she had of him. He stood next to his 1983 brand-new black Chevy pickup, his Stetson shoved back to expose his handsome face, one thumb hooked in a pocket of his jeans, the other holding his rifle, the one her mother said had belonged to his grandfather. In the photo, the sun glinted off his commemorative Winchester rifle belt buckle.

She opened her eyes and, picking up the shovel, began to dig again, but found nothing more. No wallet. No keys. No boots.

The larger missing item was his pickup, the one in the photograph. The one he allegedly left town in. Had he been up here hunting? She could only assume so, since according to her mother, the last time she saw Trace was the morning of opening day of antelope season—and his twentieth birthday.

Along with the hunting license, she'd found an unused antelope tag.

But if he'd been hunting, then where was his rifle, the one her mother said he had taken the last time she saw him?

McCall knew none of this proved absolutely that the bones were her father's. No, that would require DNA results from the state crime lab, which would take weeks if not months.

She stared at the grave. If she was right, her father hadn't left town. He'd been buried on the edge of this ridge for the past twenty-seven years.

The question was who had buried him here?

Someone who'd covered up Trace Winchester's death and let them all believe he'd left town.

Her hands were shaking as she boxed up the bones and other evidence—all except the license still in her coat pocket—and hiked back to her rig. Once behind the wheel, she pulled out the plastic case and eased out the license and antelope tag.

The words were surprisingly clear after almost thirty years of being buried in the mud since the plastic had protected the practically indestructible paper.

Name: Trace Winchester. Age: 19. Eyes: dark brown. Hair: Black. Height: 6 ft 3 inches. Weight: 185.

He'd listed his address as the Winchester Ranch, which meant when he'd bought this license he hadn't eloped with her mother yet or moved into the trailer on the edge of Whitehorse.

There was little information on the license, but McCall had even less. Not surprising, her mother, Ruby Bates Winchester, never liked talking about the husband who'd deserted her.

Most of what McCall had learned about her father had come from the rumors that circulated around the small

Western town of Whitehorse. Those had portrayed Trace Winchester as handsome, arrogant and spoiled rotten. A man who'd abandoned his young wife, leaving her broke and pregnant, never to be seen again.

According to rumors, there were two possible reasons for his desertion. Trace had been caught poaching—not his first time—and was facing jail. The second was that he'd wanted to escape marriage and fatherhood since McCall was born just weeks later.

A coward *and* a criminal. Trace solidified his legacy when he had left behind a young, pregnant, heartbroken wife and a daughter who'd never been accepted as a Winchester.

As McCall stood on that lonely windblown ridge, for the first time she realized it was possible that everyone had been wrong about her father.

If she was right, Trace Winchester hadn't run off and left them. He'd been buried under a pile of dirt at the top of this ridge for the past twenty-seven years—and would have still been there if it hadn't been for a wild spring storm.

North of Whitehorse, Luke Crawford pulled down a narrow, muddy road through the tall, leafless cottonwoods along the Milk River. The only other tracks were from another pickup that had come down this road right after last night's rainstorm.

The road ended at the edge of a rancher's wheat field, the same rancher who'd called saying he'd heard gunshots just before daylight.

Luke parked next to the fresh truck tracks. Past the tall old cottonwoods, down the slow-moving river, he could make out a small cabin tucked in the trees.

Just the sight of McCall Winchester's home stirred up all the old feelings. Luke cursed himself that he couldn't let go, never had been able to. Now that he was back in town as the new game warden, there was no way they weren't going to cross paths.

He could just imagine how that would sit with McCall.

Over the years, he'd followed her career with the sheriff's department and had heard she'd bought a place on the river. He'd also heard that she seldom dated and as far as anyone knew there was no man in her life.

That shouldn't have made him as relieved as it did.

He noticed now that her sheriff's department pickup wasn't parked next to the cabin. Had she worked the night shift last night or the early-morning one?

With a curse, he realized she might have heard the shots the rancher had reported or seen someone coming up the river road. He had no choice but to stop by and ask her, he told himself.

He sure as hell wasn't going to avoid her when it appeared there was a poaching ring operating in the river bottom. This was the second call he'd gotten in two weeks.

The thought of seeing her again came with a rush of mixed emotions and did nothing to improve his morning. He could just imagine the kind of reception he'd get, given their past. But now that he was back, there would be no avoiding each other—not in a town the size of Whitehorse.

Luke swore and got out, telling himself he had more to worry about than McCall Winchester as he saw the bloody drag trail in the mud. Taking his gear, he followed it.

RUBY WINCHESTER HAD just finished with the lunch crowd when McCall came into the Whitehorse Diner.

McCall felt light-headed after the morning she'd had. She'd come back into town, boxed up the bones and the other evidence, along with a request to compare the DNA of the bones with that of the DNA sample she'd taken from swabbing the inside of her mouth.

Even though the sheriff had told her to wait until her shift tomorrow, she'd mailed off the package to the crime lab without telling anyone. She was now shaking inside, shocked by what she'd done. Withholding evidence was one thing. Requesting the DNA test without proper clearance was another. She was more than jeopardizing her job.

But she couldn't wait months to know the truth. She'd bought herself some time before the report came back, and she knew exactly how she was going to use it.

"You want somethin' to eat?" her mother asked as McCall took one of the stools at the counter. "I could get you the special. It's tuna casserole. I'm sure there's some left."

McCall shook her head. "I'm good."

Ruby leaned her hip against the counter, eyeing her daughter. "Somethin' wrong?"

McCall glanced around the small empty café. Ruby hadn't cleaned off all of the tables yet. The café smelled like a school cafeteria.

"I've been thinking about my father. You've never really told me much about him."

Ruby let out a snort. "You already know about him."

"All you've ever told me is that he left. What was he like?" And the real question, who would want to kill him?

"What's brought this on?" Ruby asked irritably.

"I'm curious about him. What's wrong with that? He was my father, right?"

Ruby narrowed her gaze. "Trace Winchester *was* your

father, no matter what anyone says, okay? But do we have to do this now? I'm dead on my feet."

"Mom, you're always dead on your feet, and you're the only one I can ask."

Ruby sighed, then checked to make sure Leo, the cook, wasn't watching before reaching under the counter to drag out an ashtray. She furtively lit a cigarette from the pack hidden in her pocket.

McCall watched her take a long drag, blow out smoke, then wave a hand to dissipate the smoke as she glanced back toward the kitchen again.

According to Montana law, Ruby wasn't supposed to be smoking in the café, but then laws and rules had never been something Ruby gave a damn about.

She picked nervously at the cigarette, still stalling.

"It's a simple enough question, Mom."

"Don't get on your high horse with me," Ruby snapped.

"I want to know about my father. Why is that so tough?"

Ruby met her gaze, her eyes shiny. "Because the bastard ran out on us and because I—" Her voice broke. "I never loved anyone the way I loved Trace."

That surprised her, since there'd been a string of men woven through their lives as far back as McCall could remember.

Ruby bit her lip and looked away. "Trace broke my heart, all right? And you know damned well that his mother knows where he is. She's been giving him money all these years, keeping him away from here, away from me and you."

"You don't know that," McCall said.

"I know," Ruby said, getting worked up as she always did when she talked about Pepper Winchester. "That old witch had a coronary when she found out Trace and I had eloped."

More than likely Pepper Winchester had been upset when she'd heard that her nineteen-year-old son had gotten Ruby pregnant. McCall said as much.

"You're her own flesh and blood. What kind of grandmother rejects her own granddaughter? You tell me that," Ruby demanded.

"Was my father in any trouble other than for poaching? I've always heard that Game Warden Buzz Crawford was after him for something he did the day before he disappeared," McCall said, hoping to get her mother off the subject of Pepper Winchester.

Ruby finished her cigarette, stubbing it out angrily and then cleaning the ashtray before hiding it again under the counter. "Your father didn't leave because of that stupid poaching charge."

"Why do you say that?"

"Trace had gotten off on all the other tickets Buzz had written him. He wasn't afraid of Buzz Crawford. In fact…"

"In fact?"

Ruby looked away. "Everyone in town knew that Buzz was gunning for your father. But Trace said he wasn't worried. He said he knew something about Buzz…"

"Blackmail?" McCall uttered. Something like that could get a man killed.

LUKE CRAWFORD FOLLOWED the drag trail through the thick cottonwoods. Back in here, the soft earth hadn't dried yet. The wind groaned in the branches and weak rays of sunlight sliced down through them.

The air smelled damp from last night's storm, the

muddy ground making tracking easier, even without the bloody trail to follow.

It was chilly and dark deep in the trees and under-brush, the dampness making the April day seem colder. Patches of snow had turned to ice crystals on the shady side of fallen trees and along the north side of the riverbank.

Luke hadn't gone far when he found the kill site. He stopped and squatted down, the familiar smell of death filling his nostrils. The gut pile was still fresh, not even glazed over yet. A fine layer of hair from the hide carpeted the ground.

Using science to help him if he found the poachers, he took a DNA sample. Poachers had been relatively safe in the past if they could get the meat wrapped and in the freezer and the carcass dumped in the woods somewhere.

Now though, if Luke found the alleged poacher, he could compare any meat found in a freezer and tell through DNA if it was the same illegally killed animal.

In the meantime, he'd be looking for a pickup with mud on it and trying to match the tire tracks to the ve-hicle the poachers had been driving.

Pushing himself to his feet, Luke considered who might be behind the poaching. It generally wasn't a hun-gry Whitehorse family desperate enough to kill a doe out of season. In this part of Montana, ranchers donated beef to needy families, and most families preferred beef over venison.

Nor did Luke believe the shooters were teenagers out killing game for fun. They usually took potshots from across the hood of their pickups at something with ant-lers after a night of boozing—and left the meat to rot.

As he followed the drag trail to where the poacher had

loaded the doe into the back of his truck, he studied the tire tracks, then set about making a plaster cast.

While it dried he considered the footprints in the soft mud where the poachers' truck had been parked. Two men.

After taking photos and updating his log book, he packed up, and glancing once more toward McCall's cabin, went to give the rancher his assessment of the situation before filing his report.

Luke knew his chances of catching the poachers were slim. Not that his uncle Buzz would have seen it that way. Buzz Crawford had built a reputation on being the toughest game warden Montana had ever seen.

But Luke tended to write more warnings than tickets and knew he couldn't solve every crime in the huge area he covered. He didn't have the "kill gene," as his uncle often told him, and that explained the problem between him and Buzz.

The problem between him and McCall Winchester, his first love—hell, the only woman he'd ever truly loved—was a whole lot more complicated.

McCall was still considering the ramifications of her father possibly blackmailing the former game warden. "If Trace had something on Buzz—"

"I don't know that for sure," Ruby hedged. "Your father really didn't need to blackmail anyone. His mother and the Winchester money would have gotten him out of any trouble he got into."

Not this kind of trouble, McCall thought.

But she knew what her mother was getting at. Whitehorse was a small town and deals were made between local judges and some families. McCall also knew the legendary Buzz Crawford. He wouldn't have taken well to blackmail.

"So if my father wasn't worried about this poaching charge…" And apparently he hadn't been, if he'd gone hunting the next morning on that ridge. "Then why did you think he ran off?"

Ruby waved a hand through the air. "I was pregnant and crazy with hormones, out of my mind half the time, and Trace…"

"You fought a lot," McCall guessed after having seen how her mother's other relationships had gone over the years. "Did you have a fight the morning before he… disappeared?"

Ruby looked away. "Why do you we have to talk about this? Trace and I were both young and hotheaded. We fought, we made up." She shrugged. "There was no one like Trace." She smiled as if lost for a moment in the past.

And for that moment, Ruby looked like the pregnant young woman in love that she'd been in the few photographs McCall had of her—usually in uniform, alone, at the café.

The moment passed. Ruby frowned. "No matter what you've heard, Trace didn't leave because of you."

"So did he take anything when he left—clothes, belongings?"

"Just his pickup and his rifle. He would have made a good father and husband if his mother had stayed out of it. Pepper Winchester has a fortune, but she wouldn't give him a dime unless he got out of the marriage to me and made me say my baby was someone else's. What kind of mother puts that kind of pressure on her son?"

McCall didn't want her mother to take off on Pepper Winchester again. Nor was she ready to tell her mother what she'd found up on the ravine south of town without conclusive evidence.

She got to her feet. "I need to get going."

"You sure you don't want some tuna casserole? I could get Leo to dish you up some for later. You have to eat and it's just going to get thrown out."

"Naw, thanks anyway." She hugged her mother, surprised how frail Ruby was and feeling guilty for upsetting her. "I didn't mean to bring up bad memories."

"All that was a long time ago. I survived it."

"Still, I know it wasn't easy." McCall could imagine how hurt her mother must have been, how humiliated in front of the whole town, that her husband had left her pregnant, broke and alone. McCall knew how it was to have the whole town talking about you.

"It wasn't so bad," Ruby said with a smile. "Within a couple of weeks, I had you."

McCall smiled, feeling tears burn her eyes as she left, her hand in her pocket holding tight to the hunting license—the only definite thing she had of her father's—unless she counted his bad genes.

WORD ABOUT THE bones found south of town had traveled the speed of a wildfire through Whitehorse. McCall heard several versions of the story when she stopped for gas.

Apparently most everyone thought the bones were a good hundred years old and belonged to some outlaw or ancestor.

By the time McCall left Whitehorse, the sun and wind had dried the muddy unpaved roads to the southeast. The gumbo, as the locals called the mud, made the roads often impassible.

McCall headed south into no-man's-land on one of

the few roads into the Missouri Breaks. Yesterday she'd driven down Highway 191 south to meet Rocky. But there were no roads from the ridge where she'd stood looking across the deep gorge to the Winchester Ranch.

Getting to the isolated ranch meant taking back roads that seldom saw traffic and driving through miles and miles of empty rolling wild prairie.

Over the years McCall had thought about just showing up at her grandmother's door. But she'd heard enough horror stories from her mother—and others in town— that she'd never gotten up the courage.

The truth was, she didn't have the heart to drive all the way out there and have her grandmother slam the door in her face.

Today though, she told herself she was on official business. Of course one call to the sheriff would blow that story and leave her in even more hot water with her boss.

But already in over her head, McCall felt she'd been left little choice. Once the report came back from the crime lab—and she gave up the hunting license—it would become a murder investigation and she would be not only pulled off the case, but also locked out of any information the department gathered because of her personal connection to the deceased.

Before that happened, she hoped to get the answers she so desperately needed about her father—and who had killed him.

She knew it would be no easy task, finding out the truth after all these years. Her mother was little help. As for the Winchesters, well, she'd never met any of them. Trace had been the youngest child of Call and Pepper Winchester.

His siblings and their children had all left the ranch

after Trace disappeared and had never returned as far as McCall knew. Her grandmother had gone into seclusion.

The Winchester Ranch had always been off-limits for McCall—a place she wasn't welcome and had no real connection with other than sharing the same last name.

The fact that her father had been buried within sight of the ranch gave her pause, though, as McCall slowed to turn under the carved wooden Winchester Ranch arch.

In the distance she could see where the land broke and began to fall as the Missouri River carved its way through the south end of the county. Nothing was more isolated or wild than the Breaks and the Winchester Ranch sat on the edge of this untamed country.

It gave her an eerie feeling just thinking of her grandmother out here on the ranch, alone except for the two elderly caretakers, Enid and Alfred Hoagland. Why had Pepper closed herself off from the rest of her family after Trace disappeared? Wouldn't a mother be thankful she had other children?

McCall drove slowly down the ranch road, suddenly afraid. She was taking a huge chance coming out here. Even if she wasn't shot for a trespasser, she knew she would probably be run off without ever seeing her grandmother.

Weeds had grown between the two tracks of the narrow, hardly used road. Enid and Alfred only came into Whitehorse for supplies once a month, but other than that were never seen around. Nor, McCall had heard, did Pepper have visitors.

As she drove toward the massive log structure, she was treated to a different view of the ranch from that on the ridge across the ravine.

The lodge had been built back in the 1940s, designed

after the famous Old Faithful Lodge in Yellowstone Park. According to the stories McCall had heard, her grandfather Call Winchester had amassed a fortune, tripling the size of his parents' place.

There had always been rumors around Whitehorse about Call Winchester—the man McCall has been named for. Some said he made his fortune in gold mining. Others in crime.

The truth had remained a mystery—just like the man himself. Call had gone out for a horseback ride one day long before McCall was born, and as the story goes, his horse returned without him. His body was never to be found. Just like his youngest son, Trace. Until now.

An old gray-muzzled heeler with one brown and one blue eye hobbled out to growl beside McCall's patrol pickup.

She turned off the engine, waiting as she watched the front door of the lodge. The place looked even larger up close. How many wings were there?

When no one appeared, she eased open her vehicle door, forcing the dog back as she stepped out. The heeler stumbled away from her still growling. She kept an eye on him as she walked to the front door.

She didn't see any vehicles, but there was an old log building nearby that looked as if it was a garage, large enough to hold at least three rigs.

While she'd never seen her grandmother, McCall had run across Pepper's housekeeper, Enid—an ancient, broomstick-thin, brittle woman with an unpleasant face and an even worse disposition.

McCall had heard a variety of stories about Enid Hoagland, none of them complimentary. The housekeeper and her husband apparently took care of Pepper. Enid did the cooking and cleaning. Her husband, Alfred, did upkeep on the isolated ranch.

Some said the Hoaglands acted as guards to protect and care for Pepper. Others were of the opinion that the old couple kept Pepper Winchester hostage on the ranch to make sure they got the Winchester fortune when she died instead of her heirs.

McCall knocked at the weathered door, glancing around as she waited. A quiet hung over the wind-scoured place as if everything here had withered up and died.

She knocked harder and thought she heard a sound on the other side of the door. "Sheriff's Department. Open up."

After a long moment, the door creaked slowly open. An old woman appeared on the other side, and for a moment McCall thought she was about to come face-to-face with her grandmother.

But as the light flowed into the dark entry, she saw that it was only Enid Hoagland.

Enid scowled at her. "What do you want?" she demanded by way of greeting.

"I need to speak with Pepper Winchester."

"That isn't possible. Mrs. Winchester doesn't see anyone." She started to close the door, but McCall stuck a booted foot in the doorway.

"I'm sorry, but she'll have to see me unless you want me to come back with a warrant to search the house," McCall bluffed. "Tell her it's Deputy Sheriff McCall Winchester."

A malicious light flickered on in Enid's close-set gray eyes. "You're making a mistake," she said under her breath.

McCall feared the old woman was right.

A sound like the tinkling of a small bell came from deep in the lodge. Enid seemed to hesitate. "You will regret this."

McCall didn't doubt it. The older woman stepped aside and the deputy sheriff entered her father's family home for the first time in her life.

Chapter Three

Enid led McCall into what could only be called a parlor. The decor was old-time Western, the rustic furnishings dated as if the house had been sealed for more than thirty years.

McCall was too nervous to sit. She'd forced her way in here, and now she wasn't sure what she would say to her grandmother when she finally saw her for the first time.

At the sound of faint footfalls in the hallway, she turned, bracing herself, and yet she was still shocked. Nothing could have prepared her for the elderly woman who stepped into the room.

Pepper Winchester was surprisingly spry for seventy-two. She stood, her back ramrod straight, her head angled as if she was irritated. Her face was lined but there was something youthful about her. She was tall and slim, elegant in her black silk caftan.

Her hair, which had apparently once been dark like McCall's, was now peppered with gray. It trailed down her slim back in a single loose braid. Her eyes were ebony, her cheekbones high, just like McCall's.

The resemblance was both striking and shocking. McCall had had no idea just how much she looked like her grandmother.

If Pepper Winchester noticed the resemblance, her demeanor gave no notice of it. Nor was there any indication that she knew who McCall was.

"Yes?" she demanded.

McCall found her voice. "I'm Deputy Sheriff McCall Winchester."

Had the dark eyes widened just a little?

"I need to ask you a few questions."

"I'm sure my housekeeper told you I don't see visitors."

But you saw me. Why was that? Not because of the threat of a warrant. "I wouldn't have bothered you if it wasn't important. It's about your son Trace's disappearance."

"Have you found him?" The hope in her grandmother's voice and posture was excruciating. So was the fear she heard there. And yet, Pepper Winchester had to know that if there was any news of Trace, the sheriff would have been here—not some lowly deputy.

"I'm investigating his disappearance," McCall said quickly, taking out her notebook and pen.

"After twenty-seven years?" Pepper asked in disbelief. She seemed to shrink, all the starch coming out of her, all the spirit. "What's the point?"

"When was the last time you saw your son?"

Pepper shook her head, her dark eyes dimming in the dull light. "I should think you would know that, since I gave that information to the sheriff at the time."

McCall saw that this had been a mistake. What had she hoped to accomplish? She had wanted to see her grandmother. And now she had. The best thing she could do was to leave before Pepper Winchester got on the phone to the sheriff.

But she'd come too far. She couldn't leave things like this. Nor had she gotten what she'd come for. "Is there anyone who might have wanted to harm him?"

Pepper raised her head slightly, her dark eyes locking with McCall's. "Other than your mother?"

"Did your son have any enemies?"

"No." Instantly, she corrected herself. "Buzz Crawford. He hated my family, Trace in particular." Her voice broke as she said her son's name.

Again the former game warden's name had come up in relation to Trace.

"Was your son blackmailing Buzz Crawford?"

"*What?* Who would even say something like that? Your *mother*?" She raised her nose into the air. "My son didn't have to resort to blackmail. He was a *Winchester*. He wasn't going to serve any jail time. I would have seen to that."

Her grandmother's gaze flicked over her, anger and impatience firing those dark eyes, then she sighed deeply and started to walk away, signaling this conversation was over.

"Then why did you think he left town? Because you cut him off financially?" McCall asked, unable to hold back. "Or because you were demanding he divorce my mother and renounce the child she was carrying?"

Pepper Winchester spun back around, eyes narrowing dangerously. "You know nothing about my relationship with my youngest son. *Nothing*." She held up her hand before McCall could say another word. "You should leave. *Now*." With that her grandmother turned and disappeared through the door.

McCall closed her notebook and looked up to find

Enid Hoagland framed in the doorway, a smug little smile on the horrid woman's face.

"You are not to ever disturb Mrs. Winchester again," Enid said as she walked McCall to the door and closed it firmly behind her.

Standing on the front step, McCall took a deep breath of the crisp spring air. Her heart seemed to struggle with each beat. What had she been thinking coming out here to see the grandmother who had denied her all these years? Still denied her.

Letting out the breath, McCall walked to her pickup, her eyes burning. She could feel someone watching her, the gaze boring into her back. Her grandmother? Or that awful Enid?

She slid behind the wheel, anxious to get away before she shed the tears now blurring her eyes. She wouldn't give either old woman the satisfaction of seeing how much that had hurt.

PEPPER WINCHESTER STOOD at the window trembling with rage as she watched McCall drive away.

"You should have told me how much she resembles me," she said, knowing Enid was behind her even though she hadn't heard the woman approach. Trace used to say that Enid moved as silently as a ghost—or a cat burglar.

"What would have been the point?" Enid asked. "You didn't have to see her. Now you're upset and—"

Pepper spun around to face her ancient housekeeper as the patrol pickup disappeared down the road. "Of course I'm upset. Why would she come here and ask about Trace?"

"Because she believes he was her father."

Pepper scoffed at that, just as she had when Trace

told her that he'd gotten that tramp Ruby Bates pregnant. But the proof had been standing in her house just moments before.

There was no denying that McCall was a Winchester—and her father's daughter.

"You're the one who let her in," Enid complained. "I could have gotten rid of her."

When Pepper had seen the sheriff's department vehicle pull in, she'd thought it might be news about Trace and had been unable to smother that tiny ember of hope that caught fire inside her.

"She'll be back, you know," Enid warned in obvious disapproval. "She wants more than what she got this time."

Yes, Pepper suspected McCall would be back. She'd seen herself and Trace in the young brazen woman.

"So," Enid said with a sigh. "Can I get you anything?"

My son Trace. That was the only thing she wanted.

"I just want to be alone." Pepper turned back to the window, looking down at the long curve of the road into the ranch.

All this time, she'd expected a call or a visit from the sheriff. Word from someone about her son. And after twenty-seven years to have his daughter show up at her door…

Why would McCall be investigating her father's disappearance *now*? Or had that just been an excuse to come out to the ranch?

For weeks after Trace left, Pepper would stare at that road waiting for him to come down it. How many times had she imagined him driving up that road in his new black pickup, getting out, his jacket thrown over one shoulder, cowboy hat cocked back to expose his handsome face, his long jean-clad legs closing the distance as if he couldn't wait to get home.

She'd been so sure he would contact her. Eventually he would call for money. He'd known she could make his hunting violation charge go away—just as she had the others.

For that reason, she'd never understood why he would run away. She'd blamed that tramp he'd foolishly married. Trace wasn't ready for marriage, let alone a child. Especially one Pepper had been convinced would turn out to be someone else's bastard. She'd despised Ruby for trapping her son and giving Trace no way out but to leave town.

But after weeks, then months had gone by with no word, Pepper feared *she* was the reason her son had left and never came back. The thought had turned her heart to stone.

She'd walled herself up here in the lodge unable to face life outside the ranch. Worse, she'd replayed her last argument with Trace over and over in her head.

McCall was right. She *had* threatened to cut him off without a cent if he didn't divorce Ruby and denounce that bastard child she was carrying. Trace had pleaded with her to give Ruby a chance, swearing the baby was his.

Pepper sighed. Apparently, he'd been right about that at least, she thought now. She was still trembling from finally coming face-to-face with Trace's daughter. McCall.

That bitch Ruby had named the girl after her grandfather, Call Winchester, just to throw it in Pepper's face.

But there was no doubt. The girl definitely was of Winchester blood.

She frowned as she remembered something McCall had said. *"Then why did you think he'd left town?"*

McCall hadn't come to the ranch out of simple curiosity. If that were true, she would have shown up sooner.

Pepper stepped to the phone. For years, she hadn't spoken to another soul other than Enid and her housekeeper's husband, Alfred—and fortunately neither of them had much to say.

Then McCall had shown up, she thought with a curse as she dialed the sheriff's department.

LUKE SPENT A couple of hours looking around Whitehorse for the poachers' pickup before he headed south. His jurisdiction included everything from the Canadian border to the Missouri River—an area about the size of the state of Massachusetts.

For that reason, he put close to twenty-five thousand miles on his three-quarter-ton pickup every year. His truck was his office as well as his main source of transportation unless he was in one of the two boats he used to patrol the area's waterways.

This time of year, because of paddlefish season, he spent most of his time on the Missouri River south of Whitehorse. Today he was checking tags and watching for fishing violations. Fishing was picking up all over his area from the Milk River to reservoirs Nelson and Fort Peck.

For the next few months, he'd be spending fourteen- to fifteen-hour days watching fishermen, checking licenses and boats for safety equipment.

That wouldn't leave much time to catch the deer poachers, but he figured they knew that.

Tired from getting up at dawn, Luke headed back

toward Whitehorse a little earlier than usual. His place was just to the south, his parents' old homestead that he'd bought when he'd recently returned to Whitehorse. The homestead had been sold following his parents' deaths but he'd managed to get it back.

He liked to think it was a sign that he'd made the right decision by coming back here. A sign that there was a chance for him and McCall. He was building a new house on the property and was anxious for a couple of days off to work on it.

As he drove over the rise on the road, the stark skeleton of his new house set against the sunset, he slowed. The truck parked down by his stock pond didn't look familiar.

He pulled his pickup to a stop and got out, scanning the old windbreak of Russian olive trees as he did. The unfamiliar truck had local plates. As he walked past the pickup, he saw an older outboard lying in the back in a pool of oil and the broken tip of a fishing pole floating next to it.

"Hey!"

The greeting startled him even as he recognized the voice.

His cousin Eugene Crawford stepped from behind one of the outbuildings where he'd obviously gone to take a leak. He had a fishing pole in one hand and a beer in the other.

"Grab your rod," Eugene said. "Let's catch a few."

The last thing Luke wanted to do right now was fish. He needed some shut-eye. Hopefully the poachers would take a night off and let him get some rest.

"Sorry, but I've got to hit the hay," he told his cousin.

"At least come down and watch me catch a couple."

After Luke's parents were killed in a small plane crash when he was seven, his uncle Buzz had taken him in and he and Eugene were raised like brothers.

His cousin, who was two years older, had always looked out for him, fighting his battles, covering his back. In high school, Eugene had been the popular one, a former high school football star and a charmer with the girls.

Now Eugene lived in the past, high school being his glory days after an injury his freshman year in college ruined any chance he had to play pro football.

Since then, Eugene had struggled, going from one job to the next, having his share of run-ins with the law as well as women. Just recently divorced for the third time, Eugene seemed to be down on his luck, if that old beat-to-hell pickup he was driving was any indication.

"All right. But just for a few minutes," Luke said, giving in the way he always had when it came to Eugene.

"So, catch any poachers lately?" his cousin asked as he cast out into the pond and sat down on the edge of the earthen dam. It was an inside joke, something Buzz had always asked from the time Luke had become a game warden.

"A few," he answered, just as he always did with Buzz.

Eugene laughed as he watched his red-and-white bobber float on the dark surface of the water. Long shadows lay across the pond, the sky behind him ablaze with the setting sun.

Luke suspected his cousin hadn't just come out here to fish.

"Sit down," Eugene said, an edge to his voice. "You look like any minute you're going to check my fishing license."

It would be just like his cousin not to have one. Eugene liked to push the limits.

"I told you. I've got to get some sleep," Luke said, realizing he wasn't up to dealing with Eugene's problems right now, or his excuses.

"Sure. I know. You have a job," Eugene said sarcastically.

"Whatever it is, I'm really not up to it tonight."

"Yeah, you got your own problems, huh. Don't want to hear about mine." His cousin swore, reeled his line in, checked the bait and threw it back out. "I need money. I'm not screwing with you. It's a matter of life and death."

Luke sighed. "How much are we talking?"

"Fifty grand."

He let out a low whistle. "How the hell did you—"

"You're starting to sound like Buzz," Eugene said in a warning tone.

"Sorry, but that's a lot of money."

"You think I don't know that? I just made a few bad bets down in Billings and now they're threatening to kill me."

It was Luke's turn to swear. "How long are they giving you to come up with the money?"

"Six weeks, but that was two months ago," Eugene said. "I've heard they're looking for me."

"I don't have that kind of money." Luke had invested most everything he had in the house and land.

"You could put this place up. It's got to be worth a bunch. How many acres do you have here, anyway?"

Luke felt as if he'd been sucker punched. He waited until his initial anger had passed. "I can't do that," he said, turning to leave. He wasn't stupid enough that he didn't know what would happen if he put up his place for the money. "There are already two mortgages on it."

"Even ten thou would help," Eugene said, pleading.

He didn't seem to notice the tip of his rod bend as a fish took the bait.

The fish was the only one taking the bait today. "Sorry." This was one mess Eugene would have to get out of on his own.

"Yeah, sure you're sorry," Eugene said bitterly.

Luke's cell phone rang. He checked it and groaned inwardly. "I have to take this."

"Don't let me stop you."

Luke hated leaving things this way between them. He wished there was something more he could say. But the only thing Eugene wanted to hear was that Luke was going to bail him out, just as he had done too many times in the past.

Instead, as he left he pointed to his cousin's pole. "You have a fish."

MCCALL WAS ON the outskirts of Whitehorse when she got the call on her cell phone. The moment she heard the sheriff's voice, she knew.

"Where are you?" Grant asked.

"On the edge of town. Something up?" She hadn't heard anything on her radio. There was little crime in Whitehorse. The weekly sheriff's reports consisted of barking dogs, checks on elderly residents, calls about teens making too much noise and a few drunk and disorderlies.

The sheriff seemed to hesitate. "Pepper Winchester phoned me."

McCall had been waiting for the other shoe to drop. Still, it hit with a thud that set off her pulse. Hadn't she known this would happen? And yet, she'd hoped blood really was thicker than water.

"Pepper seemed to think you were on sheriff's department business, investigating her son's disappearance," Grant said. "I assured her that wasn't the case. I can understand how you might have wanted to see her."

McCall said nothing, hating the pity she heard in his voice. He thought the only reason she'd gone out there was to see her grandmother.

He cleared his throat. "She said if you came back she'd have you arrested for trespassing. I'm sorry."

McCall bit back an unladylike retort. Her grandmother was turning out to be everything she'd heard she was, and the sheriff's sympathy wasn't helping.

"It might be a good idea to stay away from the Winchester Ranch," Grant said before he hung up.

As she pulled into Whitehorse, McCall's two-way radio squawked. She listened for a moment as the dispatcher said there'd been a call about a disturbance at the Mint Bar.

She started to let the other deputy on duty pick it up since she was off the clock.

But when she heard who was involved, she said she'd take the call and swung into a parking space outside the Mint.

She heard Rocky's voice the moment she opened the bar door. A small crowd had gathered around the rock collector. As she walked in, she recognized most of the men. One in particular made her regret she'd taken the call.

Rocky was at the center of the trouble but in the mix was Eugene Crawford. At a glance, she saw that both men were drunk. Eugene as usual looked as if he was itching for a fight.

"Excuse me," she said, easing her way into the circle

of men around Rocky. Closing her hand around Rocky's upper arm, she said, "It's time to go home."

"Well, look who it is," Eugene said. "It's the girl deputy."

Eugene had been the school bully and she'd been his target. It was bad enough in grade school, but in high school it had gotten worse after she turned him down for a date.

"If you gentlemen will excuse us," McCall said, drawing Rocky away from the fracas.

"What's this about some grave Rocky found south of town?" Crawford demanded.

"Probably just a fish story like the one you told when you came in," one of the men ribbed Eugene.

McCall led Rocky toward the door. He was being the perfect docile drunk. A few more feet and they would be out of the bar.

"I asked you a question, *Deputy*," Eugene said, coming up behind her and grabbing her arm.

"Let go," she said as he tightened his grip on her. "Let go now, Eugene." He smelled of fish and sweat and meanness.

"Or what? You going to arrest me?" His nails bit into her flesh. "Try it," he said and gave her a shove, slamming her into the jukebox.

She staggered but didn't fall. "Going to need some backup," McCall said into her radio as Rocky leaped to her defense.

Before she could stop him, Eugene coldcocked Rocky, who hit the floor hard. Eugene was turning to take on the others who'd jumped in when the bartender came over the bar with his baseball bat.

It took McCall, Deputy Nick Giovanni and the bartender to get Eugene Crawford restrained and into handcuffs. Nick took Eugene to the jail while McCall drove Rocky home. He was quiet most of the ride.

"Are you sure you're all right?" she asked as she walked him to his front door. "I'd feel better if I took you by the emergency room at the hospital."

"I'm fine," Rocky said, looking sheepish. "I guess I have a glass jaw, as they say."

"Eugene hit you awfully hard."

Rocky seemed to have sobered up some. "You know that was a grave I found, don't you?"

McCall said nothing.

"I know I said I thought it was old, but it wasn't. And it wasn't no Indian grave like Eugene was saying, and I think you know that, too."

She patted his shoulder. "Get some rest." As she turned toward her pickup, all she wanted was to go home and put this day behind her.

But as she drove the few miles out of town and turned down the river road to her small old cabin beside the Milk River, she saw the pickup parked in her yard.

She slowed as she recognized the logo on the side of the truck. Montana Fish, Wildlife and Parks. She felt her heart drop as she pulled alongside and Game Warden Luke Crawford climbed out.

LUKE HATED THE way he felt as he watched McCall walk toward him. He was again that awkward, tongue-tied, infatuated seventeen-year-old—just as he'd been the first time he'd ever kissed McCall Winchester.

A lot of things had changed in the years since, but not that.

"Luke?" She stopped in front of her pickup. One hand rested on her hip just above the grip of her weapon. She was still in uniform except for her hat. Some of her long dark hair had come loose from the clip at the nape of her neck and now fell over one shoulder.

He tipped his hat. "Sorry to bother you."

She frowned, clearly waiting for him to tell her what the hell he was doing here. She had to have heard he was back in town.

"I got another call tonight about some poaching down in the river bottom," he said.

"On my property?"

He pointed down into the thicket of tangled willows and cottonwoods. "On the place down the river, but I believe they used the river road to get in and out so they had to have gone right past your place. I was wondering if you heard anything last night? Would have probably been between two and four this morning."

"I pulled the late shift last night so I wasn't around. Sorry."

He nodded and asked who else knew her schedule.

"You saying the poachers knew I would be gone last night?"

"It crossed my mind. Your place is the closest."

She leaned against the front of her pickup, clearly not intending to ask him inside. The Little Rockies in the distance were etched a deep purple against the twilight. He noticed in the waning light that she looked exhausted.

"Rough day?" he asked, feeling the cool air come up out of the river bottom.

"You could say that." She was studying him, waiting as if she expected him to tell her the real reason he was here.

But he'd said everything years ago and she hadn't believed him then. No reason she'd believe him now.

He closed his notebook. "I'd appreciate it if you kept an eye out and gave me a call if you see or hear anything."

She pushed herself off the front of her pickup. "You bet."

"The poachers are driving a pickup, probably a half ton or three-quarter-ton four-wheel drive."

"Like half the residents in this county," she said.

"Narrows it right down for me." He smiled, hat in his hand, thinking that even as exhausted as McCall was she'd never looked more beautiful. He told himself to just get in his truck and get out of there before he said something he'd regret.

She smiled, a tired almost sad smile. "Well, I hope you catch 'em."

"Me, too." He put on his hat, tipped it, and turned toward his pickup. As he slid behind the wheel, he saw that she'd gone inside her cabin. The lights glowed golden through the windows. He sat for a moment, wishing—

Mentally he gave himself a swift kick and started the truck, annoyed for going down that old trail of thought. From the beginning he and McCall hadn't stood a chance, not with the bad blood between their families. He'd been a fool to think that they did.

But for a while, she'd made him believe they were destined to be together, star-crossed lovers who'd found a way. They'd been young and foolish. At least he had, he thought as he left.

He didn't dare glance back, knowing he was wasting his time if he thought she cared a plugged nickel for him.

If he had looked back, though, he would have seen her standing in the deepening shadows of her deck, hugging herself against the cool of the night, watching him drive away.

Chapter Four

The next morning, McCall woke blurry-eyed to the sound of a vehicle driving up in her yard. She pulled on her robe and padded out to the living room as she heard someone coming across the deck, making a beeline for her front door.

It was too early for company. Had something happened?

She thought of Luke. Not him again, she hoped. Seeing him waiting for her last night had been the last straw after the day she'd had. She'd had a devil of a time getting to sleep last night and it was all Luke Crawford's fault. What the hell was he doing back in Whitehorse, anyway?

Usually, she found peace in her cabin on the river. The place was small, but the view from her deck made up for it. She loved to sit and listen to the rustle of the cottonwood trees, watch the deer meander through the tall grass along the river's edge and breathe in the sweet scents of the seasons.

Last night, though, after she'd watched Luke drive away, not even a beer and a hot bath had soothed what ailed her.

Now she realized she hadn't locked the door last night. The knob turned, and out of the corner of her eye, she saw her father's hunting license on the kitchen counter where she'd left it last night.

She quickly snatched up the license and, lifting the lid on an empty canister on the counter, dropped it inside.

She'd barely dropped the lid, when the door was flung open.

"What in the world?" she bellowed as her mother came busting in.

Her mother stopped in midstride, a cigarette dangling from one corner of her mouth. "Did I forget to knock?"

"Do you know what time it is?" McCall demanded. "What are you doing here?"

"I had to see you before I went to work," her mother snapped back. "You might remember I work early."

Before McCall could wonder what was so important that it had her mother here at the crack of dawn, Ruby enlightened her.

"I can't believe you went out to the Winchesters'. What were you thinking?" her mother demanded. "Now that old woman is threatening to have you arrested? It's all over town."

McCall leaned against the kitchen counter. "Why is it that anything I do is always all over town within minutes?"

Ruby waved a hand through the air as if it was too obvious. "You're a *Winchester.*"

McCall sighed. "Only by name." A name she'd often regretted.

"You're *Trace* Winchester's *daughter.*"

As if that were something to celebrate, McCall thought, but was smart enough not to voice that sentiment to her mother, especially in the mood Ruby was in. No matter what Trace had done to her, Ruby would defend him to her death.

"As *Trace* Winchester's daughter, I should have the right to visit my grandmother," McCall said instead and motioned at her mother's cigarette. She didn't permit smoking in her cabin. Not after inhaling her mother's secondhand smoke for years.

"Don't you want to know how I found out?" Ruby asked, looking around for an ashtray.

"Not particularly."

"That bitch Enid. She must have called everyone in town this morning, announcing that her boss was going to have you arrested."

"I wasn't arrested." But she could be soon for interfering in a murder investigation. She tried not to think about that right now, though.

Ruby, not seeing an ashtray, opened the cabin door and started to flick the cigarette out, then apparently thought better of it.

"That old harpy," she said, stepping outside and leaving the door open as she ground the cigarette into the dirt. "I thought she'd be dead by now. She's got to be a hundred. Mean to the core."

McCall poured yesterday's coffee into two mugs, put them in the microwave and handed her mother a cup as she came back in. Taking the other cup, McCall curled up on one end of the couch.

The coffee tasted terrible, but it was hot and she needed the caffeine. Her mother sat down at the opposite end of the couch. She seemed to have calmed down a little.

"I just don't understand why you would go out there after all these years?"

"Maybe I finally wanted to see my grandmother."

Ruby eyed her. "Just like that?"

"Just like that."

"And?"

"And I saw her. End of story."

"Did she even know who you were? Of course she did. One look at you and she'd see the Winchester in you."

"You never told me I looked so much like her." She hadn't meant it to sound so accusatory.

Ruby shrugged and took a sip of her coffee. Her mother was so used to drinking bad coffee she didn't even grimace. "So what did she say to you?"

"It was a short conversation before she showed me the door."

Ruby toyed with the handle on her coffee mug. "Are you going to see her again?"

Was she worried McCall would be accepted by the Winchesters when Ruby hadn't been? The idea would have been laughable if it hadn't hurt so much.

"She called the sheriff on me. Does that answer your question?"

Ruby was ablaze, cursing Pepper Winchester clear to Hades and back, not that it was anything new.

"I'm sorry, baby," her mother said. She finished her coffee and got up to rinse the mug in the kitchen sink. "But don't feel too bad. It isn't like she was close to any of her kids or her other grandkids. She's just an evil old crone who deserves to live like a hermit."

McCall didn't tell her mother that she felt a little sorry for Pepper Winchester—anyone who'd seen the hope in her eyes at the mention of Trace's name would have been.

Ruby checked her watch. "I'm going to be late for work." She looked at her daughter as if she held McCall responsible. "Promise me you won't go back out there."

McCall was saved by the ringing of her cell phone. She

found it where she'd dropped it last night and checked caller ID. "It's my boss."

"Then you'd better take it," Ruby said. "Stop by the café later."

"If I can," McCall said and waited until her mother disappeared out the door before she took the call, fearing that her morning was about to get worse.

"You're up early," Buzz Crawford said from the deck of his lake house as Luke joined him.

"Haven't you heard? Poachers never sleep."

Buzz chuckled. "You're right about that. Catch any lately?"

He'd spent the night down in the river bottom patrolling. He wouldn't have been able to sleep anyway after his visit to McCall. This morning he'd caught a few hours' sleep before coming by his uncle's.

"A few," he said, distracted at the thought of McCall.

Buzz shook his head. "You're too easy on the bastards. These guys around here aren't afraid of you. When I was warden, they knew if they broke the law I'd be on them like stink on a dog."

Luke had heard it all before, way too many times.

"So how's the fishing been?" he asked to change the subject. It was one of those rare April days when the temperature was already in the fifties and expected to get up as high as seventy before the day was over. The sky overhead was a brilliant blue, cloudless and bright with the morning sun.

Buzz, who was sitting in one of the lawn chairs overlooking Nelson Reservoir, said something under his breath Luke didn't catch and was thankful for it.

"Help yourself to some coffee, if you want," Buzz said, handing Luke his cup to refill.

"Thanks." Luke stepped into the kitchen and poured himself a mug, refilling his uncle's before returning to the deck.

A flock of geese honked somewhere in the distance and he could see the dark V of a half-dozen pelicans circling over the water. The ice had only melted off last week leaving the water a deep green.

"Walleye chop," Buzz said as Luke handed him his coffee, indicating the water's surface now being kicked up by the wind. "The fish'll be bitin'. Since you're not going to catch any criminals anyway, you might as well come fishing with me."

Luke ignored the dig. "Can't." But spending the day fishing did have its appeal. "I have to work on the house or it will never get finished." He had a couple of days off, and he planned to get as much done as possible.

"I've never understood why you bought that place back," Buzz said, shaking his head. "It was nothing but work for your father. I'd think you'd want to start fresh. No ghosts."

Is that how Buzz saw the past? Full of ghosts? It surprised Luke. The old homestead was his mother's family's place. He'd lived there his first seven years with his parents before their deaths and cherished those memories.

"You hear about those bones found south of town?" his uncle asked, then swore when Luke said he hadn't. "You never know what's going on," Buzz complained. "Anyway, it seems Rocky Harrison found some bones and was going on about them at the bar and somehow Eugene got arrested."

No mystery there, Luke thought. Eugene getting arrested had long ceased to be news.

"Rocky swore the bones were human. Probably just some dead animal. I thought for sure you might have heard somethin'."

Luke watched a fishing boat against the opposite shore, the putter of the motor lulling him as he wondered idly why his uncle would be so interested in some old bones.

PEPPER STOPPED IN front of Trace's bedroom door, the key clutched in her hand. She'd had Enid lock the room, wanting it left just as it was the day her youngest son left it.

Had she really thought he'd return to the ranch? He'd been a day short of twenty the last time she saw him. He'd promised to come to the birthday party she was throwing for him. All of the family would be there and had been warned to be on their best behavior. She had planned the huge party and, even though the two of them had fought, Pepper had been so sure he wouldn't miss his party for anything.

"You old fool," she muttered as she slipped the key into the lock. She'd had her first child at seventeen. Trace had come along unexpectedly after her doctor said she couldn't have any more children. She had thought of Trace as her miracle child.

She realized she hadn't thought about her other children and grandchildren in years. They'd resented Trace and her relationship with him. Their jealousy had turned her stomach and finally turned her against them.

With a grimace, she realized she could be a great-grandmother by now.

The door to Trace's room opened. Air wafted out,

smelling stale and musty and she could see dust thick as paint everywhere as she stepped in.

The bed was covered in an old quilt, the colors faded, the stitching broken in dozens of places. She started to touch the once-vibrant colored squares but pulled her hand back.

Her eyes lit on the stack of outdoor and hunting magazines piled up beside the bed. Trace had lived and breathed hunting. He'd been like his father that way.

Her husband, Call, came to mind. She chased that memory away like a pesky fly, wishing she could kill it.

The door to the closet was open, and she could see most of Trace's clothes still hanging inside it, also covered with dust just like his guitar in the corner, like his high school sports trophies lined up on the shelves and his wild animal posters on the walls.

Pepper stood in the middle of the room feeling weak and angry at herself for that weakness. No wonder she had avoided this room, like so many others, all these years.

But as she stood there, she realized there was nothing of Trace left here. There was no reason to lock the room anymore or to keep what her son had left behind.

Trace Winchester was gone and he wasn't coming back.

That realization struck her to her core since she'd held on to the opposite belief for the past twenty-seven years.

Tears blurred her eyes as she looked around the room realizing what had changed. She'd become convinced her son was never coming home the moment she'd laid eyes on his deputy daughter.

McCall MENTALLY KICKED herself for the position she'd put herself in as she pulled into the sheriff's department parking lot. If she'd told the sheriff up front about what she'd found and her suspicions—

When he'd called this morning, he hadn't said why he wanted to see her, just that he did, even though it was her day off. He had only said it was important.

The best thing she could do was confess all.

Except as she got out of her pickup, she knew she couldn't do that. Not yet. Once she told Grant about the hunting license, the news would be all over town.

Right now she had a slim advantage to find the killer because he didn't know she was after him yet.

Even if the killer—who she was assuming still lived in Whitehorse since few people left—had heard about the discovery of the bones, he would still think he was safe. He'd taken everything that identified the body—even her father's boots, his wallet, his pickup and rifle—all things that could have identified the body.

The killer just hadn't known about the hunting license in one of Trace's pockets, apparently.

As McCall started toward her boss's office, she hesitated. She was jeopardizing more than her job by investigating this on her own. Once she started asking questions around town, the killer would know she was on to him and she would be putting her life in danger.

But if there was even a chance that Trace Winchester wouldn't have run out on them, that he'd have stayed and made them a family, then she owed it to all of them to find out who had taken that away.

"Thanks for coming in," Sheriff Grant Sheridan said as she tapped on his open door. He motioned to a chair in front of his desk. "Please close the door."

She stepped in, shutting the door behind her. Grant leaned back in his chair. He was a stocky, reasonably attractive man, with dark hair graying at the temples, intense blue eyes and a permanent grave expression.

A contemporary of her mother's, McCall had heard that the two had once dated back in high school, but then who hadn't her mother dated?

"How are you this morning?" Grant asked as McCall sat.

"Fine." She hoped this wasn't about her visit yesterday to the Winchester Ranch but maybe that was better than the alternative.

"I talked to the crime lab this morning," he said, not sounding happy about it.

She felt her heart drop. The DNA couldn't have come back already. But Grant could have heard about the unauthorized test.

"I've asked them to put a rush on those remains you sent them," Grant said.

"A rush?" she echoed. She'd thought she'd have time. Now, her undercover sleuthing aside, once the sheriff found out about the DNA test and the hunting license she'd be lucky to still have a job. Worse, she could end up in jail.

"After what happened at the bar last night, I had to speed up the process," Grant was saying. "Apparently Rocky, with the help of Eugene Crawford, got a bunch from out on the reservation all worked up. They're convinced one of their ancestor's grave has been disturbed."

"It wasn't an Indian grave."

"You're sure?"

"Positive." She wished Rocky had kept his fool mouth shut, but it was too late for that. "Along with the bones, I found shirt snaps, metal buttons off a pair of jeans and what was left of a leather belt."

"So it was a grave," Grant said, sounding surprised. "I thought it was just bones."

He hadn't asked her and he hadn't been around when she'd mailed everything off to the crime lab. At least that was her excuse for keeping more than the hunting license from him.

His being distracted for weeks now had made it too easy. Now everything hinged on that DNA report from the crime lab.

"When you said the bones were human, I just assumed they'd been there for a while," Grant said now. "How old are we talking?"

"Hard to say." Remains deteriorated at different rates depending on the time of year, the weather, the soil and how deep the body was buried.

"More than fifty years?"

"Less, I'd say."

He was silent for a long moment. "Where exactly were these bones found again?"

She told him.

He grew even quieter before he said, "Thanks for taking care of Rocky last night. We're still holding Eugene Crawford. I understand he got into it with you. Are you all right?"

"He didn't hurt me."

"But he apparently grabbed you and shoved you?"

"He was drunk and looking for a fight," she said. "I didn't see any reason to make more of it than it was."

Grant studied her for a moment before nodding. "Well, good job at keeping a lid on things. It could have been much worse if you hadn't acted as quickly as you did. It wouldn't be the first time Eugene Crawford tore up a bar." He glanced at his watch, sighed and stood, signaling that they were finished.

McCall tried to hide her relief.

"We should have the results from the lab on those bones in a week," Grant was saying. "In the meantime, I think it would be best if we said as little as possible about the discovery, don't you agree?"

She did indeed. She couldn't help but wonder how he'd feel when he found out just whose bones they really were. If he thought there was trouble now, wait until he had to deal with Pepper Winchester.

One week. When the report came back with the DNA test, all hell would break loose. She'd give up the hunting license and let the chips fall where they may. But in the meantime, she planned to make the most of it.

LUKE GLANCED OVER at his uncle, worried. Buzz didn't seem to be taking to retirement well after thirty-five years as a Montana game warden. While he swore that he was content fishing most every day, Luke suspected he missed catching bad guys.

Buzz, who'd made a name for himself as one of the most hard-nosed game wardens in the west, had been written up in a couple of major metropolitan newspapers and magazines, helping make him a legend in these parts.

"Did Eugene get out of jail?" Luke asked into the silence that had stretched between them.

"I'm going in this afternoon to bail him out. It was the soonest they'd release him." Buzz swore under his breath. "You know who arrested him, don't you?" Luke felt his stomach clench. "McCall Winchester. The Winchesters have always had it in for our family."

And vice versa, Luke thought, but was smart enough not to say it.

"Eugene said he hit you up for that money he owes for gambling debts," his uncle said after a moment.

Was that accusation he heard in Buzz's voice? "He needs fifty thousand dollars. I can't raise that kind of money."

"He asked you for that much? When he came to me it was only thirty." Buzz swore. "He tell you anything about these guys he owes the money to?"

"No." But Luke could imagine.

"He seems to think they won't find him here. Or maybe he thinks we'll protect him." Buzz had always protected his son, to Eugene's detriment. Luke saw there was both regret and determination in his uncle's expression. "I don't have the money to give him either."

Luke wasn't sure where this conversation was headed. "He has to stop gambling, get a job—"

"Don't you think I know that?" Buzz snapped. "But fifty thousand? It would take him years to make that much at a job in Whitehorse. Meanwhile, these guys aren't going to wait on their money."

Luke shook his head, hating the desperation he heard in his uncle's voice. Eugene would be even more desperate and probably do something crazy, knowing his cousin.

"I need to get going," Luke said finishing his coffee and rising to take the mug back into the kitchen.

As he came back out, he heard the sound of a vehicle engine. Shielding his eyes from the sun, he saw a white pickup pull in, a sheriff's department emblem on the side and a set of lights on top.

Luke heard his uncle swear as Deputy Sheriff McCall Winchester climbed out.

Chapter Five

McCall had hoped to catch Buzz Crawford alone. The last person she wanted to see was Luke. But unfortunately as she pulled up to the lake house, his pickup was parked outside.

No way to make a graceful escape even if she could let the coward in her win out.

As she neared the house, she saw the two Crawford men on the deck, Luke standing as if about to leave and Buzz sprawled in a lawn chair as if he didn't have a care in the world.

She stopped at the bottom of the stairs to the deck, shading her eyes to take in the two. It hadn't escaped her notice last night that Luke had changed. He'd filled out, looking stronger, definitely confident and as always, handsome in an understated, very male way.

She could see that Luke didn't like the idea of leaving her alone with his uncle given the family history. Of course he would be protective of the uncle who'd raised him and by now he would also know about his cousin's arrest last night and who Buzz would blame.

McCall smiled to herself at the indecision she saw in Luke's expression. But was he afraid to leave her alone with Buzz because of his fear of what his uncle might do? Or her?

"I'd like to speak to Buzz alone," McCall said flashing her badge. She heard Buzz curse loud enough for her to hear.

"You coming out to arrest me as well as my son?" Buzz snapped.

Luke started down the steps to the shore. As he stepped past McCall, he said under his breath, "You sure this is a good idea?"

"I can handle Buzz." The nearness of Luke Crawford was a whole other story, she thought as he brushed on past her.

"And I can handle the deputy," Buzz said from his lawn chair.

McCall listened to the crunch of Luke's boot heels on the rocky shore before ascending the stairs to the deck.

Buzz was a big beefy man with ham-sized fists and a predilection for violence—much like his son Eugene. As the former county game warden, he'd made more than his share of enemies since he had a reputation for being a heartless bastard who would have arrested his own mother.

McCall had heard stories about him roughing up poachers, claiming they'd resisted arrest when they swore they hadn't.

"What do you want?" Buzz demanded scowling at her now as he got up and went through the open door into his house.

She stepped cautiously to the doorway and peered into the dim darkness.

The place wasn't much larger than her cabin on the river and even more sparsely furnished. The only thing on the walls other than deer and antelope mounts were framed yellowed articles from newspapers and magazines featuring Buzz when he was a game warden.

He saw her looking at the write-ups about him and chuckled. "That's what a real officer of the law looks like," he boasted as he poured himself a mug of coffee but he didn't offer her one.

She saw that he'd changed since he'd left his game warden job. He wasn't in shape anymore and he'd aged. She thought retirement wasn't working out so well for him.

"So what brings a Winchester out to see me?" Buzz asked, glaring at her.

She smiled, wondering at this hatred between the Crawfords and Winchesters. It made no sense. Especially when aimed at her since no one in town considered her a Winchester—including the Winchester family.

"I'm here about Trace Winchester's disappearance," she said into the cold malevolent silence.

Buzz had started to take a drink of the hot coffee, but jerked back at her words, spilling some on the floor and burning his mouth. He swore and put down the cup.

"Your name keeps coming up in my investigation," she said. "I was wondering why that was."

"No mystery there," Buzz spat. "Your old man kept breaking the law and I kept catching him."

"How many times was that?"

He shrugged. "I lost track."

"Really? You were the only game warden for this entire county back then. You alone had an area the size of Massachusetts to cover, from Canada to the Missouri River Breaks. It would have been impossible to catch

Trace Winchester every time he broke the law unless you made it a personal vendetta."

"Maybe he was just stupid and got caught a lot."

"Maybe. I guess it would depend on how many times you arrested him and for what."

She'd checked the arrests before she'd driven out. They were public record. "Let's see," she said taking the list from her pocket. "Littering, trespassing, improper boat safety equipment…" She looked up. "You wrote him far more tickets than you wrote anyone else in the county."

Buzz looked uneasy.

"It makes me wonder just what your relationship was with my father."

"Relationship? I couldn't stand the little—" He caught himself. "Trace Winchester was a spoiled kid who thought he was above the law. I was a law enforcement officer. You should be able to understand that."

She nodded as she stuffed the list back into her pocket and took out her notebook and pen. "When was the last time you saw Trace?"

Buzz picked up his mug again and took a sip of coffee, letting her wait. "Hell if I know. Whatever date I ticketed his worthless ass."

"You never saw him again? Like say the next morning?" she asked, her gaze riveted to his.

He stared right back. "That's right."

"You're sure about that? You didn't by any chance wait for him on a ridge south of town?" Was it her imagination or did she see fear contract his eyes?

"You deaf? I already told you. Quit wasting my time."

"What exactly is your problem with the Winchester family?"

He blinked in surprise. "Why don't you ask your

mother. Or your grandmother. Oh, that's right, Pepper disowned you."

"Actually, I don't think she went to the trouble."

He sneered at that. "Your grandfather cheated my brother out of some land. Call Winchester was a crook and a liar."

"Call's been dead for more than forty years. What did that have to do with my mother? Or my father other than he was a Winchester and spoiled?"

"I didn't say it had anything to do with your father." His smile was as sharp as the filet knife lying on the counter next to him. "If you want to know what it has to do with your mother, well, I suggest you ask her."

McCall studied Buzz for a moment, hoping he wasn't another of her mother's old boyfriends. "What happened to my father's rifle?"

Buzz jerked back as if she'd taken a swing at him. "How the hell should I know? I would imagine he took it with him when he left town."

"How is that possible? You arrested him the day before for—" she made a show pulling out her list and checking it again "—poaching an antelope before opening season. If the rifle had been used in the commission of a crime, the weapon would have been considered evidence and confiscated under the law. So you must have taken it, right?"

Buzz looked worried. "No. Maybe Trace hid it. Or maybe I just forgot. I can't remember. But if I had taken it, the rifle would still be locked up in evidence."

"I checked. It's not. Anyway, my mother swears that Trace had the rifle the next morning when he left the house to go hunting. A model 99 Savage rifle with his father's initials carved in the stock."

"You'd take the word of your mother?"

She studied him, feeling an icy chill at the malice she saw in his eyes.

Her mother had said Trace might have had something on Buzz he used as leverage to keep his rifle, but why the obvious hated for her mother?

"Was my father blackmailing you?"

Buzz went to slam his mug down on the counter but missed. The mug hit the floor, shattering. Coffee shot out in an arc across the tile, making a dark stain at his feet.

She saw he was shaking all over, even his voice. "Get out of my house. I'm done talking to you without my lawyer."

McCall closed her notebook, put it and her pen away before she stepped back into the sunlight on the deck. Even the early morning sun felt good after the cold inside.

"One more thing," she said sticking her head back into the house.

He seemed shocked she was still on his property and had the audacity to ask him another question.

"Did I mention Rocky Harrison found a human grave south of town on a high ridge from a spot where you can see the Winchester Ranch in the distance?"

Buzz didn't move, didn't speak, didn't even seem to breathe. It wasn't the reaction she'd hoped for but it was a reaction.

"What the hell does that have to do with me?" he finally demanded.

She shrugged. "When I know that, I'll be back. Keep your lawyer's number handy."

LUKE COULDN'T HELP being distracted as he filed his report on the poaching incidents. Seeing McCall Winchester again had thrown him, especially since her visit to his uncle this morning had looked official and that worried him.

As he was hanging up from making his report, he got a call from a friend in the Helena Fish and Game office.

"Something going on up there with your uncle Buzz?" his friend George asked. "A deputy by the name of Mc-Call Winchester has been looking into some of Buzz's old cases. You know anything about this?"

Luke swore under his breath. "No, what cases are we talking about?"

"Mostly those involving a Trace Winchester. Any relation to the deputy?"

"Trace Winchester was her father. He disappeared before she was born almost thirty years ago."

"Probably not strange then that she's looking into those cases," George said. "She's probably just curious. But there were quite a few tickets issued. Her father must have been a real troublemaker."

Luke wondered about that. He'd heard rumors about Trace Winchester but had figured the man's exploits had been greatly exaggerated.

"Apparently," Luke agreed, his worry increasing. He'd thought Buzz was acting strangely this morning because of Eugene's arrest and the gambling trouble. Now he wasn't so sure.

"I thought I'd let you know, anyway."

"I appreciate that." He hung up, wondering what Mc-Call had wanted with his uncle. Why, after all these years, would she be looking into some old fish and game violations against her father?

More to the point, was she just fishing? Or had she caught something that could mean trouble for Buzz?

McCALL COULDN'T SHAKE off the feeling as she left that Buzz was lying about something. She'd definitely rattled him.

While she was trying hard not to let her dislike of Buzz Crawford overly influence her one-woman unauthorized investigation, it was odd that he hadn't confiscated her father's hunting rifle. Odder still were some of his reactions.

The missing rifle seemed the key, she thought as she saw Red Harper's pickup parked in front of the Cowboy Bar.

Red Harper, according to what she'd heard, had been her father's former hunting buddy and best friend.

Red was one of those people born into a family with money *and* a good name. His father owned several farm implement dealerships across the state and had left Red a large thriving ranch north of town.

As McCall parked, she could see Red having an early lunch at the counter. If anyone would know what had been going on with her father the day he died, it should be his best friend.

The smell of stale beer and floor cleaner hit her as McCall entered the dim bar. It was early enough that only a few of the regulars were occupying the stools along the bar.

"Red," she said by way of greeting as she neared his stool.

He gave her a nod, already wary. She assumed it was the uniform. According to stories she'd heard, Red had been a lot like her father in his younger days, both from money, both unable to keep trouble from finding them.

The difference was that Red had grown up.

Trace Winchester never got the chance.

"Buy you a beer?" she asked but didn't give him time to answer as she motioned to the bartender to bring them two of whatever he was having.

"Mind if we move over to a table?" she asked. "I'd like to talk with you."

He pushed away his plate, his burger finished, and got to his feet, although he didn't look anxious to talk to her. "What's this about?"

She took a table away from the regulars at the bar and sat down. Red reluctantly joined her.

"If this is about your mother and me—"

"My mother?" McCall couldn't help the surprise in her voice. Red Harper was one of the only men her mother's age who hadn't dated her after Trace had allegedly left town.

McCall had always wondered why.

"Your mother didn't tell you I asked her out?"

She shook her head. That too was strange. McCall had lived her mother's ups and downs with men and was always the first to hear when a new man came into Ruby's life—or left it.

"Sorry, but no. Ruby can take care of herself." If only that were true. McCall had seen her mother go through so many relationships that were obviously doomed from the beginning that she didn't try to warn her off certain men anymore.

McCall, though, couldn't help but wonder why Red had decided to ask her mother out now.

Their beers arrived. When the bartender left again, McCall picked up the frosty glass and took a sip of the icy cold beer.

Red seemed to relax a little. "So what's this about?"

"I just wanted to ask you about my dad. You probably knew him better than anyone."

He nodded and picked up his drink. "There was no one like Trace."

"Is it true he was as wild as people say?"

Red smiled, flushing a little. He was a handsome man with a full head of reddish-blond hair still free of gray, blue eyes and a great smile. McCall had always liked him.

"There's some truth to the stories." Red chuckled ruefully. "He was a good guy, though. He just liked to do what he wanted. He and I were a lot alike that way."

She took another drink of her beer and waited for Red to continue.

"He liked to fish and hunt and drink and chase women." Red seemed to realize what he'd said and quickly added, "Well, until your mother."

McCall had caught his slip-up. Why hadn't she thought that there might have been another woman in her father's life?

Ruby had been pregnant with McCall, wildly hormonal, according to her, and jealous as hell, if her other relationships were any indication.

Her mother's life was straight out of a country-and-western song. If there had been another woman in Trace Winchester's life, McCall shuddered to think how far her mother might have gone to make sure no woman took her man.

Red finished his beer in a hurry, realizing he'd messed up. "I'm sorry, but I have an appointment and really need to get going."

"Why *haven't* you asked my mother out before now?"

He looked startled by the question.

"Trace has been gone for twenty-seven years," she said.

Red smiled ruefully. "Gone, but not forgotten." He shook his head. "Couldn't compete, not with her expecting him to come back at any moment."

McCall realized that Red had been competing with a ghost, even if he hadn't known Trace was dead.

"You'd be good for Ruby," she said.

He smiled at that. "Another strike against me. But thanks for saying so."

As McCall came out of the bar, blinking at the bright sunlight, she found Luke Crawford leaning against his pickup, obviously waiting for her.

"McCall," he said with a tip of his hat.

She realized at once that he'd gotten wind of her digging into Trace's old arrests for poaching and other hunting violations.

Not that she wasn't surprised to see him.

Was it always going to be like this? Her heart taking off just at the sight of him? Looking for him every time she came into town, afraid he would just appear as he had now and catch her off guard?

He'd been gone for the past ten years—since they'd both graduated from high school. The ten years apart hadn't changed how she felt. All the hurt, humiliation and heartbreak were still there at just the sight of him.

"Been waitin' long?" she asked.

"Kind of early to be drinking," Luke joked.

She knew she must smell like the bar, a combination of old cigarette smoke and stale beer. Even with Montana bars going nonsmoking it would take years for the odor to go away inside some establishments.

"You haven't been waiting out here because you're worried about my drinking habits," she said, realizing someone in the state Fish and Game Department had to have tipped him off.

"This is awkward," he said. "I heard that you're looking into a few old poaching cases involving your father."

She bristled. While all law enforcement in this part of Montana helped each other when there was trouble, this was none of his business. "Do you have a problem with that?"

"If you're targeting my uncle for some reason it is."

Well, it was finally out in the open.

"Why? Do you think he has something to hide?"

Luke shook his head as if disgusted. She saw his jaw muscle tighten and realized he was trying to control his temper.

"Look," he said finally, "the trouble with our families was a long time ago—"

"My father disappeared twenty-seven years ago—the day after your uncle ticketed him."

Luke blinked. "You're blaming Buzz for your father skipping town? Buzz was just doing his job."

"Was he? I think Buzz Crawford's reputation speaks for itself."

"What the hell is that supposed to mean?"

She sighed. "Come on, Luke. You wouldn't have been out here waiting for me if you weren't worried that your uncle is guilty of something. You know Buzz. That's why you're concerned. That's why my checking on some of his old arrests has you waiting outside a bar for me."

"Buzz took his job seriously. There is nothing wrong with that."

She met his gaze. His eyes were a warm deep brown, his thick hair dark, much like her own. Like her, he had some Native American ancestry in his blood.

McCall remembered one time when a substitute grade school teacher had broken up a fight between Luke and another boy.

"All right, you little Apache, knock it off," the teacher had said, grabbing Luke by the scruff of his neck.

"I'm Chippewa," he'd said indignantly as she returned him to his seat.

McCall had remembered the pride in his voice and felt guilty because she had never taken pride in her own ancestry. But how could she with a father like Trace Winchester, the man everyone believed had deserted his pregnant wife and unborn child? Not to mention her grandmother, who denied McCall's very existence.

"Look, I've always hated the hostility between our families," Luke said now. "I don't want to see it stirred up all over again."

She would have liked to have told him that this had nothing to do with whatever problems there'd been between the two of them—or their families, but she wasn't sure of that.

"I know my uncle can be difficult, but he took me in and raised me when my parents died. I owe him. If he's in some kind of trouble…"

"It's sheriff's department business." The second time she'd lied today, but certainly not likely to be a record the way things were going. She started to step past him.

He grabbed her arm. His fingers on her flesh were like a branding iron. She flinched and he immediately let go.

"Sorry," he said, holding up his hand as if in surrender.

She said nothing, still stunned that Luke's touch could have that effect on her after all these years.

He took a step back, looking as shaken as she felt. Was it possible she wasn't the only one who'd felt it?

Pepper Winchester hadn't been able to rest since Mc-Call's visit. She hated the way she felt, her fear making her weak. She hated feeling weak, and worse, no longer in control.

"You should drink this," Enid said, appearing with a tray. On it was a glass of juice. "It will make you feel better."

Pepper knew there would be something in the juice that would make all this go away for a while. She and Enid had never talked about the drugs the housekeeper had been slipping her over the past twenty-seven years.

At first Pepper had been grateful, wanting to escape from her thoughts, her memories, the things she'd said and done, especially in regard to her son Trace.

She took the glass from the tray and turned back to the window where she'd been standing when Enid had sneaked up on her.

She'd never questioned why Enid drugged her. No doubt to make less work for herself and her husband, Alfred. Whatever Enid put into her juice had always knocked her out for at least twenty-four hours, sometimes more.

It would have been so easy to down the juice and let herself surrender to that peaceful nothingness state.

"I'll drink it after I have a little something to eat," Pepper said. "Perhaps a sandwich. Have we any turkey?"

"I've got some ham." Enid didn't sound happy about having to go back to the kitchen to make a sandwich and bring it all the way back up. "You should have eaten the breakfast I made you."

That was another problem with the drugs Enid gave her. They had allowed the power to shift from boss to employee over the years. Enid acted as if this were her house.

Turning to face her housekeeper, Pepper considered the elderly woman standing before her. Her first instinct was to fire her and her worthless husband. But she couldn't bear the thought of having to hire strangers and she couldn't go without help.

"Why don't I come down to the kitchen for the sandwich," Pepper said. "It will save you the extra trip."

Enid studied her for a moment, looking a little uneasy. "Whatever you want. I'm just here to make sure you're taken care of."

Yes, Pepper thought, wondering at how Enid had taken care of her and what she and her husband might have planned in the future. She realized she might not be safe. Especially if Enid thought for a moment that Pepper might ever reconcile with her children and grandchildren.

While there was no chance of that, McCall's visit might have the housekeeper and husband worried. Pepper saw now that she would have to be very careful from now on.

Later she would pretend to drink the juice but surreptitiously pour it down the drain. While her hired help thought she was asleep perhaps she would do some sneaking around of her own.

Chapter Six

Determined to put Luke Crawford out of her mind, Mc-Call concentrated on what Red had hinted at—that her father had a girlfriend. If anyone would have known, it was the woman her mother had worked with twenty-seven years ago.

Patty Mason had been slinging hash as long as Ruby Bates Winchester. The two had worked together from the time they were teenagers until about the time Mc-Call was born.

Patty had gone to work at the Hi-Line Café and it was there that McCall found her after the lunch crowd had cleared out. Patty was the opposite of Ruby. While Ruby was skin and bone, Patty was round and plump with bulbous cheeks.

She smiled as McCall came in and took a seat at one of the empty booths. "Just coffee, please, and if you have a minute, join me."

Patty glanced around the empty café and laughed before pouring two cups and bringing them to the table. She squeezed into the booth, kicked off her shoes, put her feet up on the seat and leaned back against the wall.

"This is the first second I've had to put my aching dogs up all day," Patty said, wiggling her toes. "So how you doin', girl? How's your mama? I never see her any-more. Hell, probably cuz we both work all the time."

"Ruby's good." As good as Ruby ever got, McCall thought.

"She seeing anyone?" Patty was on her third marriage, this time to an elderly rancher. They had a place to the north of town on the road to Canada.

"Red Harper." This came as no surprise, McCall saw, since Patty would have already heard through the White-horse grapevine. McCall was the only one out of the loop apparently.

"You know I always thought she and Red would end up together," Patty said with a chuckle. "Sure has taken him long enough though, huh."

McCall's thought exactly. "I was hoping you could help me with something," she said, getting right to the point. "Were you working with Ruby the morning Trace disappeared?"

Patty slid her feet from the booth seat and sat up, blinking. "My goodness, girl, that was so long ago."

"Ruby said she was working the early shift."

"That's right. You know I *do* remember. It was a crazy day. We got in a busload of Canadians down here for a whist tournament." She frowned. "Wow, how many years ago was that now?"

"Twenty-seven."

"My memory is better than I thought." Patty grinned. "I remember because your mama came in late. I really had my hands full. I knew she was sick, being pregnant with you and all, but I was so mad at her."

"Did she say why she was late?" McCall asked.

"She was all rattled, you know how she gets. It was plain as her face that she and Trace had had another fight.

I wondered if she'd been to bed at all the night before, everything considered, you know?"

McCall didn't know. "Such as?"

"Well…" Patty looked uncomfortable. "The way she looked. She'd been crying and that old pickup she drove… It was covered in mud. I asked her where the devil she'd been since your mama wasn't one for driving much, especially on these roads around here when they're wet."

McCall thought of the road into the ridge south of town. "And what did she say?"

"Said Trace borrowed her truck." Patty mugged a face. "I knew that wasn't true. He never drove anything but that pretty new black Chevy his mama bought him as a bribe to leave Ruby. He took a perverse satisfaction into getting that truck dirty and staying with Ruby just to show his mama he couldn't be bought."

McCall had wondered where Trace had gotten the pickup. Now she knew. Her dear grandmother.

"So where do you think Ruby had been in her pickup?"

Patty shook her head. "You could ask her."

"She gets upset talking about Trace."

"I suppose so. Well, just between you and me, I think she'd been out looking for Trace after a big, ol' knock-down, drag-out fight," Patty whispered, although there was no one to hear. "She was upset that whole day. I felt bad for her. One look at her and you knew something big had happened. I think your mama knew he wouldn't be coming back."

RUBY CAME HOME late smelling of grease and cigarette smoke. McCall had been waiting for her. Her mother looked tired and there were blue lines on her calves from spending so many years on her feet.

McCall felt sorry for her mother and guilty. How different Ruby's life might have been if she hadn't gotten pregnant. Just as things could have been different if Trace had lived.

Or things could have turned out just the way they had.

"Didn't you work today?" her mother asked.

Had Ruby heard about her visit with Red Harper and thought McCall was checking up on her? "Nick had something come up and asked me to fill in for him."

Ruby glanced over at her as she entered her trailer, and McCall saw worry in her mother's eyes. All the questions about her father. The visit to her grandmother. Talking to Red about Trace. Now to find McCall waiting here for her. No wonder Ruby looked worried.

"I had a beer earlier with Red to talk to him about my father," McCall said as they entered the trailer, figuring Red had already warned Ruby. "You didn't tell me the two of you were going out."

Her mother shrugged. "It's just a date to a movie." She turned to look at her daughter and for a moment McCall thought her mother might cry. "Am I why you don't date?" Ruby asked, the question coming out of the blue.

She squirmed under her mother's intense gaze. "There's no one I want to go out with."

"There hasn't been anyone since that Crawford boy."

"I've been busy."

"Not *that* busy."

"Mom—"

"Fine. I know that boy broke your heart, but, McCall, it was years ago. You have to get back on the horse that bucked you off."

McCall laughed. That was exactly what her mother had been doing since her husband left her. "And how has that worked out for you? Have any of these men you dated made you forget my father?"

This time there was no doubt about the tears in her mother's eyes.

"I'm sorry. I—"

"No, you're right," Ruby said with a shake of her head. "I keep looking for what I had with Trace." She smiled ruefully as she swiped at her tears. "What else can I do, baby? At least the man you're in love with is still around and available. That should tell you something. If you weren't so stubborn—"

"You don't know anything about it."

"Don't I? I know what that boy did to you. He broke your heart. Just like your daddy broke mine." Her mother turned away and said, "You want some coffee?"

"No, thanks," McCall said as she watched her mother go into the kitchen to pour herself what was left of the coffee and reheat it in the microwave.

"Mom, I'm sorry, but I need to ask about my father."

"Fine, let's get this over with," Ruby said as she leaned against the counter and blew on her coffee to cool it. "Then I mean it, McCall, I don't want to hear any more about him, okay?"

McCall hated this, but she was afraid her mother might have found out about another woman and done something desperate, something she'd regretted all these years.

"All these years I've heard rumors, whispers behind my back, about my father. Now I need to know the truth. Was there another woman?"

Ruby put down her coffee, angry now. "You heard Trace chased girls the way some dogs chase cars, right?"

"Is it true? Did he cheat on you?" McCall knew her mother. No way would Ruby have just taken that lying down, and after what Patty had told her, McCall didn't like what she'd been thinking.

Ruby made another swipe at the tears that brimmed in her lashes. "There was talk. Your father swore there was nothing going on."

"Going on with whom?"

Ruby shifted on her feet, wrapping her arms around herself again, her mouth pinched. "Geneva Cavanaugh. She'd dumped him to marry Russ Cherry before Trace and I got together. He took it hard. Then Russ got killed and Geneva disappeared, leaving behind her two babies."

"My father didn't run away with Geneva Cherry, Mom." She could see that this had been her mother's fear for the past twenty-seven years.

Ruby began to cry. "You don't know that. They both disappeared about the same time."

McCall thought about the single grave. Wouldn't the killer have buried them together? Maybe not. The pickup was still missing, and who knew what was inside it?

"Someone would have heard from them by now if they'd run away together," she said, just for something to say.

Ruby shrugged.

"Was there anyone else?" McCall had to ask.

Her mother looked away. "Sandy."

"Sandy?"

"After Geneva, Trace was dating Sandy Thompson. That's when he and I got together."

"Sandy *Thompson* Sheridan?" The sheriff's wife? Her boss's wife? McCall stared at her mother. "You *stole* Trace from her?"

"I didn't *steal* him. You can't steal men like candy from a grocery store. I was in love with Trace. I'd always *loved* him."

"So all was fair in love and war," McCall quipped. Her mother never ceased to amaze her. This explained a lot, she realized. The cold shoulder Sandy had always given her.

Grant and Sandy had gotten married right after high school and gone away to college together. Grant became a lawyer, Sandy a homemaker. When they'd returned to Whitehorse, Grant became county attorney. Sandy had gotten involved in social activities.

McCall closed her eyes, seeing things too clearly. "You *seduced* him."

"Haven't you ever wanted anything more than life itself?"

McCall hated that Luke Crawford instantly came to mind.

"That was how I felt about your father. I would have done anything to be with him."

"Even get pregnant." McCall opened her eyes. Hadn't she long suspected this was the case?

Her mother's face fell. "Yes. Now you know the truth. I got pregnant to take him away from Sandy and force him to marry *me*."

So Pepper Winchester had been right.

Ruby was crying again. "I thought…" She stepped over to a chair and dropped into it, pulling her knees up to wrap her skinny arms around them, holding on as if for dear life. "I thought once we were a family, once you were born…" Her voice trailed off. She sniffed and McCall handed her a tissue from the box by the couch. "I guess I got what I deserved. The bad karma came back and bit me in the ass."

"You didn't deserve what you got," McCall said, fearing the killer might not agree. "Let me understand this. Trace and Sandy didn't break up until it came out about your pregnancy? How did Sandy take this news?"

Her mother mugged a face. "Sandy said Trace and I ruined her life but she seems to have survived just fine, lives in that big house up on the hill, married to the sheriff. Married him right after Trace broke up with her."

McCall frowned, unnerved by the timing. How hurt and angry had Sandy been? Hurt and angry enough to take it out on Trace?

"Mom, isn't it possible Sandy loved my father as much as you did?"

Ruby scoffed at that. "Trace was the love of my life. You haven't seen me marry anyone else, have you? It sure didn't take Sandy long to get over Trace, did it?"

Maybe that was because Trace was dead to her. Dead and buried.

Another thought struck McCall, one that sent a chill through her. Sandy had obviously married Grant on the rebound. He had to have realized that. Which brought up the question: how had Sheriff Grant Sheridan felt about Trace Winchester?

LUKE PARKED IN the shadows of the towering cottonwoods. As he got out, the breeze carried the scent of the new leaves that had just started coming out on the trees. They fluttered, making a sound like a whisper.

In the distance, a hawk let out a cry, and the forest paralleling the river fell silent. Twilight had settled into the cottonwoods. Through the thick bare branches, he could see the colors of the sunset deepening against the darkening sky.

It was early for poachers, but he'd noticed that this poaching ring seemed to be hitting at different times.

The quiet in the river bottom lulled him, his thoughts sneaking up on him as he walked along a fishing trail. There were times that he was at his most vulnerable, like now, and his thoughts turned to McCall.

She hadn't changed much from the girl he'd fallen in love with. If anything she was more beautiful. And headstrong and independent and prickly as a porcupine. She'd done just fine for herself without any help from anyone.

What was crazy was that he believed in his heart that they belonged together. If it wasn't for what had happened back when they were seniors in high school—

The sound of the rifle shot made him jump. The soft boom carried along the river bottom sending a flock of ducks rising up in a spray of water nearby.

He froze, listening, anticipating a second shot, hoping he would be able to determine which direction it had come from. The second shot came seconds later, followed by a quick third, then silence.

Luke took off running through the trees to where he'd parked his pickup. From his estimation, the shots had come from a quarter mile downriver.

At his pickup, he jumped behind the wheel and took off down the road, knowing they would hear him coming.

By now at least one of them should be up to his elbows in blood from gutting out the deer they'd shot. They would hear his pickup engine and have to decide whether to load up the deer or just make a run for it.

Either way, he would have them if their tire treads matched the plaster casts he'd made of their last three kills.

The poachers were getting more brazen, killing one

deer after another even though they must know he was tracking them. That kind of boldness often ended badly.

As he raced along the narrow windy dirt road that ran parallel to the river, Luke wished he'd taken the time to pull on his bulletproof vest. The men he was chasing would be armed.

As he came around a bend, he saw a pickup come barreling out of one of the many fishing access roads in a cloud of dust. All he was able to tell about the truck was that it was dark colored and an older model.

As Luke hit his lights and siren, he saw through the dust that one of the poachers was in the back of the truck—and the man wasn't alone.

The rising dust from the pickup made it impossible to ID the man, though—or get a license plate number on the fleeing vehicle.

As the truck took one of the tight, narrow curves too fast, Luke heard the screech of metal as a fender skinned one of the cottonwoods at the edge of the road. An instant later something large came tumbling out of the back of the truck.

Luke slammed on his brakes, skidding to a stop just inches from the carcass lying in the middle of the road.

For a heart-stopping moment, he'd thought the poacher had fallen out of the back of the pickup. But then he smelled the familiar scent of the animal's blood on the breeze—the dead deer blocking the road.

In the distance, the pickup disappeared over a rise as he watched, the poachers getting away. Again.

SANDY SHERIDAN LIVED with her husband, Grant, in a house up on the hill overlooking Whitehorse. The houses up here were newer. In Whitehorse, moving from the older homes to the hill was considered a step up in both lifestyle and status.

McCall parked in front of a split-level much like the others on the hill. She'd waited until the sheriff had left for a sheriffs' conference in Billings.

Even though it was late, Sandy Sheridan answered the door still wearing her robe and slippers, both white and fluffy. Her hair was sprayed into an updo that not even one of Whitehorse's stiff breezes could dislodge.

She'd applied fresh makeup, her cheeks looking flushed, eyes bright and ringed with mascara. McCall wondered what she was getting so duded up for at this time of the day. Or for whom.

"If you're looking for Grant, he's not here. He's at—"

"The Montana Sheriffs' Association meeting in Billings. I know. Actually it's you I wanted to see," McCall said.

"Oh?" Sandy was her mother's age, early forties, but the years had been kinder. "I guess I can spare a few minutes," she said, glancing at her watch, clearly annoyed as she stepped back to let McCall enter the house.

The house was furnished with pale furniture against white walls and drapes, giving the place a sterilized, cold feel.

"I'd offer you something to drink but—"

"I'm here about you and Trace Winchester," McCall said, cutting to the chase.

Sandy looked as if she'd just slammed her fingers in a car door. She opened her mouth but nothing came out. Earlier she'd been standing, looking impatient, now she lowered herself into a nearby off-white club chair.

"I beg your pardon?" she said.

"Oh, I'm sorry. I'd heard that you were in love with him, and I'm talking to people who knew my father."

Sandy let out a nervous laugh. "Why? That was high school."

"Some people never get over high school—or their first loves." As McCall knew only too well. "Look, I know you were dating my father when my mother got pregnant with me."

Sandy's face stiffened in anger belying her words. "That is ancient history. I really don't have the time to—"

"I should have known what I heard wasn't true. If you'd been that much in love with my father, you wouldn't have married Grant so quickly."

"I *loved* Trace," Sandy snapped, taking the bait. "We were going to get married, but then your mother…" She waved a hand through the air, hurriedly regaining her composure.

"You're *still* in love with my father," McCall said, unable to contain her shock. What was it about the man that made women love him so desperately even after everything he did to them?

Sandy looked away. "Don't be silly. That was—"

"Twenty-seven years ago. Not even time can change some things, though, huh."

"I really don't want to talk to you about this," she said, getting to her feet. "It isn't any of your business or your mother's."

Unfortunately, McCall feared it just might be. "You must have hated Trace for betraying you the way he did," she said as she rose to leave.

"I was angry. Who wouldn't be?"

"I think I would have wanted to kill him."

Sandy said nothing, her expression though said it all.

"I can see that he hurt you terribly. I'm sorry."

Tears filled the older woman's eyes. She brushed at them, obviously embarrassed and angry, and now her mascara was running.

"You've brought up a painful time in my life," Sandy said. "But that's all behind me. As you can see, I did quite well without Trace Winchester."

McCall stared at her, seeing a miserably unhappy woman behind the perfectly made-up face. "Yes, I can see that."

"Now if you don't mind…"

"What about Grant?" McCall asked, stopping at the door. "Does he know you never got over my father?"

Sandy opened the door. "Why are you asking about this after all these years? Does my husband know you're here?" She fumbled in the pocket of her robe for her cell phone.

"Don't worry, I'm leaving," McCall said, stepping past her. "I wouldn't want to make you late for your… *appointment*."

As she left, McCall glimpsed a car parked under a large old tree at the far end of the dead end street. Sandy hadn't needed to call her husband. He already knew about McCall's visit. Grant had apparently lied to both of them about going to the sheriffs' meeting.

But as McCall drove away, she wondered who Grant had been spying on—*her* or his wife.

Luke lay on the bed in his small camper trailer, unable to fall sleep. He'd planned to take a nap before staking out a spot on the river later tonight.

Through his bedroom window he could see the dark skeleton of his house and hear the breeze whispering through the beams as clouds scudded past in the gathering dusk.

He blamed McCall for his restlessness. The woman haunted his thoughts, making him ache with a need he hadn't been able to fill with any other woman. Had he thought the years would have changed McCall's mind about him? Or her feelings?

At times like this, he'd always turned to his work. He forced his thoughts to the poachers' pickup and how close he'd come to catching them earlier. He'd only gotten a glimpse of the truck as it came flying out of the fishing access, dust billowing.

The pickup was somewhere between brown and a rusted red. A good fifty years old. Something from the late fifties, early sixties. A beater. If he had to guess, he'd say a '62 Ford.

There were more than a few around in this part of the country. Hell, Buzz even used to own one.

Maybe he still did.

Luke sat up with a curse. He hadn't seen Buzz's old pickup for years. It used to be parked in the back of that old barn behind Buzz's lake house. Hell, it probably didn't even run anymore.

He swore again. He knew he wouldn't get any sleep if he didn't find out if that truck was still there. Buzz hadn't driven it in years. But that didn't mean someone else hadn't.

It was crazy. Or maybe not so crazy. He thought about that night years ago when he and Eugene had taken the pickup on a joyride. Buzz always kept the keys in the truck's ignition. Since the barn was a good distance from the lake house, they'd had no trouble taking out the pickup—and returning it—without Buzz being the wiser.

Luke had this crazy idea that someone might be using Buzz's pickup to poach deer. The irony didn't escape him. Nor would it have someone like Trace Winchester, who would have loved to rub it in Buzz's face.

Irony? Or payback?

It was dark by the time Luke parked on the road behind his uncle's old barn and killed the engine. He sat for a moment listening to the sounds of the night before he grabbed his flashlight and climbed out.

The moon was a sliver of white against the darkening sky. A few stars glittered through the veil of clouds. A breeze carried the distinct odors of the lake. Through the trees he could see the lake house. No vehicle parked next to it. Buzz wasn't home.

He breathed in the familiar scents, asking himself what the hell he was doing here about to creep around like a cat burglar.

But as he neared the old wooden structure he knew the reason he hadn't waited was that he didn't want Buzz to know. No reason to set his uncle off when Luke was probably wrong about the pickup being the one he'd seen the poachers driving.

He reached the back side of the barn before he turned on the flashlight. The lake house was on the opposite side. Even if Buzz happened to return, he wouldn't be able to see the light or hear anything from the house.

Luke slipped through the space between the two hinged barn doors. Dust motes danced in the flashlight beam that barely penetrated the dark, vast interior.

The barn still smelled of hay and manure even though it hadn't been used for either hay or livestock in years.

At a rustling sound, Luke swung around, leading with the beam of the flashlight. A cat scurried out the gap in the doors. As the dust and his heart settled back down, he probed the dark recesses of the barn with the paltry beam of the flashlight.

Luke shone the light into the dark corner where the '62 Ford pickup was always parked.

Empty.

He stared at the hole where the truck had been parked for so many years. He'd been wrong. Relief swept over him, letting him finally admit that he'd thought Eugene might have been using the old pickup.

But when had Buzz gotten rid of it? And maybe more important, whom had he sold it to?

As Luke ran the beam over the space where the truck had been parked, he noticed the faint tire tracks in the dust. The pickup hadn't been gone that long. No, not that long at all, he thought as he squatted down to touch a dark spot on the dirt floor of the barn.

The spot where the pickup had recently dripped oil was still wet.

McCALL LEFT SANDY'S, surprised how dark it had gotten. Clouds skimmed just over the treetops, the limbs whipping in the wind.

The air was damp with the promise of rain and the growing darkness heavy and oppressive. Her headlights did little to hold back the night as she left the lights of Whitehorse in her rearview mirror and drove toward her cabin on the river.

She was tired, bone weary and sick at heart. She'd forced her mother to bare her soul and found out things about her father that she'd never wanted to know.

He's dead, McCall, why can't you just let it go?

Because she couldn't. Just as she couldn't get over

Luke Crawford. She'd never believed in all that first love stuff that made good television movies. But Luke had been her first love, her only love.

Sometimes she thought about what her life would have been like if things had worked out for them. They could be married now, might even be parents.

She had a sudden image of Luke holding a baby and felt her eyes blur with tears. She rubbed them, telling herself she should be watching for deer along this stretch of narrow two-lane dirt road that wound through the large, old cottonwoods along the river, instead of bawling over what might have been.

But the night reminded her of another night ten years ago, the night she gave herself to Luke Crawford next to a small campfire beside the river. It had been the first time for both of them and so amazing that she'd known then no other man would make her feel the way Luke had.

That was the night he'd told her he loved her and wanted to marry her. She'd been so young and naive, she'd believed him, she thought now. And yet he'd been so tender, so loving—

As she came around a bend in the road, a vehicle came careening out of one of the fishing access roads. She saw the dust in her headlights an instant before she saw the vehicle.

The fool was driving without his headlights on.

She'd barely recognized that fact when the driver of the vehicle flashed on his headlights—and headed directly at her.

Chapter Seven

Luke couldn't shake his uneasy feeling as he left his uncle's barn and headed down the narrow, dirt river road. He caught glimpses of the moon through the tall cottonwoods. Clouds skimmed past overhead giving the night a surreal feel.

When he'd stopped by his uncle's cabin for a moment, he'd thought he heard the sound of a vehicle in the distance. Buzz hardly ventured anywhere other than town occasionally and then only during the day. It seemed strange that he wasn't home tonight.

Luke tried his uncle's cell phone. It went straight to voice mail. He didn't leave a message.

He'd waited for a few minutes, thinking Buzz would be home any minute, and then left, worried about what he'd discovered in the barn. He'd made a cast of the tire tracks but he hadn't needed to compare it with the other casts he'd taken from poaching sites. The distinct tracks in the dust had matched the ones from the poachers' vehicle. Someone was using Buzz's truck to poach deer, and Luke had a pretty good idea who that person was. As for Eugene's accomplice, it could be any one of his lowlife friends.

As Luke rounded a curve in the road, he saw headlights at an odd angle. His heart thundered in his chest as he recognized the pickup in the ditch. McCall?

Pulling over, he grabbed his flashlight and jumped out. The pickup's front tires were on the road, headlights angled upward, the back tires buried in the dirt of the deep, narrow ditch.

From the dust still settling on the road, Luke guessed that the accident had just happened. All he could think was that it was a wonder she hadn't rolled the truck as he rushed to the driver's side and jerked open the door, the dome light coming on.

"McCall, are you—" He never got the words "all right" out.

She came out of the pickup swinging. He felt the sharp smack of her palm against the side of his face before he could restrain her.

"What in the hell?" he demanded as he looked into her eyes, saw the fear and the anger. But it was the fear that changed everything. He'd never seen her afraid before. He remembered the only other time he'd seen her vulnerable and, like now, she'd been in his arms.

She tried to take another swing, but he had her arms pinned down. Her mouth opened to say something, but her words were lost as his mouth dropped to hers. She struggled, but only for a moment.

He felt the fight go out of her as if, like him, she'd lost herself in the kiss—just the way she had all those years ago.

Then as if reason came back to her, she shoved him away. She was breathing hard, and he couldn't tell if it was from the kiss or her earlier anger.

"You bastard," she said on a ragged breath.

"It was just a kiss, McCall." A lie. That powerful thing

between them couldn't have been more evident. For those amazing moments, she'd been kissing him back, but that could have been enough to make her even angrier.

She advanced on him. He could still feel the sting of her slap and thought for a moment she would try to hit him again.

"You ran me off the road!"

He stared at her in the glow of the lights coming from their headlights and the dome light inside her open pickup door. "Whoa. I found you in the ditch. Are you saying someone purposely ran you off the road?"

She narrowed her gaze at him. "Not someone. *You.* If you think you can scare me away from investigating your uncle—"

"Are you crazy? You can't believe I would purposely try to run you off the road. Let alone that I would try to interfere in your investigation." He saw her expression. "Yeah, I guess you can. Why should you believe me? You've never believed anything I've ever told you. Not ten years ago. Not now. My mistake for thinking you needed my help."

She took a breath and let it out slowly before glancing down the dark road. "You didn't just come flying out of that fishing access site directly at me?"

He shook his head, too angry with her and himself to speak. Why the hell had he kissed her? He'd only managed to make things worse. But once he had her in his arms, he hadn't been able to help himself.

"Then where is the other pickup?" she demanded.

"I have no idea."

"I thought…" She stared at him as if really seeing him. "The headlights came right at me, I swerved and lost control and when I looked up…"

"There I was," he said.

"I'm sorry, I guess…"

If it had been anyone other than McCall, he might have thought the driver imagined another truck. Or had been unintentionally run off the road by someone.

But this was McCall.

"I saw dust as I came around the corner," he said, trying to remember the scene before he'd realized it was McCall's pickup and lost all reason. "I just assumed you'd made the dust when you crashed in the ditch."

"A pickup came right at me."

He felt himself start. "You saw that it was a pickup?"

"The headlights. They were high, so maybe I only got the *impression* it was a truck. Wait, no, I remember the way the back of the vehicle spun out as it turned onto the river road and came toward me. It was a pickup."

As Luke looked down the dark road, a sliver of fear burrowed under his skin. He doubted it was a coincidence that he'd been looking for a pickup, heard a vehicle as he was leaving Buzz's—and one had just run McCall off the road.

What worried him was the fear that the pickup—and McCall being run off the road—had something to do with not only Buzz's truck, but also his uncle.

McCall hugged herself against the cold Montana April night and the emotions Luke Crawford had set off like fireworks inside her.

He made her heart beat too fast, her pulse race, her body ache. He had when she was seventeen. He was even more desirable now, she thought, remembering the feel of his arms around her and the kiss. She reminded herself that this was the man who'd broken her heart, but that old bitterness didn't have the bite it used to.

"I'm sorry I accused you of running me off the road."

He was standing so close she could smell his woodsy male scent. She could see that her accusation had hurt more than the slap.

She hugged herself tighter at the memory of his arms around her, the solid, strong feel of his body, his mouth on hers. "And I'm sorry I hit you."

His gaze locked with hers. "I'm sorry I kissed you."

Damn the man. She wanted to smack him again.

"Yes, I'm sorry you did, too."

"I should get my tow rope," he said, clearly upset. "I think I can pull you out with my truck."

She nodded and felt something break inside her as he brushed past her, anger in every line of his body. "Thanks," she said.

He mumbled something under his breath she couldn't hear as he headed for his truck.

McCall leaned against the cold metal of her pickup and stared at his broad back silhouetted against his head-lights. How could she have thought he would want to hurt her? Because he'd hurt her before.

She took a deep breath of the cold night air and, touching her finger to her lips, felt her traitorous heart quicken at the memory of the kiss.

His kiss had brought back the past in one fell swoop. That night beside the campfire, the stars glittering over-head, the night she'd been seventeen and so wonderfully in love.

Her skin ached at the memory of their lovemaking beside the campfire.

"McCall? You ready?"

Lost in the past, she started at the sound of his voice. Hurriedly, she climbed back behind the wheel and slammed her pickup door.

With a jolt, she realized that she'd been so shaken earlier she hadn't bothered to turn off the engine. Her hands trembled as she was reminded of the near head-on collision before she'd swerved and lost control, ending up in the ditch.

It could have been so much worse.

She saw that Luke had turned his truck around, hooked up the tow rope and was just waiting for her to give him a signal that she was ready.

She whirred down her window. "Ready when you are."

He gave her a thumbs-up before disappearing into the cab of his truck. She waited as he pulled forward, the tow rope tightening until she felt the tension stretch between them.

All these years of being apart and now they'd been thrown together how many times in the past two days? If she believed in fate…

When she felt the tow rope grow taut, she gave her truck some gas. She could hear the dirt and gravel scrape against the undercarriage, then she was hauled up and out of the ditch and onto the road, forced to hit her brakes to keep from running into the back of Luke's pickup.

Putting the truck in Park, she got out and stood between their two rigs as he unhooked the tow rope, trying not to notice the way the fabric of his shirt stretched over the hard muscles of his shoulders. "About earlier—"

"Forget it," he said, rising to his feet with the tow rope coiled in his hands.

If only she could forget.

"If you remember anything about the truck that ran you off the road…"

"Sure," she said, although she knew that wasn't going to happen. All she'd seen was dust, then bright headlights.

"I'm glad you're all right."

Both feet firmly planted on the ground. That was her.

He turned and started toward his pickup, all broad shoulders, long legs, slim hips and cowboy boots. But it was the way he moved, a long, lanky swagger…

"Luke?"

He stopped and looked back at her, waiting though wary.

"Nothing," she said. "Just…thanks."

He nodded, climbed into his pickup and drove away, leaving her wanting to pound her head against the side of her truck.

LUKE KNEW HE had to be dreaming because McCall lay next to him on the bed in his new house—the one he hadn't finished building, let alone moved into.

She was in his arms, her body warm and silky soft, scented with the sweet smells of summer. Her limbs were lightly suntanned, a sprinkling of freckles along the tops of her shoulders and the bridge of her nose.

He drew her closer, breathing her in, amazed that he hadn't lost her. He didn't question how it was that she was here with him. All those years apart seemed to melt away and he knew in his heart that this was where McCall was destined to be—with him.

Something jarred him. He closed his eyes tighter, fighting whatever was trying to pull him from the dream, knowing that the moment he came fully awake, McCall would be gone. Gone, just as she had been for the past ten years. Only this time, lost to him forever.

The ringing of his cell phone dragged him up from the dream. He stirred, still keeping his eyes closed, still fighting that moment when he would know for certain it had all just been a dream.

The phone rang again. Luke cursed and opened his eyes. The bed next to him was cold and empty.

He rolled over and snatched up the phone. "Luke Crawford." His gaze went to the lighted clock next to his bed—3:00 a.m.

And he knew even before he heard the rancher's voice that the poachers had hit again.

McCALL WOKE BEFORE DAWN. She blamed Luke Crawford for another fitful night. Showered and dressed, too antsy to sit around, she went out to examine her pickup to make sure there was no real damage.

The rear bumper was dented and filled with dirt and grass from the ditch, but apparently no real damage. With a shudder she remembered seeing the huge cottonwood trees that lined the road, fearing she couldn't get control of the pickup before plowing into them.

She was just thankful she had only ended up in the ditch. No harm done.

If only she could say as much for Luke's kiss. Damn him.

Desperately needing to get him off her mind, she got in her pickup and drove south on Highway 191. It wasn't until she'd gone a few miles that she realized she'd be driving right past his house.

She'd heard he'd bought the old Crawford place that had belonged to his parents before their deaths. Buzz had sold it to an out-of-state corporation when he took Luke in.

But when Luke had returned to town, he'd somehow been able to buy it back. She'd heard he was living in a camp trailer on the property while he built a house.

At this early hour, she was tempted to drive down to his trailer and wake him up. If she couldn't get any rest, it didn't seem fair that he should. As the saying went, misery loves company.

But she had no desire to see him. Especially after their encounter last night.

Clouds low, rain threatening, she drove another few miles before she turned off on the road that led to the ridge where she'd found her father's grave.

A cold wind rocked the patrol SUV as she sat staring at the muddy grave—and a dozen footprints around it. She'd known this would happen once Rocky told people about it. Grave robbers had scoured the area looking for curios or clues to go with their theories on whose body had been buried there.

McCall told herself it would have been worse if she'd told the sheriff about the hunting license and cordoned off the grave with crime scene tape. Everyone in town would have had to come out and see for themselves. She had to be content with the fact that she'd gotten any evidence there was and turned it all in to the lab.

Except for the hunting license.

Taking her binoculars, she climbed out and walked along the spine of the ridge. It worried her what her mother had said about Geneva Cherry disappearing about the same time as Trace.

As she walked, she looked for signs of another grave

but saw no place to bury another body. The ridge was rocky except for the area where her father had been buried.

So if Geneva had been with Trace that day and someone had gotten rid of them both, the killer hadn't buried them both here. Why bury one and not the other? Because Geneva's disappearance and Trace's weren't related? Unless Geneva had been the killer.

McCall walked out to where the ridge narrowed to a windy point. She raised her binoculars, wondering if her father had stood on this very spot looking through his rifle scope for antelope on opening day of the season.

As the Winchester Ranch came into view, McCall realized with a start that he could have been watching the house, could have maybe even seen people inside that morning.

Today the old lodge looked dark and cold under the cloak of clouds, lifeless behind the blank windows and weathered shutters.

A tumbleweed blew past on a gust, the wind howling around her, as McCall lowered her binoculars and wondered where a person might get rid of a large black Chevy pickup.

Sage- and pine-studded ridges ran out to rocky points as the land fell for miles toward the Missouri River. All those ravines. Wasn't it possible the pickup had been dumped in one? As wild as this country was it could have gone unnoticed for years.

But not twenty-seven years. Someone would have spotted it from the air or a hunter would have stumbled across it. Trace Winchester's pickup would have been known around the county—just as his antics were.

Where then? Where could you hide a vehicle so that it would never be found? She scanned the remote countryside, turning slowly in a circle, studying this unforgiving landscape.

Had the killer lured Trace out here, planning to kill him? Or had Trace's death been impulsive? Possibly even an accident? If it had been a hunting accident, why wouldn't the shooter have reported it—instead of burying the body and disposing of the pickup and rifle?

The ridge was far enough from Highway 191 that the killer wouldn't have been seen while burying the body. No need to hurry and yet the killer hadn't taken the time to dig a very deep grave. Nor had the killer taken the time to move the body to a better burial site.

Neither indicated premeditation.

So after digging a shallow grave and burying the body, then what?

Her father hadn't been out here alone. But had the killer ridden out here with him in his pickup? Or had the killer met him here? Either way, the killer needed to dispose of Trace's pickup quickly since it was so recognizable.

He would have probably gotten rid of the pickup, then come back and gotten his own rig as long as he didn't have to take the pickup far. He couldn't chance someone seeing Trace's truck, and since the only way out of here was Highway 191—

In the distance, McCall spotted something that made her pulse jump. Water the color of rust.

She focused the binoculars on the spot, her heart pounding as she saw a stock pond. Not just a stock pond, but one visible from her father's grave. The killer could have seen it or even known it was there.

How much water would it take to hide a pickup? Eight feet minimum, she estimated. As she started to lower the binoculars a windmill caught her eye and past it, a set of corrals.

She felt light-headed as she realized whose place she was looking at. The old Crawford ranch, where Luke Crawford was now building his house.

Over the wind and her thundering heart, McCall didn't hear the vehicle pull in. Nor did she hear someone approach from behind her until she felt the hand drop to her shoulder.

Chapter Eight

McCall jumped, startled. She spun around, her hand going to her holster, stopping short of her weapon as she recognized the man now standing on the lone ridge with her.

"I thought I might find you out here," Sheriff Grant Sheridan said, raising his voice to be heard over the wind. Frown lines deepened the furrows between his brows as the first drops of rain splashed down, hard and cold. "Let's talk in my rig."

McCall followed him back through the rain to his patrol SUV parked next to her pickup and climbed in, wondering how he'd known she'd be here, let alone why he'd driven way out here to look for her.

"What's up?" she asked, shaking raindrops off as she settled into the seat.

He started the engine, turning on the wipers and the heater. Rain pounded the roof and pinged off the hood.

"You tell me," he said as he looked past the rain and the rhythmic slap of the wipers toward the ridge. The rain slanted down in angry slashes, pelting the puddles already forming in the mud in front of the SUV. Fortunately the road back to the highway was rocky or they might have trouble getting out of here.

"I didn't realize you could see the Winchester Ranch from here," he said finally and glanced pointedly at the binoculars on the strap around her neck.

McCall followed his gaze to the ranch in the distance, but said nothing, her apprehension growing. Was this about Pepper Winchester?

That could explain why Grant looked worried. "Is there anything you want to tell me?" he asked.

"You mean, what I'm doing out here?" she asked, going on the defensive, fearing what had brought him all this way. "I wanted to check the site before my shift. Just as I figured, some locals have been out here digging around."

"But there wasn't anything to find, right?"

"I did a thorough search of the area the first time," she said, afraid of where this was going. "If there was anything to find, I found it."

The sheriff sighed. "McCall," he said his voice softening. "I got a call from the crime lab this morning."

She closed her eyes, surprised she was fighting tears even though she knew what the results of the DNA test were going to prove. She'd known the moment she'd found her father's hunting license in the muddy grave.

She heard the rustle of papers and opened her eyes to look over at him. He had his head down and she saw the faxed report now lying on his lap.

The patrol SUV suddenly felt too small. She lowered her window a few inches even though the cold rain blew in soaking one side of her to the skin.

"According to the report, the bones are from a male in his early twenties," Grant said without looking at her. "The lab estimates the body has been in the ground for the past twenty-five to thirty years. But I would imagine none of this comes as a surprise to you, does it."

"What about the DNA?" McCall asked, her voice breaking. "Was it a match?"

His gaze softened as he looked over at her and nodded. "I'm sorry."

Her eyes burned.

Grant cleared his throat. "I can't imagine that this was just a hunch on your part. How did you know?"

"I found my father's hunting license where the body had been buried before the rainstorm washed the remains down into the gully," she said quietly. "The license was still in the orange plastic case."

"You knew it was a probable murder scene and yet—"

"I documented everything I found with photos," she said quickly. "I treated it as a murder scene."

"You withheld evidence."

"I couldn't be sure until the DNA report came back."

He was shaking his head, clearly angry and disappointed in her. "You're my first female deputy. Do you realize how hard I had to fight to get you on the force?"

She could imagine. "I appreciate that. But he was my father, I had—"

"You're a deputy first and foremost. The moment you found this you should have roped off the crime scene, you should have come to me—"

"I bagged everything at the scene and photographed it. I knew once Rocky got back to town and started talking every looky-loo would be out here—especially if I'd roped it off with crime scene tape, and I couldn't be sure until I got the DNA report back." She took a breath. "And I knew that the minute I turned that hunting license over to you that you'd pull me off the case."

"Pull you off the case? Hell, I have no choice but to suspend you, McCall. You're lucky I don't fire you on the spot."

"I understand." She reached for her gun and badge.

He studied her as she handed over both, then pulled the hunting license in the orange plastic case from her pocket and gave him that, as well.

It was hard to give up the license, but she'd made two copies of it, knowing this day was coming. Those were hidden in her pickup.

The sheriff shook his head as he dropped the license into an evidence bag. "You destroyed any fingerprints on the license."

"The killer didn't touch it. If he had, he would have taken it along with Trace's wallet, his boots, his truck and anything else that made identifying the body possible twenty-seven years ago."

Grant didn't look any happier to hear that. "I heard you'd been asking questions around town about your father."

Had Sandy told him? Somehow McCall doubted that. But he must have wondered what McCall had been doing at his house that day.

"When I saw you headed out this direction this morning, I just had a feeling…" he said now. "I thought it had to do with the Winchesters but I never imagined…"

"My father didn't leave town," McCall said, her voice breaking. "Someone killed him and buried him out there." She pointed at the cloud-cloaked ridge. "For twenty-seven years, he was there and someone knew he was there."

"Anything else you've withheld from me?" Grant asked.

She shook her head and watched as he folded the report and put it into the breast pocket of his coat before looking over at her again.

"You have already compromised this investigation. If you care about your job, you'll take your two-week suspension and do nothing else to jeopardize your position with my department. In the meantime, this is a crime scene and you're officially suspended and off the case. Is that understood?"

"Yes." She opened her door and stepped out into the rain. The sheriff did the same, bringing with him a large roll of yellow tape and a handful of wooden stakes.

He didn't look at her as he began to cordon off the crime scene twenty-seven years too late.

BUZZ CLEARLY HAD something on his mind when he finally answered his cell phone. "What's up?" he asked, sounding impatient.

"Did I catch you in the middle of something?" Luke asked.

"No, I'm just on my way to Billings so I might lose cell phone service at any time. What's going on?"

"Billings?" Luke said, forgetting for a moment his real reason for calling his uncle.

"Eugene and I are going down to talk to the guy he owes the money to, see if we can work something out."

So Eugene was with him. "You sure that's a good idea?" Luke regretted the words the moment they were out. *None of your business.* He mentally kicked himself as he heard the anger in Buzz's voice.

"Compared to the alternative?" his uncle demanded. "Or we could just let him get what's coming to him. Is that your plan?"

Luke didn't have a plan. Nor did he think he should

be expected to. He held his tongue, trying not to let Buzz tick him off any more than he just had.

"I was calling to ask you about that old pickup you keep in your barn," he said, anxious to find out what he wanted and get off the line.

"What about it?"

"I guess I'm surprised you still have it."

"It's not worth getting rid of. Why do you care?"

"Does it still run?"

"It did last time I drove it." His uncle's irritation wasn't lost even though the line was filling with static. "Is there something you wanted?"

"We can talk when you get back. When is that?"

"Tomorrow. Listen, I'm losing you. I gotta go." And with that his uncle was gone.

Luke snapped his phone shut, worried about Buzz and Eugene going to Billings given the people they would be meeting with. Even more worried about Buzz's old pickup that should have been in the barn last night when McCall was being run off the road.

As dusk settled over the Missouri River Breaks, Luke thought about going to Billings, telling himself he needed to know the truth and it couldn't wait until Buzz and Eugene got back.

He tried his uncle's cell again to find out where they would be staying only to get voice mail. He'd have to wait until they returned to Whitehorse.

He'd spent most of the day checking fishing licenses and tags down on the Missouri. Now, headed home, Highway 191 rose up out of the river bottom to trail along the high ridges. From here he could see how the land had eroded into deep gullies and ravines as it fell to the river.

Climbing out of the Breaks, the highway skirted the

Little Rockies, the pines shimmering in the sunlight. As the land opened up into rolling prairie dotted with sage and antelope, Luke usually felt a sense of peace.

Today though, he couldn't shake the bad feeling that seemed to follow him like a threatening thunderhead. He didn't know if this sense of foreboding had to do with his cousin's gambling or the poaching and pickup.

He drove past the turnoff to his place and through Whitehorse on out to Nelson Reservoir. This time he didn't need to sneak so he drove right up to his uncle's barn.

A wall of hot air hit him as he got out of his pickup, surprised at how hot the day must have gotten up here compared to down on the Missouri River.

This time, the moment he stepped into the barn, he cut his flashlight beam to the spot where the pickup should have been.

And was.

The rusted red truck sat in the spot Luke remembered it residing for years. He felt the hood. Cold. When had it been returned? he wondered as he opened the driver's side door and glanced inside.

The keys were in the ignition—just as they always were. He shone his flashlight across the bench seat, then onto the floorboards.

Mud. A large piece not quite dry. He looked closer, hoping to find a boot print he could use. No such luck.

He searched the rest of the pickup, finding nothing unusual, then closed the door and turned the flashlight beam on the tires. By now he knew the tread of his poachers' rig by heart. They had matched the tread in the dust where this truck had been parked before it was returned. All he needed was—

Luke frowned. To his surprise, the treads on these tires *didn't* match those taken at the poaching sites. Someone had changed the tires.

He moved along the side to the truck bed. It had recently been washed out. A red flag since the rest of the pickup hadn't been washed.

Had Buzz used the truck for something? The bad feeling he'd had earlier intensified as he ran a finger along the edge of the tailgate, his finger coming away tinted red.

Blood.

McCALL DIDN'T WANT her grandmother or her mother finding out about Trace before she could tell them herself.

She'd crawled out on a limb when she'd withheld evidence from the sheriff. Now she was about to saw that limb off. But in her heart, she knew what she had to do. She knew the sheriff would wait until he had another DNA sample and report before he'd go to either Ruby or Pepper about the bones found on the ridge.

It wouldn't be enough that McCall's DNA had matched because her parentage was considered questionable. Just as it probably wouldn't be enough proof for her grandmother.

As she drove toward the Winchester Ranch for the second time within days, McCall didn't let that bother her. She owed her father this, she told herself as the green landscape rolled past.

The sky was clear, the day warm for this time of year in this part of Montana. She loved spring. It had been a long, cold winter, but this was her home, country she loved, land that she knew.

She put down her window, letting the fresh air blow

in and told herself her grandmother would see her. Enid wouldn't be able to stop her.

The nice thing about the Winchester Ranch being so far from civilization was that even if her grandmother called the sheriff, by the time he got to the ranch McCall would be gone. Of course, if Grant was determined to arrest her, he would know where to find her.

She smiled, realizing she might be more like her father than she wanted to admit.

As she turned into the ranch yard, she saw a curtain move on the second floor and the old dog came out barking and growling. *Well, they know I'm here, anyway.*

She got out of the pickup, no longer fearful of the dog. Her grandmother really should get a meaner, younger dog if she was serious about keeping people away.

She didn't even get to knock before the door was flung open. Enid, looking like an ugly old bulldog, stood blocking the doorway, her lip curled in a snarl.

"Mrs. Winchester—"

"Will see me," McCall said cutting her off. "Tell her I have news about Trace." It surprised McCall how angry she was. Her mother said she'd inherited her father's temper, and he had apparently inherited it from his mother— if the fury McCall saw in her grandmother's face was any indication when she appeared.

"You were warned not to—"

McCall waved the copy of Trace's hunting license she'd brought her grandmother. "Do you want to know what happened to your son or not?"

Pepper Winchester stopped in midsentence. Enid offered to call the sheriff and was headed for the phone when Pepper stopped her. "Leave us alone."

Enid looked as if she were going to argue. Instead,

she left in a huff, clearly furious at being sent away like hired help. McCall had to wonder again about the woman's relationship with her grandmother.

"If this is some kind of ruse to—"

"The sheriff hasn't called you?"

Pepper's hand went to her throat. "Why would Sheriff Sheridan—"

"My father never left town." She glanced past her grandmother and saw Enid lurking down the hallway, eavesdropping. "Is there somewhere we can talk in private?"

Pepper had gone very pale. McCall had the feeling that her grandmother had been expecting this visit from her, had known after McCall's last one that something other than curiosity had brought her here.

This time her grandmother led her into a small office. It appeared it hadn't been used in years, like most of the rest of the massive lodge.

Pepper closed the door but continued standing. "What is this about my son not leaving town?"

"A man named Rocky Harrison found some bones," McCall said, talking quickly, knowing any minute her grandmother could send her packing. "The bones had been washed from a shallow grave on a ridge." She stepped to the window and pushed back the curtain. "*That* ridge."

Her grandmother moved to stand by her, staring out at the ridge in the distance.

"This is a copy of what I found where those bones had been buried." McCall handed her the copies of the hunting license and the antelope tag. "The license and tag were protected because they were still in the plastic folder he carried them in."

Pepper's hands trembled as she took the pages and looked at the printing on them. She seemed to sway, but when McCall reached toward her, she quickly straightened.

"The bones can't be my son's," her grandmother said, her voice breaking. "You've made this up as an excuse to—"

"I had a DNA test run on the bones."

Pepper's gaze narrowed. "Comparing them to whose DNA?"

"Mine. The remains in that grave were my father's and assuming you're through denying I'm Trace Winchester's daughter…"

Her grandmother stared at her for a long moment before she moved like a sleepwalker over to one of the leather chairs and sat down heavily. She motioned impatiently for McCall to sit, as well.

"Why hasn't the sheriff called me about this?"

"He will be calling you to request a sample of your DNA to run a comparison test," McCall said.

"These bones—"

"Were buried in a shallow grave on the ridge. The rainstorm the other night washed them down into a gully. The hunting license was buried in the mud in the grave."

Her grandmother's hand holding the copy of the license began to tremble again. She quickly stilled it. "You're telling me that someone killed my son."

McCall nodded. "Twenty-seven years ago."

"Who?"

McCall shook her head. "It will be next to impossible to find his killer after all this time."

Her grandmother bristled at that. "I'm sure the sheriff—"

"Grant Sheridan will turn the case over to the state crime lab but with a case this cold…"

Pepper recoiled with a shudder. "If you're saying I'll never know who killed my son... Trace will get justice if it takes my last dying breath."

She'd hoped that would be her grandmother's attitude. "Then help me find his killer."

"You?" Pepper scoffed at that. "You're a *deputy*. And you haven't even been one that long."

McCall had only a moment to wonder how her grandmother had known that.

Pepper shook her head and pushed herself to her feet. "I will hire the best private investigator that money can buy."

"And you will be wasting your money."

Her grandmother's eyes widened in surprise.

"You know the people in this part of the state," McCall said quickly. "You think anyone will talk to an outsider? People up here, even if they weren't all related, are close-knit. They're even suspicious of other Montanans let alone someone from out of state. Good luck with that."

"You are certainly a brash young woman."

Like my grandmother. "I intend to find out who killed my father no matter what the sheriff or the crime lab does or doesn't do," McCall said. "But I need your help. I need to know what my father was involved in twenty-seven years ago."

Her grandmother was shaking her head.

McCall rushed on. "I might be the only person who can find out the truth. Don't you see that? I'm a local, I have some training and he was *my* father."

"What makes you think anyone will talk to you?"

McCall smiled. "I'm the black sheep of the Winchesters. Everyone feels sorry for me because I've been treated so badly by my own grandmother."

The dagger found its mark. Her grandmother looked ashamed, but only for a moment. "You seem to have done fine without me."

"I need to know everything about my father—no matter what it is," McCall continued. "Are you willing to help me or not?"

"Why don't you ask your mother?"

McCall didn't even bother to answer that. "Are we going to keep pretending that I'm not Trace Winchester's daughter?"

Her grandmother moved to the window to gaze out in the direction of the wind-scoured ridge again. "I've just found out that my son is not only dead but that he was murdered and buried within sight of my ranch."

She turned to look at McCall, her eyes shiny with unshed tears. "I'm not up to satisfying your curiosity about him right now."

"I'm sorry I had to bring you this news," McCall said. "But I knew you'd want to know right away."

Something softened in her grandmother's face, letting her grief show through.

"Are you sure you're all right?" McCall asked.

Her grandmother straightened, that moment of vulnerability gone. "You needn't concern yourself with me."

McCall nodded. "Let me know when you're ready to help me." She felt sorry for her grandmother as she left and wondered if she'd ever hear from her again. Doubtful. She was on her own finding her father's killer.

As she climbed into her pickup, she didn't see Enid, although she suspected the woman wasn't far away.

Driving away, McCall turned her thoughts to her mother and realized she had no idea how Ruby would take the news about Trace's murder.

Chapter Nine

On the way back to Whitehorse, McCall called the café. Her mother was scheduled to work a double shift. "Is Ruby still there?"

"She just stepped outside to sneak a cigarette," Leo, the cook, told her. "It's slow, so I think she's going to leave early. You want me to give her a message?"

"No, that's all right. I'll catch her," McCall said, and hung up as she came over the rise and saw the Milk River Valley—the town of Whitehorse at the heart of it.

As she drove into town, she spotted the small figure of her mother coming down the street from the café toward her vehicle. McCall swung to the curb and reached over to open the passenger side door.

Ruby leaned her head in through the open doorway.

"Hop in."

Her mother looked startled but didn't argue as she slid into the seat and slammed the door. "Shouldn't you be working?"

McCall had figured by now it would be all over town about her getting suspended.

She drove out of town headed north just because that was the way she was pointed. Out of the corner of her eye, she saw Ruby glance out the window then shoot her a questioning look.

"I got suspended for two weeks. I'll probably get fired." She looked over at her mother. "I withheld some evidence."

"You must have had your reasons. I'm sure if you talk to Grant—"

Something in the way her mother said the sheriff's first name... "That's right. You used to date Grant."

Ruby swore. "If this is why you picked me up, then just let me out now. I'm in no mood to have you give me crap about my love life or quiz me about your father." Her mother reached for her door handle. "I'm serious. Just let me out."

McCall glanced over at her mother. There was no good way to say this. "Trace didn't leave you. He never left Whitehorse at all."

"What are you talking about?" Ruby snapped. "Of course Trace left town. I wasn't serious about his mother hiding him all these years. Unless she locked him up in one of those rooms at the ranch."

"You heard Rocky found some bones south of town? They've been identified." She could feel her mother freeze. "Trace didn't leave you. He's been out there all these years."

PEPPER HADN'T BEEN up there in twenty-seven years. Small spaces terrified her, and she wished she felt up to climbing the ladder to the third floor room instead of being forced to take the old elevator.

No one had been in this wing in years judging by the footprints she was leaving in the dust. This was the only other access and the walk here had worn her out.

After McCall left, she'd retrieved her cane, hating that she needed it.

She stopped in the dark hallway. Years ago the light bulbs must have burned out. Only faint shafts of light cut through the shuttered windows as she touched the secret panel on the wall to reveal the old elevator.

The metal was cold as she pulled back the gate. Something skittered away in the elevator shaft making her shudder. She hesitated, then stepped into the tiny, cramped space, telling herself she should be more worried about the elevator's working condition than her claustrophobia.

As a newlywed, she hadn't understood the purpose of the room or why she had been told it and the elevator were off-limits to all but her husband, Call. She would later understand only too well.

The elevator smelled just as Trace's room had, old and musty, filled with ghosts from the past. As she closed the gate, she was bombarded by a barrage of memories that made her sick to her stomach.

Her breath came in gasps, her fingers trembling. She pushed the button that would take her up to the locked room.

"Pepper, why would you want to go up there again?" asked the voice in her head, a voice that sounded exactly like her husband, Call's. "What if you get trapped up there and no one finds you until the house is torn down or just falls down someday?"

Enid and Alfred were in the far wing of the house. They wouldn't have heard the elevator. Nor would they hear her cries for help. Eventually they would find her but by then—

The elevator groaned and clanked and for a moment

she thought it wouldn't rise. Then with a jerk it began to ascend.

She pressed the hand holding the cane against the wall to steady herself, the other to her mouth to keep from crying out as the elevator inched upward.

In the small, isolated space she thought she could hear voices trapped from all those years ago. The screams of her children. The incessant crying and pleading. The empty finality when the elevator stopped.

Pepper reached for the metal gate, terrified the elevator might suddenly drop as she took a step out. Miraculously it didn't move as she stepped off to find herself standing at the edge of the small room.

The room was soundproof. Not even the bulletproof window opened. Anyone sent here could not be heard outside these walls. Nor seen through the one-way glass.

The only openings were small. Just large enough for a gun barrel to fit through.

"Why in God's name did you have this room built?" Pepper had demanded when Call had once caught her snooping. She'd been pregnant with their oldest child, Virginia, at the time.

Call had been furious with her. "It's for protection."

"Against whom?"

He'd only shaken his head and escorted her from the room.

It wasn't until later that she and her children learned that the room was also for punishment.

This room was where Call had locked her the day she'd tried to leave him.

RUBY BEGAN TO cry quietly. McCall wondered what her mother was thinking, what she was feeling. Was she relieved? Angry? Or just saddened by the news? McCall couldn't tell.

Ruby hid so much. Her only passion seemed to be men. It was the only time she let her emotions out. Over men she cried, swore, broke things, poured out her soul.

Except when it came to Trace Winchester. Maybe he really had been the love of her life, just as she claimed.

McCall turned off on the road to Sleeping Buffalo Resort and drove down to the hot springs, parking in front of the bar.

"I thought you might need a drink," she said to her mother.

Ruby wiped her eyes and opened her purse to pull out a wad of ones. "I'll buy if you'll go in and get us something."

McCall wasn't much of a drinker. "What do you want?"

"Tequila. Get a pint and something to chase it, okay?"

Tequila was the booze of preference for Ruby after a breakup. It seemed appropriate given the circumstances.

McCall took the wad of ones and got out. As she closed the pickup door, she saw her mother roll down her window and light a cigarette, her fingers trembling.

When she returned with a quart of orange juice, a pint of tequila and two paper cups, her mother stubbed out her cigarette. The pickup smelled of smoke and grease and sweat.

McCall handed everything to her mother and drove down by the lake, parking in the shade of a large old cottonwood.

Ruby busied herself making them both a drink. They touched cups, eyes meeting for a moment. McCall felt the impact finally.

Her father was dead. Murdered. Nothing would ever be the same. Especially if it turned out that Ruby had killed him.

PEPPER STARTED TO step farther into the room when she was startled by movement. Something small fluttered in the far corner, making her stumble back. As she tried to still her racing pulse, she realized that the slight breeze coming up through the elevator shaft had rustled the small paper objects in the corner.

Frowning, she stepped closer. Paper party hats? They were faded with the years, but still recognizable as the tiny ones she'd purchased for Trace's birthday party. She'd bought the tiny ones for the grandchildren and had been upset when she'd seen them wearing them long before the party.

She remembered yelling at the bunch of them to get out of the house. They had scampered away.

She stared at the paper hats discarded like trash on the floor of the room, realization making her weak. They'd been in this room that they'd been forbidden to enter.

Pepper felt her anger rise as she counted the hats. Five? Had there been five children in here that day? She remembered how noisy they'd been, her two grandsons, Cordell and Cyrus, and the nanny's boy, Jack. Had they taken extra hats or had someone been with them? She hadn't invited any other children. But that didn't mean that those two horrible neighboring ranch girls hadn't sneaked over.

As she started to rise, she saw something that stopped her heart stone-cold still before it took off like a wild horse.

What she'd first thought were cracks in the plastered

wall, she now saw were words. Tiny, scrawled words scratched into the walls. They were everywhere—within child height.

Pepper closed her eyes unable to bear reading what her children had written up here while imprisoned in this horrible room.

The room had always been empty. No furniture. "It's no punishment if you fill the room full of toys or make it comfortable," Call had said.

When she'd tried to stop Call from using this room to punish their children, he'd told her he'd raise them his way, the way he'd been raised. "It's like breaking a horse. If you can't stand to watch, don't."

She couldn't stand to watch so she'd stood by helplessly for years, she thought with a shudder.

That was until Trace had come along and she'd sworn Call wasn't "breaking" this one. Trace was seven when she'd decided to leave Call, taking her youngest son and fleeing.

Call had caught her and locked her in this room for three days.

Not long after that, her husband had gone off for a horseback ride and was never seen again.

She hadn't been able to save the others. As she opened her eyes again, she felt faint and thought she might have to sit down. She grabbed hold of the windowsill and looked out at the ridge in the distance where her son's body had been buried all those years. The same spot where he'd died?

This is why she'd had to come up here. She had to know if she could see the ridge from this room.

But now she saw that it would have been impossible to see what had happened on that far ridge at this distance. She'd been foolish to think there might have been an eyewitness, someone in the family who had inadvertently seen Trace's murder.

Suddenly the full weight of her loss hit her. She felt her knees give way, and even the cane couldn't support her as she dropped to the floor.

She lay there for a few minutes, letting the dam of tears burst and fall. She wept as she had the time she'd been locked in this room and cursed her son's killer.

Finally the tears subsided. She sat up feeling dizzy and light-headed. She shuddered at the thought that she was so weak or that the past was so strong.

As she started to get to her feet, anxious to leave this horrible room and the memories within these walls, she saw a small hole behind the window ledge. Someone had dug out the chinking from between the logs and made a space just large enough apparently to hide something.

In this case, a small pair of binoculars.

With a start she worked the binoculars from the hole, wiping them free of dust with her sleeve before raising them to look out at the ridge.

Her heart caught in her throat. She fought to keep down her lunch. She could see the ridge clearly right down to the crime scene tape flapping in the wind around her son's grave.

"To Trace," Ruby said and took a drink.

To you, Dad. McCall felt the kick of the tequila. She looked out at the sky-mirrored water. From here she could barely make out Buzz Crawford's house across the lake.

"I suppose by the time we get back to town everyone will know," Ruby said as she made herself another drink.

"Count on it." This was the biggest news to hit town in some time. "Are you going to be all right?"

Ruby laughed. "Hell, yes. The bastard didn't leave me." She laughed again and lifted her glass before downing half of it. "He might have stayed, you know. Things could have been different."

She nodded. Or they might have ended the same. They would never know.

But McCall liked to think her mother and father would have made it work and stayed together. She tried to imagine having a normal family. Whatever normal was.

As it was, history would have to be rewritten. Twenty-seven years of stories based on one false assumption. McCall thought of all the whispered rumors she'd heard about her father over the years.

Trace Winchester hadn't run out on them. True, he probably would have, given what McCall had learned about him and her mother. But he hadn't and that's what counted.

A murderer had deprived her of ever knowing her father and had broken Ruby Bates Winchester's heart. That alone was reason enough to find his killer. That and all the lost possibilities.

"So how did all this get you suspended?" her mother asked after her third tequila drink.

McCall had finished her first but had passed on a second because she was driving. Even one tequila had loosened her tongue. Or maybe it was growing up with all the lies that made her want to speak the truth now.

"I found his hunting license in the mud where the bones had been buried." She felt her mother's gaze.

"So you knew it was him that first day."

"I suspected it was him."

Ruby nodded and took a drink. "What made you keep quiet?"

"I wanted to wait until I got the DNA report before I told anyone. I also knew Grant would pull me off the case once he knew for sure it was Trace. I thought I'd have more time to try to find the killer before everything hit the fan."

Ruby seemed lost in thought. "You tell your grandmother? Is that why you went out there that first time?"

"No. I just wanted to see her before she found out about the crime lab results. I'd hoped she might know something that would help me find his killer." McCall didn't add that she'd gone to the Winchester Ranch first today to give her grandmother the news. Tequila or not, she was no fool.

"You could have told me," Ruby said, sounding hurt.

"Not until it was definite."

Her mother finished her drink and stared out at the water. "You thought I killed him."

"It crossed my mind."

Ruby shot her a disappointed look, then asked, "Where exactly did you find him?"

"On a ridge south of town within sight of the Winchester Ranch. You can't go out there. It's a crime scene. I'm sure the sheriff will have a deputy posted."

She nodded. "Who would want to do that to Trace?"

"You'd know better than me." McCall saw something like a shadow cross her mother's expression. "If there is someone you suspect…"

"No," Ruby said with a shake of her head. "Will Grant be in charge of the investigation?" she asked, looking down into her drink.

"Shouldn't he be?"

It took her mother a moment. "Maybe not."

McCall felt her mother pulling away, hiding again in the past. "Mother—"

Ruby did that little shrug of the shoulders thing she did when she'd been drinking. "He and Trace didn't get along after that mess with Sandy."

McCall already suspected that. "I doubt it will matter. Truthfully? It's a cold case. Twenty-seven years is a long time. I suspect it will be impossible to find the killer."

Did her mother look relieved?

Ruby's cell phone rang. "Speaking of the devil." She snapped open the phone. "Hello?" She listened, biting her lower lip, then said, "Thanks for letting me know, Grant."

She put the phone back in her purse, unscrewed the cap on the tequila, then as if thinking better of it, screwed it back on and balled her cup up in her fist.

"Don't lose your job over this," her mother said after a moment. "Nothing can bring Trace back. It might have been better if he'd just stayed buried. I don't want you looking for his killer."

"How can you say that? Aren't you relieved that he didn't leave you? Don't you want the person who took his life brought to justice?" McCall demanded. This was the last thing she'd expected from her mother. "I thought this man was the love of your life?"

"He's gone, McCall. Hasn't he messed up our lives enough?"

McCall stared at her mother. She could see that Ruby wished her daughter had never found the hunting license in the mud at the grave site, that Trace Winchester could be buried again and so could whatever had happened on that ridge.

But unfortunately once bodies were dug up, there was

no burying them again. Even if McCall wanted to, Pepper Winchester wasn't going to rest until her favorite son's murderer was swinging from a noose.

"You know who killed him," McCall said, knowing she was thinking crazy. But she kept remembering what Patty Mason had said about the mud on her mother's pickup. Mud like on the ridge where Trace had been buried.

Ruby shook her head and sighed, suddenly looking exhausted. "Of course I don't know who killed him. But if I had to guess, I'd say it was someone Trace had pushed too far."

LUKE SANK A nail into the two-by-four and reached for another one. Restless, he'd decided to work on his house until dark. But he'd been having a hell of a time concentrating on the job.

He'd tried Buzz's cell phone a half-dozen times and left several messages. He couldn't help worrying since there had been no word.

Mostly, he was mentally kicking himself for coming back here thinking he stood half a chance with McCall. It seemed they were always on opposite sides of the fence. Now this thing with Buzz...

And yet when Luke thought about holding McCall in his arms last night, he remembered those few moments when it had felt so right. His kiss had taken her by surprise, but she'd responded and he'd felt the heat in her, that old spark of desire that had flickered like a campfire between them.

He reminded himself that she'd thought he'd run her off the road. It was like dousing himself in ice water.

Just as McCall believed he'd done something unforgivable ten years ago, and even though he'd sworn he hadn't… Yeah, trust was a huge issue between them and he doubted there was anything he could do to fix that.

But he couldn't bear the thought that McCall might be in danger and worried what might be going on. Buzz wasn't stupid enough to try to run her off the road, was he?

Luke realized he didn't know anymore. He had so many questions, and his uncle was the only one who could answer them.

Restless, he started to try Buzz's cell phone again when he heard a vehicle coming up the road. Probably Buzz, he thought with relief.

Luke shaded his eyes as he watched the cloud of dust draw closer. Definitely a pickup, just not Buzz's new one he drove.

Squinting into the sun, he saw the sheriff's department logo on the side and couldn't believe his eyes.

McCall?

He watched her drive into his yard, hoping this was a social visit, knowing it probably wasn't. Had something happened to Buzz and Eugene and she was here to give him the bad news? No, the sheriff would have called, not sent McCall.

He stood in the shade as she climbed out of her pickup. Her dark hair shone in the fading sunlight. She moved with long-legged grace toward him. And as always, he was hit with such a need for this woman that it almost dropped him to his knees.

Turning back to his work, he drove a nail into another two-by-four, warning himself not to get his hopes up that her being here had anything to do with him. Or that kiss last night.

Chapter Ten

McCall followed the sound of the hammer toward the wooden structure etched against the sunset—and Luke Crawford.

She'd driven her mother back to town in time to get ready for Ruby's date with Red Harper.

"Are you sure you're up to going out tonight?" she'd asked her mother, trying to hide her surprise. "I could rent a movie, get us a pizza—"

"No." Ruby had patted McCall's arm. "I need to see Red. I want to be the one to tell him."

McCall still didn't know how her mother was really taking the news of her husband's murder. Maybe it hadn't sunk in yet. Or maybe it had and she'd been serious about McCall dropping her investigation. "Sure. Whatever you want."

"Your father's been dead to me for a long time," Ruby had said. "I guess I just need time, you know?"

McCall had guessed so. Everyone in town would be talking about Trace's murder. Being the woman left alone and pregnant didn't garner the same kind of sympathy as being the widow of a man unjustly murdered in his prime. Ruby hadn't gotten to be the grieving widow. Until now.

Normally, McCall would have headed to her cabin,

anxious for the peace and quiet. But it was still early and there'd been one more thing she had to do.

The sun had slipped behind the Little Rockies as she spotted Luke. She glanced past him and the skeletal frame of his house to the stock pond in the distance and felt a chill snake up her spine.

Her gaze came back to Luke, and for a moment, she wanted to stop all this. She wanted to sit down in the shade with Luke, share a cold beer, watch the sun set and forget about the past, all of it, especially the part where Luke broke her heart.

She realized she shouldn't have come here feeling so vulnerable. For years, she'd built a shield around herself after Luke hurt her. But there were now cracks in her armor. Finding out that her father hadn't run out on her and her mother had opened old wounds—just as Luke had by coming back to Whitehorse.

Luke's presence had filled her head with thoughts of what could have been. What could still be if only she could forgive him.

She listened to Luke pound another nail and shelved all her crazy thoughts, especially the ones about Luke Crawford and second chances.

The air was cool in the shade. The hammering stopped. She knew Luke had already seen her coming.

As he slipped his hammer into the side of his carpenter's apron, he turned and leaned against the opening where he'd been working. "McCall," he said, the sound of it making her ache.

He looked wary, but who could blame him after last night? She bristled, reminded that all she'd done to him was slap him. Nothing compared to a kiss. She was the one who should be wary.

The sun lit in his dark eyes. His skin looked bronze against his pale yellow shirt, the sleeves rolled up to expose strong forearms. The jeans were worn, just like the boots.

He couldn't have looked more appealing or more dangerous to her equilibrium, she thought as she gazed up at him.

"What brings you out here, Deputy?" he asked.

That earlier thought of sitting in the shade with him flitted past. She swatted it away. "Your stock pond."

Luke smiled as if he thought she was kidding. He dropped the nails he'd been holding into a pocket of the carpenter's apron. "You looking to do some fishing? There's northern pike in there as long as your arm. But shouldn't you have brought your fishing pole?"

"That's not what I'm fishing for."

He raised a brow and pushed back his straw Western hat to reveal a thick pencil stuck behind his right ear. He smelled of sawdust.

"How deep would you say the pond is?" she asked, trying to distract herself from how good Luke looked and the way being this close to him made her ache.

His lips quirked in a questioning grin, humor sparkling in his dark eyes. "At the dam end? Twelve to fourteen feet. Shallower at the other end."

She nodded. Plenty deep enough. She felt a shiver of dread ripple through her. Her father's pickup was in that stock pond. With the Crawford Ranch vacant twenty-seven years ago it was the perfect place to dispose of the truck quickly.

Nor was there any reason it would have been found since the place had been bought by an out-of-state corporation and had quickly gotten tied up in some legal mess before Luke bought it back.

"Then you don't mind if I have a look?" she asked.

"Sure. What is it you're looking for anyway?"

"I've got this crazy idea there might be a pickup down there."

"In the pond?" He sounded skeptical as he untied his carpenter's apron and dropped it on the floor before he jumped down and walked with her toward the earthen dam.

As they approached, she saw that the water was the color of a rusted pickup, much too dark to see anything in its depths.

"How are you planning to— Whoa," he said as she took off her jacket and pulled off one boot. "You aren't aiming to jump in there?"

"You know of a better way to find out if the truck is down there?"

"That water will be ice-cold. It's spring fed."

She pulled off her other boot and began to unbuckle the belt on her jeans.

"*Stop.* As curious as I am to see how far you're willing to go with this, I can't let you," Luke said.

"I can get a warrant—"

"I'm not talking about *that*." He was angry with her again. "Damn it, McCall, if there's something in there, I'll find out. Whose pickup is this you think is down there, anyway?"

"My father's."

Luke blinked. "Trace Winchester?"

"He *is* my father, no matter what the local grapevine says."

"I didn't mean— Never mind." He pulled off his boots, tossing them down, then unsnapped his shirt and dropped it into the pile. She tried not to look at his bare chest.

Nor had she meant to make him angry with her again.

"I can do this without your help," she said, although she hadn't been looking forward to going in that water.

He leveled his gaze on her, eyes hard as stones. "I don't doubt you're more than capable and determined to do anything you set your mind to and that you certainly don't need me, but it's *my* stock pond. Stay here." In his socks, he padded around the dam to the side and waded gingerly into the water.

She could tell that the water was freezing cold from the way he tried not to show just how uncomfortable it was. When he reached chest-deep, he did a shallow dive and disappeared beneath the still dark surface.

McCall took off her good leather belt and dropped it on the ground, ready to go in after him if necessary. A meadowlark sang from the sage. In the distance, a truck shifted down on Highway 191. Nothing moved on the stock pond's surface.

McCall held her breath as she stared down at the water and waited.

No Luke.

She would give him just a little longer and then—

He surfaced in a shower of dirty water and swam hard toward the side, his back to her. As he climbed out, his jeans running water, she saw something in the set of his shoulders. And felt herself sag under the knowledge.

"It's down there, isn't it?" she asked as he climbed up to the dam and picked up his shirt.

LUKE SHRUGGED INTO his shirt, the thin fabric sticking to his wet skin and fought off the chill of the water—and what he'd found.

"There's a pickup down there," he said. "And it's been there for a while. That's all I can tell you."

The radio in her patrol pickup squawked. She leaned down to pull on her boots, picked up her belt and jacket and headed toward her patrol SUV without a word.

Luke swore under his breath as she called back after a moment, "I have to go. Can I trust you not to disturb the site?"

Luke picked up his boots and walked over to her, fighting his temper. When was the woman going to start trusting him?

"What do you think I'm going to do? Drain the pond? Or drag the pickup out before you get back?" he asked between clenched teeth.

Her look said that's exactly what had crossed her mind.

He shook his head, his anger suddenly spent. "McCall, why would I do that?"

"I just want to do this the legal way," she said, and he realized she wasn't wearing her badge and her gun. Why was that? "Do I need to get a warrant before I come back with a wrecker to pull out the pickup?"

"No, it's all yours."

He watched her drive away, swearing to himself. That damned woman. When he'd first seen her drive into the place he'd thought— Oh, hell, it didn't matter what he'd thought or worse, what he'd hoped. She hadn't come to see him. She was just being a cop—even if she wasn't wearing her gun or badge.

As he stomped over to the small trailer he lived in until he got his house built, he wished he'd let her go in that ice-cold pond. *Would have served her right*, he thought, his stiff jeans so cold against his skin they felt as if they were starting to freeze.

He stripped out of his clothes on his front step since he had all the privacy in the world way out here. Stark naked, he went inside and turned on the shower. As he stepped under the warm spray, he waited for it to take away some of the chill.

With McCall gone, his mind began to clear.

Trace Winchester's pickup was in his stock pond?

What had made McCall even suspect there *might* be a truck down there?

He told himself it had nothing to do with him. The place had been vacant since his parents' deaths. Luke turned off the shower and reached for a towel, finally getting why McCall had thought he might interfere with her crime scene. If that's what it was.

Buzz. McCall had been investigating him in regard to her father, and now apparently she thought the pickup in the Crawford stock pond was Trace Winchester's.

And if it was her father's truck, what the hell did that mean? Luke didn't like the implications.

Trace could have dumped the pickup before he took off for parts unknown. Or he could be inside the cab at the bottom of that pond. If so, there was little chance he'd driven himself in there by accident.

As Luke glanced out at the pond, he felt sick. A breeze riffled the surface of the water. Walleye chop, Buzz would have called it.

Buzz. Did this have something to do with his uncle? McCall apparently thought so. Luke hoped not as he reached for his cell phone and punched in Buzz's number.

Giving his uncle a heads-up wasn't interfering with the deputy or her possible crime scene. He owed Buzz at least that.

And he wanted to be the one to tell his uncle. Or maybe he wanted to judge for himself what Buzz's involvement might be based on the tone of his voice when he heard about the pickup being found in the pond.

"YOU WHAT?" SHERIFF GRANT SHERIDAN looked pale under the fluorescent lighting in his office.

"I believe I've found my father's pickup, the black Chevy missing since his disappearance," McCall said.

"Where the hell—"

"It was dumped in a stock pond not far from where his remains were found," she said.

Grant had been standing, but now he lowered himself into his office chair and motioned for her to sit down. "I thought I told you to stay away from this investigation?"

McCall stared at the sheriff. His color had returned but he still looked upset. Because she'd interfered with the investigation? Or because she'd found the pickup when he'd thought no one ever would? She realized that she was looking at everyone as a suspect.

"Aren't you going to ask where the stock pond is located?" she asked him.

His eyes narrowed. "I was getting to that. You realize I can have you arrested after I told you specifically to stay clear of this investigation?"

"Are you sure you want that kind of publicity given that it's my father who was murdered and that I'm the one who found his grave *and* his pickup?"

"You're treading on thin ice, McCall. If you don't want to lose your job—"

"The stock pond is on the old Crawford place," she said, in case there was any doubt that she didn't give a damn about her job at this point. "The ranch was vacant twenty-seven years ago. Buzz Crawford had sold it, but the new out-of-state owners never took possession." Had Buzz known that might be the case?

Grant leaned back, worry creasing his forehead as he studied her. "Have you told your mother or your grandmother about the truck?"

"No. I came straight to you. I think it would be best if neither of them was notified until there is no doubt it is his pickup. Right now it's stuck in the mud about six to eight feet underwater."

"I don't want word getting out on this," the sheriff said.

"That's why I didn't go through the dispatcher. I thought we could get Tommy over at T&T Towing to pull it out. I've already gotten permission from the new owner of the property—Luke Crawford—so a warrant isn't necessary. But I would suggest we do this now before anyone else finds out. I want to be there when you bring up the pickup."

McCall knew she had overstepped her boundaries. She half expected her boss to tell her that not only didn't he give a damn about her suggestions, but he was also locking her up for obstructing his investigation.

To her surprise, he rose from his seat, picked up his coat on the way out the door, saying, "You better turn in your vehicle and ride with me. I can give you a ride home."

Luke sat in the shade, drinking a cold beer and watching the road into his place. He hadn't been able to reach his uncle and he was growing more concerned by the minute.

In the distance, he saw vehicles coming up the ranch road. Dust rose behind them into the twilight and floated south on the light breeze.

A perfect spring evening. Unless a pickup had been found in your stock pond that might belong to the missing father of the woman you loved—and lost.

As the tow truck roared into the yard followed by the sheriff's patrol SUV, Luke rose, put down the beer he'd hardly touched and watched the sheriff climb out. Grant Sheridan had an even grimmer expression on his face than usual.

Deputy McCall Winchester climbed out of the other side.

"I understand you've given McCall permission to drag your stock pond?" the sheriff asked.

Luke nodded. "Like I told her, it's all yours." He saw McCall glance around as if looking for someone. It hit him: she'd expected him to call Buzz to warn him. And damned if he hadn't. Would Buzz be here now if he had reached him—or on his way to South America via Mexico?

In retrospect, he was glad he hadn't reached him. The way Buzz felt about McCall and the Winchesters, he thought it better to let this play out before Buzz got the news. He didn't want Buzz making matters worse. It would be bad enough if that really was Trace Winchester's pickup buried in the mud of his stock pond— and Buzz knew something about it.

As they followed the tow truck down to the stock pond, Luke couldn't help but notice how nervous McCall was. He doubted anyone else had noticed since she hid it well.

But he knew her intimately. Even making love once changed things between a man and a woman. Especially when that woman was McCall. She kept so much of herself hidden behind her tough-girl attitude. Only once had she let down her guard with him. No wonder she'd hated him after she'd thought he'd betrayed her.

"You sure you want to see this?" he asked McCall now as the sheriff went over to talk to the tow truck driver and his assistant, who was suiting up for the dive.

McCall looked over at him, frowning as if she didn't understand his concern. "My father's body isn't in the truck."

"You're sure about that?" he asked, studying her. If she was telling the truth, then why was she so nervous? Whose body did she think was going to be in there?

The diver disappeared under the water with a light, only to return moments later to come back for the cable.

Luke watched McCall out of the corner of his eye as the diver slipped under the surface. He reappeared after a short time and signaled the tow truck driver. The cable tightened as the engine mounted on the back of the tow truck began to rev.

Something moved below the surface of the water sending up bubbles then waves that lapped at the shore. Out of the rust-colored water a large pickup-shaped object emerged.

Chapter Eleven

Dark water ran from the pickup, gushing to the ground as McCall tried to see what was inside the cab. But the interior was a cave of darkness behind the slimed-over windows.

She felt Grant's hand on her arm.

"Remember the deal we made," the sheriff reminded her. "You got to come along but you stay out of it."

She nodded and took a step back as he walked over to the truck and rubbed off some of the slime to check the color. McCall had already seen that it was black. A 1983 Chevy pickup. Just like the one her father had been driving the day he disappeared.

As the water draining from the cab slowed, Grant glanced back at her. With deliberate motions, he pulled on a pair of latex gloves, then reached to open the passenger's side door.

McCall gasped as a large object swept out from the pickup on a wave of dirty water.

"What the hell?" the sheriff cried, jumping back.

McCall couldn't help herself. She stepped forward as if propelled by an invisible force, stopping short when she recognized what had been at the center of the sludge.

Waterlogged, mud-filled boots had apparently been wrapped up in a wool plaid hunting coat.

She stepped past Grant to look into the cab of the pickup but couldn't tell what else might be in there, given all the sludge.

Stumbling back, she was surprised when she felt strong arms steady her.

"Easy," Luke said.

She hadn't realized she was trembling until she felt him put an arm around her and lead her away from the truck and into the shade of his house he was building.

For a moment, she stood in his embrace, then, fearful at how wonderful it felt, moved just far enough away that he wasn't touching her, cursing her stupid pride.

Luke dusted off a spot on some lumber beside the house. "Here, sit in the shade."

She sat, feeling faint and touched by his concern for her. "I hadn't expected…" Words deserted her.

"Seeing the pickup like that must have been a shock," he said quietly as he sat down beside her—just not too close.

She'd known the pickup would be her father's black Chevy. She just hadn't known it would have this effect on her. The truck looked nothing like it had in the only photo she had of her father.

So why did it hurt so much just looking at it?

Because she knew the last person to drive it hadn't been her father—but his killer.

For a moment earlier though, she'd feared that what washed out was the remains of Geneva Cavanaugh Cherry.

She could hear Grant putting in a call to the crime lab. Now the team would have even more evidence to work with in the cold-case murder investigation. But McCall doubted there would be anything to find, given how long the pickup had been under the dirty water. Even if they did find something, she wouldn't be privy to it.

"Do you want to get out of here?" Luke asked.

She nodded and rose, turning her back on the scene beside the pond. "I just need to know if his rifle is in there."

"I'll find out. Stay here."

She stood facing the Little Rockies, the sunset rimming the mountains in deepening shades of orange and pink. A shadow began to settle over the land, over her. Seeing the pickup had made it real.

McCall started at Luke's touch.

"The rifle wasn't in the pickup," he said as they headed toward his truck. "They're talking about dragging the pond."

She nodded. She hadn't expected the rifle to be in the truck. Nor did she believe they'd find it at the bottom of the pond. All along she'd suspected the killer had taken it.

"McCall!" the sheriff called after her.

She stopped and waited as he came over to where she stood. Luke continued to his truck to wait for her, leaving the two of them alone.

"Why did you ask about your father's rifle?" Grant wanted to know.

"Because he had it with him that day. He'd gone hunting."

"You're sure he had the rifle? I thought he'd been ticketed the day before for poaching?"

"He had, but for some reason Buzz Crawford hadn't confiscated the rifle—or his antelope tag." She saw the sheriff's surprised expression. "Buzz says he doesn't recall, too long ago. But I checked. Buzz never turned the rifle in to the Fish and Game evidence department, and my mother swears Trace had it the day he disappeared."

Grant was studying her. "How did you know the pickup was here?"

"I told you, I saw the pond from the ridge. What better place to hide the truck than a vacant ranch close by?"

The sheriff pulled off his hat and raked a hand through his graying hair. He dropped his voice as he said, "I know you talked to Sandy." His gaze searched her face. "Where were you going with this?"

"I talked to anyone who had reason to hate my father enough to kill and bury him on that ridge twenty-seven years ago."

"And you thought Sandy..." He shook his head.

"Actually, I thought you had more motive," McCall said.

All the breath seemed to whoosh out of him. *"Me?"*

"You must have hated him. Probably still do."

Grant looked away. "You're wrong. I'm thankful Trace was such an incredible bastard." His gaze came back to her. "He gave me a chance with Sandy, one I wouldn't have had otherwise."

McCall felt a deep sorrow for Grant. The man really seemed to believe that he'd won Sandy.

"This ends here for you," Grant said. "Got it?"

She didn't answer, just turned and walked toward Luke's pickup. Without a word, she slid in. As Luke pulled away, she glanced back at the pond. Her father's pickup looked like some monster dragged up from the black lagoon.

"EVERYTHING ALL RIGHT?" Luke said as he drove them away. He hadn't been able to hear the conversation between her and the sheriff, but he'd watched in the rear-view mirror, and from their body language it hadn't been a pleasant discussion.

"Just great." McCall leaned back and closed her eyes. "Thanks for getting me out of there. I'm sorry about the way I acted earlier."

"You don't have to do that."

"What?"

"Pretend. I can tell this is tearing you up."

She said nothing as he turned onto Highway 191 and headed north toward Whitehorse. Luke wished she would let him help her through this, but he could tell by her silence that she'd already shut him out.

He started to turn on the radio, when her words stopped him.

"There's a reason I knew my father's body wasn't in the pickup." Her voice sounded small and filled with emotion, and when he glanced over at her he saw the tears beaded on her closed lashes. "Rocky Harrison found my father's remains not far from the stock pond."

Luke had heard about the bones from Buzz, but he'd never imagined they would turn out to be McCall's father's. Worry burrowed deeper under his skin as he recalled Buzz's interest in the find. Natural curiosity, like driving by a wreck and being forced to look? Or something more sinister?

And now Trace Winchester's pickup had been found on the old Crawford place.

Luke drove, mind racing. He wasn't sure what scared him the most. That McCall suspected Buzz. Or that she actually might have reason to.

"You're not wearing your badge or your gun," he said after a moment.

She opened her eyes and sat up, turning away to wipe her tears. "I'm suspended for two weeks. I withheld some evidence until I was certain the remains were my father's."

Luke couldn't imagine what she'd been going through. "I'm sorry." He knew the words weren't near enough. Throwing caution to the wind, he reached over and took her hand. He expected her to pull away and was surprised when her hand closed tightly onto his.

She made an undecipherable sound. He could feel her pain. But it was the anger and frustration he felt coming off her in waves that worried him. He knew this woman.

"I know what you're planning to do," he said as the road topped a hill and he could see the dark outline of the trees that meandered through the Milk River Valley. A few lights from town glittered faintly in the growing darkness.

McCall turned to give him an amused smile. He could tell she didn't think he knew anything about her. She couldn't have been more wrong.

"I know you're going after your father's killer."

"You witnessed my discussion with the sheriff. If I get involved I'll be fired."

Luke chuckled. "Like that will stop you." He saw the determination in her expression. "It won't bring your father back."

"No, there's no changing the past, is there?"

He glanced over at her, wondering if she was talking about the two of them or her father's murder.

"I have to find his killer. It's the only justice he's going to get." He could feel her gaze on him. "Why? Worried where my investigation is going to lead me?"

"Buzz didn't kill your father," he said, hoping the hell he was right.

"And you know that how?"

"What was his motive?"

"He had it in for my father."

Luke thought about all the tickets Buzz had written Trace. It certainly looked that way. But murder? "Do you have any proof?"

"Not yet."

"What if you're wrong about Buzz?" *Just as you're wrong about me*, he thought as he drove through town and took the river road to her cabin.

"One way or another, I intend to get justice for my father," she said.

He didn't like the sound of that. He pulled up next to her cabin.

"Thanks for the ride," McCall said and started to open her door. "If you're so sure your uncle is innocent, then get me a copy of Buzz's daily log for those two days. The day before hunting season opened and opening day."

Luke swore. "I can't do that."

"I know you can. But I understand why you wouldn't want to. Don't worry, I'll find another way," she said, climbing out and slamming his pickup door.

"Wait," he called as he reached over, opened his glove box and took out the Colt .45. Opening his door, he went after her. He knew this woman, knew she would move heaven and earth to find her father's killer. Nothing could stop her. Especially him.

But he couldn't let her do it alone—or unarmed—no matter where the trail led.

"I'll help you." His words surprised him as much as her. If she tried to get copies of that logbook, the sheriff would find out and she would be fired—if not arrested. He couldn't let that happen.

He grabbed her arm and turned her around to face him. Touching her was like sending a bolt of electricity through him. He felt the surge of desire rush through his veins and prepared himself for the powerful ache it left when she pulled free.

She didn't pull free this time. Her eyes locked with his. *"Why?"*

He knew she was asking more than why he would help her.

"You know why," he said as he let go of her arm. "You're the reason I came back here. The only reason."

A BANK OF low clouds made the night darker than normal as McCall watched Luke turn and leave. She felt shaken to her core. He'd come back here because of her?

The tall black limbs of the cottonwood trees creaked and groaned in the breeze against a sky as dark as the inside of a body bag.

She hugged herself against the cool breeze and breathed in the scents of the night, trying to clear her head. His confession changed nothing, she told herself, and yet she knew it did.

Suddenly she felt as if she was being propelled headlong into disaster, no longer in control of anything and completely unable to stop what was about to happen.

"Damn you, Luke," she whispered as the pickup's taillights disappeared into the darkness.

McCall rubbed a hand over her face. She was exhausted from lack of sleep, her body ached from her crash into the ditch the night before and she was frustrated and confused.

Luke was so sure his uncle was innocent.

Was she that sure that Buzz had killed her father?

All she had was circumstantial evidence at best. Anyone would have known about the old Crawford place being vacant. Anyone could have taken Trace's rifle after killing him.

Nothing she'd learned had moved her any closer to finding her father's killer. She'd learned things about her mother she hadn't wanted to know and even worse things about her father.

Her job had been jeopardized, and she wasn't even sure she wanted it back now. Maybe worst of all, she had the feeling there was no one she could trust. She'd burned bridges with everyone she knew, and now Luke had her questioning where this obsession had taken her.

She couldn't change the past. Her father was dead. Even her mother was trying to move on.

All McCall had done was stir up a hornet's nest that had left her alienated from people she cared about.

She felt like crying and had to fight the tears, knowing that once she started she might not be able to stop.

It wasn't the cold temperature tonight that chilled her to the bone as she listened to Luke drive away. She needed him, wanted him, thought she couldn't stand another night without him.

She turned, aching to call him back, wanting desperately to quit pushing him away. Their lovemaking came back to her in a rush, the feel of his body against hers, the gentle sweet way he'd made love to her.

It had been magic, bonding them together in a way she realized that had never been broken. Neither of them had been able to move on.

The past reared its ugly head, but no longer had the power it had held over her. Luke had sworn that he hadn't gone to high school the next day and bragged about "nailing" her. She'd been so hurt, so confused, so heartbroken. It had seemed so unlike him to brag to his friends but there had only been the two of them down by the river that night. It had been their secret. Word had spread the way it always had in Whitehorse, and her reputation had been ruined, though that was the least of it.

McCall had lost faith in men and love and Luke Crawford in particular. He'd betrayed her and that betrayal had kept her from trusting another man again.

Her cell phone rang, making her jump. She checked it and saw that it was a pay phone. "Hello?"

"You want to know who killed your old man?" said a low hoarse voice, clearly disguised. "Why don't you ask your mother?"

"Who is this?" She realized she'd stopped walking toward her cabin.

"Ask her about the black eye she was sporting the last time anyone saw Trace Winchester and who gave it to her."

McCall flinched as if she'd been hit. "Are you saying my father hit her?"

A chuckle. "Only because she got in the way. He was trying to hit her *boyfriend*." The line went dead.

McCall swore under her breath. *Black eye? Boyfriend?* She realized she was still carrying the gun Luke had pressed into her hand. Turning, she headed for her SUV.

With luck she could catch her mother before she went out on her date with Red Harper.

"Is something wrong?" Ruby repeated as McCall entered the trailer.

Everything was wrong and had been McCall's whole

life. She'd felt as if everyone around her had lied to her. Now she knew it was true.

"Why don't you tell me about the black eye my father gave you," she said as she stepped into the trailer.

Ruby froze. "What?"

"My father hit you."

"No. It wasn't—" She folded the dish towel she'd been using to dry the few items on her drain board and placed it carefully on the counter. "Where would you get—"

"Or was he trying to hit your *boyfriend*?" The one thing McCall had believed all these years was that Trace Winchester had been her mother's true love. Now even that was in question.

Ruby chewed at her lower lip before reaching for her cigarettes. McCall beat her to them, tossing the pack aside.

"How about the truth for once?"

Her mother shook her head. "There were things I didn't want to tell you. I wanted to spare you."

Ruby turned to open the fridge. "You want a Diet Coke?" She must have seen McCall's impatient expression, because she pulled only one out, popped the top and took a drink.

"Trace and I were having problems," Ruby said finally. "I told you about his mother cutting off his money, trying to rein him back in. He was torn. She wouldn't relent. We were broke. I was pregnant and sick and not working as much…" She took another drink, her throat working.

McCall recalled what Patty had told her about the morning her mother showed up at the café late. She'd thought from the mud on the old pickup that Ruby had been out looking for Trace.

"You said the last time you saw him was the morning

of opening day when he went antelope hunting," McCall reminded her and saw her mother's face flush under the weight of the lie.

Patty had said her mother came in late and it was plain as her face that she and Trace had had a fight. McCall had thought Patty meant: plain as the look on her face, but she must have been talking about Ruby's black eye.

Her mother started to cry. "Trace used to put his hand on my stomach and just light up when he felt you move. It was his idea to name you McCall after his father, even if you were a girl." She smiled through her tears. "He would have settled down once you were born. Would have been fine if—"

"The black eye, Mother."

Ruby finished the soda, tossed the can in the recycle bin McCall had forced on her and motioned to one of the kitchen chairs. McCall had been leaning against the kitchen counter, blocking her mother's path.

She moved now, allowing Ruby to sit down, but she could tell her mother was itching for a cigarette.

"I was fine when Trace was home, but when he wasn't…" Ruby said, turning the ashtray in a circle with her finger. "I did something terrible." Her voice cracked like the ice on Nelson Reservoir in the spring. "I went out on Trace."

"Went *out*?"

"It was just that one time. I swear. We regretted it right away."

"We?"

Her mother kept turning the ashtray, refusing to look at her.

"When did this happen?"

"The night before opening day."

McCall swore. "So you didn't see him the next morning, did you? You don't even know if he had his rifle or not." She couldn't believe this. She'd based all her assumptions about his killer on who had taken the rifle from Trace and when.

Ruby stopped spinning the ashtray. "Trace came home the night before opening day, caught us and took a punch at him. I got in the middle."

McCall sighed. Would the saga of her parents never end? "No wonder you thought he'd left you. Who is the other man, Mother?"

Ruby looked away and McCall knew. A cold chill worked its way up her spine. "It was Red, wasn't it?"

Her mother burst into tears.

Now it all made sense. Why Red hadn't asked Ruby out all these years. It had been guilt. He and Ruby had both blamed themselves for Trace leaving.

"Even if he hadn't gotten himself killed, he would have left me," Ruby cried. "Now you know why. It was *my* fault."

McCall stepped to her mother, squatting down to hug her. Ruby shook with shuddering sobs, her tears hot against McCall's cheek.

"He married you. He wouldn't have if he hadn't loved you," McCall whispered. It didn't matter if it was true or not. Not anymore. The truth was that Trace had never left Ruby. Never left either of them.

The sobs slowed. Ruby sniffed, wiped her tears.

McCall sat down across from her, feeling closer to her mother than she had in years. Ruby had cheated. It wasn't the first time a woman had done such a thing nor would it be the last. There were worse sins. Like murder.

McCall didn't stop her mother this time when she reached for her cigarettes.

"I'm sorry. I'm so sorry," Ruby said after taking a long drag and blowing the smoke out the side of her mouth, waving her hand as if that would save her daughter from the secondhand smoke.

It was hard to tell exactly what her mother was sorry for. Tricking Trace. Getting pregnant. Marrying Trace. Cheating on him. Or believing for years that her infidelity was the reason he was gone.

Whatever Ruby was sorry for, she'd paid for it the past twenty-seven years.

McCall drove home, wanting nothing more than to sleep for twenty-four hours. The cold night air did nothing to chase away her fatigue. The river bottom was quiet, the low clouds of the spring sky overhead a deep ebony.

Rounding the corner of the deck, she was almost to the door when something moved in the darkness. Mc-Call froze as a dark shape came across the deck at her.

Chapter Twelve

As Eugene Crawford stepped from the shadows, McCall knew he'd been waiting for her.

Her stomach tightened as she reached for her weapon only to realize she wasn't wearing it and she'd left the gun Luke had given her in the truck.

As she reached in her pocket for her cell phone, Eugene stepped in front of her, blocking her path with one big, heavy arm and slapping her cell out of her hand. It skittered across the deck and disappeared over the side.

"You bitch." Anger contorted his ruddy, thick features. "Because of you my father was arrested for murder."

The sheriff had arrested Buzz for her father's murder? Grant was so cautious he wouldn't have done that without sufficient evidence. He must have found something in Trace's pickup.

"I know you framed my old man," Eugene said, shoving her back against the wall of the house.

She could smell alcohol on his breath and warned herself to be careful of this dangerous man. Eugene outweighed her by a hundred pounds and had a mean streak that she'd seen all through grade school. In high school he'd asked her out, and when she'd turned him down, he'd done everything he could to make her life miserable behind Luke's back.

McCall had known that arresting him the other night at the bar would come back to haunt her. Here he was spoiling for a fight again, only he planned to win this one.

She tried to remain calm, not easy when they both knew that they were all alone out here. Even if she screamed no one would hear her, and Eugene was too big to fight.

"I'm sorry, Eugene, but I don't know what you're talking about," she said, trying to keep her voice calm.

"*Right*. You wouldn't know anything about him getting arrested and hauled off to jail for murdering the man your mother claimed fathered you."

McCall held her ground although it was hard with Eugene Crawford this close and reeking of alcohol, sweat and anger, but she knew that any show of fear would feed his need to hurt someone. And tonight that someone was her.

"If the sheriff arrested Buzz, then he must have his reasons," she said, and started to move past him.

He stopped her, slapping one large beefy palm onto the wall next to her, trapping her. He leaned in. "You always did have a mouth on you."

McCall feared how this was going to end. "You might want to consider that you are threatening an officer of the law, Eugene. Do you really need that kind of trouble?"

"After the trouble I'm already in?" He laughed, a harsh, spittle-filled laugh. "You ain't no deputy. That's right, word's out about you." He let his gaze slide down her body. "That's why you aren't wearing your gun."

"I'm only suspended. Technically—"

"Let me tell you what you can do with your *techni-*

calities," Eugene grabbed a handful of her hair in his fist, making her eyes water with the pain. "I got news for you—you were always a tramp just like your mother."

"Easy, those are fighting words," she said on a painful breath and clenched her right hand into a fist as she remembered the satisfaction she'd felt when she'd slugged this bully back in grade school for words along that same line.

Eugene sneered at her, egging her on. He wanted her to hit him so he could take some of his meanness out on her.

"This must have been a red-letter week for you," he said. "Locked up *two* Crawfords. Bet you'd like to see Luke behind bars, too, wouldn't you."

"Eugene, I have nothing against any of the Crawfords."

"You mean against *Luke*. Oh, that's right. He used to be the man of your dreams. But I took care of that. You remember in high school?" Eugene asked. "That night down by the river?"

She felt her stomach drop. The night she and Luke had made love.

"You thought he was the one who went to school the next day and bragged about bagging you," Eugene said, grinning viciously.

Luke hadn't lied. It had been Eugene. Luke had sworn he hadn't said anything. But how could she have believed him? How could she when no one else had known about the two of them making love by the campfire.

At least that's what she'd thought.

"You destroyed my reputation in high school just to get back at me for not going out with you?" Her voice broke, trembling with rage. Eugene had destroyed more than her reputation. He'd destroyed what she and Luke had shared and every dream they had of being together, not to mention her broken heart.

McCall would have tried to take Eugene on, throwing everything she had at him, even though she knew she couldn't win and would come out of the fight the worse for wear.

The only thing that stopped her was the dark figure that appeared at the edge of the deck.

"I followed the two of you," Eugene was saying, "Saw you beside the campfire." He let out a low whistle. "I said right then that I would have some of that one day," he said, gripping her hair tighter, unaware that they were no longer alone. "Guess that day has arrived." His free hand grabbed the neck of her shirt and ripped it downward.

"Get your hands off her!"

Eugene whirled at the sound of Luke's voice behind him. The look of fear on his face was almost enough retribution. Almost.

"*You* were the one who started the rumor about McCall," Luke said between clenched teeth, confirming that he'd heard. There was a cold fury in his voice.

Eugene must have heard it, too, because he released her and stepped back, raising both hands in surrender.

Why had Luke come back? Not that it mattered. She'd never been so glad to see him.

"Cousin," Eugene said, sounding alarmed. "It isn't what you think."

"I *think* you were about to rape McCall, but I asked you a question. Did you just say you were the one who started the rumor about me and McCall?" Luke demanded.

Trapped, Eugene went on the defensive, turning belligerent and confrontational. "You should be thanking me. I did you the biggest favor of your life and you didn't even know it. You could have ended up with this slut if it hadn't been for me."

LUKE FELT AS if he'd been sucker punched when he'd heard Eugene confess to what he'd done. "Do you have any idea what you did?" He took a step toward his cousin.

"Come on," Eugene said, taking a step back. "If she slept with you, she slept with everyone else in high school. She wanted what I was going to give her tonight. She asked for it."

Luke punched him, knocking Eugene down, and advanced ready to kick the hell out of him. He wanted to tear Eugene limb from limb. He'd never felt this kind of rage.

"What the—?" Eugene said, scrambling to his feet. "I was like a brother to you. She's a *Winchester*. A friggin' Winchester. I—"

Luke reached for Eugene, right hand balled into a fist and ready to strike again.

McCall grabbed his arm. "You don't want to do this," she said quietly.

"You're wrong about that," Luke said, breathing hard. "You heard him. His jealousy destroyed what we could have had. All these years…"

He started to pull free of her, half-afraid that once he started in on Eugene he might not be able to stop, and knowing it wouldn't change what had torn him and McCall apart.

"Eugene just started the rumors, Luke. I didn't trust you enough to know you were telling me the truth. And once the lies started…"

Eugene was cowering at the edge of the deck.

Luke fought to control his temper and stepped back. "Get out of my sight, Eugene, or I swear…"

His cousin scrambled over the railing, dropping the few feet to the ground and was gone into the night.

It took a moment for Luke to calm down. When he turned to McCall, he saw there were tears in her eyes.

"I should have believed you," she said.

He shook his head. "We thought we were alone. We were young, and what we had together that night scared us both." He drew her into the shelter of his arms and she snuggled against him. "I couldn't bear it though that you thought I would betray you. After that…" He was unable to put into words how miserable he'd been, how miserable he still was without her. "You should have let me kick his ass. If I hadn't come back to your cabin when I did…"

"Luke, I'm okay." She stepped back from his embrace as if she needed to get her equilibrium, to reassure herself that she was fine, that she could take care of herself.

Eugene had scared her, made her feel defenseless, and Luke knew that was a feeling McCall couldn't bear.

But it wasn't Eugene, he realized, who had her running scared. It was him. He'd hoped that the truth would change everything but now feared it hadn't.

"Don't push me away," he said, but didn't touch her.

She shook her head, tears welling in her eyes. "It was high school," she said, confirming what he'd guessed had her so afraid.

Had what they'd felt for each other back then been real? Or had they built it up in their minds, making more of it than it was? Was she that afraid to find out if those feelings for each other were still there?

"I came back here tonight because I can't bear to let

any more time go by," Luke said. "For hell's sake, stop pushing me away, McCall."

McCall KNEW THAT if she let him walk away this time, it would be the last chance for them. "I don't want you to go."

He stared at her as if afraid to trust her words. Both of them were still afraid of being hurt again; she could see it in his eyes.

But neither could deny the electricity that arced between them, she thought. The air seemed to vibrate around them. She could almost hear the low hum in the cold night air. She didn't dare touch him. Didn't dare move.

She could see in his face the same battle that was going on inside him. Had that night they'd made love so long ago just been puppy love? Nothing more?

They would never know if she let him walk away now.

"Please," she whispered and closed her eyes as he reached out and cupped the back of her neck with his large warm hand. A quiver shuddered through her as he tightened his fingers on her nape and slowly drew her to him.

Her heart seemed to stop, then take off. Heat rushed through her. Her breath came in a rush as he dragged her against his firm, solid body. She could feel the pounding of his heart.

He held her like that, his breath ragged. She heard him swallow and finally opened her eyes to look up at him.

"McCall," he whispered as he swept her up into his arms and into the cabin, kicking the door closed behind them.

As he lowered her to her feet, she slid down his body until he found her mouth. She caught her breath as he kissed her with a passion that had her toes curling in her boots.

His fingers entwined in her long hair, and her pulse thundered under her skin as he deepened the kiss. She felt his hand on her cheek, then her throat. As he released her mouth, she threw back her head and felt his fingers, then his mouth leave a hot trail down her throat to the torn opening of her shirt.

She gasped as she felt his hand cup her breast, the rough pad of his thumb rubbing her already pebble-hard nipple until she cried out, heat rushing to her center. He freed her breasts and covered them in turn with his mouth, dropping to his knees.

Later she would remember unsnapping his Western shirt, running her palms over the hard muscles of his chest, working at the buttons on his jeans.

She couldn't remember shedding her clothing, only the feel of her naked flesh pressed against his as he carried her to the bedroom, saying something about this time doing it right—in a real bed.

What she would never forget was the aching heat of desire, the need that consumed her every ragged breath. She cried out when his touch released her, and the longing started building again until she thought she couldn't bear it.

She remembered the welcome weight of him, the feeling of him filling her completely and that roller-coaster ride of desire and heart-pounding pleasure before the quaking release and that experience of ultimate fulfillment.

As she lay spent beside him, his arm around her, she memorized the feel, the smell, the sound of him, wanting to keep all of it forever. Not admitting that inkling of fear that, like ten years ago, something would drive them apart—only this time forever.

A LIGHT RAIN fell from the low clouds. Mist snaked up the river, wrapping the bare branches of the cottonwoods in gray gauze.

McCall stretched as she looked out on the tranquil scene. Strange how different it looked this morning. She realized that it wasn't the familiar landscape that had changed, though; it was her.

She felt new, like the spring leaves gracing the trees from her window—the only bright color along the river bottom.

Lying on her side, she sensed rather than heard Luke approach. The air pressure around her seemed to change. She waited for his touch, aching with anticipation.

His fingertips were warm across the cool flesh of her hip as he trailed them down the slope of her waist and up along her rib cage. She sucked in a breath as his finger brushed her breast. She took in the freshly showered scent of him. His hair would still be wet and dark against the warm brown of his skin.

As he lay down on the bed, he encircled her with his arms and drew her back against him.

She smiled, a soft chuckle escaping her throat as she realized he was wonderfully naked.

"I missed you," he whispered at her ear, his breath tickling her ear.

"Hmm," she said, leaning back against him.

"You are so beautiful, McCall."

She closed her eyes. In Luke's arms, she *felt* beautiful. Felt as if this was where she had always been meant to be. She'd never understood her mother's elusive quest for true love until this moment.

Lying in her lover's arms, McCall understood what it meant to love with such passion that you felt you would die without this man. That you would do *anything* to be with him.

Luke Crawford had ignited that kind of passion in her. For years he had stayed like a brand on her skin. She knew that no matter how this ended, she would always ache for only him. No other man would ever be able to satisfy this need.

They had talked and made love late into the night, skirting around the issue of their families and the past, except for confessions that they'd never gotten over each other.

Neither talked of the future, both of them no doubt fearful that this was too fragile. McCall was afraid of spoiling this moment if it was all they had. They had both let lies keep them apart all these years. Lies and fear that they were too young to know real love. Too young to be as serious as they'd been.

Would they have made it together had Eugene not started the rumor? They would never know.

McCall had told him why she hadn't dated, how she'd been afraid after him that she would be like her mother, going from one man to another, looking for that feeling that only Luke could give her.

"I never want to let you out of my arms," he whispered next to her ear now. "It broke my heart that you thought I could hurt you that way."

She nodded, surprised at her tears.

"Oh, McCall," Luke said, turning her around to face him. He touched his thumb pad to her cheek to wipe away an errant tear before dropping his mouth to hers. She lost herself in him just as she knew she always would.

Luke's cell phone rang and he pulled back to check his phone. "It's Buzz. I'm going to have to take this," he said as he slid out of bed, pulled on his jeans and left the room.

McCall lay in the bed staring up at the log ceiling. She'd heard Luke's quick exclamation of breath before he'd left the room. Something told her he hadn't overheard that Buzz had been arrested when he saved her from Eugene last night.

When he came back into the room, she saw the change in him.

"Buzz has been arrested," he said, retrieving the rest of his clothing from where it had been dropped last night in a frenzy of passion. He looked up. "You already knew?"

"Eugene told me. That's why he was so angry. I thought you overheard. I'm sorry."

"I guess I came in late for that news," Luke said, staring at her for a long moment. His anger had ebbed, but she could feel him pulling away. Buzz was family.

McCall watched him finish dressing, already missing him and fearing he wouldn't be back. They'd always loved each other, but ten years ago it hadn't been enough. Was it now?

"You had to have seen this coming," she said, a plea in her voice. "The pickup was in the Crawford stock pond. Buzz had access and he knew no one would be around that place. Grant wouldn't have arrested Buzz without sufficient evidence."

"Your father's rifle was found in Buzz's lake house," Luke said. "What fool would keep the weapon on his premises?"

An arrogant fool. A man who thought he was above

the law. A man like Buzz Crawford. Or from what she'd learned about him, a man like Trace Winchester. Is that why Buzz had hated her father so much? Because he reminded him of himself?

"You can't even be sure your father had that rifle with him when he died," Luke said. "You told me that Buzz couldn't remember if he'd taken it."

Her mother had lied about seeing Trace the opening morning of antelope season. Had she lied about seeing the rifle the last time she saw Trace?

Buzz had caught Trace poaching the day before. Maybe he had taken the rifle after all—and just not turned it in to evidence. Maybe her father had already been in the ground by the opening of antelope season.

"It all comes down to my father's rifle," she said quickly. "If Buzz confiscated it, then he probably wrote it down in his logbook the day before the opening of antelope season."

"Do you really believe that if he'd killed your father and kept the rifle, he would have written it down?" Luke demanded.

"Buzz is arrogant enough he might have. But at least you will know if he was in the area of the ridge that day."

"Anyone could have put that rifle in Buzz's lake house. Everyone knew he never locked his front door."

Another example of Buzz's arrogance. He was daring someone to steal from him.

"Not *anyone* could have put the rifle in his house," she argued. "Only the person who took it from my father. Come on, Luke," she said, needing him on her side. "You're afraid your uncle is guilty and worried what he'll do now that it's all coming out."

His gaze softened. "I'm just trying to make sense out

of all this." He stepped over to the bed. She felt her heart break at the thought that even now their families could come between them.

Sitting on the edge of the bed, he drew her to him, holding her tight. "I'm sorry. I have to go. I'll call you later?" He brushed a kiss over her lips, then his gaze met hers and held it and she saw the longing, the regret, the same fears she was feeling, before he turned and left.

Chapter Thirteen

Luke was allowed to go back to Buzz's cell rather than speak to him via the phones through the thick plastic partition.

He knew that it was because he was a game warden with the same training as any other law enforcement officer, but also because a lot of people still looked up to Buzz and his legacy.

Whitehorse was a small town where some loyalties never died. Just as grudges and slights never did.

"It's about damned time," Buzz said through the bars as Luke walked down the short hall to his cell. "I've been here all night. The sheriff was waiting for me the moment Eugene and I got back from Billings. I've been trying to call you for hours."

Luke had turned off his phone when he was with Mc-Call and had forgotten to turn it back on until this morning. "You could have called Eugene."

"Don't get smart with me," his uncle snapped.

Right, this was about bailing him out, and Eugene wouldn't be able to raise the money.

"Why would the sheriff arrest you?" he asked, remembering what McCall had said about sufficient evidence.

"That bastard sheriff thinks I killed Trace Winchester."

"Why would he think that?"

Buzz slashed a hand through the air in frustration. "McCall Winchester framed me. Why the hell do you think?"

Luke stared at his uncle, remembering back in high school when Buzz had found out that Luke was dating McCall Winchester. Eugene, no doubt, had told him. Eugene had probably been spying on him the whole time.

Buzz had gone ballistic. "I won't have you dating Ruby Winchester's daughter." It still made no sense, this hatred of the Winchesters over some land decades ago. Even back then, Luke had felt as if this animosity was more personal.

"How could *she* frame you?" Luke asked with a sigh.

"It was her father's rifle. One day she asks me what happened to the rifle, as if I can remember that long ago, and the next the sheriff shows up at my door with a search warrant and, big surprise, finds Trace Winchester's rifle hidden in my house. Doesn't take a rocket scientist to figure it out."

The only way Buzz could have had the rifle was if he took it from Trace Winchester. Either confiscated it when he wrote him up for poaching. Or took it when he killed him on that ridge.

Buzz was a lot of things, but Luke refused to believe his uncle was a killer.

"How would McCall have gotten the rifle?" Luke asked.

"From her mother—the person who killed Trace Winchester," Buzz said with such venom that Luke was taken aback. "She's behind all this, just getting her daughter to do her dirty work."

Luke could see that his uncle needed him to believe this. There was only one thing Luke was certain of: McCall hadn't put the rifle in Buzz's house.

"I know that look," Buzz said with a curse. "That woman's turned your head around. You've always had a weakness for the little chippie."

"Don't call her that."

"I just told you that she and her mother framed me and you're defending her?"

"And I'm telling you I don't believe it. If you locked your house—"

His uncle swore. "Just get me out of here."

"When's the bail hearing?" he asked, knowing what it would take to get his uncle out on a murder charge. Luke would have to put up his property, that's if the judge allowed bail at all.

"The hearing's this morning. Make sure I don't spend another night in jail, you hear? You owe me that."

Luke looked at the man who'd raised him, reminded himself of the sacrifices Buzz had made over the years and bit back a reply he knew he would regret.

"Just a minute," Buzz said as Luke started to leave. "The other day on the phone on my way to Billings… Why were you asking about my old pickup?"

"Someone's been using it for poaching deer along the Milk."

Buzz swore, but it didn't have his usual intensity. Nor did he seem as shocked and angry by the news as Luke had thought he would be.

He felt dread settle deeper in his gut. "Is there anything you want to tell me before I see about getting you out of here?"

"Are you asking me if I'm poaching deer or if I killed Trace Winchester?" Buzz demanded, then slammed his palms against the bars, before turning his back to Luke. "Just get me out of here."

McCALL SHOWERED AND dressed after Luke left, feeling bereft and edgy. She thought of their lovemaking and ached to be back in his arms. She'd once thought she couldn't live without him. She'd been seventeen then. The ten years apart had been hell.

But this was worse. Last night proved how they felt about each other. They were in love, had been for years. They'd come together again in the most intimate of ways, the passion blinding, the aching need to be together almost more than either of them could stand. Nothing should have been able to drive them apart.

But it had.

She'd seen how torn Luke had been between his loyalty to the uncle who'd raised him and the woman he loved. Before, his cousin had come between them. Now it was his uncle.

Whatever the old feud between the two families, it was still going strong. Why couldn't Luke see that his uncle was guilty? Because he was too close to it.

Or was she the one who was too close to see the truth?

McCall shook her head. All the evidence pointed to Buzz. He was the one who'd caught Trace poaching, and yet as much as he'd harassed her father, Buzz had sworn he hadn't taken the rifle. A red flag.

Then finding the pickup in the Crawford stock pond. Buzz would have known that the place was vacant, no one around for miles to see him get rid of the truck and hike back to the ridge. The walk back to his own vehicle wouldn't have been that tough for a man who walked hundreds of miles a year as a game warden.

Finding the rifle at his house was just the icing on the cake. The only other evidence that could put the nail in Buzz Crawford's coffin was the pages from his daily log for the days in question.

Would the sheriff have thought to check them?

She couldn't depend on Luke to help her now, she realized. When it came to loyalties, blood was always thicker than water. Luke would stand by his uncle.

When her cell phone rang, McCall hoped it was Luke. It wasn't. Nor was it her mother, who would have been her second guess. Ruby would be furious that McCall hadn't called to give her the news before everyone else in town heard about Buzz's arrest.

To McCall's surprise, it was her grandmother.

"I need to see you," Pepper Winchester said. "Can you come out here now?"

"Only if you promise not to call the sheriff this time."

A slight hesitation, then, "I apologize for that. I would appreciate it if you would drive out to the ranch. It's important or I wouldn't ask. I will have Enid make us lunch."

"You sure she won't try to poison me?" McCall asked, only half joking.

"We could make her taste it, if you like." Pepper sounded serious.

She tried not to take this invitation for more than it was. Her mother was right: she would be a fool to think that anything had changed with her grandmother. Pepper wanted something from her. The only question was what?

But going out to her grandmother's for lunch was better than sitting around hoping Luke would come back.

"Okay. I'll see you soon."

McCall couldn't help being anxious though as she drove out to the Winchester Ranch. Another spring thunderstorm had blown in and she had to shift into four-wheel drive to get down the muddy road.

She worried about ending up in a ditch again, only this time no Luke to save her since she hadn't thought to tell anyone where she'd gone.

Just the thought of Luke made her want to cry. She felt strung too tight and knew she couldn't trust her emotions.

She was tired, drained emotionally, physically and mentally. Of course she would feel this way after finding out that her father had been murdered.

That was what made her feel vulnerable and scared. Not falling for Luke all over again. She hated feeling this way. Why had she opened herself up to this again?

She knew that since finding her father's grave and realizing he'd been murdered, it hadn't really sunk in. She'd put the pieces together, found the pickup, and everything had quickly—too quickly—fallen into place after that because of the rifle. Because Buzz didn't have the sense to dump it.

Criminals were notoriously stupid. It was why so many of them got caught. Why crime didn't pay.

She realized what was bothering her. She didn't know why Buzz had killed her father. Blackmail? Blackmailers tended to get killed for obvious reasons—death being the only way to keep the bloodsucking leeches off you permanently.

What had Buzz done that Trace Winchester had found out about?

Or maybe it hadn't been blackmail. Maybe Buzz had just lost his temper with Trace. Clearly, from all the tickets he'd written Trace, he had it in for him. So who knew what had happened on that ridge?

As McCall pulled up in front of the Winchester Ranch lodge, the old blue heeler came out to growl and a curtain moved behind a window at the end of one wing.

McCall got out and, again keeping an eye on the dog, went to the door and knocked.

This time it was her grandmother who answered. Her long thick hair was freshly plaited. She wore black just as she had on the first visit, but she'd added a beautiful gold link necklace.

She looked graceful and elegant, and McCall couldn't help but notice that her expression seemed softer.

"Thank you for coming on such short notice," Pepper said. She motioned McCall into the parlor again, but this time there was a fire going in the fireplace, a welcome addition on a day like this.

McCall took the chair she was offered, noticing the scrapbooks on the coffee table in front of her.

"I have something I thought you'd like to see before lunch," her grandmother said, taking a chair next to her and opening one of the books.

McCall saw at once that the scrapbooks were filled with family photographs. Her heart leaped in her chest at the sight of four children beside Pepper, who looked young and beautiful. She was holding the baby, Trace.

The four young children were her Aunt Virginia and Uncles Angus, Brand and Worth. This was the first time she'd laid eyes on them. As far as she knew, none of them had returned to the ranch after Trace disappeared. Apparently she had cousins she'd never met, as well.

Worry as to why her grandmother was showing her these put a damper on her excitement at this glimpse into her family and her father's earlier life.

"Your father was the sweetest baby," Pepper said, touching the baby's face in the photo. She turned a page. "He was two here."

McCall stared at the photo of her father. "He was adorable."

Her grandmother smiled. "Yes, he was. I spoiled him—I know that." She turned the page, pointing out Trace in each photograph even though it wasn't necessary.

He was the handsomest of Pepper's children and clearly her favorite. She noticed what could have been jealousy in the faces of the others in one photo where Pepper was making a fuss over Trace. McCall felt a growing unease.

"Trace was such a good boy. A little wild like his father, but he had a good, strong heart." Pepper's voice broke with emotion, and she turned her face aside to wipe furtively at her tears.

McCall touched a finger to the photo of her father as a boy, seeing herself in the squint of his eyes, the cocky stance, the dark straight hair and high cheekbones.

Pepper turned the page, and McCall smiled when she saw the snapshots of her father as a teenager. It was clear why Ruby had fallen so hard for him. He was stunningly handsome, a mischievous look in his dark eyes, a swagger about him.

"He was so good-looking," McCall said, almost lamenting the fact, given what Red had told her about her father and women.

"He played football the year they went to state," Pepper said. "He was quite the athlete, but his first love was hunting."

She looked up then. "I heard you were the one who found his truck."

"It was a lucky guess," McCall said, uncomfortable with her grandmother's intense gaze on her.

"He loved that truck. I ordered it special for him. It looks nothing now like the pickup my son drove away in the last time I saw him." She cleared her throat. "I had wondered what happened to his rifle. It was his grandfather's, you know. An old model 99 Savage. It had his grandfather's and father's initials carved in the stock. How foolish of the killer to keep it, don't you think?"

It was the first she'd spoken of her son's death and Buzz Crawford's arrest. Something in her words filled McCall with a growing uneasiness.

A bell tinkled down the hall. Her grandmother closed the scrapbook and rose. Was it possible Pepper didn't believe Buzz had killed her son?

But why?

EUGENE DIDN'T SHOW up for the bail hearing, much to Luke's relief. It was just as well, since he wasn't sure what he might do to Eugene when he saw him. That thought filled him with a hollow sadness. And to think he'd felt as if Eugene was like a brother to him—like Abel and Cain as it turned out.

The judge set bail for five hundred thousand, saying he didn't believe Buzz, who had served the county for years as a game warden, was a flight risk.

Luke put up his land to raise the money to get his uncle out on bail, then got in his pickup and headed for Glasgow and the game warden district office where all daily logs were kept—including those stored from Buzz's time as warden.

He told himself he was doing this for McCall. In truth, he would have done anything for her, not that she would believe it right now. He knew from the look on her face this morning that she thought he'd chosen his family over her.

She was wrong about that.

But he was going to Glasgow for himself as much as McCall. He needed to know the truth, and he hoped it could be found in what Buzz had written in his daily logs.

A tumbleweed cartwheeled across the road propelled by a wind that lay over the grass and howled at the windows of the pickup. Luke could see another spring thunderstorm moving across the prairie toward him.

He loved the storms in this part of the country. Everything was intense up here, from the weather to the light that made the pale green spring grasses glow and warmed the Larb Hills in the distance to a dusty purple.

The storm swept across the open landscape, rain pelting the pickup, wind chasing tumbleweeds to trap them in the barbed wire fences that lined the two-lane.

As the rain passed, Luke rolled down his window and breathed in the smell of spring. The storm had left the land looking even greener, the sky washed a pale blue.

He wished McCall was with him right now, knowing she would appreciate this scene. He hadn't been able to get her out of his head. But that was nothing new. Last night, though, had only made him want her more after wanting this woman most of his adult life. Now they had a chance. Or they had had one before his uncle called.

While Luke had made his choice when he'd decided

to do this, he still felt disloyal as he entered the Glasgow FWP regional office.

It surprised him that McCall believed Buzz was a killer but that Buzz wouldn't lie about where he'd been in his warden's daily log. Was his uncle really that arrogant—and that foolish?

Twenty-seven years ago in the fall, Buzz would have probably been down in the Missouri Breaks at the far south of his jurisdiction for most of the day checking on bow elk hunters. He would be needed there more than out in the prairie looking for a possible antelope poacher.

Except, even if that's what Buzz had done, he would still have had to drive right past the road to the ridge where Trace Winchester's body had been buried. Right past the old Crawford place where Trace's pickup had been sunk in the mud at the bottom of the stock pond.

Buzz could have killed Trace Winchester, buried him on the ridge and gotten rid of his pickup in the pond.

But Luke didn't believe he had. Or maybe he just didn't want to believe Buzz would commit murder.

"Mornin' Helen," Luke said as he recognized the older woman working the main desk.

"Hi, Luke. What brings you to the big city?" she joked. "I didn't see a trial on the schedule."

"Nope, not today. I'm on another errand. I need to know where I can find the game warden daily logs from twenty-seven years ago." He knew they kept them in case a legal problem came up years down the road.

"Twenty-seven years ago? Those would be in our storage facility at the other end of town. I can give you the key. They're all filed by month and year. Do you know what date you're looking for?"

He nodded. "Shouldn't take me long."

"How is your lunch? Poison-free?" Pepper Winchester actually smiled, her dark eyes almost teasing.

"Fine," McCall said, a lie. Enid was no cook. Still, that wasn't the only reason she'd lost her appetite, she thought as she put down her fork. "Why did you really invite me out here? It wasn't for lunch or photos."

Her grandmother arched a brow as she put down her fork and pushed away her nearly untouched lunch. "Why did Buzz Crawford kill my son?"

"I beg your pardon?" McCall was taken aback by the abruptness of the question.

Pepper's direct gaze bored into her. "There must have been a reason."

McCall had asked herself the same question. "I don't know. I suppose it will come out in the trial."

Her grandmother looked skeptical. "Let's hope so. If you hear anything, you'll let me know?"

McCall nodded and was about to tell her grandmother that she'd been suspended and wouldn't be hearing much.

But Pepper stood, signaling lunch and the visit were over. As she turned to leave, she said over her shoulder, "You know the way out?"

Before McCall could answer, her grandmother had disappeared back into the gloom and doom of the old lodge.

But from the shadows, McCall caught a glimpse of Enid before the housekeeper ducked out of sight.

THE DOOR TO the metal storage unit opened with a groan. A blast of musty hot air hit Luke in the face as he reached in to turn on the light.

The long narrow building was filled with shelves from floor to ceiling, the ones closest to the door, the most recent. He entered the maze of shelves and worked his way to those from twenty-seven years ago.

According to McCall, Buzz had caught Trace Winchester poaching an antelope before the opening of antelope season. That could have meant minutes before daylight. Or the night before.

Luke pulled down the logbook for October and, stepping under one of the bare bulb lights, flipped through the book.

The notes were all written in his uncle's precise printing—until he got to the day in question. The first entry on October 20 was of Trace Winchester's poaching violation. But what had Luke's heart racing was that the entry was nearly illegible. The words ran together, looking hurriedly scrawled.

And not just that, Luke realized. The entry was written in black ink—while all the rest of the entries and those after that day were in blue.

It was a small thing and if he hadn't known Buzz the way he did, he wouldn't have thought anything of it. Buzz prided himself on doing everything neat and tidy and by the book.

Buzz had broken with routine, indicating he'd been upset and hurried.

According to his uncle's notation, he'd gotten a call from dispatch asking him to check on a possible problem on the ridge where Trace Winchester's remains had been found.

He'd responded, found Trace poaching an antelope, written him a ticket. He'd made no mention of Trace's rifle.

Luke stared at the writing until it blurred before his eyes, feeling sick. Buzz had been there and might be the only person still alive who knew what happened on that ridge that day.

Chapter Fourteen

News that Buzz Crawford had been released from jail hit the streets at the speed of light. McCall heard it at the first stop she made once back in Whitehorse after her lunch with her grandmother.

She got the feeling that everyone had believed him guilty and if not guilty, then at least *capable* of murder.

The sheriff caught her as she was coming out of the post office.

"McCall?" Grant was standing beside her car, clearly waiting for her. She thought about seeing him parked down the street from his house and wondered again if he'd been spying on her—or his wife.

"Sheriff." Had her grandmother called him about her again?

"I just wanted to let you know that Buzz Crawford is out on bail."

She wondered why he hadn't just called her. Maybe he had. She hadn't checked her messages since she feared there wouldn't be one from Luke.

"I heard," she said. "It's all anyone in town is talking about."

"Sorry I didn't let you know sooner. Luke got him out on bail."

Good ol' Luke.

The sheriff seemed to hesitate. "I also wanted to let you know that Buzz filed a formal complaint against you, saying he believes you planted the rifle in his house in an attempt to frame him. I know that isn't the case," Grant said quickly. "But he's pretty worked up. If he should come by your place, just call the department at once."

"Sure." And twenty minutes later someone would arrive at her cabin twenty minutes too late?

"Eugene got himself locked up last night," the sheriff said. "Drunk and disorderly. He hasn't made bail."

"At least Luke didn't get him out," she said, more to herself than the sheriff.

"Just watch your back." The sheriff cleared his throat. "I never thanked you for your work in finding the pickup. I'm sorry I had to take you off the case. And I wouldn't worry too much about Buzz. He's too smart to threaten you. He's in enough trouble as it is."

She wished she could be that sure of what Buzz Crawford would do. Or had done, for that matter.

WHEN LUKE RETURNED to the cabin, he found McCall standing at the edge of the deck looking over the river. She had a blanket wrapped around her shoulders and a beer in her hand.

She turned at the sound of his footfalls and he saw her expression. She hadn't been sure he would return.

"What are you doing out here?" he asked.

"Enjoying the evening." He saw she had the gun he'd given her tucked into the waistband of her jeans and wondered if she wasn't out here because she could hear anyone who approached. Obviously she'd heard that Buzz had been released from jail.

Luke had stopped by the lake house but hadn't found Buzz at home. He wasn't sure what he planned to say to his uncle. He wasn't sure what there was to say. He ended up leaving a note:

Buzz,

We need to talk,

Luke

He knew it sounded cryptic, but he also didn't want to leave anything that could be potentially incriminating. Telling Buzz about what he'd found in the logbook would have been.

After he'd left Buzz's place, all he'd wanted to do was return to McCall.

Now, without a word, he stepped to her and took her in his arms. He didn't want to talk about anything, especially his uncle. He wasn't going to let anything come between them ever again.

"I checked Buzz's logbook," he said, drawing back to look into her eyes. "You were right. The evidence is there. As I was leaving, the sheriff arrived. He took the book."

She nodded, not seeming surprised. "I'm sorry."

"Me, too."

She motioned to the cooler at her feet. "You look like you could use a beer."

He smiled and let go of her long enough to take a beer from the box and unscrew the top. He pulled on the beer, taking a long drink. She was right. This was exactly what he needed, something cold to drink, a nice view and the woman he loved.

Dark shadows were forming in the river bottom as another short spring day turned to dusk. He could hear a flock of geese honking softly from the shallows. A breeze stirred McCall's dark hair. He breathed in her scent as he snuggled against her back and slipped a hand inside her shirt to cup her bare breast.

Desire sparked along his nerve endings, firing that old familiar need in him. The passion had been there the first time they'd touched and nothing had dampened it, not even the years spent apart.

She turned to kiss him, tasting of cold beer. He dragged her to him, encircling her with his arms, deepening the kiss. Her body molded to his, and he could feel the frantic beat of her heart.

"Unless you want me to make love to you right here on this deck, I think we'd better go inside," he whispered as he drew back from the kiss.

She smiled up at him and whispered back, "What is wrong with out here on the deck?"

IT WASN'T UNTIL LATER, snuggled together under the blanket, their clothing pillowed beneath their heads and the starry night above, that they heard the sirens.

McCall sat up as she saw the flashing lights and saw where they were headed—toward the lake. "Luke?"

She'd barely gotten the word out before he was up and pulling on his clothing.

"I have a bad feeling," he said.

She had one as well as she quickly dressed and they took his pickup and headed north, following the lights of the sheriff and ambulance.

As they turned off the road, McCall saw what she'd feared. Both the patrol car and the ambulance had stopped in front of Buzz's house.

Luke pulled up in the pickup and jumped out. As he ran toward the house, McCall saw a deputy stop him.

She turned to look for the sheriff and, spotting him, hurried over.

"What's happened?" she asked.

"Buzz committed suicide."

"Suicide?" She couldn't help sounding astonished. Buzz Crawford was the least likely person she knew to even contemplate suicide. "Are you sure?"

"He left a note," Grant said. "He's the one who killed your father, McCall. He confessed. I guess, confronted with all the evidence…"

She nodded, thinking about what Luke had said he'd found in Buzz's logbook. Still, she felt shaken. Buzz had taken the cowardly way out, and while her heart ached for Luke and his loss, she was angry that she and her mother hadn't gotten to see this go to trial. This didn't feel like closure because now they would never know why.

She turned to see Luke, his face twisted in anguish as he came toward them.

"They won't let me in," he said to the sheriff. "They said he's dead?"

"I'm sorry, Luke. Buzz shot himself. He left a suicide note along with a confession to the killing of Trace Winchester."

LUKE DROVE MCCALL back to her cabin, too stunned and distraught to talk and thankful she didn't question him.

"I need to be the one to tell Eugene," he said as he pulled up next to her cabin. He leaned in, kissed her and said, "I'm sorry about your dad. You tried to warn me."

"I'm sorry, too," she said and, touching his cheek, told him to be careful before she got out of the truck.

"I need some time," he said. "I might go out to my

place at least to check things tonight. But I'll see you to-morrow, okay?"

She smiled in understanding. "Don't worry about me. Take all the time you need. I know you'll be back." She closed the door and walked toward her cabin.

He waited until she was inside before he turned around and drove through the darkness, feeling as if he'd been hit by a train.

His mind was racing. He'd found what could consti-tute evidence in Buzz's logbook. Had the sheriff shown it to Buzz? Is that why his uncle had decided to write the confession and kill himself?

Luke drove toward town, turning it all over in his head. The night was black. No stars, no moon, the clouds so low now it was like driving through cotton. He had his side window down letting the cold night air blow in.

He didn't feel the chill, only the intense sense of loss and regret. He kept rehashing his last conversation with Buzz over in his head and blaming himself that he hadn't seen this coming.

Didn't everyone say there were signs? Buzz had been acting strangely, but Luke had thought he was just bored with retirement and worried about Eugene.

Luke had never believed that a man like Buzz would ever do something like this. Murder? Then suicide? He had a bad feeling that the ones least likely to commit ei-ther were the ones who would surprise you.

For Buzz it might have been a case of the perfect storm: the arrest, his disappointment in Eugene. Suspect-ing, as Luke did, that Eugene had been using his pickup to poach could have been the last straw.

A thought crossed his mind. He scoffed at the idea but

couldn't shake a nagging feeling that the thought hadn't been as crazy as he wanted to believe.

Luke slowed the pickup on the edge of Whitehorse and headed for the sheriff's department—and the county jail where his cousin was still locked up the last he'd heard.

MCCALL FELT NUMB as she stopped on the deck to pick up the blanket she'd left there. The darkness seemed to close in along with the shock.

Buzz was dead.

She wrapped the blanket around herself and stood staring down at the river through the deep black of cottonwoods. No starlight filtered past the bare branches. No moon shone in Montana's big sky.

The only light was a ghostly glaze that shimmered on the surface of the water as it snaked past.

McCall shivered and pulled the blanket tighter as a gust of wind moaned through the trees.

It was over.

Buzz had killed her father, and while she would never know why, at least she should be thankful that Trace Winchester had gotten justice.

So why did she feel so empty, she wondered as she leaned against the railing and breathed in the rich scents from the river bottom. It was over.

Over for some, she thought. Not for Luke, though.

Suddenly she felt as if icy fingers had brushed across the back of her neck. Her stomach contracted with a feeling she was no longer alone, and that what was waiting for her in the dark wasn't just dangerous—it was deadly.

She stared hard into the black cottonwoods, listening for any hint that there was someone out there watching her at this very moment. Eugene? Had he gotten out of jail? The wind moaned through the branches, the limbs moving restlessly against the dark sky.

Taking a step back, she edged toward the front door of the house, trying to remember if she'd locked it, suddenly filled with a sense of dread.

She'd only taken a few steps when she remembered the gun Luke had given her. She'd had it earlier on the deck…

She stopped, her gaze scanning the dark shadows of the deck. She couldn't see it. Maybe Luke had picked it up. Or maybe they had knocked it off the deck earlier.

As badly as she wished she could find it, she wasn't about to take the time to look for it. Turning, she lunged for her front door, that feeling of danger too intense to ignore.

The knob turned in her hand. She hadn't locked it. Damn.

She stepped in, fumbling for the light as she slammed the door behind her, breathing hard.

There's no one out there. You're just spooked over everything that has happened. You're running scared and it's not like you.

McCall reached for the lock but froze. Had it been the soft scuff of a shoe? Or a breath exhaled? Or had she just sensed it as she had on the deck?

Whatever the reason, even before McCall hit the light switch and spun around, she knew. Someone was behind her.

"WHAT ARE YOU doing here?" Eugene said from his cell bunk when Luke walked in. "You'd better be here to get me out. Because if you've come to give me a lecture…"

Luke gripped the bars. Obviously no one had told him about Buzz yet. "I need to know something, Eugene. I told Buzz that someone was using his pickup to poach deer along the river."

His cousin leaned back on his bunk. "When did you tell him that?"

Luke swallowed back his guilt. "Right before he was released from jail."

"And let me guess. You suspect I was using the pickup. What was I doing with the deer?"

"Selling them to a client in Billings to pay for your gambling debts."

To his surprise, Eugene began to laugh. "Doesn't that sound a little too organized for a worthless ne'er-do-well like me?" his cousin asked, getting up and coming over to the bars. "Huh, hotshot game warden?"

"What are you trying to tell me?" Luke asked, afraid he already knew what was coming.

"Buzz. It was *his* idea. He was bored and if anyone knew how to poach and get away with it, it was Buzz. Why do you think we went to Billings? To unload what we'd killed." He laughed again. "Don't look so shocked. Buzz used to poach all the time when he was warden. You didn't notice how our meat supply never ran low?"

Luke stared at his cousin, remembering what McCall had said about her mother thinking Trace might have had something on Buzz he was using as leverage. "Did Buzz also mention that Trace Winchester was blackmailing him?"

Eugene grinned. "Well, if Trace was, I can tell you this much—no one blackmails Buzz for long." His cousin shook his head, giving Luke a disgusted look. "You always thought you were better than us, didn't you? Buzz joked that as great as you thought you were, you'd never catch us. Even if you did, Buzz said you'd never arrest us." He turned to go back to his cot. "When you see Buzz, tell him to spring me from the joint."

"I'm afraid Buzz isn't going to be springing anyone," Luke said. "He committed suicide tonight after confessing to killing Trace Winchester."

"Please don't do anything heroic," Sandy said, rising from the kitchen chair where she'd been sitting, waiting.

Heart hammering, McCall heard the click of the safety being flipped off on the pistol as she stared at Sandy Sheridan. Two thoughts zipped past. What was the sheriff's wife doing here pointing a gun at her? And Luke wouldn't be back tonight.

"How *did* you get the job with my husband?" Sandy asked as she advanced on her, the gun steady in her hand and pointed at McCall's heart. "Because you aren't afraid of anything? Or was it because you could twist Grant around your little finger? He always told me how much he liked you."

From the expression on Sandy's face, that had been a mistake on the sheriff's part.

"What are you doing here?" McCall asked, understanding only that she was in serious trouble. That over-caffeinated, frantic look was in Sandy's eyes, and she held the gun like a woman who knew how to use it.

Sandy gave her an impatient look. "Don't try to con me. The moment I saw you standing at my front door, I knew that Grant was right. He said you made a damned good deputy because you were bright and saw what other people didn't."

"You're both giving me too much credit," McCall said. Outside, the wind had picked up. It whipped the cotton-woods, a limb scraping against the side of the house and flickering shadows past the window. "I haven't a clue why you're here."

"Guess," Sandy said with a giggle.

A thought worked its way through the panic. "Buzz didn't kill my father."

Sandy laughed, a sound like piano wires snapping. "How can you say that? The man confessed."

No doubt at gunpoint.

McCall tried to concentrate, but the wind and trees whipping against the cabin kept distracting her. She felt too tired for this, her mind numb from shock and fear and a deep sense of regret.

How could she have been so wrong? Buzz had looked so guilty, *too* guilty. No wonder she'd felt such an emptiness when it had looked as if he'd done it—and taken the easy way out.

The sheriff was right: she *had* been too emotionally involved.

"You aren't going to tell me *you* killed my father, are you?" McCall asked. "I thought you loved him." She was only a few feet away from Sandy, but she knew better than to make a play for the gun.

"I *did* love him." Hatred flared in Sandy's eyes. "I *loved* him more than you can ever understand. I would have done anything for him. And what did he do to me? He broke my heart." She was crying now but still holding the gun aimed at McCall's heart.

McCall's mind was racing again as she tried to put it all together. "Trace felt guilty about what he'd done to you, so of course he would agree to meet you on the ridge to talk."

Sandy's eyes narrowed. "Very good."

Trace had been furious with Ruby over her little tryst

with Red, so he would have been primed to do anything his old girlfriend asked.

"But things got out of hand," McCall guessed.

"He refused to leave that tramp and you," Sandy said. "I told him you probably weren't even his baby. He thought he was just going to get to walk away from me." Her eyes took on a faraway look that turned McCall's blood to slush.

Outside the cabin, something moved across the window. Not a limb. *Someone.*

"So you killed him," McCall said, trying hard not to look past Sandy to the window again. Someone was out there headed for the front door. Luke? But he'd said he wouldn't be back. Her heart soared then dropped like a stone. Had he seen the sheriff's wife holding the gun on her? If he hadn't, he'd be walking into this deadly situation.

"What did you use? A gun, a knife, a rock?" McCall asked as she took a couple of steps toward the back of the cabin, hoping to turn Sandy so she wouldn't be able to see whoever was about to open the front door.

"What are you doing?" Sandy demanded, grabbing the weapon with both hands. "Stop moving."

"I just need to sit down," McCall said, motioning toward the kitchen chair nearby.

"You'll be lying down soon enough and for a very long time," Sandy snapped. "Enjoy standing."

"So how did you do it?" McCall asked, forced to be content with having turned Sandy at least most of the way from the door.

"I shot him if you must know."

"With the same gun you're holding on me?" McCall asked.

"As a matter of fact. Ironic, isn't it?"

The front door eased open. McCall still couldn't see who it was, but the way it opened, she was sure the person outside had seen what was going on.

"Then you buried him on the ridge," McCall said. "Took his rifle—"

"Don't be ridiculous. I left as quickly as I could, but as we were driving back to town, I passed Game Warden Buzz Crawford and remembered the vendetta he and Trace had going on. I put in a call to Fish and Game saying there was someone poaching on the ridge. I knew once Buzz found Trace dead, he wouldn't call it in. He knew no one would believe him, not the way he hounded Trace all the time. Everyone would believe he did it."

Something Sandy said stopped McCall for a moment, but she couldn't put her finger on what it was before Sandy finished. McCall could imagine Buzz finding Trace's body. He would know he'd been set up. The smart thing would have been for him to call 911, but Sandy was right. He would have looked guilty no matter what. He had motive and opportunity, and he was standing over his nemesis's dead body.

It explained why Buzz had acted so guilty. Everything was starting to make sense. "Buzz buried Trace and got rid of the pickup in the stock pond, then wrote up a poaching ticket to make it look as if my father skipped town because of it."

Sandy smiled, clearly pleased with herself.

Out of the corner of her eye, McCall saw a blurred dark shape slip in through the front door and drop behind the couch. "And you took my father's rifle."

"I thought I might need it someday. As it turned out, I did. Grant was forever boring me to death with talk about his cases. It was too easy to know exactly when to plant the rifle and make sure Buzz Crawford took the fall."

"Nice job," McCall said, horrified and yet at the same time awed by Sandy's twisted criminal mind. "But Buzz must have wondered who the real killer was." The answer came to her in a flash. "My mother."

That would explain why Buzz hated Ruby Bates Winchester so much. He thought she'd killed Trace and framed him for the murder. That's why he'd thought McCall had access to Trace's rifle and had used it to frame him.

"Bingo!" Sandy said with an unhinged glee.

"You tied it all up with a nice big bow on top," McCall said. "If you'd just left it at that, you would probably have gotten away with it. But once you murder me, you will ruin your perfect scheme."

"Oh, that's just it. I'm not quite done yet. But I will be after you write your confession, admitting that in an attempt to protect your mother, you framed Buzz and, racked with guilt, took your own life."

"You really don't think anyone is going to believe my mother killed Trace or that I framed Buzz, do you?"

Sandy burst out laughing. "Are you serious? Everyone in town has speculated for years that Ruby did it. And all of Whitehorse has questioned having a woman deputy in the sheriff's department. Everyone knows we're the weaker sex," she added with a chortle. "It will break poor Grant's heart since he is so fond of you. But that's the price he pays for hiring you in the first place."

The dark shape rose behind Sandy, and with a start, McCall saw the man's face. Sheriff Grant Sheridan?

That's when McCall remembered what Sandy had said

that had caught her attention. *We.* She'd said "*we* were driving back to town" after murdering Trace.

Sandy hadn't been alone that day when she'd met Mc-Call's father on the ridge.

McCall's gaze shot to Grant. The sheriff was out of uniform, dressed in a faded long-sleeved shirt, a pair of worn jeans and sneakers. His head was bare. He stood, arms akimbo, his usually forlorn face set in deep ridges of disappointment.

He stood behind Sandy, his weapon drawn—but pointed at the floor.

LUKE HAD STARTED down Highway 191 toward his place south of town when he'd passed, first Sandy Sheridan, then moments later, the sheriff.

Grant was driving his old pickup instead of his patrol car, and he wore a baseball cap pulled low.

Luke wasn't sure what had made him curious as he'd watched Grant in his rearview mirror. The sheriff pulled over, leaving his motor running, as if to let a car go by before he fell in behind his wife again.

He's following her, Luke thought, as Sandy turned down the river road—and Grant followed a good distance behind.

Luke swung his rig around and went after them, wondering if something else had happened. Since his talk with Eugene, he'd been so upset he hadn't been thinking clearly.

But now as he came around a curve in the road, he saw that Sandy had pulled off at the fishing access closest to McCall's cabin on the river. If there was one thing Luke knew, it was that Sandy Sheridan was no fisherman.

Even stranger, the sheriff made a quick turn onto a

ranch road, going only a short distance before pulling into the trees and cutting his lights.

Luke kept going on past the ranch turnoff and the fishing access road. As soon as he knew he was out of sight around a curve, he pulled over, cutting his lights and engine and got out.

He waited a moment for his eyes to adjust to the darkness, then he headed back down the road toward McCall's cabin, working his way through the trees. Ahead, he saw a dark figure come out of the trees from the spot where Grant had parked his pickup.

What the hell was going on? Whatever it was, it couldn't have anything to do with McCall, right?

Then how did he explain why the sheriff's wife appeared to be headed right for the cabin?

Luke had to hang back to let the sheriff cross the road and disappear into the trees, before he continued to follow the two.

He lost sight of Sandy near McCall's cabin. A moment later he saw the sheriff sneaking along the side of the cabin, then disappearing around to the deck door.

Luke followed, his anxiety growing. When he heard the first shot, he took off at a run. Earlier, during their lovemaking, he'd remembered seeing the pistol he'd lent McCall beside a flowerpot on the deck.

McCALL STARED AT GRANT, realizing he must have been the person Sandy was with that day. It seemed odd, but who else could it have been?

Grant hadn't moved. He stood with his head down, looking sick, his weapon still dangling from his right hand.

Sandy still hadn't realized they weren't alone. "Your

mother ruined my life when you took Trace away from me," Sandy said. "He wouldn't have left—if Ruby hadn't been pregnant with *you*."

McCall saw where this was going. And if Sandy and Grant had killed Trace—

The front door blew open. Grant apparently hadn't closed it properly.

Sandy swung around and saw her husband, Grant. Her finger must have been itching on the trigger because she got off the first shot.

McCall heard the second shot as she dived for the door. A bloodcurdling scream followed the report of the gunfire. Someone groaned.

As McCall scrambled toward the front door, she saw Grant trying to get to his feet. He still had the gun in his hand. Was it possible he'd shot Sandy? Or had he been trying to hit McCall?

"Stop!" Sandy yelled. "I don't want to shoot you in the back, but I will."

The third bullet ricocheted off the wall next to McCall, sending splinters into the air. McCall stopped and lifted her hands as she slowly turned around to face Sandy.

Grant, she saw, had fallen back on the floor, facedown in his own blood. Sandy had his gun—and her own. Blood bloomed from her left side, but she seemed oblivious of being hit. Grant had shot her? To shut her up? Or keep her from killing McCall?

McCall glanced at Grant, watching for any sign of life. None. Meeting Sandy's gaze, she prepared herself to meet her maker. Sandy had nothing to lose now.

She had killed Grant. Now she had to kill McCall.

There would be no suicide note. No pretend suicide.

"It's over, Sandy," McCall said, knowing her only

chance was to try to talk the woman down. "The killing has to stop. Trace is dead. Now Grant. I don't know what happened on that ridge all those years ago with my father, but I do know that you didn't mean to shoot Grant and I don't believe you would have killed Trace if it hadn't been for Grant being on that ridge with you that day."

Sandy began to laugh. "You aren't as smart as Grant thought you were. Grant wasn't with me when I killed Trace."

"Then who…"

"I wasn't the only one who hated Trace." Sandy spat out the words. "It wasn't even my idea to get him on that ridge in sight of the Winchester ranch." She smiled at McCall's shock. "They say blood is thicker than water." Sandy shook her head. "Not when it comes to sibling rivalry. Trace's own flesh and blood wanted him dead. What does that say about your father?"

"You're lying."

"How different it would have been if Trace had married me," Sandy said. "He would have changed," she said with conviction, showing just how delusional she was.

For a moment, Sandy seemed to be lost in a daydream of what her life could have been like if she'd been the one to get Trace Winchester down the aisle. Her face softened as she steadied the gun with both hands to kill McCall, her eyes moist, a smile on her lips as if seeing herself beside Trace in the small white chapel on the edge of town.

That's how she died.

McCall would later wonder if Sandy even felt the bullet that pierced her heart. Luke's shot had been true. He'd fired at the same time he'd thrown McCall to the side. Sandy's shot had burrowed into McCall's front door in the exact spot where she'd been standing just an instant before.

It had been so close that she swore she felt it brush past. Luke had saved her life.

The realization came with tears as she'd looked over at him, the two of them lying on her living room floor. He'd mouthed the words. Or at least she thought he had, since the sound of the gunshot so close to her ear had made her think she'd gone deaf.

I love you.

And then she was in his arms, and he was holding her as if he would never let her go ever again.

Epilogue

There is nothing the community of Whitehorse loved more than a scandal—unless it was a scandal followed by talk of a wedding.

It took no time at all for everyone in the county and beyond to hear about what happened at Deputy Sheriff McCall Winchester's cabin on the river.

Both McCall and Luke were considered heroes. It became clear that a lot of people hadn't liked Sandy Sheridan, especially after it came out that she'd been running around with their husbands behind Grant's back.

McCall had figured that was how Grant had ended up at her cabin. He'd been following Sandy, just as he'd been the other time she'd seen him, and was presumably aware of her transgressions. It was too bad, because McCall realized after the dust settled that Grant had loved Sandy or he would have killed her that night in the cabin—and not just wounded her.

How ironic that Sandy had passed up true love for what she thought she could have had with Trace Winchester.

The whole episode had shaken a lot of people, including McCall's mother.

"I think I'm in love with Red," Ruby had said a few

days later. "Don't worry. I'm going to take it slow. I just wanted you to know."

McCall had been touched and had hugged her mother, hoping that she had finally found a man who would do her right. If anyone could be that man, it was Red Harper.

Ruby wasn't the only one who'd been shaken by what had happened. When Luke had asked McCall to ride with him out to the house he was building, she'd been happy to go along.

He'd walked her through it, explaining what he'd planned in each room, and she saw at once that the house he'd been building was too large for one person.

"You were building this for us," she said on a shaky breath.

He smiled, and she thought that he had to be the most handsome man in the world. Her heart began to beat faster as he reached in his pocket and, shoving back his cowboy hat, dropped to one knee.

"McCall Winchester, will you marry me?"

She'd been afraid of love since she was old enough to understand that her own father had run out on her and her pregnant mother. Falling for Luke at such a young age— and thinking he'd betrayed her—had made her more than a little gun-shy.

But when she looked into his eyes and saw the love, McCall knew there was only one thing she could say.

"Yes. Oh yes!" And she'd thrown herself into his arms, ready for whatever the future held.

She hadn't been so sure about staying on at the sheriff's department. Former sheriff Carter Jackson stepped in to help after Grant's death and had asked her to stop by. He offered to reinstate her whenever she was ready to come back.

"I'm not sure I can come back as a deputy." But not for the reasons the sheriff was probably thinking. It wasn't her brush with death. It was not knowing for sure who'd been on that ridge the day her father had died.

With Sandy, Grant and Buzz all dead, she knew she might never know. She didn't want to spend her life chasing after a killer. So what kind of deputy did that make her?

"Why don't you give it some time," Carter was saying. "Don't make a decision now."

Because she wasn't her father, she nodded and said she would.

As she walked out of the sheriff's department, she was asking herself, what now? when her grandmother called and asked to see her.

"Why?" McCall asked.

The question seemed to take Pepper aback for a moment. "Must you always be so difficult?"

Diplomacy kept McCall from answering that one.

"Isn't it possible I just want to see you, perhaps congratulate you on your engagement?"

McCall drove out to the ranch, wondering if she could trust this change in her grandmother.

Maybe Pepper had found peace now that she believed Trace's killer was dead. McCall had no intention of ever telling her any different.

McCall wanted to believe that Sandy had lied. Either way she knew what that would do to Pepper. She'd lost her family twenty-seven years ago.

Recently her grandmother had mentioned contacting her family and inviting them for a visit at the ranch.

The deputy in McCall noted that such a visit would mean the suspects would be back on the ranch.

"So when is the wedding?" her grandmother asked now on the other end of the phone.

"Christmas."

"That's a wonderful time for a wedding."

A little worried about why her grandmother wanted to see her, McCall said she was on her way and hung up.

Pepper opened the door at her knock, thanked her for coming and ushered McCall into the parlor.

"Would you like something to drink? I could have Enid make us some lemonade or maybe there are some cookies around."

McCall shook her head. Was her grandmother actually nervous? "Why don't you just tell me why you wanted to see me."

"Must you always be so outspoken?" Pepper demanded, then shook her head. "You remind me of myself."

Clearly that was not a good thing.

Her grandmother glanced out the window toward the ridge across the ravine. It was lit with bright sunlight. McCall wondered how many times her grandmother had looked over there thinking about Trace, thinking that he'd been just across that narrow deep expanse all these years.

"I want you to return to the sheriff's department."

McCall blinked, surprised at her grandmother's words as much as her tone. "I beg your pardon?"

"You're too good at your job to quit."

McCall didn't know what to say.

"I think you should run for the sheriff position," Pepper continued.

"Sheriff? I'm afraid a woman deputy is as unorthodox as Whitehorse gets."

"You might be surprised what is possible when you're a Winchester."

McCall laughed. "Quite frankly, having the Winchester name hasn't really been an asset."

Pepper actually looked ashamed. "You and your mother have been treated badly and I'm sorry for that."

McCall stared at her, betting the farm that apologizing wasn't something Pepper Winchester often did.

"I can understand if you say no, but I'd like to make the offer," her grandmother said. "I would be honored if you would have your wedding here at the ranch and, if you'd not be offended, I'd like to pay for it."

McCall was speechless for a moment. "That really isn't—"

"Necessary. I know. It's so little so late."

As McCall looked into her grandmother's dark eyes, so like her own, she willed herself to be careful before trusting her grandmother.

Still, when Pepper said the words, McCall couldn't help the tears that rushed to her eyes or the sudden swell of her heart.

"I think your father would approve. After all, you are Trace's daughter, my granddaughter and a Winchester."

McCall finally felt as if that were true.

PEPPER'S ATTORNEY SOUNDED shocked to hear her voice, probably because it had been twenty-seven years since she'd called him.

"Mrs. Winchester."

"Yes, Curtis, I'm still alive," she said drily, though her lawyer sounded as if he had one foot in the grave. He'd retired years ago, turning his practice over to his nephew.

"I need you to do something for me. Not your nephew."

"Of course." He sounded resigned to whatever it was she wanted.

"Find my family. I want to see them."

He made a surprised sound. "That's wonderful, Pepper. Mending ties with your family is so important at this age. I know you won't be sorry."

She was already sorry and said as much.

"I want you to contact each of them—use your letterhead," Pepper told the attorney. "I've written down what I want you to say on my behalf. Enid will deliver it tomorrow. Do you think you can handle that?"

"I would think this means you are writing a new will."

"Don't think, Curtis. Just do what I ask and make sure no one finds out the terms of my will until I'm gone."

"Of course everything in your will is confidential. You and I are the only two people who know the terms."

"Make sure it stays that way. You will let me know when you have the addresses and the letter ready to mail." She hung up before he could offer any further pleasantries and reread the letter her lawyer would be mailing out.

She nodded to herself, pleased. It would bring her grandchildren back to the ranch. Of course it could also bring the others. She would deal with that when she had to.

What would all of them be like now? Either greedy or curious, she hoped, since the letter would lead them all to believe she was dying and about to divide up her fortune—but only to those who returned to the ranch as she requested.

That, she assured herself, would lure them all back to the Winchester Ranch where she would be waiting for them.

As she looked toward the rocky ridge in the distance,

Pepper Winchester knew it was no coincidence that her son had been murdered in sight of the Winchester ranch.

Just as it was no coincidence that a pair of binoculars had been hidden in the third floor room.

As she watched the sun set over the Montana prairie, she swore on her son's grave that once all her family was back on the ranch, she would find out who under this roof twenty-seven years ago had betrayed him. Then there would be hell to pay.

* * * * *